SEIZED

ELIZABETH HEITER

MIRA®

ISBN-13: 978-0-7783-1862-0

Seized

Recycling programs
for this product may
not exist in your area.

Copyright © 2016 by Elizabeth Heiter

For questions and comments about the quality of this book, please contact us at
CustomerService@Harlequin.com.

www.MIRABooks.com

Printed in U.S.A.

Praise for the novels of Elizabeth Heiter

"Elizabeth Heiter does her research, and it shows in this superb FBI thriller. With a ripped-from-the-headlines plot and excellent characterization, *Seized* is a true winner. Don't miss it."
—J.T. Ellison, *New York Times* bestselling author of *What Lies Behind*

"Gripping from the first page, *Vanished* will keep you on the edge of your seat all the way to its searing conclusion. Heiter has given us a roller coaster of a thriller, sure, but this novel is also a rich and harrowing story of the psychology of evil and those who strive to stop it, insights that will stay with you long after you've finished the book. And what a heroine we have in Evelyn Baine!"
—*New York Times* bestselling author Jeffery Deaver

"A handsomely crafted mixture of police procedural and thriller, *Vanished* is a book whose events will haunt you well after you finish."
—*Mystery Scene Magazine*

"Elizabeth Heiter rises to the top of [a crowded field] featuring serial killers with her sterling *Vanished*... A splendid and scary read."
—*Providence Journal*

"*Hunted* is a nonstop, thrilling read that will leave you breathless, and Evelyn Baine is a sharp and gutsy heroine you'll want to follow for many books to come."
—Tess Gerritsen, *New York Times* bestselling author of the Rizzoli & Isles series

"*Hunted* is a terrific, gripping, page-turning debut by a talented new voice in suspense. A great read."
—Allison Brennan, *New York Times* bestselling author

"Elizabeth Heiter has written a thriller that grabs readers from the first page...*Hunted* is a fast read because the pages fly by as the narrative gets more and more exciting and suspenseful."
—*Book Reporter*

This book is for my uncle Tom Dunikowski and my aunt Andy Hammond. Thank you for your belief in me, your support no matter what, and for always being there when I need you.

Dear Reader,

Welcome to the world of The Profiler! If you've already read the first two books in the series, thank you for returning as Evelyn Baine tackles what looks like a routine investigation—until it lands her on the wrong side of a hostage situation and in the middle of an emerging terrorist threat. If this is your first visit to the series, Evelyn's story began in *Hunted*, where she tracked down a deadly serial killer known as the Bakersville Burier and learned just how deadly it can be to get inside the head of a killer. In the sequel, *Vanished*, Evelyn tackled the case she'd waited most of her life to investigate—the disappearance of her best friend—when the Nursery Rhyme Killer resurfaced after eighteen years of silence.

Seized marks the return of Evelyn and fellow agent Kyle McKenzie as a case takes them to the remote Montana wilderness. Writing this story meant delving into new research, including cults and brainwashing techniques, survivalists, homegrown terrorism and how to profile a person's next move by his or her past actions. I hope you enjoy the result!

After *Seized*, Evelyn will be back for a brand-new adventure, and I hope you'll continue to come along for the ride. You can keep up with me and the books (as well as get extras and join my newsletter) on my website at elizabethheiter.com. You can also find me on Facebook at facebook.com/elizabeth.heiter.author and Twitter as @ElizabethHeiter. I love to hear from readers.

As always, my heartfelt thanks for reading!

Elizabeth Heiter

FBI Terms and Acronyms

ASAC—Assistant Special Agent in Charge. Working directly under the SACs (Special Agents in Charge) who run divisions or field offices, the ASACs run programs.

BAU—Behavioral Analysis Unit. The BAU is where FBI "profilers" (the official name is Criminal Investigative Analysts) work. BAU is a part of CIRG (Critical Incident Response Group) and is located at Aquia. BAU agents provide behavioral-based support to the FBI, as well as other federal, state, local and international law enforcement agencies, including profiles of unknown subjects (UNSUBs).

CIRG—Critical Incident Response Group. CIRG provides rapid response for crisis situations around the country and integrates tactical, negotiations, behavioral analysis and crisis management resources. BAU (Behavioral Analysis Unit) and HRT (Hostage Rescue Team) are part of CIRG.

CNU—Crisis Negotiation Unit. Also part of CIRG (Critical Incident Response Group), CNU trains the FBI's field office negotiators and deploys with HRT to domestic crises. CNU's motto is *Pax Per Conloquium* (Resolution Through Dialog).

CODIS—Combined DNA Index System. It describes the FBI's program for DNA databases, including NDIS (the National DNA Index System), which contains DNA profiles from federal, state and local sources.

ERT—Evidence Response Team. ERT agents are specially trained FBI agents who collect evidence at crime scenes. Being on ERT is a secondary position, so these agents also work regular special agent duties.

HRT—Hostage Rescue Team. Also part of CIRG (Critical Incident Response Group), HRT is part of the FBI's tactical response for crises. Unlike SWAT, their members work full-time as HRT agents and respond to incidents involving hostage rescue, barricaded subjects and high-risk arrests. Their motto is *Servare Vitas* (To Save Lives).

OPR—Office of Professional Responsibility. OPR reports directly to the deputy director of the FBI. Its role is to identify misconduct within the FBI and manage investigations and discipline related to misconduct.

RA—Resident Agency. The FBI has 56 field offices across the USA and in Puerto Rico, and approximately 380 resident agencies, smaller FBI offices spread across the country.

SA—Special Agent. Special agents investigate violations of federal laws and assist state and local law enforcement. There are more than 13,000 special agents (as part of more than 35,000 FBI employees).

SAC—Special Agent in Charge. SACs run field offices, with the exception of the largest offices—LA, NYC and DC—which are run by assistant directors in charge, ADICs, because of their size. Within the bigger offices, SACs run divisions under the ADIC. SACs also lead special groups, such as HRT.

SSA—Supervisory Special Agent. SSAs run squads. Each field office of the FBI has numerous squads, broken up by type of investigation: white collar, intelligence, counterterror, violent crime, etc.

SWAT—Special Weapons and Tactics. All FBI field offices have SWAT teams and special agents who are SWAT members do so as an ancillary duty, in addition to work on a regular squad. SWAT agents handle high-risk tactical operations.

SEIZED

Prologue

The Freedom Uprising was coming.

John Peters had waited a long time for this. He could feel the anticipation building inside him, and he wished he could share it with someone other than Bobby Durham.

John glanced at his partner, perched silently in the passenger seat of the truck, arms crossed over his chest, supplies packed in at his feet. Bobby was okay, as partners went. Not exactly a strategic thinker, but he was a die-hard believer. He'd do whatever was necessary to complete the mission.

Still, John wished his half brother was here, the man who'd brought purpose to his life.

He lowered the window, let the familiar scents of dirt and pine and fresh snow creep into his nostrils as he drove. It was so close now. One more day in this place, and then he could move on, begin the mission.

If only he could be the one to end it, be there for the final target and see it with his own eyes, instead of just on the news. But he'd be the one to start things off. And they'd start off with a bang.

He smiled at the thought and felt Bobby's curious gaze.

"Are you ready for this?" John asked.

"Damn right I am," Bobby replied, his young voice full of boastful confidence.

"When we get back you'll need to clear out your bunk. Everything goes."

"I know. The maps, the guns, the supplies." Bobby repeated John's words from earlier. "I'll get rid of everything. We'll be set as soon as we've got the go-ahead."

"Good." Before they left, John would double-check, of course, and he'd empty his own bunk, too, although he never wrote anything down. He kept it all where it belonged, locked in his mind, where no one could accidentally discover it.

Never leave behind anything they can use.

The reminder ran through his head, but he didn't need reminding. He'd been training for this mission all his life. He just hadn't realized his true purpose until recently.

And his purpose was great. The lesson he would help teach this country was crucial.

"No one will suspect a thing till we get back." Bobby's words interrupted his thoughts.

John grunted noncommittally. Bobby was willing to die for the cause, but John knew the kid imagined himself returning a hero.

John was resigned to the truth. They'd never be coming back here. If they made it through their mission alive, they'd spend the rest of their days in hiding. But it would all be worth the sacrifice.

He pictured the final target, the one he'd never get to personally see, and he felt his anticipation shift into something hard and powerful and bigger than any one person.

He'd seen a video of the target once, from a long time ago, taken with a shaky old video camera. An elite group of men, so cocky and righteous. Standing on land that wasn't theirs, using bullets to enforce their pretend authority.

He could almost see them now, still thinking they were untouchable. Thinking their bloody hands had somehow come clean.

They were wrong.

And soon, very soon, the whole world would know it.

1

Lee Cartwright wanted to kill her.

Evelyn Baine didn't need to be a profiler with the FBI's elite Behavioral Analysis Unit—BAU—to know it. All she needed to do was stare into Cartwright's angry, narrowed eyes and look at the snarl quivering on his lips, the thrust of his jaw as he leaned toward her across the table.

The bare bulb flickered overhead, deep in the bowels of the Montana State Prison. The distant chorus of prisoners' voices reached her ears, but it was just the two of them in the tiny, dingy interview room. Just her and the convicted bomber. They were separated only by a flimsy table and a pair of standard-issue handcuffs. Those were bolted to the table, but looked as if they'd barely closed around Cartwright's meaty wrists.

His eyes skimmed over her once more and she knew exactly what he saw—a perfect victim.

She gave him steady eye contact, refusing to react as he flexed his hands. He seemed to be testing the strength of those cuffs. The fact that Cartwright wanted to kill her was one of the reasons she'd been chosen for this interview.

Lee Cartwright had been convicted of bombing two black churches and one mosque. Two people had died, and dozens more were injured. It was his way of sowing fear; like a lot of bombers, he wasn't just targeting a specific group, but also seeking notoriety. He'd wanted people to fear *him*, the man who'd been dubbed the "Nail Bomber" because of the materials he used.

He was antifederalist and anti-anyone-who-wasn't-white. Sending her—a biracial federal agent—was her boss's way of telling Cartwright that he didn't call all the shots. The idea was to piss him off enough to get him to brag. He'd told prison officials that he had a copycat, and the FBI wanted to find out if it was true.

The other reason the head of BAU, Dan Moore, had sent her was that she was on his shit list.

Interviewing felons, even felons who claimed a copycat was contacting them, wasn't usually a BAU job. But the file had crossed Dan Moore's desk and apparently it looked like yet another suitable punishment for her refusal to follow orders three months ago.

She'd never been his favorite person; she was too young, too female and too poor a team player. He'd always treated her like the newbie who needed babysitting, but lately, it had gotten much worse. Lately, she felt as if she wasn't even on the team anymore.

Worse, she wasn't sure she wanted to be. And that was something she'd never questioned, not since the time she was twelve years old and her best friend, Cassie, had gone missing.

"I have nothing to say to you," Cartwright muttered for the third time in the half hour they'd been having this little staring contest.

"You told two guards you had a copycat, Lee. You

said you wanted to talk to someone about it. I'm here. Talk to me," Evelyn pressed, trying to sound earnest.

The truth was, she felt discouraged. She'd already asked the warden about Cartwright's incoming mail and his visitors. Since the only person who visited him was his mom, and his mail had never been flagged as suspicious, she was pretty sure his request was more about attention than a real threat.

But someone *had* been setting off explosions in the Montana wilderness about an hour away. There was no indication these had anything to do with Cartwright—he used a distinct method for creating his bombs, as telling as a signature, that local law enforcement hadn't found this time.

The current explosions were a nuisance, but they'd happened far from anyone. And the reality was, this area had several groups with fringe militia ties, and explosions like the ones in the wilderness had happened before. Cartwright's claim of a copycat was unlikely.

Still, he'd been convicted of hate crimes and murder. If there was even a tiny chance he was telling the truth, someone had to check it out.

That someone shouldn't have been her. There was no reason to fly her across the country when there were perfectly capable agents here, and the case didn't need a profiler at all.

And she was tired of the bullshit assignments when there were plenty of real cases she could be profiling.

Maybe, if she could ever get back to those legitimate cases, she could figure out whether she still belonged. Maybe it would tell her if, after finally unraveling what had happened to her best friend when she was twelve, she had any drive left for profiling.

Cartwright did nothing but snarl back at her, the muscles flexing in his prison-pumped arms.

Evelyn held in a sigh and leaned forward. "Who's been contacting you, Lee?"

"I'm not telling you shit."

Frustration built up. He should've seen her—exactly the kind of person he'd love to target at one of his bomb sites—and wanted to brag about the copycat. They hadn't expected him to hand over a name, but they *had* expected him to taunt her with whatever he might know. Assuming the threat was real, which seemed more and more unlikely.

This complete refusal to talk was surprising.

"What's your copycat planning to target? If he's really copying you, he doesn't seem to be doing a good job." She tried to appeal to his vanity and his need to prove himself at the same time.

Cartwright scowled at her. "Forget about it."

"Did you teach someone how to make a bomb?" she asked, leaning back in her chair. She tried another route. "It's not like you used the most sophisticated method we've ever seen."

"Yeah?" he barked. "Have *you* tried it? Packed in all those nails...?" He cut himself off and smirked at her. "My method was just fine."

"But not so complicated that you'd need to teach someone else to do it, right? I mean, they could just figure it out on their own?" It probably wasn't true. Cartwright had used easily accessible materials to create his bombs, but they'd been sophisticated in the detonation. The FBI hadn't seen anything quite like them before—or since.

"Whatever," he said. "I didn't ask for you. I got nothing to tell you."

"Why? Because there is no copycat?"

"Believe what you want."

"I believe you're wasting my time," she snapped, bracing her hands on the table and leaning forward again so she could glare at him.

In that instant, he lunged toward her, shooting out of his chair and driving his elbow at her face.

She leaped back, cursing herself for not properly gauging the distance he could move while tethered to the table. But she wasn't fast enough and his elbow clipped her cheek. It sent her flying backward.

She slammed against her chair, then tripped over it, falling onto the ground, her head slamming the concrete floor.

Behind her, she heard the guard wrestling with the locked door. Cartwright's grating laugh sent fury racing through her veins.

She should've expected it. Cartwright had nothing left to lose. Thanks to a lenient judge, he'd avoided the death penalty, but he was never leaving this place.

She got to her feet before the guard had the door open, and resisted the urge to react. Instead, she righted her chair and sat back down as though everything was fine, waving the guard off. "Does it bother you that this is the worst you can do? Is that why you're making up claims of a copycat?"

His face flushed an angry red and a vein in the center of his forehead popped up. "Get out."

"If you're not making it up," she challenged, ignoring the way her cheek throbbed, "then prove it."

"I didn't make any damn claim to the Zionist…" He cut himself off again, blew out a noisy breath.

But she knew what he was going to say. *Zionist Occupational Government.* It was what a lot of fervent antigovernment groups called the federal government. She tried not to roll her eyes.

"I have nothing to say to you," Cartwright finally finished.

She stared at him a minute longer, but a year and a half as a profiler—or behavioral analyst as they were officially called—told her she didn't have anything to gain here. Her six years before that as a regular special agent told her she needed to find a real case.

"Nice talking to you, Cartwright," she said, the sarcastic response so different from the way she would've handled an interview like that three months ago.

Cartwright just sat there, jaw and arm muscles flexing in unison, and Evelyn stood and motioned for the guard.

The keys jangled in the lock again for so long Evelyn was glad Cartwright had only winged her with his elbow. Eventually the door opened and the guard beckoned her forward.

She moved to his far side, practically sliding along the wall as he led her down the hallway, past a row of cells. They were in the supermax portion of the prison, filled with lifers, which made them especially dangerous. But the inmates were a lot less likely to lodge spit—or other bodily fluids—at a guard they had to deal with every day than a visiting federal agent.

Luckily for her, the guard was six feet tall and as broad as a small car, making her five-foot-two, one-hundred-and-ten-pound frame virtually invisible. Still, the catcalls and obscene comments trailed behind her, leaving an imaginary layer of filth under her loosely tailored suit.

"You get anything good from Cartwright?" the guard asked, sounding completely uninterested in the answer as they reached the front of the prison.

He was slow getting her weapon out of the locked box where she'd had to leave it when she entered, and Evelyn shifted her weight impatiently. Less than two hours in this building and already she felt desperate to breathe fresh air.

How must Cartwright, who'd been locked up for three years of a life sentence, feel? Was that why he'd claimed he had a copycat? To waste the government's time and amuse himself? With someone like him, it was entirely possible.

Evelyn hooked her holster back onto her belt and tugged her jacket down over it. "Thanks. Nothing useful from Cartwright."

She checked her watch. A few hours to grab a late dinner, pack up and catch her flight. She'd follow up with the warden when she was back in Virginia.

As soon as she stepped outside, Evelyn drew in a lungful of fresh, clean air, shivering in her wool suit. It was twenty degrees colder in Montana than in Virginia, and a light dusting of snow covered her rental car. The sun had begun to sink while she was inside, and the parking lot looked eerie in the semidarkness.

As she hurried toward her car, her fingers seemed to drain of warmth as fast as her breath puffed clouds of white into the November air. She strode away from the fenced area around the prison, anxious for the heater in her rental—and saw someone standing beside her car.

She could tell from twenty feet away that person was in law enforcement, probably FBI. It was the way she stood, angled to see any approaching threat, the way she held her hand near her hip, where her weapon would be holstered.

Evelyn glanced down at her watch again as she reached her car. The Montana State Prison wasn't exactly a short jaunt from the closest FBI office. Which meant this agent wanted something. Evelyn's stomach grumbled as she sensed her chance for dinner slipping away.

"Evelyn Baine?" the woman asked. She stuck out a hand and shook with the precision of a military officer and the force of someone used to working in a predominantly male profession. "I'm Jen Martinez. Salt Lake City office."

She flashed a set of FBI credentials and Evelyn squinted at them. "Good to meet you."

Jen frowned as she dropped Evelyn's hand. "What happened to your eye?"

Evelyn gingerly touched the tender spot high on her cheek where Cartwright had winged her. It was swelling underneath her eye. "An accident. What can I do for you?" She tried not to shiver outwardly as she crossed her arms over her chest to preserve whatever warmth she could.

Jen must have lived in the area long enough to be used to the cold, because she looked comfortable, even with her blazer unbuttoned. She was a few inches taller than Evelyn, with white-streaked blond hair pulled into a bun nearly as severe as the way Evelyn wore her own dark hair. She probably had fifteen years on Evelyn, and everything about her, from the laser-sharp gaze to the polyester-blend suit, screamed longtime law enforcement.

"When I heard BAU was sending a profiler to talk to Lee Cartwright, I had to come and get your input."

"You have some insight into Cartwright's copycat?"

Jen waved her hand dismissively. "No. But I do have another situation where I'd like a profiler's take."

Evelyn looked pointedly at her watch. "My flight takes off in a few hours." Actually, it was four, but that wasn't a lot of time to fully review a case and give case agents a profile of their perpetrator.

Not to mention the fact that she wasn't supposed to review a case at all until it was vetted at the BAU office and brought to her officially. Then again, maybe Jen had a case that would allow Evelyn to use her profiling abilities for a change. "Did you bring the file with you?"

"Not exactly," Jen hedged. "I was hoping we could take a ride."

Evelyn moved from one foot to the other, trying to generate more warmth. "Where?"

"Ever heard of the Butler Compound?"

"No."

Jen's lips tightened. "Figures. I've tried to get BAU to look more closely at it a couple of times, but I keep getting denied."

Probably for good reason—but Evelyn didn't say that. The BAU office received hundreds of requests every single week, from federal, state and local law enforcement offices all over the country, plus the occasional international request. There was simply no way to take them all on. And many of them genuinely didn't require a profiler.

"If…" Evelyn started.

"You're here." Jen cut her off, hands on her hips. "Just take a look, would you? There's something there. I know it, and I need help."

The desire to follow procedure, to do things by the book, rose up hard. Once upon a time, she'd been a stringent rule-follower. But the desire to contribute again as a real profiler—to get out of limbo—was stronger.

"Tell me what you want," Evelyn said. "And where's your partner?" As a profiler, Evelyn didn't have one, but that was rare. Like most law enforcement, the FBI liked to pair up their agents.

Relief rushed over Jen's face. "I'm between partners. Mine just transferred to another office. But I heard you were here, and I couldn't miss this chance." She suddenly seemed to notice Evelyn shivering. "Want to get out of the cold?"

"Yes."

Jen laughed and nodded at the battered SUV next to Evelyn's rental. She beeped open the doors and climbed inside, turning on the engine. "Hop in."

As Evelyn got into the passenger seat of what was obviously Jen's Bureau-issued vehicle, she flipped the heat up to high, then said, "Give me the basics."

"I can do better than that." Jen buckled up, gunning it out of the parking lot.

A bad feeling came over Evelyn—the strong, sudden certainty that she was heading into something she shouldn't. It mingled with annoyance that Jen had tried to trick her, instead of just asking Evelyn to go somewhere.

"Where precisely are we going?" she demanded, buckling up even as she debated asking Jen to turn around.

"Butler Compound," Jen replied.

"How far is it?"

"About an hour," she answered, but from the way she said it, Evelyn could tell it was actually longer. "And then I'll drive you right back."

Evelyn frowned down at her watch. If she missed her plane, she'd be even higher on Dan's shit list. Which hardly seemed possible.

And if she was going to leave BAU, she wanted it to be *her* choice, not because Dan Moore had kicked her out.

Jen must have seen her annoyance. "I want you to see the place for yourself," she blurted. "Maybe then BAU will finally believe it's not just some harmless cult."

"What do you think it is?"

Jen glanced at her, intensity in her eyes, then back at the road. "A threat."

"This is remote," Evelyn said, staring out her window at the woods. The trees were thinning as they climbed in elevation, but it was still wilderness. The sun had fully set now, so she found it hard to see much beyond the headlights of Jen's SUV.

They'd been driving just over an hour, and Evelyn had seen nothing more than the occasional lean-to or shack. Snowcapped mountains rose up in the distance. The view was beautiful, but she couldn't imagine anyone living out here.

"Yeah," Jen agreed. "Very remote. Good place to hide out, away from prying neighbors. Away from law enforcement, too."

Jen had finally hung up the call she'd taken almost as soon as they'd gotten in the car, which had prevented

Evelyn from getting any more information about why they were going to the Butler Compound. But she'd learned plenty about Jen from her half of that conversation.

"That was your supervisor, huh?"

"Yes," Jen said. "And before you ask, no, I'm not supposed to be doing this. He thinks I'm running down a lead on another case. Which was probably obvious from that call. He has no idea I tracked you out to the prison."

Evelyn nodded. "He may not know about me, but he knows what you're doing."

"What?" Jen whipped her head toward Evelyn, and the SUV jerked. She corrected quickly on the poorly maintained road. "Why do you say that?"

"I could tell from your call."

"You could hear him? What do you have, bat ears?" Jen asked. She'd taken the call on her Bluetooth, instead of putting it on speaker.

"No. But that's what makes me a profiler," Evelyn replied. "Trust me, Martinez. He knows."

It had been obvious from the way Martinez had kept repeating answers to the same questions about her location. Detailed questions, as though her boss didn't believe a word she was saying.

"Shit," Jen muttered. "He warned me to stay away from this."

"Want to tell me what I'm getting into here?"

"Okay. So, the compound is pretty isolated, as you can tell. This group is cut from the same cloth as Cartwright." She glanced over at Evelyn. "Which reminds me, while we're there, call me Jen. Not Martinez. Just Jen. That's how they know me."

Evelyn shot her a disbelieving look. "They *know* you?"

"Yeah, I've been out there a couple of times. Kind of unofficial, doing the rounds, that sort of thing. They come out and meet me, talk for a while. Usually Butler himself, sometimes with a few of his followers."

"And they bought your reason for visiting?"

"Oh, yeah. Salt Lake City is a big field office, but this area is sparsely populated. People around here are used to law enforcement periodically making goodwill calls."

Evelyn frowned, but didn't argue.

"You ever work at an RA?" Jen asked.

Evelyn shook her head. Most agents now started at one of the bigger field offices, but back when Jen had begun her FBI career, they were still sending a lot of newbies to resident agencies, smaller satellite offices.

"Well, I have. Place quite a bit like this actually, out in Nevada. And it was par for the course, law enforcement checking in on everyone now and then."

Evelyn nodded, still not sure it was a good idea for Jen to be making these visits. On the other hand, direct contact was the best way to get information on a potential problem group.

"Anyhow," Jen continued, "my last partner and I introduced ourselves as FBI, but with first names only. No reason to tell a bunch of racists that I'm married to a Hispanic man."

"They're going to love *me*," Evelyn muttered. Her mother was of Irish-English descent, but her father had been Zimbabwean. There was no hiding her heritage.

"Yeah, well, the profiler who showed up being a big, white, Aryan-looking guy was probably too much to hope for. Don't worry. The most they'll do is glare at you."

"That'll be fun," Evelyn said, already regretting that she'd agreed to this as she glanced at the dashboard clock. She didn't really mind the animosity of suspects—that was pretty common—but this visit was sounding more and more like a bad idea.

And if the most she had to fear from them was the evil eye, what kind of threat were they?

"The leader, Ward Butler, was friends with Lee Cartwright when they were kids," Jen explained as she sped along the barely paved roads.

Evelyn stared at her. "You know Cartwright's claiming he's got a copycat, right?"

"Yeah, I heard. I wouldn't take anything that guy says at face value, though. He's not exactly the type who'd warn the government. He's more likely to watch the news from prison and cheer when it happens. Or taunt law enforcement, acting like he knows who's copying him, just to get a rise out of us."

"Okay," Evelyn said. "I can see that. But if Butler and Cartwright are friends…"

"*Were* friends," Jen corrected her. "Like twenty years ago. They grew up together, but there's no indication they've been in contact in a *long* time. Then they had a complete falling-out when Cartwright went violent, and Butler started his compound."

"So you're saying Butler's group isn't violent," Evelyn said, getting frustrated. "Why are they a threat?"

"They haven't been violent *yet*," Jen replied. "But I think they're going to be."

"Why? And how long have they been nonviolent?"

Jen slowed the SUV and turned off onto a dirt path.

"Just because they've been quiet for a few years doesn't mean they plan to stay that way. Butler refers to the place as a 'refuge' for other survivalists. And we have a lot of those—people who want to live off the land, with no interference from anyone. Most of them wish they'd been born a couple of centuries ago, with no law except maybe a local sheriff, and the chance to be as isolated as they want."

"I know about survivalists," Evelyn said. "And sure, some of them are a problem, but plenty of them just want to be off the grid. Leave them alone and they leave everyone else alone."

The SUV bounced along the potholed trail, and Jen's silence dragged on until she said, "You know the Unabomber's cabin was only about twenty miles from here? His neighbors probably thought *he* was harmless and just wanted to be left alone."

Evelyn held in a sigh. "You still haven't told me why you think this particular group is more dangerous than any of the dozens of other cults we've got."

Jen's knuckles whitened on the steering wheel. "You're too young to remember some of the crap from the nineties, but…"

"I know enough." Evelyn could see where this was going. "And yes, there's been an uptick in homegrown terrorism chatter over the past few years, but…"

"Officially, the Butler Compound is a low threat," Jen broke in. "The FBI thinks Butler is more likely to feed his followers Kool-Aid than plan an attack against anyone. But I've been around cults. One of my very first assignments was in Waco, Texas." She gave Evelyn a meaningful look.

"The Koresh disaster? You were there?" David Koresh and his followers had been in a fifty-one-day siege after Bureau of Alcohol, Tobacco, Firearms and Explosives agents tried and failed to deliver a warrant. Koresh and his followers had fired on the ATF agents and barricaded themselves in the Apocalypse Ranch—a name that should've set off warning bells from the start. The FBI's Hostage Rescue Team had eventually surrounded the place. In the end, Koresh and the cultists had set their own compound on fire, and most of them died.

"Yeah, I was there. Mostly getting senior agents coffee, but trust me, I have experience with cults. I heard the crazy ranting, I saw the few cultists who came out, I saw the place burn. Hell, I even walked through crowds of protesters and had egg thrown at my face. But this compound is different. It's got some of that same creepy vibe, but I'm telling you, this is more than a simple cult. There's just something *off* about the place. I *know* there's more happening. And I'm not going to be the FBI agent who overlooks it."

No wonder BAU had refused to take on the file. The Butler Compound had already been evaluated and Jen had nothing but her gut to say there was a genuine threat.

Evelyn was probably going to find a group of survivalists who wanted nothing to do with her or Jen. She'd come home with nothing useful from Cartwright, and an unsanctioned side trip that would make her miss her flight.

Jen must have sensed her frustration, because she said defensively, "See for yourself."

The SUV rounded another bend and the compound seemed to appear out of nowhere. It was a larger building than she'd expected in such a remote place, and much more sophisticated, too. Usually survivalists built small, and used the materials they found in their immediate vicinity. Not this group.

The compound looked more like an aboveground bunker than a house. Windows were barred as if they lived in the city instead of the wilderness, and there was a tower at the center, rising high in the air, that Evelyn hadn't seen until they'd gotten close. But if anyone was up there, they would've seen her and Jen coming for miles—a single set of headlights approaching through the darkness.

Evelyn peered through the windshield, squinting at the rooftop. "Are those…?"

"Solar panels," Jen broke in. "Yeah. Judging from the chimneys, they have a couple of fireplaces. And I know they've got some massive generators, but they're not hooked up to the grid at all. As far as we can tell, they have no electricity and no internet. They've even rigged their own system to bring in water. They're *totally* off grid."

What a way to live, Evelyn thought but didn't say. Then again, there were plenty of cultists who lived without electricity while their leader had excessive luxuries.

And this group was supposedly made up of survivalists, so maybe they really didn't need modern comforts.

The compound was nestled at the base of a steep, curved peak that would prevent anyone from approaching on either side. The rest of it was surrounded by a tall, chain-link fence, topped with barbed wire. But the gate at the entrance hung open.

"Well, this is kind of weird," Jen said as she drove in.

"What is?" Evelyn asked, sitting straighter.

The group had cut down trees to put up the fence and

to keep anyone from scaling a tree to hop over it; inside they'd left the environment alone. There wasn't much more than a few scraggly pines, but they were still big enough for someone to hide behind. No one emerged. She didn't see anyone at all. A nervous shiver crept up Evelyn's spine.

"Usually they meet me at the gate," Jen said, her tone wary.

"How often have you come here?" And how clearly had she advertised her suspicions?

"Just three times."

That would make her interest obvious, Evelyn figured. But where *was* everyone?

"Maybe BAU was right about the Kool-Aid," Jen joked. Her voice held no humor.

She parked close to the compound, took out her cell phone and started to call someone. She had her door open and was hopping out of the vehicle before Evelyn could suggest they wait.

Swearing, Evelyn followed. Even if Jen had made her suspicions obvious, she knew the people better than Evelyn did. They'd talked peacefully with her in the past, so theoretically they wouldn't overreact to having her return.

Regardless, Evelyn didn't like it. Not the open gate, not the stillness of the place, not Jen's stubborn insistence that there was danger here.

Cold air stung her throat as soon as she slammed the car door behind her. Either because it was later now, or because of their elevation, it felt another twenty degrees cooler up here. In the Montana wilderness, she needed more than a wool suit and a pair of low heels.

She'd taken barely five steps when her fingers started to throb from the cold.

Still, she unbuttoned her suit coat for quicker access to the SIG Sauer P226 strapped at her hip.

Jen followed the set of thick tire tracks that ran off the hard-packed trail and into the looser dirt. As she stepped around the corner of the building, she called out, "Hello?"

Evelyn picked up her pace to follow when she heard Jen exclaim, "Hey, I know you!"

Then Jen walked around the corner again, this time backward, with her hands up and held out to her sides.

Evelyn reached for her weapon, but before she could unholster it, a man came into view.

He was nothing more than a big blur of angry features and camo, because all she could focus on was the modified AK-47 aimed directly at Jen.

2

"What are you doing here, *Agent* Martinez?" the armed man demanded, his voice a deep, harsh rumble.

Next to her, Jen jerked at the news that Butler knew her last name. Then she tried to recover, and her voice was surprisingly calm as she took another step backward, both arms up and out. "Just a friendly visit. Nothing more, Ward." Ward Butler, Evelyn realized as her eyes adjusted to the darkness. The leader of the Butler Compound. The man Jen suspected of being a homegrown terrorist.

Standing there now, holding an illegally modified weapon, wearing a thick, scruffy beard and dressed in camouflage and a skull cap, he looked like one.

"Drop that," Butler barked, ignoring Jen's conversational tone entirely.

Jen's eyes went to her phone. The readout was lit up, probably because she was on the line with whoever she'd started to call in the car.

"Drop it now!" Butler yelled, his voice echoing across the compound.

As the phone fell from her hand, Butler casually

redirected his AK-47 and shot it, midair, blasting the phone to pieces.

Instinct made Evelyn lurch backward, and she went for her weapon.

Before she reached it, the AK-47 was pointed at her.

"I wouldn't do that," Butler warned. "Hands up."

As Evelyn raised her arms, they started to tingle. Because of the cold or because she'd seen how good a shot Butler was, she wasn't certain.

Although Jen's boss certainly suspected she'd come up here, he probably wouldn't expect her back at the office for hours. Maybe not until tomorrow.

And no one knew where Evelyn was.

"Let's try this again, Agent Martinez," Butler said slowly, a sarcastic emphasis on the word *Agent*. "What are you doing here?"

Most cult leaders were charismatic. Narcissistic sociopaths, too, but they had to be able to conceal that. They had to exude enough charm to get a group of people to give up everything they owned and follow them.

Not this guy. As far as Evelyn could tell, he was a hundred and eighty solid pounds of pure menace.

She didn't have much experience with cults, but Butler was setting off all kinds of alarm bells. If he was a cult leader, where the hell were all his followers?

"I'm at the end of a shift, Ward," Jen said. "I'm taking my new partner on the rounds." She lifted her shoulders and gave a little smile. "You know, to meet all the neighbors before we head back to the office."

Butler turned toward Evelyn, looking at her with a disgust he didn't bother to hide. "You're the newbie in the Salt Lake City office?" he asked, skepticism dripping off every word.

"That's right," Evelyn replied, uncomfortable with Butler's tone. Had he mentioned the field office to let her know he was familiar with how the Bureau worked? Or was there more to this?

Jen put a little steel in her voice when she said, "There's no need for this to get ugly."

A sneer crossed Butler's face. He didn't move his gaze from Evelyn as he told Jen, "You made it ugly."

The force of his hatred had Evelyn stumbling back on her heels, and Butler's sneer turned to a tight smile.

But instead of saying another word to her, he looked at Jen again. "This is private property. Trespassing without announcing yourself isn't very smart." He made an apologetic face. "You're likely to get yourself mistaken for an intruder and shot."

Chills danced across Evelyn's skin. After Butler's display with the phone, she absolutely knew there was no way she could get her gun out of its holster before he pulled the trigger on both of them.

If he did, she'd never get the chance to decide what to do about her FBI career. Never get to say goodbye to her grandma. Never get to figure out where her brand-new relationship with fellow agent Kyle McKenzie was headed.

She should've taken more time off after solving her friend's case. She should've extended that vacation with Kyle, never mind what the FBI wanted. She thought of that quiet, secluded beach, with nothing for miles but ocean and sand and Kyle's deep blue eyes staring back at her…

For that one brief week, she'd felt like a different person. Someone whose life wasn't completely consumed by her job. Someone who didn't have an overwhelming need to chase down the demons of her childhood until they were all she could see.

She'd felt *normal*, something she couldn't remember feeling in a long, long time. Not since her best friend had disappeared from her life, which had started her down the path to becoming a profiler.

With Kyle, she'd felt as though the whole world was finally beginning to open up. Then she'd gone back to work, thinking everything would be different.

But for the past three months, she'd felt lost. Without purpose. A feeling she'd never experienced in her life.

And now, here she was, back in the job that had taken everything she had. And if she didn't get her profiling instinct back, it just might take her life.

"Now toss over your gun. Real slow," Butler said.

Jen reached for her weapon and Evelyn tensed as she watched. She readied herself to dive for the ground if Jen didn't toss it. Readied herself to reach for her own gun as a desperate last effort if Butler's finger moved inside the trigger guard of his AK-47.

Jen hesitated only a second before tossing the gun into the brush.

Then the sudden rumble of a powerful engine sounded from around the corner. A big black truck hurtled past her, close enough to blast heat across her back and rip hair loose from her bun.

It kept going, through the gate and out of the compound. A moment later, another man turned the corner, arms swinging loosely, an AK-47 slung over his shoulder.

This guy looked like a cult leader. Taller and leaner than Butler, he had sandy blond hair that curled around his ears and a face that was probably attractive when he wasn't scowling.

Evelyn risked a glance at Jen, wondering who the newcomer was, but Jen stayed silent.

Still, Jen and Butler were obviously familiar with each other, so this must've been the person Jen had spoken to when she'd first left the SUV. The one she'd claimed to know, sounding surprised.

"We've got to take care of them," Butler said in the sort of casual tone that was more appropriate for ordering dinner than discussing the murder of two federal agents.

The new guy shook his head. "I don't think you should do that."

"They could ruin things for us."

"It's a problem," the blond guy agreed. He was dressed in camouflage, too, but wore no hat or gloves. Although his pale skin was ruddy from being outside, he looked comfortable.

Evelyn spoke up. "There's no problem here."

"Shut up!" Butler shouted at her. "This is the start of everything," he said to his companion. "It doesn't matter what we do with these two."

"Killing them will just bring more feds," the other man argued as Evelyn tried to work out his role.

Other than as a possible voice of reason. She inched her hands down slightly, praying that this guy could convince Butler to let them go.

If this *was* set up like a typical cult, maybe he was a trusted higher-up who took orders from Butler and enforced them with the followers? Cults often referred to guys like that as lieutenants.

Evelyn glanced quickly around. But if she was right

about that, where were the followers? Were there any? If so, why hadn't they appeared when the gunshot went off? And what did Butler mean when he said this was "the start of everything"?

"That one—" Butler waved his gun at Evelyn "—is the newbie. The other one, Jen Martinez here, has been sniffing around our place for months."

"Who cares? We're not doing anything wrong," the new guy said smoothly.

Except owning illegal weapons, but Evelyn didn't mention that.

"Well, *now* I can't let them leave," Butler said, and there was a little too much glee in his tone.

Evelyn glanced at Jen again, willing the other agent to look at her. How were they going to get out of this? Did Jen have *any* kind of connection with Butler or the new guy that she could use?

Talking seemed like their best bet, especially now that there were two cultists with weapons and Jen was unarmed. But Evelyn couldn't decide which approach to take.

Jen kept her gaze firmly on Butler. "Of course you can let us leave," she told him. "You haven't taken things too far. Not yet. Let's keep it that way."

"Maybe you should lock them up," the blond guy suggested, ignoring Jen. "Drive their vehicle out of here."

"Why would you need to do that?" Evelyn asked. "If nothing's happening—and we certainly haven't seen anything that would require our attention—why would you want the FBI out here searching for us?" Before he could respond, she added, "And if you think her supervisor doesn't know we're here, you're mistaken. This is the first place they'll look if we don't show up in the next hour."

Butler shrugged. "Can't be helped." He nodded at his lieutenant. "Maybe you're right about hanging on to them for a bit. Check them, Rolfe."

"Ward." Jen tried again as Rolfe frisked her for any hidden weapons. "I've always been straight with you. This isn't necessary."

He ignored her and then Rolfe was standing behind Evelyn, close enough to make all her muscles tense. He emptied her holster and took her cell phone. Then he patted her down so thoroughly that Evelyn knew he was practiced at carrying concealed.

She was convinced he had another weapon on him. Not that she could do anything about it.

He gestured toward the building, and she and Jen began walking in that direction. Jen looked shell-shocked and furious, but she stared straight ahead as her shoes crunched on the frost-covered grass. She made no further effort to protest, almost as if part of her was glad they were getting to see inside the compound.

Butler walked close behind them, his AK-47 leveled inches from Evelyn's back.

"You staying?" Butler asked gruffly, and it took Evelyn a minute to realize he was talking to Rolfe.

She frowned and glanced over her shoulder.

Rolfe had fallen into step behind Butler, but his eyes locked on Evelyn's as soon as she looked at him.

She stumbled, then averted her gaze. Why wouldn't Butler's lieutenant stay? Unless he wasn't a lieutenant. Unless he had some other role at the cult. But what role would require him to leave? Then again, why had the driver of the truck left?

What the *hell* was going on at the Butler Compound?

* * *

"You're going to Montana," the head of BAU told Greg Ibsen as soon as he walked through the door of his boss's office.

"What?" Greg stopped abruptly in the dull gray room. "Did Evelyn's interview with Cartwright give us something?"

Greg tried to keep the surprise out of his voice. He'd been a profiler with BAU a long time. Long enough to know when Dan Moore was sending someone on a long-shot assignment as punishment.

Dan frowned at him, probably able to read every thought running through his mind, since he was a profiler, too. "No." He tapped his pen against the towering pile of legal pads on his desk. "There's another situation in Montana."

"If Evelyn's already there, maybe she should take it," Greg suggested. He'd trained Evelyn, and he knew her as well as anyone could. Whatever the case was, she could handle it. And if Dan didn't start giving her real assignments again soon, he was afraid she'd leave the unit.

"Too late. She's on her way back," Dan dismissed him, draining his cup of coffee as if it was water. "You'll probably pass each other in the air. Besides, she doesn't have much experience with this kind of case."

"What is it?" Greg asked, dreading the call home he'd have to make, telling his son, Josh, that he'd be missing his first hockey game. Greg's family was used to it; this was the life of an FBI agent. But it still wasn't easy to hear their disappointment, shaded with resignation—as though they'd *expected* him to cancel.

"The Salt Lake City office has an agent who went

off on an unsanctioned call. Her boss says she's got a hard-on for the Butler Compound, a cult out in the Montana wilderness that's technically under the Salt Lake City office jurisdiction. He's pretty sure she went there. About an hour ago, her supervisor got a call from her. Apparently, she didn't say a word when he picked up, but he heard part of a conversation, then a gunshot."

"Okay," Greg said slowly. "And they want a profiler because…?" It sounded like they needed the Salt Lake City SWAT team, fast.

"Because they haven't had contact with the agent, and they don't know her status. They aren't a hundred percent sure she's there, and the cult is a survivalist group. Completely antigovernment and, although they've never displayed aggression before, these people are skilled with their weapons. The Salt Lake City office is afraid a show of force will start a firefight."

"Then shouldn't I be reviewing the Butler Compound information from here to give them a profile?" Greg asked. He didn't mind going to Montana if they really needed him, but he didn't see how being on-site would help in this case. Especially since there wasn't even a confirmed "site" yet.

Dan sighed and opened the top drawer of his desk, where Greg suspected his boss kept endless bottles of antacids. But instead of popping any, Dan closed the drawer again, looking pensive. "You're heading out with a CIRG contingent. A hostage negotiator and a group from HRT."

The Critical Incident Response Group was a special group within the FBI, made up of teams that could respond instantly to any serious emergency, anywhere in the United States or abroad. BAU was part of CIRG, the only part not located in Quantico, the next town over.

If he was going with a hostage negotiator and a bunch of Hostage Rescue Team agents, that meant someone high up expected things to turn very, very bad. The kind of bad that required more than just a local SWAT team. The kind of bad that required HRT agents, who did absolutely nothing but train for and execute tactical missions.

Unease settled in Greg's stomach, along with the hint of anticipation that always came with a new case to profile. That was what had kept him in BAU for going on nine years. "What don't I know?"

"Most of it you *do* know," Dan replied, just as his phone began to ring. He tapped a button to silence it. "We're looking to avoid an armed standoff here. But if this agent is inside that compound, we have to get her out."

Greg nodded. The last time someone from the antifederalist movement had stood up to the government, it had become a media spectacle that seemed likely to turn violent at any minute. But the FBI, as well as local and state police, had walked away.

That incident in Nevada had driven all the wackos out of the woodwork. They'd shown up to pledge their support to the rancher who'd refused to move his cattle off federal land. And then they'd hidden in the surrounding brush, aiming rifles at federal agents from all directions and posting the images online.

It was a miracle no one had fired a shot. Greg knew the chances of another ending that peaceful were slim.

"I assume I need to head over to Quantico?" Greg asked, starting for the door.

"Hold on," Dan said, his tone weary. "There's one more thing."

"You have a file on the Butler Compound?"

"Yes, but it's thin. We evaluated the group last year, at the request of this Martinez agent, the one who's missing now."

"And?"

"And we considered them a low threat, basically a cult that wanted to be left alone to live without federal interference. They're bound together by their desire to live off the grid. There's probably a religious component tying them together, too, although we don't have evidence of that yet. It's a group that wouldn't strike out unless the government showed up on their doorstep, but a genuine danger if that happened. Vince did the analysis."

Vince was one of their old-timers, a legend who'd finally retired and gone into the private security consulting business a month ago. BAU was still looking for his replacement.

"That's good, as long as we can stay off their doorstep," Greg said slowly, because he sensed something worse was about to follow.

"Martinez kept insisting Butler was a Bubba."

Bubba was slang in law enforcement circles for a homegrown terrorist.

Greg was skeptical. "She thought a cult leader was a Bubba?"

"Not just him," Dan replied. "The whole group of them."

"That'd be pretty unusual, especially for survivalist types."

Precedent said that kind of personality—an extremist antifederal homegrown terrorist—was a lone wolf. Someone who'd try and fail to fit into fringe militia and survivalist groups, then finally set out on his own to wreak havoc.

Not a cult member, who looked to a leader to provide identity. And certainly not a cult leader, who derived power and purpose from having a group of people to do his bidding and treat him like a god. If that cult leader sent his followers out to commit terrorist acts, he'd be breaking up his little kingdom. With no one left to worship him, what would be the point of his cult?

Greg took the file Dan handed over. "You now think Martinez could be right?"

"No. But I think her constantly going there for answers might've pushed the group into endgame mode. We could be looking at people who are ready to barricade themselves in their compound and defend it to the death. Or mass suicide."

Greg frowned, suddenly understanding why he was being sent to Montana. "And if there's a chance Martinez is there, we have to go in, anyway."

Dan nodded grimly. "Exactly."

3

"We need to move," Jen whispered as a faint sliver of light tracked over the right side of her face and onto the floor.

"We need a *plan,*" Evelyn countered just as quietly. "They took your car keys. We're in the middle of the wilderness, without supplies." Cold as it was inside the compound, which felt like it didn't have any heat, at least it was well-insulated. Outside, it was much, much colder. Which could mean frostbite and death from exposure.

"Besides," she continued, "even if we get the SUV started, I'm guessing they've closed that big gate by now, and they're going to hear us. You saw what kind of shot Butler is."

Jen eased the door closed again.

They'd been locked inside a storage room in the compound, off the side entrance. Butler and Rolfe had left them here twenty minutes earlier, so with any luck they'd gone straight to bed. Or to some room far away in the compound.

But Evelyn didn't know anything about the place, including who else was there, or where a weapon or car keys might be located. And given the layout—with that big lookout tower on top of the building—she suspected someone would spot them long before they got to the gate.

"I have a plan," Jen said as she tucked strands of hair back into her bun. She'd broken six bobby pins before managing to unlock the door.

"Yeah, what is it?" Evelyn asked, grabbing her arm before she inched open the door again. "Do you have any idea how many we're up against here?"

When they'd first been shoved into the room, they'd sat silently, their ears pressed against the door, listening to Butler and Rolfe talk. Rolfe had convinced Butler not to kill them—for now.

But Evelyn had heard the words *leverage* and *stall for time*, which made her nervous. Especially since she still wasn't sure what was going on here.

Because as much as Jen insisted they were terrorists, she had no real evidence. And nothing to support her theory except her gut.

To Evelyn, the place might not have seemed like a typical cult headquarters, but it didn't seem like a terrorist hideout, either.

Once Butler and his lieutenant were gone, Evelyn had tried the door handle, discovering without surprise that it was locked. While Jen worked on it, Evelyn had tried to question her. But Jen had been uncharacteristically silent, pensive as she'd shimmied the bobby pins into the lock.

Rubbing her arms for warmth, Evelyn tried questioning her again now. "How many cultists are there?"

"I don't know," Jen whispered. "Maybe a dozen. Maybe two dozen. I've never gotten inside before."

"I didn't see anyone besides Butler and Rolfe."

"Trust me. They're here," Jen said, her tone certain.

"Did you recognize Rolfe? Is he Butler's second-in-command?"

Jen frowned. "No. Not him. I've never seen Rolfe before tonight. But I recognized the one driving the truck."

Evelyn leaned closer. "Who was he?"

"I'm not sure." She sounded frustrated. "I know I've seen him before, and he doesn't belong here. He's not a survivalist. I'm sure I know him in connection with work. I can't remember exactly where I've seen him. But it'll come to me."

"Okay. Well, do you think the fact that you recognized him had anything to do with Butler freaking out? Or was it just because we're on his land and we saw him carrying illegal weapons, something we could charge him on?"

"I honestly don't know. Let's talk about it later. Right now, we need to go." She peeked out the doorway again, then nodded at Evelyn and stepped through it.

Holding in a curse, Evelyn followed. She squinted in the dim light of the hallway, before glancing back.

"Wait," she told Jen, noticing bottles of bleach and other cleaning supplies in the cabinet. Maybe there was something in there they could use.

But Jen must not have heard her whisper, because she was still moving. And she was moving in the wrong direction. Farther into the compound instead of back toward the exit.

Evelyn hurried after her, running on her tiptoes to avoid clicking her heels on the wood slat floors. A pair of sconces, mounted on the walls and giving off less light than a twenty-five-watt bulb, cast shadows as she hurried forward. Grabbing hold of Jen's sleeve, she demanded, "Where are you going?"

Jen tried to shake her off. "I'll never get another chance to be *inside* this place. We have to see what's in here."

Evelyn gripped the older woman's sleeve tighter. "Butler wants to kill us. We need to get out of here. And we need a plan, because driving out the gate seems like a long shot."

"I'm not leaving," Jen insisted. "I already told you. I'm not going to be the person who missed a threat inside our borders. This is my chance to get real intel on these people. And this is *your* chance to get a close-up look and give me a profile."

"Damn it," Evelyn muttered as Jen pulled free and darted through the doorway ahead.

Was this how her own colleagues felt working with *her*? Evelyn knew she had a reputation as someone who wasn't a team player, and she could admit to herself that it was deserved. But Jen's tunnel vision was ridiculous.

This was a really bad idea. Why the hell had she agreed to come with Jen? She should've left the prison, gotten some dinner while she wrote up her report about yet another worthless assignment, then gone home.

She could've been asleep on the plane now, getting a little extra rest so she could stop by the nursing home where her grandma lived on the way to work in the morning. Instead, she was sneaking around inside a damn cult. Chances were, if they came across Butler without his more even-tempered friend, he'd use them as target practice.

Controlling her frustration, Evelyn followed, still on her toes and cursing her low-slung heels. She couldn't leave another agent behind.

When they turned the corner into a larger room, Jen thrust out her arm and blocked Evelyn from moving any farther.

Jen put a finger to her lips and nodded toward the other end of the room.

Evelyn blinked, urging her eyes to adjust faster. This room was even darker than the short hallway, but it was big. She looked around at the three large tables, the shelves stacked with canned goods, water and MREs and a big lockbox near the back. The kind of lockbox meant to hold weapons. Unnerving, but not exactly unexpected for survivalists who carried around AK-47s.

She squinted at Jen, trying to figure out what she'd seen—and then she realized. Voices from somewhere beyond this room. Evelyn strained to make them out.

"—for bringing the supplies, Rolfe," someone said.

"Not a problem," Rolfe returned.

"I saw that feeb drive up again," the first guy said. It wasn't Butler, so Evelyn assumed he must be one of the cultists.

She glanced at Jen, who was frowning at the slur.

"It's taken care of," Rolfe replied.

"It's a sign," the first guy said, anticipation in his voice. "She's the first of them, isn't she? A Babylonian."

Swear words lodged in Evelyn's throat and she clamped her teeth together to keep them in, but she couldn't stop herself from shaking her head at Jen.

The other agent's jaw had gone slack with surprise.

This group was deeply mired in cultist philosophy; taking a page from the Book of Revelation, they subscribed to the idea that the end times would be heralded by the arrival of "Babylonians." It wasn't the first time Evelyn had heard of a cult twisting the Bible, claiming that "Babylonians" were law enforcement officials and a sign of the apocalypse. This was the clearest indication yet that they were dealing with a regular cult, and possibly one that would fight to the death to protect its land.

"No," Rolfe said, sounding exasperated. "She's an enemy, but she's been handled."

A weird response if Rolfe was the second-in-command and expected to follow Butler's preaching, which apparently included a focus on the end times.

Evelyn frowned. This place was full of inconsistencies. But if Butler believed their arrival heralded the end times, she wasn't going to give him any excuse to take action.

She gripped Jen's sleeve again and tugged, gesturing back the way they'd come. If Rolfe was telling the cultist that Jen had been handled, it could mean more than just locked in a closet. It might mean that, despite his words to Butler, he expected them to be dead soon.

Jen took one last look around the huge, well-stocked room they'd entered. To Evelyn, it seemed like the domain of a group who planned to ride out a rough winter in hard terrain, not a terrorist plot in the making.

She nodded and the two of them spun back toward the hallway. In a pair of gym shoes and with longer strides, Jen made it down the hallway and to the back door faster.

Evelyn was still a few feet behind her, heart thudding and toes aching as she tried to run silently, when the back door opened from outside.

Framed in the open doorway was Ward Butler, holding his AK-47 in one hand and Jen's car keys in the other. There was shock on his face, followed by rage.

As Evelyn slid to a stop in the center of the hallway, Butler calmly shook his head. Then he lifted his machine gun and fired.

"We've got a problem."

The words echoed through Kyle McKenzie's earphones as he slithered through the hole they'd cut at the bottom of the six-foot fence surrounding the Butler Compound. That definitely wasn't what he wanted to hear at 6:00 a.m. as he snuck up on a group known to have stockpiled weapons.

Dampness seeped through his HRT-issued flight suit, and he fought back exhaustion. After arriving in Montana after a last-minute flight from Quantico, they'd joined the rest of the team in setting up an immediate perimeter around the Butler Compound. Now he and his partner, Gabe Fontaine, were tasked with getting closer.

"A problem. What else is new?" Gabe muttered, close behind him.

It had been nonstop since they got to Montana. They couldn't confirm that Special Agent Jennifer Martinez, a twenty-three-year veteran with the FBI, was in the Butler Compound at all. The place had no working phone, and the leader, Ward Butler, had no cell phone registered in his name. So far, the cultists had ignored the battle phone the negotiator had tossed over the fence, as well as the requests to talk through the bullhorn.

For all they knew, no one was even here. The place looked like a ghost town, with the compound shut tight and no response at all to the FBI's arrival.

Basically it was a clusterfuck. No one knew anything useful, they couldn't talk to the cultists—who might or might not be terrorists—and they couldn't storm the place.

As he stood, Kyle swept the area in front of him, using his night-vision goggles. Fog had crept in, meaning his NVGs were set to Active, so they could bounce an infrared light off any objects in front of him.

Without that, he couldn't see much of anything. But if the cultists had their own NVGs—which was entirely possible with a group of survivalists—they'd be able to see the beam. They'd be able to see him.

Worry about what you can control, Kyle reminded himself as he inched slowly forward through the dry, stiff pine needles and a layer of frost. Every step was precise, careful, silent. The survivalists might have the equipment, and they might be practiced at living off the land, but they didn't have his training.

Snipers were in position on the peak behind the compound, with eyes on the tower, which had remained empty so far. HRT was acting on the assumption that no one knew they were trying to get a closer look.

"We think we've got another agent inside." That was the voice of Sam "Yankee" McGivern, the Assistant Special Agent in Charge who ran HRT. His tone was dire and he paused long enough that Kyle froze.

"Mac," Yankee continued, "the warden over at the prison just called BAU. Evelyn's rental car is still in the lot. One of his guards saw her get in Jen's vehicle hours ago. She never made her plane."

Dread rushed over him, but he shoved it back and kept moving, until he was behind the cover of a pathetic-looking fir tree. "Anyone been able to reach her?"

"No. We're not getting anything from Jen's phone, but Evelyn's cell pings off a tower around here, and we've got a lock on Jen's vehicle, a few miles away from the compound. We just sent agents to check it out."

"Okay," Kyle said, instead of the string of curses he wanted to let loose. *Mind on the mission*, he reminded himself.

He understood why Yankee had wanted him, in particular, to know. Every one of his teammates, listening on the call, would realize why Yankee was telling him, too. From the second he'd met Evelyn, a year and a half ago, he'd been drawn to her. Initially it was because she was so serious, so focused on work and nothing else, that he couldn't help teasing her. But her allure had soon become very different.

It had gotten so bad that even his boss knew he was interested—how could he not, when Kyle found regular excuses to jog over to the BAU office at Aquia to see her? What none of them knew was that, finally, Evelyn was interested in return.

She was the one who'd wanted to keep the fact that they'd started seeing each other three months ago a secret. Agents in the Bureau could date, but they couldn't date and work in the same squad. And although BAU and HRT were different units, they traveled together regularly for critical missions.

The rules there were murky; Evelyn's determination to protect her job above all else was not.

Or at least it hadn't been, for most of the time he'd known her. Ever since they'd returned from solving her friend's case, she'd slowly begun to lose the intense drive that had drawn him in from the second he'd met her. Her boss *had* been giving her bullshit assignments, but the old Evelyn would have fought him on it. The new Evelyn just took them. Lately, he hardly recognized her.

"Keep us updated," Gabe said into his mic, which reminded Kyle that he'd gone silent for too long.

"Let's move," he whispered, treading carefully from the cover of one scraggly, snow-dusted tree to the next. They didn't know exactly what they were dealing with here, but what they *did* know was that survivalists were talented at making booby traps, and cultists were notoriously paranoid. Not a good combination.

Kyle kept up his painfully slow, steady pace until they were close to the large building at the back of the compound. Behind him, Gabe moved just as silently; the only reason Kyle knew he was there was from years of working together.

Finally, Kyle's hand grazed the solid exterior of the building. Was Evelyn in there? Was she okay?

"Technical coverage coming up," Gabe whispered into the bone mic at his throat. He slipped a hand into one of the pockets in his flight suit, and then pressed it against the building wall, leaving behind a sophisticated eavesdropping device that actually looked like a fly.

The communications technicians who worked with HRT were not only geniuses, they also had a sense of humor. Too bad that, right now, Kyle didn't find much of anything funny.

Gabe tapped his arm and Kyle moved around the corner, toward the side where they'd be at the highest risk of being spotted. Kyle watched every step, and nodded his NVGs at a set of deep tire tracks that rounded the bend and stopped near a steel door. Big tracks, probably from a large truck.

He couldn't keep himself from looking back at the door, and his desire to test the lever made his hands tense around his MP-5. His feet seemed stuck in place as his need to search for Evelyn intensified.

Then Gabe was beside him, pointing forward because this close to the compound they didn't even want to whisper.

Forcing himself to move, Kyle passed the door, rounding another corner. He almost wished someone would appear outside and engage, so he'd have an excuse to go in there and get Evelyn out.

But the compound remained eerily silent.

Still beside him, Gabe pressed another bug to the wall, moving a little faster now. They needed to place two more bugs, then go back the way they'd come. It would start getting light soon, and they had to be out of here before anyone inside woke up.

Assuming anyone was in there at all. So far, they had no indication of it. There'd been no response to their calls, and the snipers hadn't been able to pick up anyone at the windows. Shades were drawn over all of them, and it was dark inside, with no hope of spotting even shadows.

Was it possible they'd fled before HRT had landed in Montana?

As Kyle moved away from the building and behind the cover of a tree, Yankee's voice came over his radio again. "The technical coverage is picking up voices from the building. Head back here, guys."

Desperate for information on Evelyn, Kyle moved even faster. He told himself to slow down, but he couldn't seem to do it as he darted from the cover of one tree to the next, following their original route.

Then a hand slapped him hard on the shoulder, and

Kyle spun around, his heart thudding a tempo that sounded like *stupid, stupid, stupid*.

But it was just Gabe. "Sorry," he mouthed.

In return, Gabe whispered, "Don't move." He lifted a fallen tree branch off the ground and held it out a few inches past Kyle's foot. When he pushed it down, a piece of metal snapped over it, breaking the branch in two.

Bear trap, Kyle realized, nodding his thanks at Gabe. That would've done irreparable damage to his foot. And ended his career in HRT.

Keeping watch for more booby traps, Kyle slowed down, feeling antsy every second he wasn't back in the Tactical Operations Center—TOC—set up outside the fence.

Finally, finally, he followed Gabe back under the fence, then jogged over to the temporary post that would manage tactical decisions. Inside the large tent, his boss looked up, expression grim, at Kyle and Gabe's entrance.

"What is it?" Gabe asked from behind him as Kyle's voice refused to work and fear stampeded through his veins.

Yankee put down his earphones and stood, his head skimming the top of the tent. "We've got at least a dozen voices inside the compound."

He moved forward and placed a hand on Kyle's shoulder. "We don't know any details right now, but they just talked about a dead federal agent."

4

"You brought this on yourself."

Evelyn focused hard, trying to bring the world into focus, but pain sliced through her head and Ward Butler seemed to sway in front of her, wavering as if they stood on the bow of a ship. He was still holding his AK-47, and Evelyn felt nauseated as she touched the side of her face, where he'd smashed her with that gun, knocking her out. But first, he'd taken a shot.

The memory rushed over her, the panic of seeing Butler appear in the doorway, having no time to run, nowhere to hide. The horror of watching him spray bullets, of seeing Jen go down. The fear of thinking she was next.

She'd run for Jen, anyway, slipped in her blood and hit the ground hard. That had probably saved her life, because Butler's next barrage of bullets had gone over her head.

Then he'd strode to her side, and just when she thought it was all over, there'd been a yell and he'd slammed the butt of his AK-47 into her face instead. She had no idea how long ago that had been.

"Where's Jen?" she managed to ask. Moving her jaw

made pain travel down her neck, but she kept blinking and eventually Butler came into focus.

The compound was dimly lit, either darker than it'd been before, or her vision was compromised. The coppery smell of blood was in her nose, the residual taste of fear in her mouth.

"Martinez is dead," Butler replied, no remorse in his voice.

Evelyn gulped in a deep breath, even though she'd known. Blood clogged in her throat and Evelyn choked on it, realized the inside of her mouth was bleeding badly, that her jaw might be broken.

She tipped her head and spat out blood, got a full breath. "Why?" she rasped.

Butler smiled—a hard, tight, angry smile. "Shouldn't you be asking if you're next?"

Before Evelyn could form a response, he stepped aside, and Evelyn's range of vision widened. She discovered she was still lying on the ground where she'd fallen. She jerked, trying to push herself up as she saw all the blood surrounding her. Jen Martinez's blood.

It was dried on her arms, soaked through her suit. There was a lot, still sticky in places, but much of it hardened, like a brownish-red cast over her skin.

Just as she was getting off the ground, Butler jammed a booted foot into her chest, knocking her back down. Back into the pool of blood.

Panic burst inside her, a desperate need to move, to escape the feel of another agent's blood. To escape the fear that she could have prevented Jen's death, that she'd signed her own death warrant by following Jen here. She tried to ignore it, and instead focus on assessing.

How long had she been unconscious?

She looked around frantically, praying that by some miracle Butler was lying, that against all odds Jen had survived this kind of blood loss, but she wasn't there. Standing in the doorway where Butler had been when he'd shot her was Rolfe.

"We need this one," Rolfe said, and his eyes darted to her, lingering just long enough for hope to bloom.

They'd kept her alive so far. It hadn't been Butler's idea, because he'd tried to shoot her. And that shout she'd heard seconds before he'd knocked her unconscious teased at the edges of her memory. She had to assume it was Rolfe, asking him to wait. She locked her eyes on him, trying to make a connection.

Butler shrugged at his lieutenant, radiating power and rage and something else, something Evelyn couldn't quite pinpoint. "So you said. And you could be right, considering what they've brought to our doorstep."

His grip on his weapon suddenly tightened. "Deal with her. I'm going to talk to everyone." He glared at Rolfe, almost as though he was daring him to disobey, then turned and moved deeper into the compound.

As he walked away, her panic began to subside and new sounds penetrated. Some kind of thumping, like metal against wood, and the low mumble of too many voices. So, there were more people in here. The rest of the cultists?

She struggled to hear, to gauge how many cultists were here, what she might be up against. But her ears were still ringing, and it was hard to tell. There might've been a dozen, might've been a hundred.

Evelyn watched Butler go, and the world started to sharpen. She couldn't see anyone, but they had to be gathered in that large room she and Jen had walked into earlier.

She saw movement in her peripheral vision and turned to discover Rolfe holding out a hand to her.

She hesitantly put her hand in his, and he yanked her to her feet so fast that she fell into him. She automatically threw her free hand up to brace herself and landed flush against his chest. He was lean, so she hadn't expected the taut muscles underneath her hand. Still, there was something else, something that didn't belong.

He moved away from her, but not before she realized what he had on underneath his camouflage shirt. A shoulder holster.

"Come with me," he said, not giving her a choice, because he hadn't let go of her hand. He pulled her with him as he began walking in the opposite direction Butler had gone.

He passed the utility closet where she'd been stuck with Jen, and she felt new hope flare inside her—hope that he'd open that big steel door and just push her outside. After watching Butler shoot Jen, she'd prefer to take her chances in the inhospitable Montana mountains than stay here. Frostbite and death from exposure be damned.

But instead of opening the door, he suddenly whirled around, and pushed on the wall, which popped open into a new hallway. A door without a handle, practically invisible in the dim light.

Before she could move, he grabbed her around the waist, then lifted her up easily and set her down on the other side of the doorway. She didn't have time to protest; he took her hand again and started pulling her along.

She glanced behind her in time to see the door slide quietly shut, in time to see something shimmer along the ground in that doorway. She squinted, trying to make it out. A trip wire? *Inside* the compound?

She stumbled and righted herself, eyes forward, though she couldn't see anything.

It was even darker in this hallway, and quieter. Evelyn followed blindly, intensely aware of her hand crushed in Rolfe's, the squish of her shoes every time she took a step, Jen's blood between her toes.

Where was he taking her? What did he plan to do with her?

She opened her mouth to ask, but what came out was, "Where's Jen?" She didn't think Butler had been lying about her death, but what had they done with her body?

She sensed more than saw Rolfe glance back at her, before he stopped, opened a new door and dragged her inside.

"She's gone. I'm sorry. She shouldn't have brought you here. Now we're going to have to figure out what to do with you."

He finally released her and wiped the blood off his own hand on his pant legs. He did it distractedly, as if the blood didn't bother him. Or worse, as if he was used to it.

Then a dim light came on, illuminating a small, sparse room. Wooden shelves along one wall were lined with stacks of neatly folded utilitarian clothing, bars of soap and threadbare towels. She turned, discovering buckets and shovels stacked against another wall.

"There are smaller sizes in the left corner," Rolfe said as she heard the door close. "Those should fit you. Go ahead and change."

She spun around to find him standing close to her in the tiny room, anger and annoyance etched on his face. But at Butler or her? She wasn't sure.

She backed up, bumping the shelves hard enough to send a splinter through the sleeve of her suit and into her arm. "Can you wait outside?"

He crossed his arms over his chest. "Leave a cop alone in a room full of potential weapons? I can't do that. Come on, change. You don't want to wear that."

She hesitated, and he took a step back, leaning against the door, his eyes steady on her. "Just pretend I'm not here."

She felt an acute sense of discomfort, but the reality was, she had no idea how long she'd be here, or if they'd decide to toss her outside. In this weather, she'd be better off in warm sweats than her blood-soaked suit.

Evelyn shivered as she slid her suit jacket off, watching Rolfe carefully for any sign of sinister intent. She ripped the splinter out of her arm. The camisole she wore underneath her jacket had splotches of dried blood, too, and Evelyn yanked it over her head, replacing it with a sweatshirt that hung down to her hips. But it was warm. And dry.

Rolfe shifted his gaze to the wall as she changed out of her pants. The back of her underwear was sticky with blood, but she wasn't changing out of those in front of Rolfe, no matter how indifferent he seemed. Quickly, she stepped into a pair of big gray sweatpants she had to cinch tight at the waist. They pooled at her ankles as she put on a pair of thick wool socks.

Her skin felt tight where Jen's blood had soaked through her clothes and dried, but at least she wasn't drenched in it anymore. When she reached down to pick up her suit, Rolfe grabbed her arm, stopping her.

"Leave it. You don't want that."

He was right. Covered in Jen's blood, it would've gone straight in the trash if she was at home. She didn't need it, anyway. Butler had already taken her weapon, handcuffs and cell phone. She had no way to protect herself, and no way to call for help.

The only way she was getting out of here alive was if she convinced someone to let her go. And Rolfe was her best bet, since he was the only reason she was still breathing.

Stuck this close to him in the small room, she could see the tiny lines under his hazel eyes, and she had a sudden, unexpected flashback to college. To another pair of hazel eyes, eerily similar.

Except for his blond hair, Rolfe looked a lot like Marty Carlyle. The older brother of one of her best friends, and her first serious boyfriend. Someone she'd thought she could trust, who'd broken her heart.

She took a step backward, bumping into the shelf again as Rolfe's grip tightened on her wrist. She couldn't trust Rolfe, either, but she needed him to trust her. She needed him to connect with her.

And yet…if he was a racist who hated the federal government, why had he convinced Butler to let her live at all?

"Let's go," he said.

"Where?" Talking made her jaw throb, and she probed a raw spot on the inside of her cheek with her tongue, tasting more blood. With her free hand she gingerly touched the side of her chin, but even that slight touch was painful.

A hint of a frown curled his lips, and now that she'd noticed the resemblance to Marty, it was all she could see. Marty was Jewish, though, and Rolfe would surely have hated him, too.

"What's so funny?" Rolfe asked.

"Nothing's funny," she snapped before she'd thought it through. A federal agent was dead, a federal agent who'd been right about one thing. Something strange was happening at the Butler Compound.

But it was better not to remind him of Jen, so she said, "Butler's followers aren't going to want me among them. You can't want me here, either, a black woman…"

His eyes seemed to bore into her as he studied her too closely. "One of your parents is white. That's true, isn't it?"

She nodded, not sure if that improved things or made them worse.

"I don't care about that, anyway."

She frowned, and knew he'd seen her disbelief. "Butler…"

"I'm not Butler."

She tried to tug her hand out of his grip, but his fingers tightened around her wrist. "You're his lieutenant, aren't you?" she demanded, before figuring out a real strategy.

Some emotion flashed in his eyes at her words. Anger? Regret? Cunning?

She couldn't tell. Did he resent Ward's position as leader? Was Rolfe hoping to overthrow him? That would be a hard sell in a cult, but at least Rolfe didn't seem to want her dead. Still, she didn't want to be in the middle of a power play. Especially with Ward Butler surrounded by survivalists who'd chosen to leave behind everything they knew, and live where and how he demanded.

There were lots of different kinds of survivalists, and most of them prided themselves on being able to live off the land. They knew how to hunt. And they knew how to kill. Most of them didn't make a habit of killing people, but they hated the federal government, and anyone who represented it. She didn't want to discover what they were capable of doing to her.

"This may be Ward's place, but we're not what you think."

"Explain it to me, then," Evelyn said, trying to sound earnest. The more clearly she understood the dynamics, the more likely she'd be able to profile the players. And if she could do that, maybe she could get out of here alive.

Just when she thought he was going to shake his head and drag her off somewhere, probably back to the supply closet—although undoubtedly he'd tie her up this time—he spoke. "This isn't a *cult*." He spat the word out, as though it was dirty, beneath him.

She'd never used the word *cult*. Was he denying what others had called them? Or was he more intelligent than she'd suspected? She mulled that over as he continued.

"I'm not Ward's lieutenant or anything else. It may be Ward's land—and it's definitely Ward's rules—but everyone who lives here made the decision to come because they all share one thing. They want to be left alone, to live how they choose, without interference from a government we don't recognize."

He scowled at her, then started to pull her forward.

She dug her heels in, sliding forward, anyway, in the wool socks. "Just let me go. I promise, I..."

"You know Butler's not going to allow that, Evelyn."

Her name on his lips made her uncomfortable; it sounded as though they knew each other. As though he and Butler weren't holding her against her will. But he'd claimed *Butler* was doing it, so maybe she could find an ally here.

"You realize it's illegal to keep me here against…"

"Illegal?" The skin around his eyes crinkled, and she had the distinct feeling he was trying not to laugh at her. "You *trespass* on land that doesn't belong to you, and then you have the nerve to claim *we're* doing something wrong? We have every right to protect our land, every right to protect our liberties against a tyrannical government. You have no authority over me."

He took a breath, and then shook his head, visibly composing himself. "What happened with your friend was wrong, though, and I'm sorry."

She didn't want to talk about Jen—didn't want to remind him of the trouble he could be in—so she tried another tactic. "What good does keeping me here do? You said yourself I don't belong. So, let me go, and…"

"Keeping you in here keeps your friends out there."

Before she could ask what friends, he tugged on her wrist, harder this time, making her lose her balance as he opened the door and pulled her out.

"If you let me leave, they have no reason to come in," she insisted, her heart rate picking up. Whoever was outside—if Rolfe was telling the truth—was probably here because they'd realized Jen was missing. Would they have any idea *she* was in here?

Rolfe pulled her back the way they'd come, stopping at a room smaller than the closet. She discovered it was a bathroom. Survivalists with indoor plumbing—thank goodness.

"Why don't you wash your hands?" he suggested softly.

She lifted them, palms up, and saw the blood caked in the creases of her hands. Hurrying to the sink, she turned on the water, not even caring that it was freezing, and scrubbed and scrubbed until her hands hurt.

"I think you got it out," Rolfe said, turning off the water and passing her a threadbare towel. After she'd wiped her hands, he nodded and led her down the hall again.

As he opened the hidden door, a voice boomed over a bullhorn. "Ward Butler, this is Adam Noonan, from the FBI. We just want to talk. Please pick up the phone we tossed in."

Evelyn's pulse accelerated. Adam was from the Crisis Negotiation Unit. And if CNU was here, surely HRT was, too. Which meant Kyle was here.

Hope began to build again. If anyone could get her out of here, it was Kyle and his teammates.

"Ward." Adam's voice came over the bullhorn, and it sounded as if he'd been talking for a while, maybe during the time she'd been unconscious. "Let's start a dialog, one leader to another."

"Moron," Rolfe muttered, then said to her, "Watch your step." He lifted his feet carefully over the taut wire, finally dropping her wrist.

She followed, resisting the urge to rub her arm, then asked softly, "Doesn't it seem a little dangerous to have a trip wire inside?"

He gave her another of those mocking smiles. "You've never lived off the land, have you?" He seemed equally disgusted and perplexed as he added, "You wouldn't last a day if your comforts suddenly disappeared and you had to try to survive off what the mountain had to offer. You'd be dead before dawn." With that chilling prediction, he turned and kept walking, clearly expecting her to follow.

It was the first time he'd put real space between them. She couldn't stop herself from looking at the back door, within running distance, but Rolfe had an AK-47 slung over his shoulder and something else strapped under his camouflage shirt. And she had no idea how far away HRT was. Most likely they'd set up a perimeter outside the fence. Too far to run without being shot in the back.

Still, her whole body tensed as she tried to decide if she had a better chance of outrunning Rolfe out there than she did of weathering Ward Butler's temper in here.

"I wouldn't do that," Rolfe warned, without turning.

She walked a little faster, toward him, even as a voice in the back of her mind told her she'd missed what might have been her only chance to run. "What does living off the land have to do with a booby trap inside your own home?"

Did the other cultists know it was there and always remember to step over it? Or was this a part of the compound only Butler and his lieutenants were allowed to enter?

If so, that was a hell of a way to keep out your own followers.

She glanced back at it one last time, wondering what would happen if it was tripped. Wondering what else was behind that door that she hadn't been able to see in the darkness.

"Keep moving," Rolfe said instead of answering her question, and she had to increase her pace to keep up with his longer stride.

She followed him back down the dim hallway, toward the room where she and Jen had seen the supplies and weapon lockboxes. As he stopped in the doorway, she discovered that the room was now filled with cultists.

There were about twenty of them, and they were all men. Evelyn did a double take, looking for any women or children, but saw none. A cult without women or kids was unusual. And although survivalists could be loners, they were equally likely to prepare a bunker for an entire family. Did this cult not have any families or were they somewhere else?

The men ranged in age, but otherwise they looked the same to her. They were all white, their eyes glued to Ward Butler, who stood facing them, radiating power.

There was plenty of camouflage in the room, and a lot of weaponry, casually slung over shoulders. Everything from AK-47s to shotguns to bows and arrows. Most of the men wore thick facial hair and had rough, weathered skin and angry expressions.

The anger seemed to intensify as Ward Butler announced, "Here she is, our own personal symbol of government tyranny who thought it was her right to enter uninvited into our refuge."

Twenty faces swung her way, and all that fury directed solely at her made Evelyn instinctively take a step backward.

"Kill her," someone shouted and, as one, the group surged toward the doorway. Toward her.

* * *

"The shit's really hit the fan," Sam "Yankee" Mc-Givern, the head of HRT, announced as he walked into the Tactical Operations Center.

TOC was a glorified tent, but inside were state-of-the-art communications devices, hooked up to satellites that worked even in the inhospitable Montana wilderness. Greg's spot was crammed into a corner of the tent, next to the negotiator, Adam Noonan. He glanced around, realizing Adam had left the tent without his noticing.

Then he raised his eyes from his pop-up desk, seeking the sound of Yankee's booming voice. At six and a half feet, the man's head scraped the top of TOC, and he exuded strength, exactly the kind of figure FBI headquarters probably loved having as the lead in their version of special operations. He even had a scar running across the left side of his face, marring otherwise completely smooth, dark skin.

He strode through TOC, weaving around the operators and directly over to Greg, who sat a little straighter.

The sounds around him filtered back in again as his focus lifted more fully from his laptop. HRT agents, a Special Agent in Charge from Salt Lake City and support staff were all working frantically around him, but with a common discouraged slump to their shoulders. From outside the tent, Adam's voice came over the bullhorn.

Greg wrapped his hands around his thermos, hoping warmth from the coffee would penetrate where his gloves were failing. Judging by the temperature of the thermos, he needed a refill. "What now?" Greg asked

Yankee, hearing the exhaustion and worry in his own voice.

It was approaching midmorning, and despite Adam's repeated attempts to contact the cultists, no one had responded. But somehow, word had spread about what was happening here, because the protesters and news crews had appeared in much bigger numbers than they'd expected.

Meanwhile, Greg had spent the time trying not to think about Evelyn, the closest thing he had to a partner at BAU. Instead, he'd been reading and rereading everything he could on the Butler Compound and its members, hoping he'd find some way to help her. Assuming she was still alive.

He tried to push the thought aside, but it had been intruding for hours now, ever since word had come down that the cultists had been overheard talking about a dead federal agent. He needed to focus on whatever he could do to help Adam make a connection with someone inside; if the group wouldn't talk to them, it limited their options significantly.

Details about the compound members were sketchy at best. According to the old profile written up by BAU, Ward Butler was a hard-core survivalist with a handful of weapons possession, resisting arrest and tax evasion charges lodged against him over the years. He'd spent some time in jail, but had always gotten out, and as the years went by, he'd slipped farther and farther off the grid. He'd risen to the top of a local militia group before dropping out entirely and forming his compound, supposedly a gathering place for like-minded survivalists.

As a fringe militia leader, he fit the bill. Obsessed with weapons, antigovernment, believing that society would ultimately crumble and he'd need a bunker and the skills to live off the land. A man seeking power in a like-minded community. But he didn't seem like a typical cult leader—primarily because they tended to be charmers. They were usually as good at manipulating words and ideas as they were people. Ward Butler, on the other hand, had an outright angry, almost antisocial personality. But then, there were as many cults as there were personalities.

"There's something going on inside," Yankee said in his deep Southern drawl. Apparently, his nickname was ironic, given to him by the other members of HRT.

"What is it?" Pinpricks of pain shot through his fingertips as he gripped his thermos harder, and he realized his hands were frozen. Apparently, the heating system in TOC couldn't handle the Montana mountains.

"Take a listen, would you? I want an assessment." Yankee nodded at the headphones, discarded on Greg's desk, that would hook him up to the parabolic mics.

"Mic three," Yankee added as he hurried back the way he'd come, to talk to the Special Agent in Charge who'd arrived from the Salt Lake City office.

Greg traded the thermos for his earphones. As soon as he slipped them over his ears and turned to the right mic, a flurry of loud, angry voices made him cringe. It was hard to understand anyone with all of them talking at once, but one voice stood out.

"We need her alive," the man yelled over the fray.

Her. They had to be referring to Jen or Evelyn. One of them was still breathing. Relief and fear coursed through him in equal measure as his eyes were drawn to the picture brought in by an agent from the Salt Lake City office.

Jen Martinez was a forty-five-year-old mother of two. In the picture, she seemed happy and confident, a grin on her face and her arm around the waist of her husband of more than twenty years. Standing on either side of the couple were their kids. A daughter in high school and a son in middle school. The daughter resembled her mom, in appearance and attitude. The son took after his dad—or would, as soon as he emerged on the other side of his current awkward stage.

Every time he looked at the photograph, Greg felt the immediate need to avert his eyes. It was too close to the pictures he kept tacked up in his cubicle back at Aquia, of his wife, Marnie, and their two children, Lucy and Josh, the same ages as the Martinez kids.

He'd made the call to Marnie on the way to the plane, and she'd given the phone to Josh. His son had put on a good front, but Greg had heard his disappointment. Josh's very first hockey game, and he'd missed it. Worse, Josh had sounded hurt, but not surprised.

Greg loved his job. He couldn't imagine leaving it. But he spent too much time away from his kids—time he was constantly trying to make up to them when he was home.

If his partner was alive, that meant Jen Martinez was never going home to her children.

His eyes were drawn once more to the photo, to the kids who were waiting to hear if they still had a mother. Then he forced himself to look away, forced his mind back on the mission.

He glanced over at his cousin Gabe, a member of HRT who'd recently come off shift and was listening through his own earphones, frowning. He remembered the years after Gabe's mother was killed overseas. She'd just been in the wrong place at the wrong time during a spree shooting.

Greg's parents had tried to help Gabe and his sister get through it, while their dad grieved by pushing everyone away. Greg recalled all the times Gabe had spent at their house, staying in Greg's old room while he was away at college. All the times Greg's parents had spoken about the hell Gabe and his sister and father were going through. *Shut it down*, Greg told himself.

"We know who's talking?" he asked loudly. Who was trying to keep Evelyn or Jen alive?

Gabe looked up, his angular face creased with concern. He shook his head and went back to jotting notes.

Through Greg's headphones, the flurry of voices continued. Some were arguing that they should throw her outside, let her fend for herself—an idea quashed by a voice Greg *did* recognize. He'd spent hours online searching for feeds of Ward Butler, and he'd found a few. Mostly old militia meetings, and they'd told him that the man was definitely radical, even for fringe militia. They'd also told him that Butler had a distinctive growl of a voice, as though his vocal cords had frozen years ago and never properly healed.

Ward's deep voice cut through the followers', reminding them that the FBI was outside, and insisting that if they let her go, the FBI would invade.

There was a surge of voices, mingled with other sounds—booted feet on hard floors, the slap of something against skin, guns being racked.

Then the distinctive *boom* from a shotgun blast split the air, and Greg instinctively sank lower in his seat.

Around him, HRT agents lurched to their feet and swarmed the entrance to the tent. A mad rush of big men trained in specialized tactical response, each carrying sixty or so pounds of equipment, all trying to race outside at once.

Over his headphones, the shuffling of feet and the loud arguments continued, and it took Greg a minute to understand. The gunshot hadn't come from inside the compound.

It had come from the FBI's perimeter.

5

Evelyn gasped for breath, the smell of blood and sweat and too many bodies squeezed closely together burning her nostrils. Pressed against the rough, hard wall, with Rolfe's back against her, and her heart pounding, she could barely breathe.

The cultists had chased them back into the hallway, had managed to flank her and block her way before she could make a run for it. Somehow, for some reason, Rolfe had stood in front of her, trying to convince Butler to keep her alive.

A few of the cultists had stayed in the main room or followed and leaned against the wall, as if waiting for the show to start.

But most of Butler's followers had entered full-on mob mentality. If Butler was still giving orders, she couldn't hear him over the roar of the other cultists. Their screams all mingled together, becoming little more than a blare of words she couldn't make sense of.

Until someone shouted, "String the bitch up!" Then a rope came lassoing from somewhere to her right, passing behind Rolfe and snagging her bun, snapping tight. It wrenched her head hard enough that if it had gone around her neck, she'd be dead. Then the rope slipped off.

"Try again!" someone demanded. "Make an example of her!"

"Feeb!" someone else screamed. "How do you like your false power now?"

"Babylonian!" A third voice, shrill and excited, rose above the others. "Your time has come! We'll defeat your evil army!"

"Stop with the Babylonian bullshit," a tall man with a knife in his hands and a scowl on his face snapped back. "She's just another government pawn, trying to take from others. We need to make her pay for it, like Ward always says."

"Back off!" Rolfe shouted with so much rage and authority that the crowd actually did take a collective step backward.

But it didn't last. The cultists surged forward again almost immediately, and in front of her, Rolfe's hands locked around his AK-47.

To protect her? Evelyn didn't know, but it probably wouldn't matter. Just Rolfe against more than a dozen frenzied survivalists? Even if he handed her a weapon—which he wasn't likely to do—it wouldn't be enough.

A strong hand wedged itself between her and Rolfe, gripping her upper arm and trying to wrestle her free.

Evelyn pushed hard against the wall, and managed to get her hand up, digging her short nails into the man's wrist as hard as she could until his grip loosened. But just as fast, there was someone else on her other side, reaching for her, too.

Then Ward Butler's distinctive growl cut through the noise, so loud and angry it made her jump.

"Enough!"

As one, his followers stopped, but Evelyn didn't have to see them to feel the blast of hatred aimed at her. Rolfe's body eased forward a little, finally allowing her to draw a full breath, but setting panic free. She latched on to the rough folds of his camo, hoping to keep him there. He was all she had besides Butler's whims protecting her from a lynching.

"We hang on to her for now," Butler said, and a grumbling that sounded like an angry lion's roar filled Evelyn's ears.

Still, the crowd eased farther back, and most of them returned to the main room where Butler had preached earlier. Rolfe moved away from her, too, pulling out of her shaky grasp with ease.

He left her there, trembling in the hallway. A few scowling cultists prevented her from running for the door as fast as she could. Although it occurred to her that if they had trip wires inside the compound, there was probably something at the back door.

Evelyn slid along the wall, the three men who'd stayed behind tracking her closely as she slunk into a corner of the room. She didn't want Rolfe out of her sight.

He was at the front now, standing next to Butler, talking. Evelyn turned to scan the rest of the room, and discovered that the other men had taken seats at the three tables and were talking among themselves as if nothing had happened, suddenly as docile as a group of survivalists could get.

Her heart rate wasn't as quick to decelerate, and she pressed a hand to her chest as she swiveled her head, looking for the next threat.

Snippets of conversations drifted her way as the sound of her heart pounding in her ears slowly faded. Some of the men had moved on to mundane topics, like how brutal they predicted this year's winter would be, the best methods for finding food on the mountain and where to scavenge for supplies. Others still grumbled about letting a federal agent live when they needed to teach the government a lesson. A handful just eyed Butler and Rolfe with interest.

The few who'd stayed behind in the hallway still stood within arm's reach. The guy with the lasso—a small, heavily bearded man, probably in his twenties, with beady eyes and a snarl—kept glancing between her and Butler. The other two were calmer, hands lingering near their weapons, but displaying no obvious fury. More of Butler's lieutenants?

She squinted at them, trying to remember where they'd been during the mob, although she hadn't been able to see much around Rolfe. She had no idea if they'd swarmed her or if they'd been among the few who'd stood back and watched, ready to jump in or break it up, depending on Butler's orders.

"...question me!" Butler's furious voice caught her attention. Evelyn shifted her head toward him again, straining to hear, but he quieted down as Rolfe, his back to her, gestured with his hands. He seemed to be arguing aggressively.

New worry rushed into her mind. What would Butler do—or have his followers do—to Rolfe if he didn't obey orders? And what would happen to her without Rolfe?

How the hell had she let herself get mixed up in this mess? Would she have recklessly accompanied Jen if she hadn't been looking for a way to decide whether she still belonged in BAU? Or would she have done what Dan wanted and headed home on schedule?

Was this just one more sign that it was time to move on? To leave profiling behind for good? To leave the FBI?

To start over somehow? Of course, that meant she'd have to figure out what she wanted to do—who she even *was*—without the mission that had been driving her since she was twelve years old.

The very idea made her uneasy. The need to find out what had happened to Cassie had pushed her through college, through her advanced degrees, through the FBI Academy. It had motivated her to work impossible hours, striving for a perfect record, until she'd been accepted into BAU.

Now, her desperate need to solve Cassie's case was gone, because she'd done it. What was left?

She'd never know unless she could make it out of here alive, Evelyn reminded herself as she tried to hear what Rolfe was saying.

"…need her! Don't forget why you're here," Rolfe's voice carried toward her.

"This isn't how it was supposed to go," Butler boomed. "Not *here*! This place was supposed to stay invisible." Then he seemed to realize how loud he was being, and glanced around as Evelyn wondered what exactly his words meant.

Ward caught her eye and Evelyn lowered her head, but not before she saw him look back at Rolfe and give him a toothy, insincere smile.

"I never would've let them kill her," Butler said, clearly intending for her to overhear as he added, "Not yet."

Rolfe said something in response, but all Evelyn caught was an ominous-sounding, "Don't forget what we agreed," before he stalked away from Butler and toward her.

"Let's go," he barked, grabbing her arm and dragging her along with him back the way they'd come.

She stumbled, trying to catch her footing. "Where?"

"You want to stay with me or them?" Rolfe replied, the fury in his tone telling her now wasn't the time to test his determination to keep her alive.

"You," she whispered, as if she had a choice.

"That's what I thought," he said, still pulling her along so fast she had trouble keeping up.

The beady-eyed guy with the lasso spat at her, but kept quiet as Rolfe dragged her back the way they'd come.

He slowed down just long enough to let her step carefully over the trip wire, and the way he glanced at her gave her the impression that his anger was directed more at Butler than at her. It was hard to tell how far they'd walked in the semidarkness, but Evelyn thought they'd passed the closet where he'd brought her earlier to change.

How big was this place? And where were they going?

She could sense Rolfe's mood in his painful grip, so she didn't ask, just let him push her through another door and shut her inside. She heard him storm off, and as soon as he left, she reached out blindly and tested the handle. It was locked. A second later, footsteps approached again and she listened as something scraped the floor as it was wedged under the handle from outside.

She stood in the darkness, waiting for her eyes to

adjust. No matter how much she strained, she couldn't see anything at all, not even shapes. She gave up and stretched out her arms. Her right hand bumped into something wooden, sending another splinter into her arm. She ignored the pain, sliding her hand forward, identifying shelves. They were lined with plastic containers, but she couldn't guess what might be in them.

Carefully, she took a step to the left, and immediately bumped into another shelf. So she was probably in a different closet, like the one they'd originally shut her in with Jen.

What had they done with the other agent? Evelyn sucked in a deep breath, suddenly afraid to move backward. What if Jen's body was in here with her?

As a profiler, she'd seen a lot of death. Usually in crime scene photos, as she consulted from her office in Aquia, but up close and in person plenty of times, too.

In her job, getting called in on a case meant the death was probably gruesome. During her year at BAU, she'd seen depravity she couldn't possibly have imagined.

But she'd never had to watch another agent being shot, then been drenched in her blood. She'd never been locked in pitch darkness, hoping not to stretch out her arm and encounter a body.

Panic threatened, and Evelyn tried to ignore it, to think. Her best chance of getting out alive was to profile the people inside the compound, to understand them well enough to predict what they'd do next.

It was easy to see that Rolfe was her best ally. But why? What kind of lieutenant so openly questioned his leader?

The survivalists who'd chosen to live here did seem united in their hatred of the federal government, in the "prepper" ideology—the idea that they needed to be prepared for the collapse of civilization. Maybe instead of trying to go it alone, they'd banded together to ride out the end times together. They all appeared to be single, without families, so perhaps this was the family unit they'd created instead. Maybe those things formed the basis of the cult structure, instead of a typical religious belief, since they didn't seem to share a religion.

Was it enough? Preppers who'd put their faith in Butler as a leader? Except the conversation she'd overheard between Butler and Rolfe went through her mind as she absently tried to yank the splinter out of her arm. Butler had talked about the compound as though it wasn't the only place he controlled.

Could Jen be right? Could they be more than a cult? Could there be a terrorist connection?

Evelyn sighed, sinking slowly to the ground, feeling her way before she sat. She wrapped her arms around herself for warmth as she considered.

The mob of cultists who'd come after her had been disorganized, abrupt. Could a group consisting of members who didn't share a religious connection band together effectively enough to fuel a terrorist ideology? Could they really follow orders and act on their leader's plan?

Images flashed through her mind. The frenzied delight in the eyes of the man who'd hoped to lynch her. The shrill voice and sudden furor of the one who believed her to be a Babylonian heralding the arrival of an apocalypse. The grim, disgusted tone of the guy who just hated agents of the government.

They were unlike any cult she'd ever seen or studied. Unlike any terrorist group she'd come across.

There was no real unity here. So what kept them together?

When the FBI didn't just go away, would they turn on one another? And what would that mean for her?

"Move, move, move!" Yankee yelled, leading from the front as he raced toward the perimeter.

Kyle finished strapping on the extra weaponry he'd set down after coming off shift. The MP-5 slung over his back, the extra Glock strapped to his chest, the magazines on one thigh, flash bangs on the other. Hopefully he wouldn't need any of it.

He raced up next to Yankee, his breath puffing clouds of white into the frigid Montana air, his boots crunching in the frost, his gaze swiveling left and right. As far as he could tell, no one had breached the perimeter. But nothing was certain, and he pulled his MP-5 to the front for easier access.

"We have intel?" Gabe asked their boss.

"All we know is that someone took a shot near the perimeter the local police established." As more HRT agents joined them, Yankee continued. "We don't know who fired. We don't know what the target was, or if anyone was hit." Yankee's speed increased, but his voice remained calm. "Remember, unless there's an *immediate* risk of loss of life, no one fires. We're not giving them any excuses."

The local PD was handling the perimeter, along with agents from the Salt Lake City FBI. What made this different from most standoffs was the fact that they were dealing with a lot more than just reporters and camera crews.

Antifederalist numbers had risen rapidly in the past

few years, and they'd proven their willingness to flaunt their beliefs at other standoffs around the country. Unfortunately, it wasn't *just* beliefs they were flaunting, but also an arsenal of weaponry that rivaled HRT's equipment. And the know-how to use it.

The Salt Lake City office had already beefed up security at the perimeter twice since HRT had arrived early that morning, and reports had come back that the crowd of protesters was still growing. And too many in that crowd had come armed for war.

Kyle's stride faltered as he finally caught sight of the perimeter. "Shit," he mumbled, and kept going, gripping the stock of his gun, knowing that if he had to fire it casualties would be too high.

There was no other outcome, not with the sheer number of people pushing their way toward the perimeter. The sound seemed to reach him all at once, the roar of twenty-five furious voices without a united message.

How had they gotten here so fast? This part of Montana was remote, isolated. The population was fewer than five hundred and most of them didn't live here year-round.

Some of the crowd had come in heavy winter coats and carried handmade signs. Those were the ones who would eventually give in to the need for warmth and head home, watch the outcome on TV. But about half the protesters were wearing serious outdoor gear, mostly in camouflage colors, and they were armed. A cursory sweep of the crowd showed him a few shotguns, some handguns and far too many rifles. He glanced around and spotted additional shooters perched in the spindly pine trees.

"Get the negotiator here," Yankee said into his mic as he looked up into the trees. "The profiler, too."

Kyle glanced across him at Gabe, whose jaw had clenched at the mention of his cousin.

"We've got protesters with radios," Yankee muttered. "Are they talking to one another or did we miss something?"

Were all these people here because of an antifederalist principle, and not Butler specifically? That was definitely possible, given the number of fringe militia groups and antigovernment extremist movements in the area. Or could Butler be giving orders from inside the compound, bringing supporters here himself? Did he have a bigger reach than they'd realized?

If Butler could contact the outside world, that might explain the size of the crowd. Then again, it could also be due to the reporters jostling for position amid the protesters.

Kyle stared up at the closest shooter, braced near the top of a pine tree. It swayed under his weight, but he seemed at ease, holding a semiautomatic in gloved hands, a radio painted in camo colors strapped high on his chest along with enough extra ammunition to take on an army. A canteen was hooked to his waist next to a sheathed knife, and he wore a bulletproof vest under all the packets of ammo. He caught Kyle's gaze and seemed to smile, though it was hard to tell through the heavy salt-and-pepper beard. The pine tree bounced as he lifted his weapon higher, lining it up with Kyle's head.

Kyle instantly tensed. His gut reaction was to swing his own weapon into position…and to wish he'd taken the time to grab his helmet. But this guy could hit a target; Kyle didn't need to see him try to know that.

He had fringe militia written all over him. A helmet wouldn't make any difference. And aiming his own weapon could set the supporter off, give the guy an excuse to shoot first.

So, instead, he kept his MP-5 clenched close to his body, aimed down at the ground and said into his bone mic, "Inactive shooter, pine tree, at my three o'clock."

"Got him." Wyatt Thompson, the brand-new sniper on their team, came back immediately.

Kyle had no idea where Wyatt had positioned himself, but Wyatt's father was a big deal in the army and apparently Wyatt had learned to shoot around the time he'd started walking. He was one of the best shooters they'd ever seen in HRT. The tension in Kyle's shoulders loosened instantly, even as a reporter pointed directly at him, and then the cameraman behind her swung his lens to film them.

"There go your future undercover jobs," Gabe joked, sounding calm as always, a hint of amusement in his tone.

Kyle resisted the urge to look over at his partner and roll his eyes. Hopefully someone on the FBI's media team would stop that coverage from going anywhere, but undercover work wasn't in his future, anyway. He planned to stay in HRT until they forced him to retire.

"I've got news on Jen's car." Greg's voice suddenly came over Kyle's radio and he pushed his hand over his earphone, although he could hear perfectly. The screams of the protesters seemed to fade into the background as his hands clenched his weapon too tightly.

If they'd found the car, did that mean they'd found Evelyn or Jen? Or, God forbid, a body?

"Evelyn's cell phone was inside the SUV, but nothing else," Greg said, his steady profiler voice giving nothing away, even though it was his closest friend in BAU who was missing. "The SUV was abandoned a couple hundred yards off the road. Someone was clearly trying to conceal it, and I doubt it was Jen or Evelyn."

Someone from the Butler Compound had taken the SUV, probably hoping to hide the connection between the agents and the compound. Probably after they'd killed one of them. But which one?

"Mac!" Yankee yelled, and Kyle realized he'd stopped moving, that his teammates were still advancing toward the perimeter.

The Salt Lake City agents had brought in police barriers to halt the crowd, but several of them had been knocked over, and the agents and local cops had been pushed back twenty feet. The crowd was still swarming toward them.

"Where the hell is the negotiator?" Yankee demanded.

"We've got movement in the tower." Wyatt's voice came over the mic before anyone could reply about Adam's whereabouts. "It's not Butler, but the subject is armed. He can definitely see the protesters from there. A picture is coming at you," he finished, and Kyle knew that last part was for the support staff in the tent, whose job it would be to try and identify the guy.

"I'm here!" a voice panted behind Kyle, and he recognized Adam an instant before the negotiator raised a bullhorn to his mouth and addressed the crowd. "We need you to move back behind the barricades. This is private land."

"It's not *your* land," the protester closest to Kyle screamed. The Salt Lake City agents and the local cops moved backward, slipping behind the lines of HRT but staying close, some of them readying riot shields.

"Brothers!" They heard a new voice over a loud-speaker blaring from the compound. Ward Butler's stones-on-a-grinder voice.

The crowd suddenly quieted, going still, their faces lifted toward the sound. "Thank you for showing your support today. We stand united against a tyrannical government. An *illegitimate* government!"

A cheer rose up from the crowd as Yankee looked back at Adam. "Get their attention."

"We have a bigger problem," Greg said over the mic.

"Where are you?" Yankee asked.

"Back at the tent. We identified the man in the tower. He's small-time in the states' rights movement, but he's got a handful of arrests under his belt, and a very active blog."

"And?" Yankee asked through his teeth.

"Unless Butler's changed this guy's tune drastically since his last blog post a month ago, he's convinced the end times are coming. His blog is full of fictionalized accounts—Babylonians in the form of government agents storming the strongholds of the righteous and the battle to end it all. By his account, the FBI's arrival is a sign of the apocalypse. That's gotta be Butler's view, too."

Kyle glanced at his partner. If they stormed the compound, the cultists would fight to the death. And if there was a federal agent alive inside, she'd be dead as soon as that happened.

He looked back at the crowd, still waiting silently, anticipating Butler's next words. If those words urged his followers to fight, could HRT hold them back? And even if they could, would it matter? Or would Butler begin his endgame?

6

The closet door opened fast, and Evelyn scrambled to her feet, her fists instinctively coming up, even though she knew it was futile.

Ward Butler stood in the doorway, a furious glower on a face that already seemed permanently bent in a sneer. "Move," he growled, gesturing for her to come out from the corner.

She squinted; the dim light in the hallway seemed bright after the total darkness of the closet. She considered refusing, but it wouldn't help her.

Stomach churning, she stepped slowly toward him, peering down the hall. She'd expected a crowd of cultists, begging for another try at a lynching, but it was quiet. Not even Rolfe was with Butler this time, and it made everything seem ominous in a different way.

"Let's go," he said, pointing with his rifle back down the hall, over the trip wire and into the main hallway, which was also empty.

"Where?" she asked, glad to discover her voice didn't squeak. It came out strong and clear, as if she still had some say in what happened to her.

"Upstairs," he replied, and he opened another nearly invisible door, revealing a curving staircase.

The lookout tower. She'd wondered how they accessed it. Did he plan to throw her off it?

No, she decided as he slammed the rifle barrel into her back when she didn't immediately start climbing.

The force of it shoved her forward, and she hit the first step with her shins, then went down on her hands. Her knees hit the edge of the metal stair, shooting pain through her legs and up her spine.

She pushed herself to her feet and began climbing, sensing more than hearing Butler behind her. The rumble of his voice reminded her of driving too fast over loose gravel, but he moved silently, with stealth, like a man who was used to stalking prey in the mountains.

He wouldn't throw her out the window; it wasn't high enough. She might survive that fall.

He was taking her up there so the FBI surrounding the building would see her. He was showing his hand, betting it was good enough to get him whatever he wanted.

Her pace quickened. Maybe she could tell them something, give them some kind of message.

But what? Her mind blanked. What did she really know that they wouldn't already have discovered themselves?

Before she could come up with anything, Butler was jabbing her with the rifle barrel again and she stepped into the lookout room. It was a tiny space, with barely room for two people to stand, but there were windows on all sides, and the sloping mountains toward the entrance provided a view well into the distance.

Ward didn't climb up into the room with her. He stayed on the stairwell, just out of sight of any snipers who might be watching. He kept his rifle aimed at her, despite the fact that there was nowhere for her to run, no room to fight.

She spun in a slow circle, looking through the windows, knowing for certain that an HRT sniper was staring back at her. Probably several. But wherever they were, she couldn't spot them.

She took in the steep mountain behind the compound, protecting the cultists on two sides. It was covered with new snow, and in other circumstances, it would have been a gorgeous view. A little stark, but this was nature in a purer form than she usually got to see, mostly untouched by man.

She turned toward the front of the compound, and saw a crowd of protesters. Their features were blurred from up here, but signs rose above them. Facing the protesters was a line of men and women, some in blue; they had to be FBI and local police.

While she was locked in the closet, she'd heard Butler's puffed-up voice talking about how the protesters were ready to fight the police, that all he had to do was say the word. She'd scooted closer to the door when she heard Rolfe reply, trying to make out his words, but he'd kept his voice so much softer than Butler's. She still wasn't sure what he'd said; her best guess was "Not yet."

She'd also heard them say something about April 19—a date a lot of antifederalists held in high regard. She couldn't tell what they'd been saying about it. That had worried her, because violent believers had used April 19 as a battle date—it was when the raid on Waco had happened, when the Oklahoma City bombing had happened. But April was a long way off, and right now she had other problems.

As she gazed out the window, she saw that the protesters were contained, although there were more of them than she'd expected. She could see the signs bouncing up and down, but there was no mad rush toward the compound.

The sound of Adam Noonan's voice made her jump, even though she'd heard him speaking all morning. She looked up at the sky, at the sun casting pink over the mountains. Was it evening already? The hours had blended together while she'd hunched in that closet, trying to create a strategy to stay alive.

"Mr. Butler, let's meet face-to-face." Adam was pushing the same message Butler had ignored all day.

To Evelyn's surprise, Butler lifted his own bullhorn, one she hadn't even realized he was carrying. "We have your agent. It's within our rights, when someone trespasses on our land, to execute them."

Evelyn felt her whole body jerk, and instead of looking at Butler's other hand, the one still holding that rifle, she looked past him, down the staircase. But it was empty. No Rolfe to talk Butler out of killing her. Was Butler's plan to shoot her while her friends watched, too far away to do anything about it?

"Let's talk about what you want, Ward," Adam said, and nothing in his tone revealed that he'd known her for the entire time she'd been at BAU—not quite two years. He sounded neutral, invested only in making peace between Butler and the government.

That was his job, but it still left a sour feeling in Evelyn's gut. She studied the distance to the protesters now, the distance to any police presence, and knew for certain that HRT would never be able to storm the compound. Not before she was killed.

Adam's negotiation skills—and her own profiling abilities—were her only real chance.

"I want you to leave us alone!" Butler bellowed, and down below, the protesters roared their approval so loudly that their voices seemed to echo around her.

"You have to know that if you kill me they'll come for you," Evelyn told Butler quietly, staring him dead in the eyes, trying not to let him see her fear. Trying to think like the profiler she was, the profiler she'd always wanted to be.

He dropped the bullhorn to his side and snarled back, "Let them try."

"*You* might survive," she lied, keeping her voice slow and even. "But what about your followers?"

He smirked. "They're willing to die for what they believe in. Aren't you?"

She pointed out the window, in the direction of the protesters. She couldn't see the reporters, but she knew they were there. And she knew what Butler wanted the world to think—that the FBI had come after them for no reason, forcing Butler's hand. "You shoot me, and it'll go on the news. How's anyone to know you didn't invite me in here just to kill me? You've let Jen in before. That's probably not the PR you want for your cause."

Ward's lips twisted downward, and his gun lowered, too. "My people will know."

"Are you sure about that?" Evelyn pushed. She wasn't positive it was the right move, but she didn't see any other.

"Yes," he replied immediately, then smiled. "It doesn't matter, anyway. I'm not going to kill you. Not here. Not now."

He raised the bullhorn again. "You come in here,

and she dies," he warned, then tossed the bullhorn at her feet and headed back downstairs.

Apparently, the negotiations were over.

The cultists were glaring at her.

For the past five days, that was the worst they'd been allowed to do. Butler's exact orders to his followers when he'd brought her down from that tower were, "No one touches her. It isn't time."

Ever since, she'd lived in fear of when that time would come. When she'd end up like Jen, whom Butler had most likely dumped somewhere on the mountain so she'd be hard to find.

Evelyn walked slowly into the large room where they all gathered for meals, nodding her thanks as Rolfe slipped an extra Meals Ready-to-Eat into her palm as he walked past her. She kept her head down, avoiding the cultists' resentful glares as she sat in the far corner and peeled open the MRE, what military forces ate on missions.

She slurped down the room-temperature liquid quickly, as much to avoid focusing on how disgusting it was as to prevent anyone from taking it away. Beef and potatoes, she recognized, trying not to gag.

Her raw throat stung as she forced down the mushy MRE, and her hands were ice-cold, but that was nothing new. Even in the sweats Rolfe had given her that first day, she couldn't remember when she'd last been warm. She'd caught a cold the second night, which was only getting worse. She spent most days actively trying not to shiver.

The nights were a little better, because Rolfe had insisted to Butler that he'd watch her. At first, she'd been half relieved it wasn't Butler and half afraid of what Rolfe might want. Especially when, instead of locking her back in a closet, he'd zip-tied her to his tiny, metal-framed bed, apologizing the whole time. She'd tried to fight him initially, but he was far stronger than she'd expected.

Thank goodness, once he'd had her arm tethered, he'd just piled blankets on her—until she was actually warm—then dumped one on the ground for himself. Ironically, she'd felt safer during the past five days while tied to a strange man's bed than while walking with limited freedom around the compound. Particularly after Rolfe had whispered to her that first night, "I'll try to protect you. Just keep your head down, and try to stay away from Butler."

She couldn't completely trust Rolfe. He was Butler's lieutenant, and she needed to remember that. It didn't matter that he seemed to genuinely care that she not get hurt, or that he seemed to regret what had happened to Jen. It didn't even matter that she suspected he could be having second thoughts about the path he'd chosen. He was still part of Butler's cause.

But he was the best ally she had in here, and she found herself looking for him each day, relief settling over her when she spotted him nearby.

She could hear the typical angry whispers at the tables around her. Ever since Butler had taken her up to that tower, she'd been allowed to walk around the compound freely. Or at least as freely as she could with the constant gaze of the cultists on her, the constant fear that one of them would disobey Butler—or that Butler would change his mind.

She'd spent as much of the past five days as she could

trying to gather any information that might help her or HRT, hoping she could get it to them. But her days were still structured. She was expected to be in the crowd when Butler preached, to be at the tables when food was passed around, to follow Rolfe back to his room when the sun went down. Still, she'd tried to figure out the cultists' long-term plan, the best points of entry for HRT and whether the cultists had a strategy in place if the compound was breached. Unfortunately, there were so many eyes on her that she hadn't learned much.

Lately, all Butler wanted to do was preach his lifestyle over the bullhorn, to anyone who might be listening, inside the compound and out. She knew the protesters were still there, because every once in a while their voices would rise to a fevered pitch and she could hear them. They seemed to be feeding Butler's ego even more.

He'd demanded that he be given the opportunity to tape a message for the local news outlets, and the FBI had agreed. Since she hadn't seen a TV in here, she had no idea if they'd actually played it, but judging by the triumphant grin she'd seen on Butler's face the next morning, she suspected they had. Or at least he believed they had.

It reminded her of too many cult standoffs she'd read about before she joined BAU. A cult leader with sudden media and law enforcement attention who thought that gave him all the power. But like the rest of them, eventually he'd tire of preaching. Eventually it would be time for action.

She thought back to Jen's joke about the cultists drinking Kool-Aid, and the memory made her wonder again what Butler had done with the other agent's body.

She forced her mind off it, because it wasn't important. Jen was dead. It was just her now.

And regardless of what the original BAU assessment had been, Evelyn didn't think mass suicide was going to be the final outcome. The cultists here were long-time survivalists; their plan would be to fight. Some of them probably wished they'd never come. But she could tell others were already itching for the chance to prove their skills to the agents outside.

They'd never believe they stood no chance against HRT. Undoubtedly there'd be casualties on both sides. But Evelyn knew she'd never see the fighting. As soon as Butler decided it was time to go on the offensive, she'd be expendable.

Swallowing the last of her MRE and suppressing the urge to cough, she stood and tossed the container in the nearest trash can. Then she walked slowly out of the big room, trying not to attract attention. Her feet were chilly, even in the wool socks, and her calves ached from walking on the hard floors without shoes.

She felt the eyes of the cultists on her as she moved, could make out snippets of their whispers. They were restless—that much she knew—tired of Butler's preaching and the FBI surrounding their home.

"This isn't what I signed up for," one of them said, and Evelyn glanced back to see him whip a knife out of his pocket and snap his wrist, sending it straight at the back wall. It flew between two of the other cultists, then stuck in the dart board on the wall.

His tablemates cheered, and he turned and stared meaningfully at her.

She spun around and picked up her pace, hurrying into the hall.

Another voice rose, just enough for her to catch the end of his sentence before she moved out of hearing range. "…promised me some action."

What had they thought when they'd come here? Evelyn forced herself not to glance back, forced herself to keep walking as normally as she could.

She didn't look around at all until she'd reached the end of the long hallway, where she crouched down and carefully opened the gun port she'd discovered yesterday. Just a circle on the wall that opened far enough to slide the barrel of a rifle through. Yet another sign that Butler would fight rather than surrender. Yet another sign that he saw this place as his Babylon—the place of the final battle. The place of Armageddon.

She looked both ways, then pulled it open, shifting her body to block the view from anyone who might come down the hall. She knew she didn't have much time. They wouldn't leave her alone for long, even after showing her how they'd booby-trapped the exterior doors with shotguns, rigged to fire if the doors were opened. No one was getting in or out, not without a lot of time to carefully remove the booby traps.

Cold from the floor instantly seeped through her clothes and pinpricks raced up her legs to her skull. She tried to ignore her discomfort as she put her mouth near the port and spoke directly into it. "The doors are booby-trapped," she whispered, hoping someone could hear her.

She knew how HRT worked. There would be parabolic mics on the compound; she just didn't know where. But she figured her best bet was to project her voice outside.

"There are twenty men in here," she continued. "All

I can get are first names, so nothing you can run in the system, but they carry weapons at all times. They have additional arms and ammunition under their bunks."

With the limited freedom she'd been given over the past few days, she'd learned that all the cultists except Butler and Rolfe bunked together in a room off the main hallway, in one long row, two high.

The top bunks were so close to the ceiling that the men couldn't sit on them without bumping their heads. The bottom bunks—when lifted—revealed storage for two.

She'd seen the racist with the lasso lift his bunk one day, and discovered that it hid a full survival kit. Everything from a stack of MREs, extra wool blankets, first aid kits, gas masks, water purification tablets, duct tape, two knives, two pistols, two rifles and enough ammunition to support an entire army unit.

He'd noticed her looking at it, and promptly slammed it shut. She'd run out of the room, but not before realizing that all the bunks hid storage compartments. She didn't dare try to loot from them; she was too closely watched.

Still, it made her wonder. Was all that ammunition to fend off looters in the end times? Or had Ward Butler been hoping for a standoff with the federal government all along?

"What are you doing?" Rolfe barked, his voice low but furious.

Evelyn dropped the port opening and tried to leap to her feet. She wasn't up before Rolfe reached her. How had he approached so silently?

His fingers latched around her upper arm, digging in

until she yelped. "You shouldn't have done that. What are you thinking, Evelyn? What if Butler had seen you?"

He pulled her through the hidden doorway, barely slowing enough for her to leap over the trip wire. She saw Ward Butler on the other side.

The hallway had more light than before, and she wanted to look around, to inspect the area, which only Butler and Rolfe seemed to enter. But she couldn't take her gaze off Butler.

He had a frenzied light in his eyes. She'd seen it before—in an orphanage director who'd been accused of molestation and set his own building on fire, then watched as it burned, the kids still inside. In a human trafficker who'd been arrested, but refused to divulge the location of a truck of "merchandise" that had come over the border with no one to meet it. In a man who was about to be indicted for defrauding his company of millions and decided to go on a shooting spree at the company board meeting.

Butler knew he was cornered, but he didn't plan to go down alone.

"What's she doing in here?" Butler snapped.

"I'm locking her up again," Rolfe answered, and tried to pull her past Butler.

But the leader grabbed her other arm, the two men playing tug-of-war with her until the joints in her arms ached and Butler said, "I want to make an example of her."

"Then we have no leverage," Rolfe told him.

"We have *all* the leverage," Butler replied, actually smiling.

"If you kill me, the FBI has no reason not to breach," Evelyn put in quickly.

"They know about the booby traps," Rolfe added.

"What?" Butler's gaze whipped from Rolfe to her and back again. "Which ones?"

"On the compound doors," Rolfe replied.

There were more booby traps? Connected to that trip wire she'd just jumped over? Outside, on the ground surrounding the compound? Or somewhere else entirely?

"How'd they find out?" Butler asked, his expression frantic and then suspicious. "And how do you know?"

"I have my ways," Rolfe answered, not looking at her as he said it.

He'd heard her trying to give HRT information. And he was protecting her from Butler again. Why? Because he was smart enough to know she was their only leverage, and that despite their skills and weaponry, the FBI could still overpower them? Because he didn't want to die in here? Evelyn squinted up at him, her gut insisting there was more to it.

Could he possibly be that different from the rest of them? Could he be doing this simply to save her life?

Butler scowled back at Rolfe, and finally dropped her arm. "Fine. I'm going to talk to my people. Do what you want with her."

He strode away, and Rolfe pulled her farther down the hall, past the closet where he'd brought her to change on the first day, back into his room, where she'd spent the past five nights.

Tiny and sparse, it contained nothing more than a stack of supplies and a single metal-framed bed covered with a pile of threadbare wool blankets he'd brought for her. And the single blanket he'd spread on the ground for himself.

She shivered. It was even colder back here than in the main part of the compound, but Rolfe never seemed to notice.

"Sit." He pushed her onto the bed. Instead of sitting beside her, he stepped backward, leaning against the far wall.

"You're only making this harder on yourself," Rolfe said, his voice neutral, not furious the way his grip had suggested.

"Keeping me here is keeping the FB—"

Rolfe cut her off. "The FBI isn't going to leave us alone if we let you walk out of here. But Ward *will* kill you if you don't quit antagonizing him. Can't you see that he doesn't recognize the value of keeping you alive?"

"And you do?" *Why?* She didn't ask.

"Obviously, or you'd be dead several times over," he snapped back.

Then he took a visible breath, blowing out a puff of white into the air that made her realize the cold wasn't all in her head. It was freezing in here. The cultists were just acclimated to it.

"You seem like a good person. What would make you become a lackey for the FBI?" he asked, almost conversationally.

"What would make *you* become a lackey for someone like Butler?" she responded immediately, then cursed herself.

A sardonic smile curved his lips, and there it was again, that bizarre resemblance to Marty Carlyle. On the rare occasions when she used to speak before thinking, Marty would give her that same smile.

That was so long ago now. After Marty had broken her heart back in college, she hadn't seen him again for years. Then, suddenly, her friend's brother had returned to DC, divorced from the woman he'd left her for, and wanting another chance.

She'd said no. She tried not to repeat her mistakes. But she hadn't expected the jolt—half old betrayal, half regret—she'd felt when he'd shown up, looking so similar to the way she remembered him. Like a dark-haired version of Rolfe.

She shook the memory clear. "You have to know Butler is—"

"High on his own power?" Rolfe interrupted. Not giving her time to formulate a reply, he strode over and sat down beside her.

The thin mattress sank under his weight and she scooted to the left, putting space between them. She glanced at the closed door beside her, the room seeming miles away from the cultists. She couldn't even hear them from back here.

But she wasn't afraid of Rolfe. Not really. Not the way she was of Butler and the other cultists.

Here was her chance, a faraway whisper in her mind insisted, a voice that used to be strong and clear. Her profiler's voice.

If she had any chance of unraveling what was really happening here, of keeping herself alive and ending this standoff peacefully, she had to connect with Rolfe.

"Why are you here?" she asked, then cringed at the clumsy question, uncomfortable this close to him on the bed. He usually kept a careful distance, and she knew it was to keep from scaring her.

He leaned back, crossing his long legs in front of him. "A better question is, why are *you* here? What does the FBI care about a peaceful group of survival-

ists living in the middle of nowhere? We're not bothering anyone."

"We only came for a goodwill visit," Evelyn said,
sticking to Jen's original story.

A smile quirked his lips. "Bullshit." He moved toward her fast, in one smooth motion, getting in her face.
"Something specific brought you all the way out here."

He stared at her, and she fought the instinct to back
away. "I'm new. I'm supposed to meet…"

He laughed, shook his head and stood. "You're a
lousy liar." He checked his watch. "Last chance."

"Okay, fine. You tell me why…"

"Nope." Rolfe glanced at the closed door. "We're not
negotiating. Get up."

Slowly, she did, following his gaze to that door. They
were alone. They were far from the other cultists. Yes, he
was her only ally inside this compound. And yes, he was
bigger than her, and he was armed. But she was trained.
Could she take him down? Fast enough, silently enough?

He looked back at her, and shook his head again.
"I can see what you're thinking, and I'll save you the
trouble. My training is better than yours. I'm trying to
keep you alive here, but you come after me and I'll be
forced to fight back. I may not want to hurt you, but I'm
sure as hell not going to let you hurt me, either. Don't
mess with me, Evelyn."

Chills crept over her skin at his matter-of-fact tone.
Movement caught her eye and she looked down, spotted the small blade he held in his right hand. She hadn't
even seen him take it out.

As fast as he'd pulled the knife out, he slipped it back
in his pocket. As though he'd never actually intended

to hurt her, as though he just wanted her to know that he *could*.

She looked back up into his eyes. And suddenly, of all the things she wasn't sure of—what was really happening at the Butler Compound, how to keep herself alive, whether she had it in her to remain a profiler— one thing she knew with absolute certainty.

Rolfe was not what he seemed.

7

Evelyn was startled awake, and her lungs seemed to rattle as she drew in a breath. Instead of getting up, she curled into a tighter ball on the floor, trying to preserve warmth.

She was locked in a closet again. This time it was Rolfe's closet, where he'd stuck her after Butler had burst into the room the other night. He'd seen her and Rolfe talking together and he'd stared at the zip tie on the bed, then given Rolfe a nasty look.

"She's not here for your entertainment," Butler had snapped at Rolfe. He'd dragged her into Rolfe's closet and locked the door.

It was smaller than the closet he'd stuck her in before, and as far as she could tell, Rolfe didn't keep anything in it. She recalled the stack of supplies next to his bed, and wondered if someone had cleared them out, expecting her to take their place. Somehow that didn't seem right to her, but she couldn't think of any other explanation.

That wasn't all she couldn't do. She couldn't gather information about the cultists from in here, couldn't do much of anything besides lie on the floor and hope Butler forgot about her again.

She couldn't tell how much time had passed, since the light never filtered in, but she was pretty sure she'd been inside the closet overnight. It made her wonder where Rolfe had gone, because she'd expected him to open the door as soon as Butler left. She was also pretty sure, going by the temperature inside the closet, that it was against an exterior wall.

She'd spent just over a week inside the compound, and already she felt far removed from her life in Aquia, from her role as a federal agent. The only reassurance she had that the FBI hadn't given up on her and gone home was times like this, when Adam's voice reached her from a bullhorn, through that wall.

Adam sounded weary, as if he had little hope that Butler would ever respond. Suddenly, she heard Rolfe, moving around in his room. She opened her mouth to call him, to ask for something to drink.

"Damn it! This isn't what we agreed!" Butler's growl penetrated the closet walls.

Evelyn instinctively froze, not wanting Butler to hear her. Not wanting to remind him she was here.

"It's almost time," Rolfe said, and although his tone was relaxed, the words themselves were ominous.

Rolfe was much quieter than Butler, but if she strained, she could make out his words. Time for *what*? And how had Rolfe ended up with Butler? He was obviously Butler's only lieutenant, but he questioned the leader regularly—and protected her, even openly, in front of the followers. Why did Butler put up with him? Was Rolfe holding something over Butler? Or had he proven himself too successfully in the past for Butler to let him go now?

More than that, though, she wondered what Rolfe's

motivation was. Why had he kept her alive? Was it because Butler had become too fanatical for him? Did he want to get out?

She knew the FBI had parabolic mics set up on the compound—although she had no idea how much they could hear from inside the thick walls. But Rolfe and Butler probably realized they could shoot her and the FBI wouldn't know unless they came in. And if that happened, it was over for her, anyway.

Rolfe had told her his training was better than hers. What did that mean? Survivalist training?

Was it possible that he was working as a police informant? She quickly rejected the possibility. She didn't know why, but she would've bet good money that Rolfe wasn't on the local police's radar.

Then who had trained him? Before she could come up with a theory, Butler's voice penetrated the closet again and seemed to wrap around her like barbed wire.

"What about *my* plans? You think this is only about you? You think you're in charge here? That any of these men would follow *you*? I could demand your death right now, and that would be the end of it."

"Then everything you worked to build would be for nothing," Rolfe replied calmly in a tone that made Evelyn imagine he was holding that tiny blade between his fingers again.

He'd purposely drawn her attention to it when he'd pulled it on her, but he was right about his training. She'd never seen him palm it in the first place.

And that was something she *was* trained to see. At the FBI Academy, she'd spent time in hand-to-hand combat. She'd learned how to spot when someone was carrying, how to protect her own weapon, how to take a hit and remain standing. But wherever Rolfe had learned to fight, he'd learned well. She just hoped he'd continue to protect her, that he'd never actually turn on her.

Her stiff body began to ache from holding so still, but she tried to ignore it, tried to hold back the cough scratching its way up her throat until her eyes watered. *Don't remind Butler you're in here*, Evelyn chanted in her head.

She might not fully understand Rolfe, but she had a good read on Butler. Rolfe was right; Butler was high on his own power, and that made him dangerous—to his followers and particularly to her. Her breath come faster with her fear, and it felt unnaturally loud.

"You're trying to make sure that my empire's going to be for nothing now, aren't you?" Butler shouted.

"I'm not the one who shot Martinez. Why the hell did you do that?"

"She *saw* him. What choice did I have? We couldn't let her walk out of here. She could've ruined everything." There was a pause, then Butler added, almost petulantly, "Maybe I should've let her."

"Maybe you should have," Rolfe said, his voice still so calm and even that Evelyn knew it had to be pissing Butler off.

"She recognized him."

There was another long pause after Butler's words and Evelyn lifted her head, trying to hear Rolfe's response. Butler was obviously talking about the driver of the truck. Why did it matter if Jen recognized him? Her body, stiff from lying on the floor all night, spasmed as she stretched closer to the wall, and she dropped her hand to the floor to brace herself. But it was too late. She'd made a noise.

"Son of a bitch!" Butler snarled. "The fed's still in there?" The closet door was wrenched open.

"You told me to leave her there," Rolfe said, and his voice seemed unusually tense. Because of what Butler had said about Jen recognizing the guy? Or because he didn't want to protect Evelyn from Butler again?

Evelyn squinted against the dim light coming into the closet, and scooted backward, although there was nowhere to go.

Butler stood in the doorway, practically filling it with his bulk, a furious glower on his face. The modified AK-47 strapped diagonally across his chest and the pistol hooked to his waist didn't look as threatening at that moment as his huge fists, opening and closing as if he imagined her neck locked inside them.

Just when it looked as though he was going to stride into the closet and try to do exactly that, she saw Rolfe's hand clamp down on his shoulder. "Leave her alone," Rolfe said so harshly that it sounded like an order.

Fury raced over Butler's features, and for a second Evelyn thought he was going to take a swing at Rolfe. Instead, he stepped backward and slammed the door.

Plunged into darkness again, she felt her breath stall in her lungs as she waited for what he was going to say or do next.

But all she heard was the door to Rolfe's bedroom opening, then that slammed, too. Butler was gone.

Or at least she assumed it was Butler. She slowly drew in air, listening for Rolfe. For several minutes, she heard nothing at all, and when she'd decided they must've left together, she heard the creak of Rolfe's mattress.

When everything went silent again, she realized Rolfe was probably wondering if Butler was going to turn on him for his disobedience.

Evelyn wondered that, too. But as the silence dragged on, she remembered Butler's words. He'd said Jen had seen *him*. The driver of the truck.

Evelyn had forgotten about him until they'd mentioned it. She was almost certain he hadn't returned to the compound. Was Butler worried that someone would connect the driver—whoever he was—to this place? Was he wanted by police?

She rejected that as the problem. Butler had been arrested multiple times, and he claimed not to recognize federal law. He probably wouldn't blink at harboring a fugitive, because anyone he let in here would break the same laws he did.

Then what?

Ward and Rolfe kept talking about some event, kept saying it was almost *time*. But time for what?

Mass suicide or an attack against the agents outside seemed the obvious answers, but neither of those would have anything to do with the truck driver. Unless he was supposed to attack the surrounding agents from the other direction?

Panic fluttered through her, but dissipated as quickly as it had come. There was no way for Butler to have anticipated her and Jen's arrival, no way for them to anticipate that the FBI would be surrounding their compound.

So it had to be something else.

Butler's words to Rolfe on her first day suddenly came back to her—Butler asking Rolfe if he was going to stay. The memory made her squirm with discomfort. What was she missing? Why wouldn't Rolfe stay?

There were too many inconsistencies here.

She thought of Jen, and in that instant, she could feel every drop of dried blood she hadn't been able to wash off her skin. Rolfe had let her wash her hands, but when she'd tentatively asked about a shower one day, Rolfe's gaze had darted back to the cultists and he'd shaken his head, telling her simply, "I think that's a bad idea." Now the vestiges of that blood felt like a physical reminder of every accusation Jen had made about the group.

Evelyn had tried to keep an open mind, but nothing about the group fit the usual definition of terrorism. Unless she'd been thinking about it all wrong…

Her nerve endings buzzed, her exhaustion fading abruptly. *Maybe Jen was right.*

What if the Butler Compound didn't look like a cult or a terrorist group because they weren't exactly either one? If Rolfe didn't normally live here, if he came and went unlike the rest of the followers, it would explain a lot. The tense relationship between him and Butler. The way the cultists reluctantly obeyed him, but didn't really seem to know him.

Evelyn scooted into a sitting position, wrapping her arms around her knees as she tried to work it all out. Rolfe could be a recruiter. Perhaps he was in charge of bringing Butler new followers, and then Butler used the compound to mold them and send them out into the world to fulfill his agenda.

Could that be it? And if so, was there a chance Rolfe didn't know quite what he'd gotten himself into? Maybe he was just trying to bring survivalists together, not understanding until it was too late that Butler was creating an empire.

And was that truly Butler's agenda? He was antifederalist, so if Jen was correct, he'd probably follow in the footsteps of traditional homegrown terrorists. Not the kind BAU had been seeing more of lately—Americans who'd borrowed ideology from other cultures, like radical Islam—but individuals whose hatred for the federal government found battle cries in people like Weaver and McVeigh.

The bombs! She'd come to talk to Cartwright because he'd been bragging about a copycat. But it was way more likely that he'd heard about the bombs on the news in the prison common area and wanted some attention. Cartwright had been locked up for three years, with only his mother to visit him. He had some deranged fans, but he was mostly forgotten.

The Butler Compound, on the other hand, was close enough to the recent bomb sites. They hadn't shown Cartwright's signature, but they could be practice sessions by homegrown terrorists planning to stage an attack.

The words she'd heard Butler and Rolfe repeat so often over the past week suddenly had a new and frightening meaning.

It's almost time.

The insistent buzzing of Kyle's phone jolted him instantly out of a combat nap. It was already clutched in his hand, so he held it in front of him, squinting as the light came on, and he read the terse text from Yankee. Mac, get to TOC.

He lurched to his feet inside the small sleeping tent HRT had pitched for agents who were off rotation. Less than an hour ago, his team had come off shift, and after more than a week of sleeping in brief increments on the hard Montana mountain, he felt constantly exhausted.

He'd gotten into the habit of lying down wearing most of his gear, so he only had to grab his weaponry as he wove around his teammates curled up in their sleeping bags in the cramped tent.

Gabe, on the ground at his feet, didn't open his eyes. "Want me to come with you?"

"Watch your phone," Kyle answered as he opened the tent flap, letting in a blast of wind that made a few of his teammates grumble. "I'll let you know."

He and Gabe were partners; they usually operated as a pair. Yankee calling only him, and while he was off shift, meant it probably wasn't an HRT assignment at all. It was probably about Evelyn.

His pace quickened until he was running toward TOC. When he pushed open the flap and strode inside, the atmosphere in the tent, always packed full of Special Agents and support staff, seemed more tense than usual. Yankee stood in the center of the tent, giving orders over his radio to the HRT team currently set up around the compound. But he paused as soon as he saw Kyle and waved him over.

"Go see Greg," Yankee said. "Evelyn's talking again. And we think she's talking to you."

Kyle double-timed it through the tent, moving impatiently around the support staff members who were working frantically, taking up too much space. Greg was in the corner of the tent, deep circles underscoring his eyes and a scowl on his normally easygoing face.

"What's happening?" Kyle asked.

Greg took a headphone off one ear, leaving it on

the other, and rubbed his eyes. "We got Evelyn on mic again. She's near the second bug you placed."

Kyle frowned. "Near the second bug" meant she was toward the far back of the compound, where they never heard any of the cultists' voices except those of Ward Butler and one other guy. Usually the two of them spoke in hushed tones, and they had a frustrating tendency to move into areas the mic couldn't pick up before they said anything of interest. Assuming they ever said anything of interest.

But overnight, Greg had picked up Evelyn's voice back there. Far away from most of the cultists might be good—less opportunity for them to come after her again. Or it could be very bad—cloistered with Ward Butler, a man prone to dramatic, instantaneous mood changes.

"We know what's back there yet?" Kyle asked.

Greg shook his head. "Best we can tell, it's the area reserved for the cult leader and his lieutenant. He only seems to have one, which is a little odd, but his group of followers is pretty small. The bug doesn't work well back there, so Evelyn must be close to an exterior wall right now. We picked up her voice a minute ago. She was asking for you."

Kyle sat next to Greg, in Adam's vacant chair. "What do you mean?"

"She must know you're here."

"Okay. And?" Kyle tried to cover his impatience as he stomped his feet to generate some warmth, wondering what was wrong with TOC's heating system. Of course she knew he was there. He hadn't seen her up in the tower a few days ago, but the snipers had confirmed her location, which told him she'd seen HRT.

She probably hadn't been able to spot him, but she was familiar with his schedule. His team was on call now, so he'd be pulled in for any crisis.

"She'd know a profiler would come, too," Greg added. "But she'd have no way of knowing it was me."

Kyle just nodded, not wanting to get into a pissing match with Greg, who was usually above that sort of behavior. But Evelyn and Greg were like informal partners; BAU technically didn't work in pairs like most FBI units. Maybe he didn't like the fact that Evelyn was trying to talk to Kyle instead of him. Still… "What did she say?" Kyle reached for a spare set of headphones. "Is she talking now?"

"No," Greg replied. "But she was speaking a minute ago, and I expect she'll start again. So far, it sounds totally random. I think someone must be nearby and she doesn't want whoever it is to understand what she's giving us."

"Tell me," Kyle insisted.

Greg pushed a piece of paper toward him, with words and time/date stamps, and read aloud, "Mac. The beach. The snack bar. Mac. The beach. The snack bar. It's going to be soon."

Okay, she was definitely talking to him. She'd worked with HRT before and knew their MO; she'd be aware they'd get mics on the compound. She'd know they'd do their best to cover as much of the place as possible, so she had to be hoping she was somewhere the mics would pick her up. He frowned and looked up at Greg, who was staring back at him expectantly.

"That mean anything to you?" Greg demanded, stress making his words sound hard and abrupt. One hand clutched his headphones over his right ear, the other was wrapped around a thermos as if he was trying to crush it.

Her words *did* mean something. But they didn't connect to a cult full of trigger-happy survivalists.

After Evelyn had solved the disappearance of her childhood friend—the case that had been haunting her most of her life—she'd shocked the hell out of him by taking him up on his suggestion that they go on vacation together. He'd said it as a joke, assuming she'd never agree. Then she had, and they'd both taken time off, not informing the FBI that they were planning to visit the same beach.

If they *had* shared that information with the FBI, there would've been questions. And paperwork. And, Evelyn was afraid, reassignment.

When Kyle didn't immediately answer, Greg pressed him. "It has to be a code. She's trying to tell you something. What is it?"

Greg would never put Evelyn's career in jeopardy, but Kyle knew that admitting he and Evelyn had gone on vacation together—even if Greg already suspected—wasn't wise. Everything that happened in TOC got recorded in one way or another. It all ended up in after-mission reports.

"We talked about her vacation," Kyle hedged, and as he said it, he realized how odd her colleagues at BAU must have found it when she actually took time off. Until recently, pretty much her entire life had been tied up in her job. "She did mention a little snack shack on the pier."

It was the place they'd stopped for a bite to eat the first day they'd arrived. They'd sat on that deck, sharing boiled peanuts and sweet tea and their life stories, while they let the spray of saltwater wind dance around them. He'd never seen Evelyn more relaxed, less guarded. At that moment, he thought he'd truly gotten through to her—which he'd been trying to do since the day she'd shown up at BAU a year and a half ago.

"Anything special about it?" Greg asked, then before Kyle could answer, he muttered, "It *has* to mean something. Otherwise, she's losing it. We have no idea what her condition is in there."

That was something Kyle had been trying not to think about. The snipers had reported that she seemed to be in decent health, without visible injuries, but they hadn't seen her since she'd been up in that tower. Too many things could have happened, back where HRT couldn't hear. Assault, torture, rape. He forced himself to focus and looked down at the paper in front of him again. "'It's going to be soon,'" he read aloud. "Yeah, this has to be code."

But what did the snack bar on the pier have to do with a group of cultists?

He frowned at Evelyn's words, frustrated.

"Tell me about it," Greg said. "Describe the place."

Kyle's eyes darted back up to Greg's and he realized it didn't matter how he tried to hide his involvement with Evelyn. Greg had known before they'd come to Montana. And somehow Kyle would've bet a lot of money that Evelyn hadn't told him.

Kyle's interest in Evelyn had long been an open secret. But there was nothing open, nothing overt, about Evelyn's interest in return.

The guy was a hell of a profiler. Kyle was suddenly very glad Greg was here.

He pictured the small red building, perched at the

very end of the pier, looking as if a strong wind might blow it into the ocean. The food had been wonderful, all Southern comfort stuff. But there hadn't been anything remarkable about the place at all, except...

"Bubba's Bar," Kyle recalled. "The place was called Bubba's Bar."

The color drained from Greg's face. "Are you sure?"

Kyle nodded, instinctively gripping the stock of his MP-5 a little tighter.

"Bubba." Greg swore, dropping his headphones and gesturing frantically for Yankee and the Salt Lake City SAC, some guy with pockmarked skin and a permanent scowl whose name Kyle couldn't remember.

The two men ran over, both still giving orders over different radios. "What is it?" the SAC demanded.

"We think Evelyn's trying to tell us *Bubba*," Greg said.

"And that *it* will happen soon," Kyle added.

"Bubba," the SAC from the Salt Lake City office repeated slowly. "She thinks Agent Martinez was right?" Skepticism and regret colored his voice as he glanced back and forth between them. "You're positive?"

"Yes," Greg replied firmly.

"A homegrown terrorist attack," Yankee said, dread in his words, but a cool, analytical expression on his face. "And she hasn't told us exactly when? Or what the target is?"

Greg shook his head, while Kyle stared intently at his boss. They'd been to these calls before, and he knew Yankee well.

Before Yankee could say anything, Kyle reminded him, "If we go in, the *first* thing Ward Butler will do is kill Evelyn."

"This changes everything." The SAC sighed, then stepped a few feet away, barking into his radio even as he dialed someone on his cell phone.

If Kyle had to guess, he'd say the SAC was calling SIOC, the FBI's Strategic Information Operations Center, based in a windowless, forty-thousand-square-foot room in the center of FBI headquarters. If they were going to convert what was currently a surveillance mission into a tactical operation, it would be SIOC's decision.

"If there's an attack planned on US soil and the only people who have any information about it are in there…" Yankee gestured in the direction of the compound, where there'd been nothing but silence from Butler and his followers for seven days.

"Butler's people are heavily armed. We go in there, and it's going to be *bad*," Kyle said, desperation squirming in his gut.

He liked action. The worst part of HRT's job was the "hurry up and wait" part. But he also knew groups like this. HRT had experience with groups like this.

The best way to preserve life was to wait them out, waste God knew how much taxpayer money rather than human lives. Including the lives of Butler and his misguided followers.

Normally, he'd be all for taking the chance when it came to real intel on a potential terrorist threat. But he'd been up close to that compound, had seen some of the booby traps—and Evelyn had told them there were more, rigged to all the exterior doors. It would take too long to breach.

Panic rose up, and he jammed his hands into his

pockets to keep from clenching them. There was no way they'd be able to get to Evelyn before Ward Butler could.

Yankee shook his head as the SAC rejoined them, looking even grimmer than he had a few minutes earlier. "Evelyn's a profiler. Hopefully those skills will keep her alive if the cultists come for her."

"She's a federal agent," the SAC broke in, his tone harsh and final, his own agent still missing, presumed dead at this point. "She knows the risks. We've got agents searching for chatter. We get any kind of confirmation, and this standoff is over. We breach."

"It's time."

John Peters stood, folding the last of his belongings into his small duffel bag, and clicking the Off button on the TV remote.

Despite how long he'd prepared, how long he'd waited for this day, he'd still expected to be nervous when it finally arrived. Instead, he felt a strange calm, and a deep conviction that his actions would be the start of something monumental.

His name would go down in history.

Bobby Durham—not a strategic thinker, but a die-hard believer—gestured with disgust at the TV. The news had been running regular coverage of the standoff at the Butler Compound. "You see what's happening there?"

"It's irrelevant."

Bobby didn't get up from the other single bed, just planted his hands flat on the cigarette-stained, paper-thin comforter. With his white-blond hair cropped close to his face and light blue eyes wide over a freckled nose, he looked like a college kid. That was probably why he'd been chosen. People were too distracted by the freckles and the baby face to really notice the other details about Bobby.

The weather-roughened hands, the wiry muscle snaking through his arms, the jailhouse tattoo peeking out of his collar. The way he moved those baby-blue eyes, ever watchful, a hardness to them if you looked carefully enough. The messenger bag he clutched a little too close to his chest whenever he picked it up, even in practice.

But at the moment, the usually unflappable Bobby seemed wary. "We haven't heard from him."

"And we won't," John said. "He's not going to contact us while the FBI is swarming. We stick to plan."

"But…"

"Move," John ordered, not bothering to remind Bobby who was in charge.

Bobby might have the jailhouse creds and the "whatever's necessary" determination, but John had the right connections. If not for John, none of them would've known how to put together that little device in Bobby's bag. Not with this kind of sophistication.

And for the message they wanted to deliver, they couldn't rely on brute force or peaceful protests. They needed an elegant message, a demonstration of exactly what they were capable of doing.

"Got it," Bobby said, no more hesitation in his tone as he grabbed that messenger bag and slipped the strap carefully across his chest.

"We're not coming back," John told him, not for the first time. "Leave nothing behind, okay?"

"It's all in the truck," Bobby replied, heading for the hotel door without a backward glance.

John followed him out, taking one more look behind him before he shut the door. This fleabag motel would be the last comfortable, remotely civilized place they'd stay. From here on out, they were going off the grid.

Frankly, he preferred off the grid.

They'd parked the truck out back, behind the motel where the security cameras were clearly fake and the lightbulbs had long ago burned out. In the darkness, he and Bobby worked side by side, carefully smoothing on the decals for a mom-and-pop plumbing business that, if checked, would actually trace back to a real business with some questionable investors.

Then they were off, driving through the rest of the night. They parked just outside the city to wait out the morning, even stopping at a great little bakery in the suburbs, and then drove downtown right before the lunchtime rush.

With the brim of his baseball cap pulled low over his eyes, his heavy beard dyed an unnatural reddish-brown, John drove past the target once.

Bobby barely moved as they passed the building, only looking at it from his peripheral vision. But John knew he wanted to smile at the number of employees streaming out for lunch, bundled up in heavy jackets over their suits in deference to the light snow. And at that glass. All that beautiful glass.

"It's time," John said, pulling to a stop one block away. "I'll meet you three blocks down."

"Got it," Bobby said, carefully smoothing a sticker onto the front of his backpack with gloved hands.

Just before Bobby left the truck, John glanced down at that sticker.

FREEDOM UPRISING it proclaimed in bold red letters.

He couldn't help himself. He smiled as the door slammed and he watched Bobby walk casually back toward the site.

Three blocks away, he parked the truck and waited. After ten minutes, he checked his watch. After fifteen, he spotted Bobby striding nonchalantly toward him.

Perfect timing. Bobby was back inside the truck and the two of them were winding leisurely out of town before they'd even heard the explosion.

Behind him, the sky suddenly went dark as smoke curled upward. For an instant, there was an unnatural stillness, as though time was frozen. Nothing moved except that gray blast as it slowed, settled and billowed outward. Then, over the ringing in his ears, he heard the screaming.

He remembered to slam on his brakes and glance around, as if surprised, before continuing on his way.

He ducked his head, in case he was caught on some traffic camera footage, and didn't even crack a smile as Bobby crossed his arms over his chest and declared, "Phase One is complete."

8

Kyle stood at the edge of the Butler Compound gate, beside a brand-new hole in the fence, trying not to shiver as big, wet snowflakes plopped on his nose. He couldn't see the other HRT team, but he knew they were on the opposite side, beside their own entry point. Nerves trembled in the pit of his stomach as he gripped the stock of his MP-5 and waited for the signal to move.

Around him, the surroundings were dark under a heavily clouded sky, just the green glow of his night-vision goggles illuminating his teammates. Ever since word had come down that they were going in, his world had dimmed to nothing more than the voices in his ear-buds and the primed, focused silhouettes of the HRT members beside him.

They'd gotten the official approval fifteen hours ago, only minutes after the bomb had detonated outside the ATF field office in Chicago. He'd been off shift then, so one of his teammates had gone to a newsfeed on his smartphone, and instantly the images of pain and death had blasted through the small HRT tent.

The building's structure had remained sound—the bomb had been well-designed, but way too small to take down a large building. It had exploded during lunchtime, with a hundred federal employees nearby. The architecture of the ATF building relied heavily on a modern mix of clean lines, steel and expansive, gray-toned windows. Either the bomb's design had been intended to shoot projectiles directly into the many windows, or the bomber had gotten lucky.

Watching the footage of the blast's aftermath play on repeat, Kyle didn't think for a second that the bomber had relied on luck. He hadn't been going for the building. He'd been going for the people. He'd been going for the federal agents.

And he'd succeeded. Kyle was never going to forget the sound of the woman closest to one of the cameras, screaming as she ripped a piece of glass out of her face and blood dripped down her side from more glass embedded in her. She stumbled toward the street, then finally collapsed as the smoke from the bomb billowed around her. Kyle clutched his MP-5 tighter, until his fingers started to tingle and his breath came too fast.

Focus on the moment, he reminded himself. *Focus on getting Evelyn out of this compound alive.*

They'd waited until 3:00 a.m. to begin the breach. Natural biorhythms meant that if the cultists—terrorists, Kyle mentally corrected himself—inside were keeping to a regular sleeping schedule, they'd be in deepest REM sleep now. The technical coverage that HRT had planted provided limited access, but it had told them the group mostly kept normal schedules.

There'd been no reaction inside to the explosion in Chicago, although as far as the FBI could tell, the group had no TV or radios, no connection to the outside world. Still, there'd been a different tone to Butler's preaching that afternoon. A manic excitement as he promised that their cause had just changed forever.

Either he had access to the outside that the FBI hadn't found, or he'd known the bomb was coming.

It had been the final confirmation the FBI's Strategic Information Operations Center needed to approve a tactical breach of the compound. Between Evelyn predicting a bomb connected to the compound and the leader's frenzied speech soon afterward, the likelihood of a connection was too strong to ignore. HRT was going in.

Now, as Kyle willed his heart rate to settle back into its regular rhythm, Yankee's slow Southern lilt came over his earbuds. "TOC to all units. You have compromise authority and permission to move to green."

Instead of slowing, Kyle's heart hammered even faster. This was it. Once compromise authority was given, there was no turning back. They were going inside, and they weren't coming out until they had full control. Until everyone inside was either in handcuffs or body bags. Except, *please God*, one federal agent they all prayed would come out alive and unharmed.

Maybe, if they got really, really lucky, that number would be two. Although Butler had talked about a dead federal agent, until they actually found Jen's body, they weren't counting her out. If she was still capable of being rescued, they had every intention of bringing her home to her family.

Instead of taking off at a full run, Kyle followed his teammates through the small hole in the fence, stepping carefully in the footsteps of the man in front of him. If someone stepped on a bear trap or other booby trap along the way, he'd be left behind. Once they had permission to move to green, nothing could prevent them from entering the compound, not even the injury—or death—of one of their own.

He walked silently, slowly, his boots leaving tracks in the four inches of snow. It had started falling yesterday and still hadn't stopped. The covering of white would make it harder to see any traps on the ground, but as Gabe came to a sudden halt, Kyle knew someone had. A flick of Gabe's wrist, and the entire team took one step left before continuing, past the cover of the last scraggly pine trees and into the open.

On the other side of the building, the second HRT team was moving in the same painstakingly slow manner. It was planned so they'd reach the side and front doors at exactly the same time. But Kyle had to force his feet not to move faster, not to dart around Gabe and his other teammates and make a mad, suicidal dash for the door.

Kyle viewed this moment as the most dangerous— more than standing a few feet away from a door as it was blasted off its hinges, more than trading shots with a group of armed zealots. The danger wasn't so much to his team. If they were spotted by someone inside or any of the remaining die-hard protesters at the perimeter, he trusted their snipers to remove any threat. The danger was to Evelyn. As soon as Butler realized they were coming, he'd do one of two things—use her as a human shield or put a bullet in her head.

Knowing what he did about Butler, Kyle suspected the man would be too cocky about his own skills, too angry at the FBI's entry and too quick to act instead of think. He'd kill her.

The last thing Greg had done before HRT strapped on their gear and headed for the compound entrance was to look Kyle directly in the eye. His voice had cracked as he'd said, "Bring her out alive."

Kyle couldn't even be sure where she was. After hours of hearing her talk to them in code from the back of the compound, they'd listened tensely through the mics as Butler suddenly dragged her out of wherever they'd been keeping her. All the indications were that she hadn't returned.

It didn't mean anything, he told himself. He had to believe she was still alive and well, had to believe Butler hadn't pulled her into some area their technical coverage didn't reach and shot her. He had to believe he'd be able to keep the promise he'd made to Greg.

He had to believe he'd get her out of there, hold her in his arms again, convince her that their relationship was worth taking public.

Suddenly, they were at the compound entrance. He didn't fully remember crossing the open field, walking directly in Gabe's footsteps, hearing only the sound of his own breathing because of his earplugs. Now, along with the rest of his team, he took one step left, so they weren't directly lined up with the door as the agent in front slapped a rectangular charge in the center.

Gabe raised his hand, and his boss's voice came over his headset, and then Kyle heard nothing but the blast of a steel door being blown off its hinges. Pieces of the door flew past him, and he felt the heat of it singeing his skin through his flight suit.

At the same time, Kyle heard the angry blast of a shotgun.

He didn't need the instruction to "Go, go, go!" He was already on the move, stepping over the trip wire stretched low along the doorway. He glanced up at the shotgun someone had jimmied in the opening, then he was moving past it, lifting his MP-5 into firing position now that no teammate stood in front of him.

His vision narrowed to just his field of fire, the area directly ahead—his area. His teammates had other slices of the field. All he had to worry about was whoever entered his field of fire. All he had to do was take them out of commission—temporarily by arresting them if they laid down their weapons or permanently by shooting them if they didn't.

Initially, as he raced down a dim hallway toward a bigger room straight ahead, he thought there'd be no one to confront. He thought that maybe they'd truly surprised the group out of sleep, and the cultists would be slow to wake and grab weapons. That perhaps HRT would be able to get to the group's sleeping quarters and have them all cuffed without firing a single shot.

But then the first bullet whizzed toward him, so close he actually felt the air as it missed his head by a fraction of an inch. He scanned the immediate area, looking for the threat, but saw no one.

Crouching low, he continued forward, just as a small, cylindrical object came flying toward him. It bounced at his feet, and he didn't have time to do more than glance down and recognize a familiar green shape before it exploded.

Then his ears recoiled at a high-pitched ringing and his whole world turned brilliant white.

A loud *boom* blasted through the air, even louder than the gunshots that seemed to have been going on forever but had probably started less than five minutes ago. A high-pitched screeching invaded Evelyn's ears.

Pain ratcheted through her head and her ears closed up, as if she was on a plane that had changed altitude.

She pressed more tightly against the shelving she was tethered to, and glanced right. Toward the sound of weapons firing, a full-out battle she was having a hard time hearing.

HRT had invaded.

She'd known it the second she'd heard a different blast a few minutes ago that had jolted her from sleep. It had to be the front door blowing off its hinges. She'd actually been expecting it, ever since Ward Butler's bizarre afternoon speech. It had been high on rhetoric and low on detail, but the cocky grin on his face told her something big had happened.

If she was right, that something was a bomb.

She'd lurched upright, her arm asleep from being raised above her head. After dragging her out of the closet yesterday, Butler had pulled her back into the main part of the compound, parading her in front of his followers. She'd looked around frantically for Rolfe, the voice of reason, but he wasn't there. Then she'd steeled herself, expecting Butler to take her to the front of the room and kill her.

In what might be her last minutes, she'd regretted all the things she'd never done, all the hours she'd spent cloistered in her FBI cubicle, trying to make up for the fact that eighteen years ago her best friend had been kidnapped, and she'd been left behind. She'd regretted that she'd never really tried to create a life outside of work, not until recently. Her vacation with Kyle had been…special. She'd felt like a different person. Maybe the person she would've become if Cassie hadn't gone missing—and if she'd never learned that she was supposed to have been taken alongside her best friend.

But she didn't know how to be that person. Now that she'd solved Cassie's case, she wasn't sure she knew how to return to the life she'd made for herself at the FBI, either.

Still, the biggest regret she'd had as Ward Butler dragged her to the front of the room, that unnatural glee in his eyes, was that she'd be leaving her grandma all alone. The grandma who'd raised her, who'd rescued her from the hell that was a dingy apartment with her alcoholic mother and her string of questionable boyfriends. The grandma with dementia, who probably wouldn't understand where Evelyn had gone when she suddenly stopped showing up at the nursing home. The grandma who had no one left in the world to visit her but Evelyn.

So, she'd turned to Butler, ready to beg for her life, only to discover she was nothing more than a prop. He didn't even look at her as he ranted about federal power, his grip on her arm going from bruising to bone-crushing. Then he'd talked about the blow they'd struck today, and she'd known the end was coming, that the FBI had heard him and would be sending in HRT.

One way or another, she'd known it would all be over soon.

Now, as the battle raged on, past the room where the cultists gathered to eat, Evelyn tried to stay calm and figure out her options. She was in yet another closet, this one off the back of that main room, surrounded by bags of MREs and bottles of water, a zip tie tethering her to one of the shelves.

Frantically, she fumbled with the few remaining bobby pins in her bun, yanking one out and sending a curtain of dark hair cascading around her face. She jammed the bobby pin into the zip tie as hard as she could, trying to break the lock.

Nothing happened.

Swearing, she kept shoving it into the mechanism, until she missed and stabbed her wrist instead, then yelped and dropped the bobby pin. It wasn't working.

Panicked, she stared at the closed door. The closet opened into a little room with no apparent purpose at all. But that room had two different doors. One was behind her, and had to lead into Butler and Rolfe's private area. The other led into the main eating area, where she could hear the sounds of a fight raging again as her ears began to clear.

The followers had evidently unearthed the weapons from under their beds and run toward the main room, shooting. But what about the leaders? As far as she knew, there was no back entrance. A side entrance, yes, and a front one. But nothing in the back, where Butler and Rolfe liked to hide out. If Butler hadn't joined the fighting yet, he had only two options. The door through which Rolfe had always taken her—which was too close to where HRT must have breached—or the door near her. She hadn't heard it open. But if he came this way now, with the fighting in full force and his men surely going down, she knew he'd pause long enough to shoot her.

Giving up on trying to unlock her wrist, she tried tugging her arm downward, trying to break the tie instead. Pain ripped through her, sharp and insistent, traveling from her shoulder to her fingertips and back again. Ignoring it, she pulled again, wrenching her whole body away from the shelf.

Then she tripped and fell, hitting the other wall as the metal shelving came down on top of her, MREs and water bottles raining all around her. The force of it knocked the air from her lungs, and tears flooded her eyes at the sharp pain in her back.

Squirming under the shelving, she discovered that the zip tie had broken in the fall. She shoved at the weight on her back, but the unit was heavier than she'd realized. Finally, she squirmed out from underneath it, scraping the metal edging along her back hard enough to tear her sweatshirt and her skin. She vaguely registered that she'd probably just made a lot of noise, but she hadn't really heard it over the gunfire and the persistent ringing in her ears.

Hoping no one else had heard it, either, Evelyn leaped to her feet and started to race for the door. For the tiny room off the back of the gathering area, and beyond it. For the HRT agents sent in here to get her out safely. For Kyle, who would do whatever it took to bring her home. And not just because he was dating her—because it was his job. But she stopped before she reached the door.

The gunfire was nonstop, punctuated by screaming and thuds that had to be men going down, probably never to get up again. She couldn't walk into that. And to get to the HRT agents, she had to go *through* the cultists. She'd never make it.

Instead, she slowly eased open the closet door, pressing her face against the opening and peering into the little room. The little *empty* room, she saw, relief settling over her as she pushed the door fully open and stepped inside. Just as fast, her relief faded. She still had to make it out of here alive.

And she knew firsthand that every man in the compound had at least one knife, one rifle and one pistol to his name. She had nothing, not even shoes.

She glanced around the little, pointless room. The compound was filled with more weapons than everyone at her office at BAU owned collectively—and legally—so it was surprising that there was nothing here at all.

She looked at the other door. The door that led to the back area, reserved for the leader and his lieutenant. There was a good chance Butler was there. But so was Rolfe.

She was trying to decide which direction to take when something slammed against the other side of the door leading into the main room, and the ringing in her ears started to subside. HRT was gaining ground, pushing the cultists back. Butler's men would come in here soon.

Evelyn grabbed the door into the back area and yanked, praying she wouldn't discover Butler standing there, holding an AK-47 and wearing the sinister expression he'd had when he'd shot Jen. She saw nothing except darkness. The bulbs that had lit the walls earlier were out, but she squinted hard and realized this door led to the other end of the hallway, closer to Rolfe's bedroom than Butler's suite.

Hope surged. If she could get to Rolfe, he'd keep her alive. She was pretty sure he'd wanted no part of Jen's death, that he didn't want to see her hurt. Her gut told her he was her best chance.

She squinted through the doorway, noticed the glint of a wire and leaped over it, into the forbidden area of the compound. As her feet hit the hard flooring, something latched onto the back of her sweatshirt.

She dug her heels in just as a voice called out, "I've got her!"

Glancing behind her, she saw a group of cultists rushing into the tiny room, most of them bleeding, all of them carrying weapons. Lasso Guy had his fist locked in her sweatshirt and she slid backward on the wood floor, not getting any traction with her socks.

She dug in harder, desperately trying to squirm free, to stay out of range of that trip wire. But he was stronger than she was. One more yank and she slipped, hitting the ground, feeling the wire cut into her ankle.

A blast went off too close to her, and she instinctively flinched. But the booby trap hadn't been aimed her way, into Butler's sacred area. It was aimed into the common space. Behind her, the man who'd tried to lynch her a week ago dropped to his knees, eyes wide with surprise and pain as red darkened the front of his shirt. Then he slumped to the ground, eyes still open, staring at nothing.

Evelyn looked upward, to the gun fastened onto the doorframe. It was probably still loaded. From the shock on the other cultists' faces, they hadn't known it was there.

But now they knew how to avoid it.

Evelyn scrambled to her feet, racing toward Rolfe's bedroom, followed by the pounding of heavy booted feet.

Panting, she grabbed the door handle to Rolfe's room and yanked it open, rushing inside. The room was empty. Rolfe wasn't here.

She spun back around as the door opened again, and three cultists slid into the room. Two aimed pistols at her as the third slowly advanced, tossing a switchblade back and forth from one hand to the other.

The guy with the knife gave a half grin, half snarl that made his thick beard quiver. "No one here to protect you now," he gloated as she backed up, hitting the wall.

Then he lunged.

9

Where the hell was Evelyn?

Kyle's ears were ringing under his earplugs, and his vision was still compromised from the flash bang that had exploded so close to him. The cultists were using exactly what HRT used, to temporarily blind opponents, to set off a noise just under the threshold of shattering eardrums. Usually it disoriented them enough to give HRT a chance to get control, ideally without firing their weapons.

At least it hadn't been a real grenade. Considering who they were up against, Kyle knew he'd gotten lucky. This group probably had real grenades.

They were well-stocked. And they hadn't been sleeping. Instead, they'd been ready for the assault, already stationed at optimal vantage points as HRT agents charged in through the two most obvious entry points—the only two doors. And they'd planned silently, maybe suspecting listening devices, because TOC hadn't heard them say a thing.

Even now, as HRT finally got control of the main room, lined with tables stacked high with the kind of weaponry that would drive ATF ape-shit, Kyle was feeling the effects of that flash bang. He probably should have been out of the fight. He might have taken himself out, except that too many of his teammates had gone down with worse injuries. And Evelyn was still in here somewhere.

He moved forward, ignoring the scent of gunpowder seeping into his nostrils, the curl of smoke in the room from so many weapons being fired in a closed space. Other HRT members would restrain the remaining cultists here. His job was to keep moving.

He pushed on, trying not to think about the blood he was tracking through. He nodded at Gabe to follow him into a smaller room off the main gathering area. Once he stepped inside, he found a dead cultist and he paused a minute to frown at the man, who'd bled out from a gunshot. But HRT hadn't made it this far. Which meant he'd been taken out by one of his own. Why?

Kyle kept his weapon leveled as he finished surveying. To his left was an open door leading into a closet. Empty, with a large shelving unit on the ground, bottles and MRE bags spilled all around it. A smear of blood across the floor, as though there'd been a fight.

Straight ahead was a door that had to lead back into the area where HRT had planted another bug. Ward Butler's area.

Gabe wrenched open the door. He was about to walk through when Kyle grabbed a fistful of his partner's flight suit and pulled him back a step. "Trip wire," Kyle said into his mic. He pointed at the ground and Gabe stepped over the wire as Kyle relayed the information to the rest of the teams.

They entered a hallway that would have been pitch-black except for his NVGs, which bathed it in eerie green instead. Nearby, a door. And behind that door...

Kyle strained to hear and Gabe nodded back at him, his expression hard. Someone was in there.

Scanning the floor, watching for more trip wires, Kyle moved forward, his pulse quickening. They'd heard Evelyn back here before. Could she be here now?

Kyle positioned himself on one side of the door, with Gabe on the other. Then Kyle nodded, and Gabe pulled the door open and Kyle went in, stepping high to avoid any wire.

All at once, everything seemed to both slow down and happen at double-speed. Two cultists standing with their backs to the door began spinning toward him, raising their weapons. Behind them, on the ground, Evelyn grappled with a big camo-covered guy wielding a switchblade.

She was underneath him, squirming and kicking, both hands clenched around his wrist, trying to keep the knife away from her as he rained punches on her with his free hand.

Kyle turned back to the other cultists. "Drop the weapons!" he yelled, giving them precious milliseconds not to fire on him.

But instead of looking afraid or resigned, fury and the hope of glory and a hint of desperation flew across their faces instead, and the pistols came up higher.

He and Gabe fired at almost exactly the same second, and both cultists dropped to the ground. Kyle had no time to wish they'd surrendered instead, because the last guy in the room had hauled himself to his feet, one hand locked around Evelyn's waist. The other held that huge knife to her neck. She panted from exertion after fighting him, the vein in her neck pulsing, the tip of the knife pressed against it.

"It's over," Gabe said, his voice soft and reassuring.

"It's not over," the man snarled, his knuckles whitening around that knife, pressing a little closer, a little deeper, until a small drop of blood appeared on Evelyn's skin. "You come near me and I split her open. You'll be mopping up her blood for a week."

"Put the weapon down and step away from her," Kyle ordered. He kept his own voice calm, not showing the cultist any of the panic racing through him as he shifted his own MP-5 higher, sighting on the man's nose. On the one tiny, precise spot that would take him down instantly, no dying twitch. No last-second movements that would drive that knife into Evelyn.

Kyle tried not to look at her, dressed in too-big sweats, gaunt and bruised, her eyes wide, one hand gripping the man's wrist, hoping to force that knife away from her neck. He kept his focus on the man behind her, watching for any movement in his hand, intent on his face.

She was still alive. He was damn well going to make sure she stayed that way.

"You have no other options," Kyle told him, inserting as much power and confidence into his tone as he could. "You move that knife at all—except to drop it—and we drop you. Look at your odds. It's the only way you walk out of here. You don't need to die today."

The man's hand quivered, and Kyle felt his own finger tense against the trigger as the man's chin jutted up. The cultist didn't want anyone to doubt his courage, Kyle realized. He'd die to prove a point, to prove his loyalty.

Loyalty. The word stuck in his mind and Kyle flashed

back to that trip wire he'd stepped over, to the cultist shot in that tiny room, far from the fighting. And Kyle knew he could end this peacefully.

The words wanted to tumble out, but he forced himself to speak slowly, clearly, to try to save this man's life. "Don't die for Ward Butler. He's someone who'd hide, let his men do his fighting. He set that trap, the one that killed your friend. Right?"

The man's hand shook again, the knife rocking against the thin skin covering Evelyn's carotid artery. There was indecision in his eyes, and the anger of betrayal.

"Don't let Butler kill you, too," Kyle pushed.

The man's eyes darted from Kyle, to Gabe, down to Evelyn and back again, then the fury in his eyes overtook the indecision. "It never would've happened if you hadn't come in here! Fucking feebs!" His grip on the knife tightened, and it started to slice.

Kyle pulled the trigger.

The sound of a bullet blasted through her ears like the unexpected pop of a firecracker, making her shudder. The hand holding the knife against her neck seemed to lose all animation and the knife clattered to the floor. The man behind her dropped, too, just fell away with a thud as he landed on the hard floor.

Evelyn stumbled forward, almost falling. She touched her neck gingerly, carefully, and came back with a smear of blood.

Panicked, she pressed more firmly, looking for the wound.

"You're fine. You're okay."

The deep, familiar voice registered before the words did, and Evelyn stared up into Kyle's face. He was in a helmet and goggles and weighed down with a crazy amount of weaponry—rivaling the men in the compound—but it was him. Her vision blurred and she moved forward until he caught her arms.

"It's a scratch. He didn't cut you badly," Kyle said, steadying her, his gaze searching hers as if he was trying to make sure she really was fine.

From behind her, Evelyn heard Gabe say, "He's dead."

She started to turn, but Kyle pulled her forward, clamping one hand around her arm. "I'm getting you out of here," he said, urging her through the doorway and down a hall.

She squinted, trying to see, but it was too dark after the dim lighting in Rolfe's room. Instead, she just followed Kyle as he tugged her along. The compound smelled like an indoor firing range after heavy use, and the acrid scents seemed more prominent without sight.

When they reached the doorway to that small room she'd seen after leaving the closet, light finally filtered in and she wished it hadn't. The man who'd grabbed her was still lying on the ground, a permanent expression of pain and surprise on his face. As Kyle began pulling her into the room, she tugged back, warning, "There's a trip…"

"It's been removed," Gabe said from close behind her. Kyle gave her a nod, the hard expression on his face telling her no one was getting past him.

Relief overwhelmed her in that instant. Kyle was with her. She was getting out of here. Finally.

This was her tenth day inside the compound. But it felt as if she'd been there much, much longer.

Then the relief faded and all the questions rushed in.

What was waiting for her outside? What had they done with Jen? What act of terror had Butler authorized?

They moved quickly, sidestepping the dead man on the floor, and Evelyn tried not to look down at him. Even though he'd tried to lynch her, she hadn't wanted him dead. Behind bars, definitely, but...not like this. She jerked her gaze up and kept going.

Kyle led her into the main room and her eyes watered instantly at the much heavier smoke. She vaguely registered Kyle telling her to watch where she stepped; she looked down to find the once-faded pine plank flooring stained with blood, little red rivers still running. It had seeped into the cracks and veins of the wood, and Evelyn knew from experience that it would never come out. Even if the floor was scrubbed until the blood was no longer visible to the naked eye, it would still be there, proof of what had happened here.

Men lay on the ground amid those stains, and not just cultists, but FBI agents. Some of the men were moving; more stared sightlessly at the ceiling.

Numbness swooped in, hard and fast, and Evelyn focused on putting one foot in front of the other. On leaving this place for good.

When she finally stumbled out of the Butler Compound, she thought she'd find quiet. She stepped into the fresh snow just as the sun began to rise, sending streaks of pink and purple into the sky. The gorgeous colors reminded her of being on vacation at the beach, and it seemed somehow wrong that the same sunrise was here, too. The light reflecting off the sparkling snow seemed too bright and painful to her eyes after more than a week in the dim compound.

She'd expected to be greeted by other FBI agents,

maybe the negotiator and some other federal agents who'd led the cultists off in handcuffs to be questioned. She'd thought her tense shoulders would relax, waited for a sense of relief to arrive.

Instead, as she took that first step outside, in socks and sweatpants, sinking into four inches of snow, she was met with angry shouting. A line of local cops and federal agents stood with shields against an approaching group of protesters. They were fewer in number than she'd seen in the tower, but it looked as though the ones with handmade signs had gone home. The ones carrying shotguns had remained.

She saw them pushing forward, slamming against the agents and cops with the kind of fury she knew should have sent her running. But all she could do was move slowly, mechanically, one step after another, let the numbness fill her. Some part of her still seemed to be inside that compound.

She could still feel the rush of air from the bullet that had whizzed over her head. Still smell the unmistakable mix of smoke and blood. Still feel the trembling in her hand as the arm she clutched, belonging to the man who'd held a knife to her throat, as he dropped away from her, suddenly motionless.

She'd seen death up close before. Too many times. Usually victims she was profiling in order to find their killers. In those cases, she almost always came in after the fact. But she'd faced the possibility of death herself, too. She'd fought for her life more than once, been willing to take someone else's if it came to that. It was part of the job.

But she'd never had someone, alive and angry, pressed so close to her one second, then falling dead the next. Never had a bullet, shot by a colleague—a man she was dating—pass so close to her. Close enough that, had it gone a few inches awry, she would've been the one to fall to the floor, dead.

"Move!" The demanding voice in her ear startled her, and only a strong grip on her elbow kept her from slipping in the snow.

Kyle was beside her, looking fierce in his full battle gear, determination on his face as he dragged her forward, putting himself between her and the onrushing protesters.

In that second, the world snapped back into focus. The cold surged up from her sopping wet feet, setting ice in her veins, until she could feel every follicle on her head. Pain rushed forward, pinpricks of heat in her back and her arm and her head. The furious screams of the protesters filled her ears, and she started to run, Kyle's arm keeping her from going down in the snow.

"Go! Go! Go!" someone behind her yelled, and soon she was being shoved into a big white tent, crowded with support staff and a few Special Agents. They all dashed around in a frenzy, taking up too much space, talking too loud, sounding too frantic.

Evelyn could hear screaming and gunshots outside, but everything faded into the background as Kyle inspected her from head to toe, still gripping her arm. "Are you hurt?"

"I'm fine. Really," she added, trying to smile.

"We'd better go," Gabe said, and Kyle squeezed her arm. Then he was gone. Probably to help manage the protesters. Or to bring in the cultists, the ones who were still alive.

She started to follow, not sure exactly why, but wanting to *do* something, and wanting to keep Kyle in sight. Before she could get to the tent door, Greg was there, his arms wrapped around her in a tight hug as he called for blankets.

He smelled like sweat and wool, and although she wasn't much of a hugger, some of the tension she'd been carrying eased. Next to her grandma and her two friends from college, Greg was the closest friend she had. Hell, he was her emergency contact. She hugged him back, and closed her eyes against the sudden tears.

"Evelyn, are you okay?" Greg pulled away from her to study her face, and she recognized his expression.

She saw the relief that she was alive, the residual stress, the hint of distraction, as part of his brain still focused on his role as a profiler. But she also saw beyond that; he was studying her for signs of trauma.

"I'm fine," she said again, but her lips trembled when she tried to form a reassuring smile.

Vaguely, she realized that he must have been here all week. That would explain the jeans and coffee-stained sweatshirt he had on under his open coat, the light beard on his face.

"Blankets!" Greg called again, more insistently this time, and then someone was draping a heavy comforter over her shoulders. The weight of it seemed too heavy and she felt her whole body slump.

Still, she tried to straighten when Yankee pushed his way through the tent, grabbing his sleeve. "What's the status? What's happening? How many did we lose?"

Kyle's boss looked ready to shake her off, but something in her expression must have changed his mind— probably the dread she was feeling at the idea that HRT agents had died coming to rescue her.

"No casualties. We do have some serious injuries, though. It's still dangerous out there. The compound's under our control, but the protesters are the new threat."

Then he did pull his arm free and hurried through the tent, calling out orders Evelyn didn't register because she was too busy digesting his words. No HRT agents had died. She felt her shoulders slump a little more, another tiny bit of tension slipping free.

A pair of support staff members bumped into her as they passed through, and Evelyn stumbled. She felt off balance, maybe because she'd gotten sick in that compound, or maybe because of the sheer stress of constantly worrying that Butler was going to run in, raise that AK-47 to her head and fire.

"Come and sit down," Greg said, drawing her into the corner as the support staff parted to let her through. He pushed her into a chair and then someone was bringing her clean socks and shoes.

As she took off her wet socks and put on the new, warm ones, she asked Greg through her scratchy throat, "What's happening?"

"Your warning was right."

Dread sank to the pit of her stomach, even though she'd known it from the moment Ward Butler had dragged her into that main room and started his egotistical, babbling speech.

"It was a bomb, wasn't it?" Those damn explosions they'd blamed on a copycat of Cartwright's, when all along it must've been Butler's followers practicing for the real thing. As Greg nodded, she tried to get back into Special Agent mode. Tried to think like the profiler she was supposed to be. "What was the target?"

"ATF office in downtown Chicago."

"Casualties?"

"Sixteen. And two dozen more injuries. It was strategic timing," Greg told her. "They hit at lunchtime. And there were a lot of projectiles. Plus, all the glass in that building…"

"Any thoughts on why they chose that specific target?"

Greg shrugged and she noticed the wan color of his skin, the slight tremor in his hands, likely from too much coffee while he profiled the Butler Compound members. He looked worn down, as if he'd physically aged since the last time she'd seen him, in Aquia a week and a half before.

Greg frowned at her question. "Other than hard-core survivalists having very strong feelings about their right to bear arms and being opposed to ATF enforcement? Not really. And we haven't found any specific connection Ward Butler has to Chicago."

"Any leads on the bombers?"

Disappointment flitted across his face. "We were hoping you'd be able to help us with that."

She shook her head. "Jen saw someone leave when we arrived. She said she recognized him, although she couldn't place him. I think he might have been the bomber, but I didn't see him."

"A survivalist?" Greg asked, turning to his laptop and beginning to type.

"No. She said he wasn't one of them. I think that's why she noticed him. She claimed he didn't fit. She didn't know why he'd be at the compound."

Greg's fingers stilled. "That's odd. If he didn't belong, why would he act as a bomber for them? You figure he's some sort of freelance guy?"

Evelyn frowned. It didn't make sense. Sure, you could pick up a traditional killer-for-hire, someone who'd take out a target with a gun or a knife. But a bomber?

Before she could come up with a theory, Greg asked, "Did you get any more from her about why he didn't fit? And what about Jen? Is she…?"

Evelyn swallowed back the image that instantly arose at his question. Jen, skidding to a halt as Butler appeared in the doorway. The hard smile that had lit up Butler's face as he'd lifted that AK-47. She shuddered, remembering how Jen had gone down. Her hand went to her jaw, to the still-tender spot where Butler had slammed that gun into her face, knocking her out. She was astonished she hadn't broken her jaw or lost any teeth.

"Butler shot her," Evelyn choked out, then coughed, hoping Greg would think her cracking voice was because she'd caught a cold. It was at least partly true.

He frowned back at her and she knew he wasn't fooled. "She's dead?" he asked quietly, his voice barely above a whisper.

Still, the support staff closest to them went silent, their faces swinging toward her, full of dread.

Evelyn nodded, her motions feeling stiff and forced. "She has to be. There was a lot of blood." Some of it was still caked in her skin, so deeply embedded she felt like it would never come out. Just like the blood in the compound flooring.

Greg turned away from the laptop, taking her hands in his through the folds of the comforter. "You're not sure?"

"He knocked me out. I came to and she was gone. But he used an AK-47, at close range. She couldn't have survived that. And the blood..." Greg nodded grimly, moving to type something again, and Evelyn could see some of the support staff turn quietly away, wiping their eyes. They were from the Salt Lake City office, Evelyn realized. They'd known Jen, worked with her, befriended her.

Jen Martinez was impulsive, dedicated, determined. She got an idea about a case and she refused to let it go, regardless of what anyone else thought. Evelyn knew she shared many of those qualities. She could imagine herself befriending Jen.

"I'm sorry," she whispered.

"It's not your fault," Greg reassured her.

Evelyn nodded, looking away, hugging the comforter more tightly around her so Greg wouldn't see that she didn't believe him. She could have refused to go with Jen. She should have told the other agent to turn around as soon as they reached the open compound gates. She should've stopped her before she'd walked around the building.

But she hadn't.

If she'd been a better profiler, she would've seen the signs, could have prevented this whole mess.

"Don't go down that road," Greg said.

She lifted her head, her eyes meeting Greg's, and she realized he could probably read every thought running through her mind. He'd trained her, back when she'd been a newbie in BAU, and *he* was a hell of a profiler.

She finally gave voice to the fear that had been eating at her for the past few months, ever since she'd found the truth about what had happened to Cassie. "I don't know where I belong anymore."

Her words came out small and lost. Exactly how she felt right now.

She didn't even really know who she *was* anymore, not when she'd defined herself by her role as a profiler for so long, and by her desire to become one before that.

She put up a hand to stop Greg from saying anything, because the truth was, nothing he could say would change how she felt.

Greg didn't have a chance to respond, anyway. An HRT agent she didn't know well burst into the tent, carrying another agent over his shoulder, blood all over both of them.

Evelyn felt herself instantly recoil. They looked like they'd come off some faraway battlefield, not a remote patch of otherwise peaceful wilderness in Montana.

"Status," Yankee demanded, shoving his way to the front of the tent and helping the second HRT agent— who was thankfully still alive—off his teammate's shoulder. A support staff member ran over, carrying a huge first-aid box, and Yankee said the guy had been an EMT before he joined the FBI.

The HRT agent still standing told him, "Roger was hit. The bullet slipped behind his Kevlar. We tied it off, but he needs a hospital. We've got some other bad injuries out there, too. A few casualties." His gaze darted briefly around before he added, "No agents were killed, but four of the local cops are dead. I can't tell you how many injuries, but we have some other gunshot wounds that are bad. The protesters are getting worse. We need backup."

Yankee spun back toward the interior, yelling at the Salt Lake City SAC. "Call your SWAT teams up here!" He was putting on combat gear himself as he contin-

ued. "And get a medevac en route as soon as we clear
them to land."

Then Yankee followed his agent through the door of
the tent, giving Evelyn a view outside.

The brilliant white of the snow was spattered with
red. Advancing in a tangled mass were protesters, police officers, Salt Lake City agents and HRT agents. It
was chaos, and Evelyn realized she'd been so busy talking to Greg she hadn't really noticed the nonstop blast
of bullets. Kyle was out there, somewhere in that mass
of officers and angry civilians. Fear latched onto her.

Someone pressed a familiar object into her hand and
Evelyn glanced down as the tent flap closed behind
Yankee. A pistol. If HRT and the locals couldn't keep
the protesters back, they'd reach the tent soon.

Evelyn looked up again, suddenly seeing the hardened faces of the veterans around her, the fear in the
eyes of the rookies who hadn't yet learned to hide it.
She dropped the blanket from her shoulders and readied her weapon.

10

The blast of a shotgun going off too close made Greg flinch, then instantly hit the floor, along with everyone around him. Everyone except Evelyn, who remained standing, her gaze fixed blankly on the new hole blasted through the top of the tent as big, wet snowflakes drifted slowly through it.

Greg reached up, grabbed her hand and dragged her down beside him. "Evelyn!" he yelled. "Focus!"

She looked numb, dazed, like victims he'd encountered in his nine years working at BAU. He could practically read the dumbfounded thoughts floating through her mind. *She'd made it out of the compound. She was supposed to be safe here.*

But none of them were safe, least of all the agents in the fray outside, among them his cousin Gabe. Greg said a silent prayer for Gabe, and for Kyle, whom Greg had known ever since Gabe and Kyle were paired. Then he concentrated on something—someone—he actually had some control over. Evelyn.

"We'll deal with whatever happened inside later," he told her in the voice he used with his son, Josh, when he knew he had to be both firm and understanding.

"Right now, you need to get your head in the game. You hear me?"

She nodded, getting a better grip on the pistol someone had given her. Working for BAU, neither of them had much need for weapons anymore, even though they carried them. Still, he and Evelyn were two of the few people in the room who had the training and authority to use FBI-issued weapons at all.

Around him, support staff members who didn't carry weapons, and had no experience in the middle of a shootout, huddled tensely together. The Salt Lake City SAC was on a phone and the radio at the same time, talking into both, and pausing periodically to give instructions to a support staff member nearby. That woman ran, hunched over, back and forth between two computers and the SAC.

A couple of the support staff had the wounded HRT agent in a corner, and they huddled protectively over him, even as he tried to lift his MP-5 and get to his feet. Just like an HRT agent, to want to be in the fight, no matter what. Just like his cousin would be doing, if he were injured.

Trying to put Gabe out of his mind, Greg glanced worriedly at Evelyn, then urged her forward. "Come on. It's you and me," he reminded her. The SAC carried a weapon, too, but was too busy to use it. The same was true of a few other Supervisory Special Agents in the tent, although all of them had one ear to a phone and one hand on the weapons at their hips.

She gave a hard nod, and some animation came back into her eyes, a hint of the determination that usually radiated from her.

There was more shooting, and some shouting, and

Greg couldn't tell if it was getting closer or starting to move away. His mind drifted to his family, to his phone call with Josh, telling his son that he couldn't attend his first hockey game. Would that be the final memory Josh had of him?

He tensed, panicked at the idea of leaving his wife and kids behind, of making Lucy and Josh go through the trauma of losing parents again. Whatever they did or didn't remember or feel about their birth parents, it was still a loss, and Greg didn't want to add to it. He and his wife, Marnie, wanted to be the stabilizing force in their lives.

Yes, the FBI required him to carry a weapon. The FBI authorized him to use it, if necessary. But most agents—unless they were on SWAT or HRT—never did, except during practice.

He held his gun a little tighter, just as the tent flap opened. Greg lifted his weapon, noting from his peripheral vision that Evelyn did the same, that even though she wobbled on her knees, her aim was steady.

His finger slipped inside the finger guard, and then he instantly pulled it away, his heart jackhammering against his chest.

An HRT agent whose name Greg couldn't remember strode into the tent, a furious expression on his face as he dragged a cuffed protester in with him. "The rioters are under control now," he panted. "We just thought you'd want to know."

Greg let out a long, relieved breath as he stood up. Beside him, Evelyn lowered her weapon and stood, too, her gaze shifting past the agent to the closing tent door.

One of the Supervisory Special Agents stepped forward as a few support staff got shakily to their feet.

"What's the status?" the SSA demanded. "We have SWAT coming in from Salt Lake City."

"Don't need them," the HRT agent said, still sounding winded. "A few of the protesters took off, but they won't be back. We've got everyone else in custody."

"What about our guys? Are the HRT agents all okay?" Greg asked at the same time the SSA demanded, "What was the protesters' goal? To shoot every member of law enforcement who went into the compound?"

"Not exactly," the agent replied. "They were trying to *liberate*—" he rolled his eyes "—the people we just arrested."

"It's our God-given right to…" the protester started, but Greg cut him off.

"Our guys?" Greg persisted. Was Gabe okay?

"No casualties," the HRT agent said. "We still need a medevac." He gave the closest SSA a pointed look.

"I'm on it," the SSA said. "We have it standing by."

"Good," the HRT guy said, and before Greg could press for more details, he added, "Everyone stay put for now." Then he hurried out into the snow again.

Slowly, the rest of the support staff stood, glancing at one another hesitantly as the big SSA with the buzz cut who looked like he could be HRT himself began yelling into his phone. Then, seemingly as one, they got back into gear, as though nothing had happened, returning to their computers and getting on phones.

"Come on," Greg said to Evelyn, casting one last worried glance at the closed tent door before heading to his own laptop.

"It's already on YouTube," one of the support staff told him as he righted his chair, which had toppled over, and got back on his computer.

"What is?" Evelyn asked, confusion on her face.

"This," the staff member said, throwing her hands wide. She shook her head as she joined two others on the ground, trying to keep the HRT agent from moving around too much.

Judging by what he was saying about going back outside, the makeshift tourniquet was working.

"What was she talking about?" Evelyn asked.

Greg turned his laptop toward her, typing in a few search terms, and there it was. "Someone taped what just happened outside. It's on the internet."

"What?"

She leaned closer, but Greg didn't hit Play. He didn't want to see it.

"It's not the first video. There've already been several, focusing on protesters hiding in trees and aiming weapons at the federal agents. Some kid with a graphics program got hold of one of them, overlaid sounds of gunshots and pasted a red explosion over an agent's face. Damn thing went viral."

"It went *viral*? The group must be getting some pretty bad press, then."

"I wish," Greg said. "But we're the ones getting the bad press."

"What?" Evelyn slapped her hands on her hips, staring down at him. "How is that possible? Butler is a *terrorist…*"

"They don't know that," Greg reminded her. "We can't release the connection to Chicago. We can't *prove* the connection. Frankly, all we have is your gut on that."

"But…"

"So what the public sees is the FBI, out in force and dressed in combat gear, surrounding a compound in the middle of the wilderness. We can publish all the press releases we want about the situation—but we went light on the federal agents being held hostage, because we didn't want to put you or Jen in extra danger. Butler may not have a large following himself, but the number of people who are speaking out to support him is huge."

"Survivalist numbers are on the rise," Evelyn mused. "But still…"

"It's not just survivalists. It's other extremist right-wing groups, too, who see us surrounding a quiet compound— *storming* a quiet compound—and they've been making all kinds of press statements."

"And the news is taking them?"

"Hell, yes," Greg said, surprised at the naïveté of her question. "Anything that gets viewers. But public opinion isn't our problem right now. Our problem is Butler. And whatever he's got planned next. Until we get Butler himself in here, you're our best source of information."

Evelyn nodded, sinking into the chair beside him. "Okay. And when you get Rolfe. He'll be helpful." She clutched her hands together, still looking dazed. "What do you need to know?"

Greg busied himself pulling up a new file on his computer, to keep her from seeing his frustration. When were they going to get the old Evelyn back? It wasn't just this case, either. He'd been covering for her, making excuses, for weeks.

A sour feeling lodged in the back of his throat. Maybe she really had nothing left, no passion for profiling anymore. And with a job this demanding, this emotionally draining, you *had* to have a passion for it, or you'd burn out.

He pushed the worry aside. Evelyn had been a natural when she'd joined BAU. He had to believe she'd get her drive back.

"Tell me everything," he said.

Before she could start, the tent door opened again. Greg jumped to his feet, hoping it was his cousin.

But it was a different HRT agent, this one from his cousin's team. A big guy named Charles, with a wife and three kids at home.

A few weary-looking Salt Lake City agents came inside after him, one of them clutching his arm to his chest. The other guy said the medevac helicopter had landed, and two support staff members helped the HRT agent to his feet. His face looked bloodless as he walked slowly out the door.

Charles moved aside to let them pass, then announced loudly, "We've got the badly wounded heading out in medevacs. Anyone else who's injured is waiting for the ambulances. We're taking any cultists and protesters who don't need medical attention to the local police station for questioning and processing."

"What's the plan...?" one of the support staff began to ask, but the Salt Lake City SAC interrupted, pointing at Evelyn.

"You need to get down there and help."

"I'm not sure that's a good idea," Greg said. "She needs a medic to check her out first." Once he knew she was okay physically, he wanted her story before she started getting information from others.

"Too bad," the SAC snapped. "You're going, too."

Greg crossed his arms. He had a reputation as an easygoing guy, and usually he tried to further that reputation. But the Salt Lake City SAC wasn't his boss.

And he didn't put up with bullshit; he didn't care what the guy's title was.

Evelyn stood, grabbing his arm before he could say anything. "I'm okay. I don't need a medic. And I want to go. I want to talk to Ward Butler—while he's the one who's imprisoned, instead of me."

Charles snorted, looking annoyed as he swiveled back toward the door. "That's not happening," he called over his shoulder.

Evelyn stood, started to follow. "Why not?"

"Ward Butler is dead."

The closest police station was much larger than Evelyn had expected, and much farther away. After a bumpy, hour-long ride down the mountain, she'd found herself walking into a modern building with a bustling police force that handled a huge area of Montana. It was rural, so although their square footage was challenging to patrol, the number of people they were protecting was relatively small. Apparently, their biggest crime problems were drug dealing, domestic violence and, oddly, hate crimes.

She wondered vaguely if that was because of the Butler Compound members. A young officer, heavily bundled in a thick coat, led her down a hallway that reeked of disinfectant. The heat was blasting, but she was still cold in the sweatshirt and pants she'd had on for ten days. Greg trailed behind her more slowly, and she could sense him taking in all the details of the police station—including the self-congratulatory plaques lining the walls, and the patrol officers passing by who were giving them curious, slightly hostile glances.

Was it because the FBI was being blamed for what

had happened up at the Butler Compound? Or because some of their own had been killed today? She ducked her head, figuring it probably was, and unable to totally blame them for their anger, even if it was misplaced.

"Here you go," the officer told Greg, and her partner stepped into a room with an SSA from the Salt Lake City office.

Evelyn kept going, walking silently beside a different SSA—one who handled the sole terrorism squad at the Salt Lake City office. Finally, the officer opened a door at the end of the hallway and gestured her inside. "We'll bring the prisoners in to you," he said, then turned back the way he'd come.

"Do we have a list of the dead yet?" Evelyn asked as she entered the bare room, which had nothing but a long white table and four chairs. "How many are on there, besides Butler?"

The SSA—Evelyn dug around in her memory for his name, coming up with Lucas Halstrom—tapped away on his BlackBerry, then looked up at her from where he'd taken a seat at the table. "So far, they've confirmed thirteen of Butler's men dead, and seven in custody—seven from the compound, anyway. I'm…"

"What about Jen?" Evelyn broke in.

He shook his head, and his fingers stilled against his phone. "Still not accounted for. The assumption is that they took her off-site to bury her. We're bringing up a canine team." He rubbed his temple, then added, "They're supposed to text me as soon as they find her."

He cleared his throat, steadied his voice and continued. "Some of those in custody are injured, so they're actually at the hospital and not here. Looks like we'll get to talk to three now."

Three men out of twenty. Evelyn shivered, remembering when most of those twenty men had surrounded her in the compound, calling for her death. Now many of them were gone, and with them, a lot of the FBI's possible sources of information on any future terrorist attacks Butler was planning.

"What about Rolfe?" Evelyn asked. Nerves cramped her stomach as Lucas shook his head again.

"I don't have any confirmed IDs on the dead yet. Pictures will be coming, in case you can identify anyone, but right now I've just got the basics. We've got Evidence Response Team agents in the compound, along with a medical examiner."

"Okay." Evelyn sat at the gleaming white table, under bright fluorescent lights, her eyes hurting after a week in semidarkness. She felt useless without her weapon, phone or credentials. At least, she told herself that was why she felt useless, that if she got her gear back, she'd feel more like the Special Agent she was. "Let me know as soon as you hear."

"Who's Rolfe?" Lucas asked, squinting at her. "What's his last name?"

He stared at her intently, his hazel eyes gleaming with suspicion, and Evelyn could tell he was a solid SSA. He knew she wasn't telling him something.

She shrugged, looking away from Lucas so he wouldn't see her hope that Rolfe was among the living. He'd saved her life repeatedly, and he was their best chance for real details about additional targets, since he was the second-in-command. She couldn't help hoping he was still alive. She refused to think too closely about why.

"I have no idea what his last name is, but as far as I

could see, he was Butler's only lieutenant—or his recruiter, if my theory's right. Which, given the bombing, I assume I am. If anyone can tell us details about the plot, it's Rolfe."

Lucas nodded, and typed a text into his phone. He was a huge guy, with big, blunt features—a flared nose, flattened on top, a long, lined forehead and a prominent chin—and he looked like he belonged in SWAT, rather than behind a desk. When it had seemed as though the protesters were going to come into TOC, he'd been on the phone, one hand clutching his weapon, a furious scowl on his face. He'd looked ready for battle. She wondered if he approached his cases that way.

He typed as they waited for the first of the three men they'd get to interrogate, and Evelyn turned her attention back to Rolfe. She wanted him to be alive because she'd formed a bond with him, she realized. He was antifederalist, probably a closet racist despite his denials about that, and he'd participated in holding her hostage. Yet she felt sick at the thought that he might be dead.

She groaned in disgust. She wasn't supposed to get Stockholm Syndrome. That was for untrained victims who spent years in captivity. Not FBI profilers who spent a week and a half held hostage by men she'd known were up to no good before she even got there.

"What's wrong?" Lucas asked, and Evelyn saw that he'd finished his text and was staring at her again.

She was saved from having to explain when the door opened and the same young police officer reentered, leading a cuffed cultist.

The cultist was also young, maybe early twenties, with a shaved head and tattoos peeking out from his shirtsleeves. He had deep brown eyes, filled with apprehension, and he was chewing on his lip as the officer sat him down at the table. He fidgeted, gazing down at his cuffed hands—and away from her.

Right about now, he was probably hoping she hadn't seen him on the edge of that crowd ready to lynch her, sticking close to the wall. As though he wasn't sure he wanted to be part of it, but didn't want anyone to think he wasn't going along, either.

He probably expected her to be furious with him, to want to use her federal power to do whatever she could to punish him.

Instead, she smiled, although it felt a little unnatural. But this guy was young, very likely new to the movement. There was a good chance he didn't have any serious arrests on his record before now. If she didn't alienate him, she could get information from him.

The officer dropped a folder on the table in front of Lucas—no doubt containing the kid's name and any details they had on him—and then left the room.

As the young cultist continued to fidget and stare down at his hands, Lucas picked up the folder and leaned back in his seat. She moved closer, reading along.

The cultist's name was Shaun Porter. Twenty-two. A few arrests over the years for vandalism, trespassing and a DUI. The officer's notes indicated that he'd grown up in a middle-class family nearby and had always been a quiet, shy kid. He'd slowly begun falling into fringe militia groups once he hit high school. His parents had tried to file a complaint when he'd moved out to the Butler Compound a year ago, but there wasn't really anything the police could do, since he was of age and had gone voluntarily.

Beside her, Lucas closed the folder and leaned forward, which meant he wanted to take the lead. That made sense. He was white and male, two things Shaun would identify with—but Evelyn spoke first. She wanted him to think she didn't remember his actions inside the compound. She wanted him to think she didn't hold a grudge.

"I'm Evelyn. We didn't really get a chance to meet inside, Shaun. This is Lucas."

The kid gave her an incredulous look, and Lucas spoke up, his voice low and easy, his tone conversational. "So, Shaun, tell us about the bomb."

Shaun raised his head, surprise in his eyes, followed by suspicion, and Evelyn tried to keep her own disbelief off her face.

No warm-up at all? Did Lucas figure the shock approach would work or was he just fed up after being in a tent listening to Butler preach for a week? After being warned by Jen that there was a threat inside, and dismissing her?

She glanced sidelong at Lucas, wondering if he'd been Jen's supervisor. Wondering if he was carrying around guilt for her death now.

"What bomb?" Shaun asked, petulance in his tone as he braced his cuffed hands on the table. "You're not pinning some shit on me I didn't do."

"Oh, don't worry," Lucas said, his voice calm. "We have plenty of shit to charge you on that you *did* do. Like the deaths of four policemen."

Shaun blanched, his already light skin going even paler. "No way! I didn't kill anyone."

"How do you know that?" Lucas demanded, banging one fist on the table, his voice going hard. "Can you track the bullets you fired? Because we can. Forensics are a fascinating thing, Shaun. We'll be able to track every bullet from every individual gun."

"Then I have nothing to worry about," Shaun said, but his voice quavered underneath the bravado.

Evelyn started to jump in; Lucas was faster. "Give us the information we want on the bomb and we'll make you a deal."

"I don't…"

"Right now," Lucas snapped. "There's a time limit on this offer and it expires in about two seconds."

"I don't know anything about a bomb!" Shaun said, his eyes wide as his gaze went back and forth between them, settling on her, pleading. "I don't. I swear."

Lucas leaned back in his seat. "Time's up."

The door to the room opened and another Special Agent—Evelyn hadn't even realized he'd been watching the interview—grabbed Shaun by the arm and pulled him toward the door.

"Hey, wait! I don't know anything about a bomb! And I didn't shoot anyone! I want to talk to my parents!" Shaun insisted, but the agent just kept dragging him along until they were out of the room, the door shut behind them.

Evelyn turned to glare at Lucas. "What the hell was that?"

"We talked about this in the car," Lucas reminded her. "We're doing the interviews because the cultists will know you, and hopefully your presence will make them nervous. I've got the terrorism background, so I'll ask the questions, and then move them on to the next interview. He was a waste of time. He didn't have any information for us. He's too young, and too new. Butler clearly didn't share his plans with everyone. But someone else can dig into this kid for other information. You and I have to focus on the bombings. You've got the profiling skills. I don't claim to be able to do that. So, if you disagree with me on a subject, you jump in. Otherwise, we're moving them through. We have no idea if—or when—another bomb might go off."

More quietly, he added, "And if by some miracle, Jen—Martinez—is still alive, I want to find her."

"Okay," Evelyn said slowly. They'd received those instructions on the way over, although admittedly, she hadn't paid as much attention to the details as she should have. She'd been distracted by the incessant thoughts running through her head.

Was Rolfe still alive? Who the hell had killed Butler? Had he died in the skirmish with HRT? Or had his own men killed him, after they'd learned he'd set up booby traps against *them* if they dared enter his sanctuary? Three of them had followed her into Rolfe's room, but she had no idea how many more had been behind them, who might've kept going and tracked Butler down.

They still didn't have any real answers on that; if they did, no one was telling her.

She shifted in her seat to face Lucas. "Any news on who killed Butler?"

He frowned. "It wasn't us. We found him in the far back room, what looks like his bedroom. Our best bet is that one of his own killed him. His throat was slit."

Evelyn shuddered, remembering the guy who'd held a knife to *her* throat.

But she'd watched that cultist come into the back area, watched him die by Kyle's bullet. He wasn't the one who'd killed Butler. Of course, in a group of survivalists, they all knew how to use a knife. It could've been any of them. And after Butler had set up booby traps and deserted them in the firefight *he'd* dragged them into, they probably all had reason to want him dead.

"You have any ideas on a good candidate?" Lucas asked, just as the door opened again.

The same police officer brought in another cultist. This one was older, midfifties or so, with a jagged scar across his cheek that looked as though he'd stitched it closed himself. His camo was streaked with blood, and his face was lined with fury.

"I have nothing to say to you," he told them as soon as he sat down. He leaned back in his chair and scowled and, no matter what Lucas asked, wouldn't say another word.

When Lucas asked about a bomb, a frown crumpled the man's forehead, but otherwise he made no response. Finally Lucas rolled his eyes, shook his head and said, "We're finished," and the same agent from before came in and dragged the cultist out.

"This is going well," Lucas muttered when the door closed.

"The bomb surprised him," Evelyn said.

"Yeah, I agree. He didn't know about it, either." He turned to look at her. "You think only Butler and this Rolfe guy knew?"

"Maybe. If the compound was meant to be a recruiting ground, maybe the men there didn't even know it. There was a huge variety of beliefs in there—it's what struck me as odd about them as a cult. They didn't seem to share a core philosophy. But they were all survivalists, all antifederalist. Rolfe could have picked them out and delivered them to Butler, who observed them, then pulled out the ones he thought were good candidates."

Lucas nodded. "It's actually a smart method, if you're right. It keeps the majority of them in the dark in case anything goes wrong. And it lets Butler pick out the most die-hard of the group and send them off to do his bidding."

"What if we're taking the wrong approach here?" Evelyn asked. "Maybe instead of asking about the bomb, we need to ask about members who left suddenly in the past few months."

Lucas pulled out his phone again, and typed another message. "I'm passing that on to the agent handling the more intensive interviews. We'll stick with the bomb for now." He started to put his phone away, then it beeped at him and he took it out again. "We have information on the dead."

Evelyn leaned close as he pulled up images on his phone. Thirteen of them, thankfully close-ups of their faces that, for the most part, didn't reveal the gruesome nature of their deaths. Tension knotted her gut as Lucas clicked slowly past face after face, all of them slack with death, taking away some of the anger she was used to seeing.

When he finished, she shook her head, her hopes rising. "Rolfe isn't there. He must be among the injured. We can interrogate him. He should be able to tell us about the bomb."

"Good. I've got those images, too, taken at the hospital. You point him out and, unless he's on the operating table, we'll bring him here now." He clicked a few more buttons and opened a picture that showed a cultist, probably midthirties.

Evelyn remembered him mostly as the guy who'd handed her some tea one day, telling her gruffly that she looked like she could use some. Now he had a cast on his arm, stitches on his leg and a bald patch on the side of his otherwise shaggy blond hair where another line of dark thread marched.

"Not Rolfe," Evelyn told Lucas, and he flipped to the next picture. She shook her head through three more pictures and then glanced expectantly at Lucas when he didn't go to the next shot.

"Who else?"

"That's it," Lucas said.

"What do you mean? Where's Rolfe?"

"You missed him. He must've been in one of the pictures of the dead."

"No. He wasn't."

Lucas sat a little straighter. "Then he must be our final uninjured cultist."

As if on cue, the door opened and the young cop came back in, pulling a limping man behind him.

The man looked up at them, exhaustion and defeat on his face as he settled into the chair across from them.

"We've been waiting for you, Rolfe," Lucas said.

The man gazed back at him blankly and Evelyn shook her head. "That's not Rolfe."

"It has to be."

"Well, it's not. You must have missed someone."

"We didn't *miss* anyone," Lucas said. "Twenty men, plus Ward Butler. They're all accounted for."

"No, they're not." Agitated, Evelyn got to her feet. "Where the hell is Rolfe? If we want to know about that bomb, we need Rolfe."

11

"Maybe he's still hiding somewhere in the compound," Lucas said into his phone.

Kyle's face, exhausted, with a smear of blood on his cheek, stared back at them from the phone's tiny screen. "We'll keep searching, but I've got to tell you, we've hit all the rooms. If he's hiding, it's someplace pretty small and well-hidden. And we're being very careful about anything we open. There are still a lot of booby traps in here."

"Are you all right?" Evelyn asked, ignoring the perplexed frown Lucas gave her.

"No worries," Kyle replied, and she wasn't sure if he said that because he was on the job and no one knew they were dating, or if this was just normal enough for an HRT agent that he *was* fine.

"Is the place still guarded?" Lucas asked. "Is it possible this Rolfe guy hid until the raid was over, then snuck out after everyone left?"

Kyle swung his phone around so they could see his surroundings. "Yeah, we're still here. Two HRT teams, minus six members in the hospital. Plus the SWAT team that was on the way from Salt Lake. They didn't make it in time to help with the protesters, so they're watching our perimeter now. We also have ERT agents, and the Salt Lake City SAC's on scene. It's crowded. This Rolfe guy didn't climb out from under a bunk somewhere, gather up a stash of weapons and walk out the front door. If he's still inside, he's tucked away somewhere clever. It might take a while, but we're going over the whole place, top to bottom."

"Good," Lucas said. "He has to be there somewhere, and you need to find him. If Evelyn's right, he's the only person who'll be able to tell us if there are more attacks planned."

"We're on it," Kyle responded.

"Great," Lucas replied, then closed the call before Evelyn could thank Kyle for coming in to get her, for shooting the man who was ready to slit her throat. Before she could find a way to ask anything more personal.

She hadn't had a chance to talk to him after the protesters had been arrested. The higher-ups had been pushing her to get to the police station to start questioning, and HRT had been working nonstop, removing booby traps and making sure everyone was accounted for.

She'd seen Kyle from a distance, walking beside Gabe, who looked like he was limping a little but otherwise seemed fine. Kyle had glanced at her and nodded, his way of reassuring her, but things felt different between them. They'd felt different since she'd gone back to work.

She knew it was her. *She* was different. Kyle had spent so long trying to convince her to go out with him, and once she'd agreed, he'd been patient with her demand for secrecy. At the beginning, his asking her out had been a joke, but that had slowly changed. Now that she'd let herself open up to Kyle, maybe her baggage was just too much for him.

"Evelyn!"

"What?"

Lucas frowned again, worry and annoyance warring in his expression. "You need a break? You want a sandwich? Or maybe some coffee or pain pills? You seem…distracted."

"No, I'm fine. Sorry." Her throat still ached, despite the two cups of hot tea Greg had gotten her from TOC. She felt the persistent need to sneeze, and there was a rattling in her chest whenever she breathed. Her jaw hurt, her back hurt, her arms hurt. But that was nothing compared to her frustration. "Let's see what the other interviews have turned up." She headed for the door, and heard him mumble something unintelligible under his breath before he got up and followed.

In the hallway outside, Greg was talking to the young officer who'd brought them the cultists to question.

"I'll check it out," the officer told Greg, looking far less hostile than he had when he'd met Lucas and Evelyn.

Trust Greg to make everyone like him, Evelyn thought as the officer walked toward the front of the station. She wished she had that talent.

For her, reading the behavioral cues at a crime scene and tying them to a particular type of person had always come naturally. It was like a puzzle she had to unravel. But the part of the job that required her to work with local law enforcement and get them to trust her? That had always been much harder.

"What's he checking out?" Lucas asked.

"Any information they have on a local named Rolfe. It's not exactly a common name," Greg said. "Maybe we'll get lucky."

"So the longer interviews didn't give us anything?"

"Not yet." Greg clutched a foam cup close to his face, as if he was breathing in the steam from the coffee, trying to suck the caffeine out of the air. "And as far as I can see, none of these guys know anything about the bomb. Either that, or they're all damn good actors."

Lucas snorted, crossing his arms over his massive chest. "The kid, the angry old-timer and the guy who needs a doctor but is too proud to admit it? I doubt that." The amusement faded. "If they didn't know about the bomb, then it sounds like we're out of luck until we find this Rolfe character."

"What do we know about Rolfe?" Evelyn asked. "From my perspective, he acted like Butler's second-in-command, but I've been wondering if he was the recruiter for Butler."

"Probably not," Greg said. "According to the interviews, most of the cultists—or whatever you want to call them—resented Rolfe. They're painting a picture of a guy who showed up whenever he felt like it—which they claim wasn't very often—and suddenly became Butler's right hand. Someone who just popped in for a day or two and started bossing them around, then left again for months."

"He brought new members when he showed up?"

"No."

"No? Then why did he come and go?"

"No one seems to have any idea. But they've all got identical stories about how they grew their membership. They say new members were recruited by existing ones or by Butler himself. They don't call it recruiting, of course, just 'discovering like-minded people.' It sounds as though the cultists didn't understand who Rolfe was, why he showed up or why they were supposed to go along with anything he said."

"So he's not a recruiter," Evelyn said slowly. She looked from Greg to Lucas. "Then what is he?"

"Butler recruits, Rolfe trains and we have a third unknown person who's the mastermind?" Lucas suggested.

"That's too complicated for a homegrown terror plot," Greg argued. "It might make sense if we were talking about a group who traveled to other countries for training, then came back here to act. We've seen some of that. Of course, then the trainers are overseas and it's more diffuse. But for a traditional, far-right-wing terrorist? I mean, survivalists in general don't play well with others."

"Sure, but look at what Butler's built," Evelyn reminded him.

"A place to ride out the Armageddon together. Safety in numbers, when the unprepared masses come after them," Greg said as Lucas stared at him incredulously.

"What?" Greg demanded. "You head up the Salt Lake City's terror squad, right? Your office has tracked some of these guys over the years. You know how preppers think."

"Yes," Lucas said. "And I agree with you. But Evelyn believes they're connected to the Chicago bombing. Which means either there's *some* kind of conspiracy here. Or we're wrong, and the bombing has nothing to do with this group."

Greg shot her an apologetic look and asked, "If these

guys were motivated to join up with Butler—to hunker down and ride out the end times—why the hell would they train to *go out* and attack? The true Bubbas are loners, the guys who *don't* fit in these groups because their ideas are too extreme. I believe Evelyn. She's one of our best profilers. But that means we're missing something here."

"Maybe that's it," Evelyn mused, trying to ignore the thought that perhaps *she* was the one who was missing something. When Greg looked confused, she clarified, "Exactly what you said about the real Bubbas not fitting any group. These people had *huge* differences in their belief systems. They weren't united, except as survivalists. Maybe that was Rolfe's purpose. Butler lured them in, then picked out the extremists and had Rolfe come and check them out. The ones who fit, Rolfe took away to initiate."

She remembered him telling her that he was sorry she'd been pulled into the compound, sorry for what happened to Jen. "Or maybe Rolfe didn't know what he was really getting into."

"If he's the only lieutenant, and he was the one coming and going, he knew," Greg said.

She nodded. She didn't really want to believe it, after Rolfe had protected her, but it was the most logical explanation.

"You think there's a third guy in this leadership or not?" Lucas asked.

"I don't know," Evelyn said. "That would mean ceding a lot of power to Butler and Rolfe. Terrorists don't usually rely on democratic leadership systems."

"Well, mostly the power would be ceded to Butler," Greg pointed out. "Rolfe could have just served as a liaison or deliveryman between the two. Because otherwise, Rolfe would be an equal player, and I doubt he'd let Butler boss him around the way he did if that was true."

"A third person might explain the connection to Chicago," Lucas said thoughtfully. "We can't find any link between Butler and the Chicago ATF."

"I'm not sure there needs to be one," Greg said. "It could be symbolic. Or just strategic. Something they knew they could access, and a softer target."

"A *mall* is a softer target," Lucas muttered. "Chicago ATF should have been pretty secure."

"It was," Greg argued. "They went for the people outside. Like the Boston Marathon."

The three of them were silent a minute, and Evelyn took in the grim expressions on Greg's and Lucas's faces. She hadn't seen the footage from the Chicago explosion yet, but she'd seen the feeds from the Boston Marathon. No matter how many cases she profiled for BAU—hundreds of serial killers, child abductors, arsonists and bombers—there was some level on which, academic understanding aside, she just didn't get how one person could knowingly inflict that kind of pain on another.

But there was one thing she did know, and not just because of her master's degrees in psychology and criminology, or her extensive training from the FBI. It had more to do with a gut-level understanding she'd always had in these sorts of cases. "They're going after another target."

"And that's why we're rushing these interrogations," Greg said.

"Why do you sound so certain?" Lucas asked Evelyn,

absently stroking his sidearm, as though he was itching to use it on any threats that might appear.

"If they went to this much trouble to recruit, it's not just about one attack. This is part of something bigger. It has to be."

Lucas held up both hands. "That's assuming Butler is connected to the attack. Now, we're acting on the belief that you're right, since the bombing came just after you warned us, but I have to tell you, I've been on the phone with the Evidence Response Team inside the compound."

"And?" Greg prompted when he paused.

"And they've found nothing there to connect Butler to the attack. Not a single thing."

"Evelyn knows…"

"I'm not saying she's wrong," Lucas broke in. "But we need a concrete connection, or we have to broaden our search. Obviously, there's a team in Chicago already working other angles, but the Bureau's putting out some serious manpower on the basis of a single agent's gut feeling."

"Two agents," Evelyn reminded him quietly. "Don't forget Jen."

Lucas clamped his lips in a tight, angry line, as though he was trying to restrain a flurry of furious words.

But Jen Martinez had died because she was convinced everyone around her was missing a valid threat. And she'd been right. Evelyn wasn't about to let anyone forget it, herself included.

When Lucas finally spoke, there was something sad in his voice. "Jen wasn't even on the terror squad. She never should've been at that compound." He turned and walked away before Evelyn could respond.

Evelyn began to follow, but Greg grabbed her arm. "He feels guilty enough, Evelyn. Let him be."

"Maybe he *should* feel guilty," she muttered, not really sure why she felt such animosity. Maybe because she felt guilty, too. She hadn't believed Martinez, either.

She shivered, from the cold that seemed to hit her at random intervals, or more guilt. She hugged her arms around herself, wishing she'd had something besides the cult sweat suit to change into. But although someone had picked up her car and her luggage, she hadn't had time to get it. She hadn't had time to stand under a scalding hot shower, either, to scrub and scrub until she no longer felt the filmy layer of Jen's blood on her.

"You sure you're okay?" Greg asked. "We can still take you to the hospital."

"I'm fine. What do we know so far about Chicago?"

"Well, here's the latest." Greg opened his phone, typed in a command and turned it to face her.

She leaned close, staring at the image. It looked like pieces of a heavy cloth, torn apart and pieced back together, with a filthy sticker pasted on one part that was still whole.

"It's the backpack that contained the bomb."

"The sticker…"

"It says Freedom Uprising," Greg said. "That sound familiar?"

Evelyn frowned, trying to remember. She started to shake her head, and then a memory teased her. She'd been asleep, tethered to Rolfe's bed, when she'd heard Butler and Rolfe talking. Their voices had been distant, as though they were down the hall, but they were arguing. Butler had said something…something…

What was it?

As hard as she concentrated, the memory wouldn't rise to the surface. "Maybe. I'm just not sure."

Greg tried to hide his disappointment, and she tried to pretend she hadn't seen it. There was way too much she wasn't sure about, and she couldn't remember when she'd last slept, or eaten an MRE. She glanced back at him and admitted, "I think I need a break. Some food, a shower, some new clothes."

Greg nodded. "I'll get an officer to drive you. I'll call you if anything breaks."

"Thanks."

She was just heading down the hall toward the front of the station, a sudden exhaustion weighing down every step, when Greg's voice reached her.

"Wait! Kyle's on the phone with more information for us."

She hurried back, and Lucas appeared from the other direction. She gave him a nod, hoping she hadn't already soured their working relationship, and he nodded quickly back at her before turning his full attention to Greg.

"What's up, Mac?" Greg asked, holding out his phone.

This time it was just on speaker, no video, and Evelyn wished she could see Kyle's face again, if only to reassure herself that he was still okay.

"We think we've gotten rid of all the booby traps." She could hear exhaustion in each word. "We've checked in every closet, under every bunk. It's definite. There's no one else. Rolfe isn't here."

"Maybe he was never there," Lucas said quietly after Evelyn had left for her hotel. Just Lucas and Greg remained in the police station's too-bright, oddly clean break room.

"What?" Greg paused in lifting what he figured must be his tenth cup of coffee that day to his mouth, and stared back at Lucas, uncomprehending. "Who?"

"This Rolfe guy. Look, I know Evelyn is your partner…"

"Technically, she's not," Greg said. "But Evelyn wouldn't make up the presence of a terrorist! Besides, we asked the other cultists in interviews about Rolfe. No one denied he existed."

"None of them actually said he was there during the raid, either," Lucas pointed out. "Maybe he'd already left and Evelyn just heard his name. I think we have to ask ourselves, *Is she reliable?* I mean, the place was surrounded. He couldn't have escaped and there's no one inside."

"Of course she's reliable," Greg insisted, setting down his coffee cup as his driving need for caffeine was overshadowed by his need to protect his closest friend in BAU.

Lucas raised one hand, leaning forward from his spot on a big, cushioned chair in the corner. "Look, man, I'm not saying she'd mislead us on purpose, but you saw her. She's in bad shape. Has she told you what happened in there?"

"I got the quick and dirty version," Greg said. The truth was, he knew Evelyn had been holding a lot back. Most likely, it was just because she was a private person, and she couldn't stand the idea that anyone might feel she wasn't up to the job. As a woman in law enforcement, she probably *did* have to worry about that more than most men. But they needed all the details; in an investigation, you never knew what small bit of information might hold the key to closing the case.

"Okay, so it's probably worse than she's admitting," Lucas pressed, and Greg couldn't argue with that.

Knowing Evelyn, it was a lot worse than she was admitting.

"The cultists went after her a few times. We heard the nasty mob when we first arrived, screaming about killing her. Maybe she hallucinated this guy's presence."

Greg started to protest, but Lucas said, "Hear me out. Maybe she hallucinated someone who was protecting her, because she needed a way to distance herself from what really did happen."

Greg swallowed back his instant response and tried to be objective. He'd seen that very thing happen with victims who'd been held captive. They'd convinced themselves of a person's presence, someone the FBI could *prove* wasn't there. They'd needed a way to protect their minds, to replace the memory of what had actually happened, so they could make it through something horrible.

But Evelyn was a trained profiler. Regardless of what she'd faced in that compound, he had to believe she'd still be able to separate reality and fiction. Besides, they'd had audio on her part of the time. "We heard someone defend her," Greg reminded Lucas. "That wasn't her imagination."

"Doesn't mean it was this Rolfe guy. It could've been anyone in there. There could've been a combination of people doing the things she's attributing to Rolfe. Come on. We have absolutely *no* evidence this guy was in there."

"What about the room where Mac found her? It

was *someone's* room. It had to be Butler's second-in-command, given the location."

"ERT is printing the room," Lucas said. "And I'm not saying he doesn't *exist*, just that maybe he wasn't there at the time. She heard the group talk about him. From what we learned in the interviews, nobody liked this guy, so she could've imagined him as her savior. The other possibility is that we already have him in custody—or the morgue—and she doesn't want to turn him in."

"Why wouldn't she turn him over?" Greg demanded, but he didn't really need Lucas to tell him the answer to that one.

Evelyn was showing clear signs of Stockholm Syndrome. If she felt indebted to this Rolfe guy and didn't want to get him in trouble, that meant he was still able to *get* into trouble.

Greg didn't believe for a second that Evelyn had hallucinated the guy—but refusing to identify him, either consciously or subconsciously?

They'd positively IDed the three guys who'd been in the police station for questioning; however, that hadn't happened with everyone at the hospital yet. "We'd better make IDing everyone a top priority," Greg suggested.

Lucas nodded, hunching over his phone as he typed out a quick text to someone. "Do you think she's fit for duty?"

"Yes," Greg answered immediately, and even though he *wasn't* a hundred percent certain, he couldn't take that concern anywhere. Not without potentially damaging her reputation or her career. She was already putting both in jeopardy herself, between going into the compound and her recent apathy toward profiling.

"Oh, shit," Lucas said, and Greg realized he'd lost focus.

He glanced over at the other agent and discovered Lucas was still looking at his phone. "What now?"

"News of Butler's death has leaked to the press."

"Shit," Greg echoed. "Let me guess. The public…"

"Is blaming us," Lucas finished. "Yep. This is an even worse public relations disaster than we thought it would be. We should've waited. We shouldn't have gone tactical. I sure as hell hope this doesn't impact our investigation."

"Nothing we can do about it," Greg said, not commenting on the tactical decision. Still, he had a bad feeling about what was yet to come. "We need to focus on finding this Rolfe guy. And on our agent. Any word on the search for Jen?" He purposely didn't say what he knew Lucas had to be thinking—they weren't searching for Jen. They were searching for her body.

Lucas gave a hard, fast shake of his head, clutching his hands together in his lap. "Nothing. They still haven't found her."

Greg sighed, knowing every hour that passed without locating her was one more hour her family had to wait for news that couldn't be good. "Evelyn says Jen was shot that first day, before we arrived. They could have driven her out of the compound. We've only got a rough estimate of how far they could've gone. It's a big area to cover."

"I know." Lucas looked down at his lap. "Meanwhile, our office is getting calls from her husband every hour on the hour. He's a nice guy. He's…" Lucas swallowed hard, shook his head. "She's been here a long time, so everyone knows him, too. And their kids…"

He trailed off, and Greg waited silently, giving him a chance to recover.

The ringing of Lucas's phone startled them both. Lucas jumped, then frowned at the number on his call display. "It's the JTTF in Chicago."

After the bombing, a Joint Terrorism Task Force had been formed immediately, made up of ATF, FBI, local police and probably several other agencies Greg didn't know about. He leaned closer to Lucas, hoping the JTTF had a solid lead in the bombing investigation. "Speaker?"

Lucas nodded and took a loud breath, clearly trying to get his emotions in check. Then he hit Answer and said tiredly, "Supervisory Special Agent Lucas Halstrom. You've got SA Greg Ibsen from BAU on the line, as well."

There was a pause, then a deep, rumbling voice came over the speaker. "Fred Lanier here. Lucas, we're officially pulling you into the task force. We want you running the Montana angle. We've also asked for the other profiler, the one who was inside the compound. We want both of you in Chicago tomorrow morning for a briefing."

Lucas opened his mouth, then shut it. He said simply, "Yes, sir."

"I'm not sure that's wise." Greg jumped in before Lucas could hang up the phone.

"Why not?" Fred asked.

"Evelyn was held hostage for a week. She needs time to recover. She should be checked out at a hospital. She…"

"I spoke with her supervisor at BAU," Fred interrupted. "She hasn't been taken out of the field. She's coming. Get her on that plane."

Greg prepared to keep arguing, but Fred hung up.

Lucas glanced at him and sighed. "I'll keep an eye on her," he promised.

Greg nodded, trying to look grateful. Inside, he was just worried. Would Lucas's presence help? Or would he question every recollection of her captivity, every theory she brought to the table?

Evelyn was already teetering on the edge of leaving the FBI. Deep down, Greg could feel it, even if she wasn't ready to admit it.

Would this push her over the edge?

12

"Where do you expect the next bombing?"

The question came from Fred Lanier, head of the JTTF in Chicago. Rumor had it that he was an old-timer in the Chicago terrorism squad, with a nonstop work ethic and no sense of humor. He sat at one end of a long, rectangular table in an interagency coordination room at the FBI field office in Chicago. Evelyn was at the other end, and there was quite a distance between them.

The entire task force stared back at her just as intently as Fred. A line of agents with matching bloodshot eyes, parked in front of laptops and well-used coffee mugs, waited for her to give them the break they needed.

When she'd arrived, the first thing that had struck her was how much this place resembled every other FBI field office she'd ever visited. Gray, industrial carpeting. Boring white walls. Cubicles sectioned off by squad. A whole lot of agents and support staff crammed into the space. And the persistent buzz of voices, rising and falling like a strange symphony.

Now, she tried not to fidget as she faced something else that was similar to every visit she'd made to a field office in the past year. As a BAU agent, if she visited other offices, it was to consult on a case. Which meant she was used to being asked questions that were nearly impossible to answer. She was used to being the center of attention, with a group of law enforcement agents watching her with unrealistic hope or unearned distrust.

Today, it rattled her more than usual.

"I can't tell you where the next bombing's going to be," she answered, trying not to let her voice tremble. "All I can say is that I expect one."

"How soon?" someone from ATF demanded.

"I don't know."

"Okay," the same ATF agent said, sounding frustrated as he braced his elbows on the table, deep brown eyes boring into hers. "Then tell me this, will ATF still be the focus? Or do you think they'll go after a different type of target?"

"I don't have the answer to that, either. But it'll definitely be a federal target."

Lucas spoke up. "Why?" he asked. "Because Butler is a survivalist? What if he hated anyone who didn't agree with his philosophy? Who's to say his next target won't be civilian?"

She opened her mouth to answer. Everything she'd been asked to provide was based on the theory that the ATF bombing had been masterminded by Ward Butler. But that was all it was—a theory.

She believed it, although she knew there was doubt within the JTTF. Probably rightfully so. No evidence had come out of the compound yet to support her theory, so the timing *could* have been coincidental. A good investigation had to focus on all the possibilities. As a profiler, it was her job to make sure they focused on the most likely direction.

Before she could speak, Fred smacked his hands against the table, looking impatient as he drew everyone's attention. "Since Butler is dead, even if there'd been more attacks planned, will they actually happen?"

Everyone in the room seemed to hold their breath as Evelyn considered the questions. "There was no one fundamental belief inside that compound," she finally said slowly, forming her answers as she spoke. "But I'm convinced Butler was recruiting hard-core survivalists—the fringe element—which means he was looking for something specific. And *Butler's* strongest hatred was for the federal government. If he was in charge…"

"True." Fred cut her off, obviously wanting the answer to *his* question. "I agree with you there. If he was the mastermind of the Chicago bombing, his plan would be centered on federal targets. But setting aside the fact that we can't prove he had anything to do with it, let's run with your theory for a minute and focus on this. Since he's dead, if he did have more bombings planned, would his followers still go through with them?"

The room silenced as everyone stared at her again.

This question was trickier. In theory, Butler had pulled out the die-hard element, so they'd be committed to his cause. Then again, news was bound to break that Butler had booby-trapped his compound against his own followers. Whether the bombers would *believe* he'd done it was one thing, but if they did, would they scrap any additional bombings they had planned?

"We need to find a way to publicize how Butler turned on his followers, and quickly," she offered. "It would be best if it doesn't come directly from us."

"Because they'll expect us to lie," Lucas said, nodding. "They hate the government, and they're suspicious of anything we say. I agree. That information *can't* come from us, or they'll think we made it up, and it could actually make them *more* committed. Maybe we can use some of the surviving cultists instead, and have them go on the record with the media."

"Look into it," Fred ordered Lucas. "Now, let's move on to the bombers." He flicked on a laptop, and the screen's image projected across the room, against the bare white wall. "We've got some security camera footage from the bombing that we've pieced together. It's not great—the bomber keeps his head down most of the time—but everyone take a look."

He hit Play and Evelyn swiveled in her seat, watching intently as a grainy picture flickered on the wall. A snapshot frozen in time, of a man wearing a thick, dark-green coat, wearing a baseball cap pulled low over his forehead, a blue bag slung over his shoulder. A hint of a tattoo peeked out between the collar of his coat and the bottom of his hat.

"Are we running the tattoo?" she asked. If he'd ever spent time in prison, that could provide a clue. Prison officials logged tattoos and other identifiable marks. Going through all of it would be a project, because inclusion of convicts' tattoo information into the FBI's database was voluntary, so not all prisons uploaded theirs. If it wasn't in the FBI's database, they'd have to start searching state by state, but it might be worthwhile.

"We're checking on it," Fred confirmed. "This one came from a security camera across the street. Here's the next one."

He clicked to a new image, of the bomber bending down near the ATF building, setting his bag on the ground a few feet in front of a tall concrete pillar.

Another click and there he was again, leaving without his bag.

A sick feeling welled up in her at seeing this image, taken before the bomb exploded, this chance to recognize the unattended bag and act. But no one had, and it was too late now. Too late to undo the sixteen dead, the twenty-four injuries—including one to a seven-year-old boy who happened to be walking by with his mom at the time of the blast.

"And then we have this," Fred concluded, flipping to the last image, of a big black truck at an intersection.

The bomber was in the passenger seat, and another man sat beside him.

Evelyn leaned even closer. This was the first she'd heard of a second man being involved.

"We just received this image," Fred said before Evelyn could ask. "And we'll be going live with it on tonight's news, asking the public for help in identifying these men. Unfortunately, we don't have a license plate hit, because they were smart enough to muddy it up."

Anticipation started to rise. Evelyn could feel it in the room around her, in the shuffling sound of suit coats as agents leaned forward, in the collective breath the whole room seemed to take. This could be the break they needed.

The image wasn't great. There must've been something wrong with the traffic camera, because there were pixels missing on the driver's face, but the image of the passenger was fairly clear. He was bent slightly forward, the hat still shading his eyes, hands crossed smugly on his chest. His nose and mouth and more of that tattoo, which snaked around the front of his neck, were visible. Someone might recognize him. At the very least, putting the image on the news should drive both men into hiding, away from public eyes. Away from public targets.

She felt the excitement ripple through the room again, and knew the rest of the agents had to be feeling the same thing. Releasing these pictures would inevitably bring hundreds, if not thousands, of tips someone would have to sort through. But maybe they'd get lucky and one of those tips would lead them to the bombers.

"This is a good break," Fred said. "But let's not get lazy. I want these assholes in custody *now*. I don't want another Eric Rudolph situation."

Evelyn nodded. The Olympic Park bomber had spent more than five years living off the land in the Appalachian wilderness after setting off the bombs that killed two and injured more than a hundred people. He'd been on the FBI's Most Wanted list, wasted a huge amount of FBI resources and was finally caught by a state trooper on a fluke. Like the Butler Compound members, he had survivalist training.

"But I don't just want these two bombers. I want the whole plan, and I want to be *damn* sure we have the entire network. If this was Butler's work—" Fred glanced at Evelyn "—and I'm not a hundred percent convinced it was, then we have a pretty unusual recruiting network here. Effective, but unusual."

"Not really," Evelyn said. "In certain ways, cults and traditional terrorist groups operate on the same mentality. Cult followers can be as dedicated as suicide bombers. We've seen enough cultists kill themselves or others because their leader demanded it. And we may not have a lot of examples of cultists dabbling in terrorism, but the examples we do have are extreme. Think about Aum Shinrikyo."

In the midnineties, a group of cultists had released sarin gas in a Tokyo subway at the height of morning rush hour. A dozen people had died, and thousands had gotten sick. Afterward, the group's status had officially been changed by the US from "cult" to "terrorist organization."

Around her, some of the agents nodded thoughtfully.

"It's a similarly dangerous mind-set," Lucas said, jumping in. "And terrorist groups often have a distorted view of religion at the center of their recruiting methods. Cults do, too. Both usually have someone in a leadership role who's charismatic and strategic. A leader who's egotistical, but someone a group of people would follow without question."

Lucas's words rolled around in her mind, and she fidgeted. Butler was egotistical, that was for sure. But did he fit the rest of the criteria?

Despite their similarities, all cults were different. All terror groups were different. Was she leading them down the wrong path?

As if he could read her thoughts, Lucas glanced over at Evelyn again. "I'm not completely convinced Butler's behind this, either, but there is precedent here. There's a reason we watch these groups."

"So, if this is a cult that's morphed into terrorist activities, we're probably looking at individuals willing to die for their cause," an ATF agent said, sounding dismayed.

"Yes," Evelyn said, trying to push aside her sudden doubts. She'd been right about the bomb. That couldn't be a coincidence. "And they'd also believe that killing hundreds—or thousands—of people in the name of their cause is worthy."

"But if we tell the bombers that Butler betrayed them, that he betrayed his own people…" Lucas said hopefully, raising his eyebrows at her, as if he wanted her to expand on that.

Why had Butler done it? Evelyn wondered suddenly, realizing she hadn't really thought about it. Why would Butler sabotage his own followers? Maybe the booby trap had been placed there in the event of a raid. Perhaps he'd done it because, if it came down to it, he could talk the talk, but he didn't actually want to get caught up in the fighting. The memory of him shooting down Jen in the hallway, the glee on his face as he'd done it, immediately erased that idea. Butler had shown he wasn't averse to getting his hands dirty. He liked it.

Was it because he didn't want any of the remaining cultists to survive an attack and turn against *him*? Maybe he was worried someone would discover he was using the compound as a recruiting base, and not the survivalist mecca he'd promised. He could've been worried that the already armed men would turn on him if they somehow found out. That was a possibility. What she knew for certain was that he was an egomaniac. She doubted he'd ever consider the idea that his followers would question his plan. He'd think he was smarter than all of them.

So maybe it was because the only followers he'd cared about were out doing his bidding, anyway. And if the compound was raided, he didn't want any of the others to survive it.

But if that was the case, he was diluting his own power. It was why she hadn't believed Jen in the first place—because a cult leader's power came from his followers. From the men who locked themselves in a compound with him, looking up to him like a god, willing to do anything he asked. Without them, what was the appeal?

Her theory was based on the idea that Butler was sending out his real disciples, and keeping the ones who failed the test behind with him. But that was an odd approach, unless his plan was much longer-term and they'd interrupted him.

Except that the Chicago bombing was the start of it all. So it was a strange decision for him to stay behind with the men he *hadn't* chosen. Sure, he might've thought he had more time to get away, but he hadn't acted as if he'd *wanted* to. He'd seemed to love his reign inside the compound, even—or especially—when it was surrounded. He'd reveled in it. His preaching had increased the longer the HRT agents were there, and he had protesters and a big audience, complete with news crews. Evelyn frowned as she thought it over, that persistent nagging in her mind telling her she was missing something important. Because Butler hadn't acted as if he wanted to leave. And if he was the leader of a terrorist group, he should've had an exit strategy. He should've wanted to escape, to continue his attacks, to continue his bigger plan.

No, Butler hadn't wanted out of the compound at all. The only person who'd seemed stir-crazy, the only person with any power who *hadn't* wanted to be there, was Rolfe.

Memories raced through her mind at lightning speed. Rolfe telling Butler, "We need this one," referring to her after Butler had shot Jen. Convincing Butler to keep her alive, to use her to hold the FBI at bay when Butler had wanted to shoot her on the spot.

Rolfe screaming at the cultists to back up when they came after her. Rolfe protecting her from them with his own body. Immediately after Rolfe's protest, Butler demanding his cultists stop.

Rolfe telling Butler that he needed Evelyn. A distraction. Telling him that she was a useful bargaining chip. *Buying time.*

"Rolfe wasn't *convincing* Butler to keep me alive," she said, nausea swirling in her stomach as she realized she'd been completely duped by Rolfe.

She'd believed him. She'd believed he was exactly what he seemed. She'd believed he was her only ally inside the compound. She'd actually run for him instead of her own colleagues when the raid started.

Disgust at herself roiled inside her.

"What?" Fred demanded, and she blinked, discovering that he was scowling at her.

She looked around and saw that she'd interrupted whatever he'd been saying. But she kept going, forcing herself to straighten in her seat. "Rolfe wasn't talking Butler into keeping me alive. He just wanted it to appear that way. Really, he was *giving orders*. They were disguised as requests, because he didn't want anyone to know his true role."

Lucas squinted at her. "What do you mean?"

"Butler wasn't the real leader. It was Rolfe."

13

"What?" Lucas whirled around. "What do you mean, Rolfe is the real leader? From what I can see, this guy is a ghost."

Fred looked back and forth between them, a scowl on his naturally craggy face that made him seem even more formidable. "Someone explain to me how the cult leader *you* called a terrorist—" he jabbed a finger toward Evelyn "—is now just a lackey."

"I didn't say he was a lackey. Not exactly," Evelyn hedged. "He was legitimately in charge of the compound. He was legitimately in charge of recruiting." Confidence filled her as the things that had been bothering her fell into place. She tried to ignore the self-doubt that tagged along behind it, the knowledge that Rolfe and Butler had fooled her so completely the whole week and a half she was inside, under their power. "Butler was perfect for recruiting. It put him in the position of power he wanted. It gave him followers. And he got to choose the followers best-suited to Rolfe's plot."

"Okay, wait a second," Lucas said before she could continue. "Where the hell is this Rolfe guy? HRT still hasn't found him, and there's no way he walked out of that compound without anyone seeing him."

"He must have," Evelyn argued, even though she cringed at the idea that she was bad-mouthing HRT. That, in a roundabout way, she was bad-mouthing Kyle. It was their job to make sure no one got out, except in handcuffs.

And she already felt she'd betrayed him, in some subtle way, by running deeper into the compound when they'd raided, instead of toward him. If she was right this time, she'd tried to rely on a terrorist leader.

What did that say about her as a profiler?

"I don't see how it's possible for Rolfe to have gotten out," Lucas said, crossing his arms. "Unless he left before the place was surrounded. There were two doors. Two HRT teams breached those doors. What'd he do, walk right past them?"

"I don't know," Evelyn shot back, although she knew Lucas was correct. There shouldn't have been any way for Rolfe to walk out of that compound. Two doors, blocked by HRT agents, and windows with bars. So why couldn't they account for him? Still, she argued, "We haven't found Jen, either, but we know she was there."

"That's a little different," Fred said quietly. "They could have removed her body before HRT even arrived. In fact, that's the most likely scenario, since we found her vehicle a few miles away from the compound."

"It's all quite logical," she insisted. "Rolfe has the charisma." The first time she'd met him, she'd thought that *he'd* been the one who looked like a cult leader, not Butler. He obviously hadn't used it on the other cultists, probably didn't want them to realize his true role, but he could turn it on. He'd turned it on for her.

She tried to shake off the memories. "All the times I thought he was arguing with Butler, he was actually telling Butler what to do!" But how had she let him dupe her so thoroughly? It was her *job* to be able to see behind people's masks, to understand what they really were.

"Are you coming up with these theories on the fly?" She must have looked insulted, because Fred added, "I need to know how sure you are about this, since it changes everything. If we were operating on the theory that Butler's death might have stopped future attacks…"

"Yes," she agreed. This *did* change everything. "Rolfe's not dead."

"We don't actually know that," Lucas put in. "What?" he asked when she glanced at him. "We have no idea where this guy is, so who knows? Okay, yes, we assume he's alive, but…"

"Not the point," Fred interrupted him, then turned back to Evelyn. "How sure are you?" he asked again.

A heavy weight seemed to press down on her. It was a weight she felt often—the responsibility to be right all the time. It was an impossible expectation, but that was the job. If she was wrong, and the case investigators followed her advice, she could help a killer go free. She could give terrorists time to set off another bomb.

She thought hard about her new theory. If Rolfe *was* the leader, his comings and goings from the compound made sense. He was coordinating with his bombers, and coming to the compound to evaluate possible new recruits. She frowned, trying to remember what she'd heard Butler and Rolfe talk about when she'd been locked in Rolfe's closet.

They'd discussed Jen having seen someone. They had to be talking about the driver of that truck. A big black truck, she recalled. Just like the truck in the traffic camera footage from downtown Chicago.

Rolfe had been angry that Butler had shot Jen. Evelyn was suddenly distracted by the fact that they'd never said anything about disposing of her body. She was surprised that hadn't come up. Did it mean there was a chance Jen was still alive?

She dismissed the thought. She'd watched Jen go down, watched her get hit by a bullet shot out of an AK-47 at close range. She'd awakened in a puddle of the woman's blood. Jen *had* to be dead.

But if Rolfe had arrived to see the two Chicago bombers off from the compound, then where had he been before? Was it a sign that there were others out there, poised in different cities, waiting with their own bombs?

"Evelyn!" Fred snapped. "Is Rolfe the leader or not? Is this a low-likelihood theory or a definite?"

"I can't guarantee it," she said softly, wishing she could. "But I think he is. And I think there are more bombers."

"More bombers?" an ATF agent barked. "More *bombs*, or more bombers?"

"More bombers," she repeated. "These two in Chicago must've been the ones who left the Butler Compound when Jen and I showed up. I didn't see inside the truck, but it was the same color as the one in the footage…"

"Black?" The agent cut her off. "There are a *lot* of black trucks in Chicago. Besides, the one in the footage had some kind of logo on it. A plumbing company apparently. We've got agents running it down. Was it a company truck you saw?"

"I don't know. But the logo could have been a fake."

"It's possible. We're running that angle, too."

She continued. "A black truck leaves the compound when I arrive and then a week later a black truck is connected to two bombers? Logo or not, that could be a link. Anyway, Rolfe wasn't always at the compound. I think he came because of them. And if he wasn't there before, there's a good chance he has other bombers in place."

"Well, this just gets better and better," Lucas muttered under his breath.

"How many?" Fred asked tersely, reminding her of her boss as he tossed back a pair of pills—aspirin, maybe—and washed them down with coffee.

She shook her head. "I'm sorry. I still need to go through everything. We need to finish interviewing the survivors from the cult. I just…"

"I know, I know," Fred said. "Every investigation is easier with enough time. And we appreciate you flying down here immediately after your ordeal."

She preferred not to discuss her days inside the compound, but thankfully, he kept going.

"Obviously, time isn't something we have." He looked down at his watch. "Let's finish up this briefing and then I want you two—" he lifted his gaze to her and Lucas "—back in Montana, running those leads. I want calls twice a day, minimum, even if you have nothing to report. And if you get anything crucial, I want you to wake me up at 4:00 a.m. if you have to. Understand?"

"Yes, sir," Lucas replied.

"Okay," Evelyn agreed, trying to sound upbeat, confident.

She didn't want to go back to Montana. As much as she wanted to play a part in bringing down Rolfe and anyone he might have working for him, she didn't want to go back and talk to the men who'd held her captive for a week and a half. She didn't want to think about all the mistakes she'd made along the way. Following Jen into that compound. Trusting Rolfe. Not realizing sooner that she'd profiled everything wrong. Was there still more she was missing?

A voice cut through her thoughts. "Hey, we've got something!"

Evelyn glanced over to see that it was the FBI agent sitting beside Fred who was talking. He was a definite FNG—fucking new guy, in FBI parlance—and he was practically wriggling out of his seat in his enthusiasm. She leaned forward. "What is it?"

The agent looked down at his laptop again, then up at Fred. "The FBI lab just sent some information on the bomb."

"What do we know?" the ATF agent, who appeared to be in charge on their end, asked. "Do we have a signature? Fingerprints? Source information? What?"

"We have a signature."

Everyone in the room turned toward the new agent. A signature on a bomb was as good as a fingerprint. It was a distinct method of creating a bomb that pointed to a specific person, someone with a history of setting bombs.

"What's the signature?" Fred demanded.

"It belongs to a guy named Lee Cartwright."

Cartwright hadn't been lying. He had a copycat. The news still rattled around in her mind, a full twenty-four hours after she'd learned it, along with the memory of visiting him inside that prison.

She was back in Montana. The FBI had booked her a hotel close to the field office, not sure how long she'd be staying. Right now, she was bundled from head to toe after she'd finally made a stop at the local sports store. She'd picked up what was left in stock after a week of agents visiting—winter boots a size too small, a winter coat a size too big, a ridiculous-looking hat complete with ear flaps, gloves she couldn't wear while holding a pen and layers of clothes. Every time she got dressed to go outside, she felt clumsy and uncoordinated. But it was better than constantly freezing.

During her trip to Chicago, TOC had been mostly disassembled. The tent was still there, but inside it was a shell of what she'd seen after the raid on the compound. A few pop-up tables and chairs, closed laptops, a handful of support and ERT agents. They'd been talking quietly and she'd felt like an interloper, so a few minutes ago she'd stepped out into the snow.

Greg had returned to Aquia last night, pulled back for another pressing case, a serial arsonist on the east coast who was targeting police officers' homes. Adam, the negotiator, had gone home, too; so had the Salt Lake City SAC and most of his agents. At this point, the various investigations were happening more from offices than out at the compound. Unless you were in evidence collection. Or the profiler assigned to the task force.

HRT had gone home, too. And because she'd been pulled out of Montana so fast and sent to Chicago, she'd missed seeing Kyle again. She'd called him from the airport, but it had gone straight to voice mail.

She felt a hollowness in her chest knowing there was a space between them that hadn't been there before. Knowing it was her fault.

Some part of her was glad they hadn't had a chance to talk yet, because she hadn't decided what she was going to say. Would he ask why she'd been at the back of the compound, seeking refuge in Rolfe's room, instead of running for him?

Why did it suddenly feel like a million years ago that she'd stood on that beach beside him, thinking about the freedom of her future, instead of only a few months?

Everything felt different since she'd been rescued from that compound. Her entire life felt somehow more remote, as if she was removed from everything that had come before. She hadn't even spoken to her grandma yet, and she felt guilty that she'd found it easier just to talk to the nurses.

That hadn't been intentional; the only time she'd been able to call between interviews with cultists and the flights, her grandma had been asleep. Mabel Baine didn't know Evelyn was in Montana, anyway, and wouldn't have been worried. Much of the time, her grandma didn't even know where *she* was.

Still, ever since her grandma had gotten sick when Evelyn was seventeen, it had been Evelyn's turn to care for her. The dementia wasn't always there, and she needed to try calling her again soon. Maybe hearing her grandma's voice would help make *her* feel more normal.

Trying to set aside her personal concerns, she surveyed the area around her. The excessive HRT equipment was gone now, from the helicopter to the box trucks to a couple of heavy-duty assault vehicles that could probably punch holes through walls. Without them, the landscape looked wide and barren, like it had when she'd first arrived with Jen.

Evelyn spun in a slow circle as huge snowflakes plopped lazily onto her face, then slid icy fingers down her neck and inside her coat. She stared at the beautiful rise of the mountains off in the distance. Stark rocks jutting toward the sky, dusted with snow that had to be several feet deep, but from here looked like a light sprinkle. In the other direction, she saw sparse woods that got denser as they went down the mountain, until they became a thick, green forest. A good place for men to hide and evade the FBI. A good place to set off practice bombs.

But how had they copied Cartwright's bombs? His signature was distinctive. It was specific, and it wasn't simple to replicate. And in theory, no one would try unless they'd actually seen Cartwright's designs.

The problem was, Cartwright hadn't had a partner. He'd been a loner, a "lone wolf" type who, in the three years he'd been in prison, had been visited only by his lawyer and his mom.

The lawyer was a court-appointed defense attorney who'd been way out of his league on Cartwright's slam-dunk case. But he had a reputation for being honest. Not someone who'd risk his career or his freedom by passing information from Cartwright to a survivalist group.

As for Cartwright's mom, she was nearly seventy. Evelyn had plans to see her later in the evening, but a preliminary search showed no criminal history. Somehow Evelyn couldn't see a seventy-year-old woman handing off bomb-making instructions to a survivalist group, either.

That meant the most likely way for one of Butler's—

or Rolfe's, she corrected herself—followers to have gotten the details was from someone *else* inside the prison. Someone Cartwright had told about his bombs, who'd passed the knowledge on.

Salt Lake City agents were beginning to investigate that, by comparing the names of the known followers to visitors at the prison. The problem was, they had no idea what the names of the Chicago bombers were. They didn't even know Rolfe's full name. And unfortunately, dusting Rolfe's room for prints hadn't gotten them a hit in the FBI's Next Generation Identification program, which had just replaced their Integrated Automated Fingerprint Identification System. That meant Rolfe didn't have a criminal history to find. Which was going to make it a hell of a lot harder to find *him*.

Evelyn's phone buzzed and she pulled off her top layer of gloves with her teeth so she could answer. "Evelyn Baine, BAU."

The words slipped off her tongue with such familiarity, but somehow they sounded wrong now.

"It's Lucas," the agent said, obviously out of breath. "Are you at the compound?"

"Yes. Where are you?"

"Back at the office. Look, you need to get inside the compound. They found something."

"What?" Evelyn asked, just as the flap of TOC opened and two ERT agents and a support staff member went running past her, toward the compound entrance.

Evelyn started to follow, keeping Lucas on the line, wondering how he'd heard before her when she was the one who was actually on-site. "What is it?" she repeated. She picked up her pace, trying not to slip in her too-small boots as she crossed the foot-high snowdrifts.

"I want survivalists!" Lucas barked, not talking to her. "I don't care who they visited. Anyone on that prison visitor's log who has survivalist connections goes on a list, and I want it on my desk yesterday."

"Lucas," Evelyn said. "What did they find?"

"An escape route," Lucas told her. "Get in there and find out more." He hung up before she could ask anything else.

Evelyn scowled, dropped the phone in her pocket and pulled her heavier glove back over her numb fingers, then began to run. She slid a few times before she made it to the door, where she had to trade her boots for footies over her socks and sign the log. Then she was back inside the compound.

She'd never been claustrophobic, but she suddenly felt caged in, as though there wasn't enough space and there wasn't enough oxygen. If she moved down the hall and to the left, she'd be looking at the spot where Jen had died. If she moved closer to the main room, she'd be standing in the spot where the cultists had tried to string her up.

"In the back," one of the support staff told her when she didn't move. "Butler's room."

The one room in the compound where she'd never been. But she knew how to get there. Strange, though, that an escape route had been discovered in Butler's room, when Rolfe was the one who'd gotten away.

Her feet felt like lead, but she nodded at him and started walking. The compound was much brighter than when she'd been held captive here, since the FBI had set up portable lights everywhere. It had been so dark before, they probably worried about missing evidence.

She continued through the main room where the cultists had eaten, where Butler had stood up front and made his final, grandiose speech before the HRT raid. Then she went into the tiny room off the back of it, that little space with no apparent purpose except to separate the cultists' living spaces from the leaders'. She glanced briefly at the closet where Butler had stuck her that last night, remembering how furious Rolfe had been when Butler grabbed her.

It came back to her in a sudden flash, the absolute fury in Rolfe's eyes. She'd remembered recoiling from him, and then immediately hoping he'd win the argument, fearing that the reason for his anger was that Butler planned to kill her.

When Rolfe argued, he usually won. At the time, she'd assumed it was because he was logical in his arguments, a trusted lieutenant, but now she knew—or at least suspected—otherwise. That time, Butler had insisted, and he'd played the best card he had—the followers were loyal to *him*, not Rolfe. At his word, they'd turn on Rolfe.

Rolfe had sent her one last unreadable glance, then nodded at Butler, who'd dragged her out of Rolfe's room and into the main area. It was the last time she'd seen Rolfe. As far as she knew, it was the last time anyone had seen Rolfe.

She opened the door into the leaders' area and looked up at where the gun had once been rigged, and then down where the trip wire had been positioned. Both were gone now, in evidence bags at the Salt Lake City office.

Evelyn stepped through and walked down the hallway, finally stopping at the open door to Butler's room. She felt frozen, as though she was breaking some kind of rule by entering his space. That feeling angered her and she forced herself to go in.

Fear washed over her as soon as she walked into the room, and she stiffened against it. Butler couldn't hurt her now.

She glanced around, wondering where everyone was. The room was empty, and it occurred to her that maybe the support staff member had meant to tell her to go to Rolfe's room. But while she was here, she wanted to take a quick look around.

It was a lot like Rolfe's room, only bigger, presumably because Butler spent more time at the compound. Same wood-slat flooring, same closet door, same metal-frame bed with a simple mattress. Except where Rolfe's room had been nearly empty, Butler's was packed with stuff. For a survivalist, he wasn't exactly living light.

He had his own private stash of water, MREs and blankets. There was an evidence marker that Evelyn remembered from the log; the space it marked had held stack upon stack of boxes filled with ammunition and weapons. Apparently, most of them had been full, but some had guns missing, and the FBI didn't think they could all be accounted for in the weaponry used against the raiding HRT force.

Against the second wall was his bed, a side table with a well-thumbed Bible and a knife. The opposite wall was lined with bookshelves. She came closer, taking in titles on everything from survivalist guides to law enforcement evidence collection methods to advanced mathematics.

She frowned, not having pegged Ward Butler as an academic. Putting on a pair of latex gloves, she took out one of the math books and opened it. On the title page, written in thick, precise penmanship, were the initials *RS*.

Did the books actually belong to Rolfe and not Butler? Her gut said they did, but if so, why were they in Butler's room? Had Butler taken them while Rolfe was away from the compound? Or had Rolfe given them to Butler for some reason?

"Evelyn!" someone called, and she jumped as the closet door opened and an ERT agent stepped into the room. "We're in here."

The closet door opened wider, revealing a closet almost identical to the one in Rolfe's room—a small, rectangular space with shelving units on one side and not much else. Except in this closet, the floorboards had been pulled up, and Evelyn suddenly got goose bumps. Because under those floorboards wasn't dirt like there should have been. Instead, there was a doorway, with stairs leading underground.

"This is it," she said. It had to be. "This is how Rolfe escaped."

14

"I can't believe I didn't think of this," Evelyn muttered as she walked down the circular staircase into the low tunnel beneath. If it hadn't been under a survivalist compound in the middle of nowhere, she might have figured that whoever created this had tunneled right into an existing system. It looked like the inside of a city's water piping system, or at least her idea of it, with a rounded metal top and sides. Only the ground was dirt.

The people who'd made it had known what they were doing, and they hadn't wasted space. It was a way out, definitely not meant for comfort. Even at only five foot two, she had to hunch over in the tunnel. There was no room to stand straight, and if she stretched her hands out to either side, she almost touched both walls at once.

"Why would you have thought of a tunnel?" the ERT agent beside her asked. He was decked out in a full-body evidence-collection outfit, including a mask that made his voice sound eerie.

"Survivalists build bunkers," she replied simply, her own voice tinny and unnatural as it echoed against the metal.

"Isn't that where we just were?" he asked, gesturing above him.

"That was the compound. Survivalists often build underground bunkers, stocked with supplies, an air filtration system and weapons. A place to ride out an Armageddon or some other catastrophe. A lot of them worry about a nuclear blast or something else that would make the air above unsafe."

Her anger made it hard to breathe. She should have suggested there could be an underground portion of the compound days ago. She should've *realized* it days ago.

She was way off her game.

"This doesn't look like a doomsday bunker," the ERT agent said, shining his flashlight down the tunnel, which seemed to narrow even more but clearly went on for quite a distance. "It looks like an escape route."

"The question is, was it Butler's escape route or Rolfe's?" she mumbled.

"It was in Butler's room," the agent reminded her. "We looked in Rolfe's room and we didn't find anything like this. Based on your analysis of the leadership structure, we actually pulled up floorboards in there as soon as we discovered this. Before we came down here."

"Maybe *this* is why we found Butler with his throat slit," Evelyn suggested. "So Rolfe could use his escape tunnel."

"You think Rolfe killed Butler?"

Evelyn shrugged. "Butler is dead and Rolfe is missing. I'd say that's the most likely scenario."

She wondered if that had always been Rolfe's plan. To stay there long enough for the raid to start, to ensure the Butler Compound would be destroyed, eliminate the only other person inside who knew about the real plan and then disappear.

That would definitely help him cover his tracks. The

raid would be a distraction, bringing FBI resources to the compound, while the bombers got into position. Rolfe probably hoped the FBI would have to split its resources, and that they'd never connect the two investigations at all.

Killing Butler had the added benefit that if the bombs *were* ever connected to the compound, the obvious suspect would already be dead.

Could Rolfe really have expected everything to play out that way? Once Jen had shown up and recognized the driver, everything had changed. But Rolfe could have disappeared right then and there. Yes, it left Butler as a potential liability, but staying was more of a personal risk for Rolfe.

Except that *Rolfe* was narcissistic, just like Butler. He'd have to be, to think he could lead a successful terrorist plot of this kind. He simply assumed he'd be able to pull it off. And so far, he had.

"Let's see where this tunnel leads," Evelyn said despite her tension at the idea of traveling down that long, dark tunnel.

"Wait," the agent said before she could take a step. "Look." He pointed the flashlight down and to her side.

The two of them knelt down, their knees almost touching in the small space, and Evelyn spoke first, her voice quiet. "Blood."

"A lot of it," the ERT agent agreed. "Dirt's been kicked over some of it, but whoever came through here was seriously injured."

"Do you think Rolfe was hurt when he went after Butler?" Evelyn asked.

"I doubt it. Butler's throat was cleanly slit. He was holding a gun, but he trusted the person who killed him.

He let that person get close. He didn't have any defensive wounds on his arms or hands. I didn't see anything under his nails, and there's no evidence he tried to use his weapon. No bullets lodged in the walls in that room. There was a significant amount of blood, but my guess would be it was all from Butler."

"Okay." Evelyn knew it would take time—and DNA tests—to confirm that. Probably more time than they had.

"But Rolfe must have hurt himself badly somehow," the ERT agent said as he swung the flashlight slowly across the blood-saturated ground. "Or, at least, whoever came through here was badly injured."

"It had to be Rolfe," Evelyn said. "He's the only one we're missing." She frowned. Unless it was Jen's blood. But why would they have brought her body out this way?

"Not necessarily," the ERT agent disagreed. "Maybe someone else took refuge down here during the fighting, then came back up."

"No one was allowed in that part of the compound except Butler and Rolfe," Evelyn told him.

"And you, right?" The flashlight swung up, shining on her face.

Evelyn squinted into the light. "Yes, but I definitely wasn't ever down here." *That* she would have remembered. She'd been locked up belowground once before, during a previous case. Just the thought of it, the feeling of dirt raining down on her until she couldn't breathe, made her sweat inside her winter gear. She felt a dread she hadn't expected as she stared down that tunnel again. "Do you think this is how they took Jen's body out of the compound?"

The agent swung his light back that way, but it didn't extend as far as the tunnel went. It wasn't bright enough to show whether there was more blood on the ground, either. "Possible. I'm going back up for a better light and then we'll get some more agents and walk it. You can come if you want, but you'll have to follow behind us. I don't want you trampling anything."

"Okay." Evelyn tried not to rankle at the implication that she'd walk over evidence. Still, she understood; as an ERT agent, it was his job to protect any physical evidence, just like it was hers to see the behavioral evidence.

As he handed her the flashlight and went back up the tiny, winding metal staircase, Evelyn swung the light slowly around. It didn't look like most of the survivalist bunkers she'd seen. And she'd studied plenty of them in photographs, when she'd created a profile last year for a survivalist who'd abducted his kids after he'd lost custody and visitation privileges. His reaction to losing them legally wasn't to fight it, but to grab them and go to ground.

That guy had built a series of bunkers in the wilderness, and Evelyn had gotten a crash course in how little a person needed to survive, and what someone could create out of a hole dug in the ground or drilled into the side of a mountain.

But every example she'd seen had been fashioned for someone to actually live in. Obviously, that had never been the intent here. Hearing sound above her, she aimed the flashlight up again, to find the ERT agent descending, along with a few others dressed in the same full-body gear.

"Let's see where this goes," the ERT agent said,

flicking on a lantern so bright it made Evelyn cringe as the tunnel suddenly blazed with brilliant white light.

The ERT agents moved carefully past her, a tight squeeze in the small space, and started down the tunnel in a line, all of them hunched low as they walked.

Evelyn took a deep breath, fought off the threatening panic and followed.

Evelyn squeezed her eyes shut, pressed a hand against her racing heart, and tried to calm her desperate gasps of breath. She bent down inside the tunnel, feeling tiny drops of dirt splash against her head, and the panic kept rising up, stronger and stronger.

The feel of being underground during that earlier case, the feel of dirt falling on her, all of it crashing around her until she was buried beneath it… Until she couldn't breathe at all. Until…

"Evelyn!"

A hand clamped on her arm and she yanked free, almost falling. The hand closed around her elbow again, and she lifted her head to see the ERT agent's masked face inches from hers.

"Evelyn. You okay?" He peered at her with equal parts concern and disbelief.

She nodded, trying to get control of herself. "It's just the dirt," she muttered.

He frowned at her, glancing at the ground. "You find something?"

"No. That dirt." She started to point upward, but realized as his flashlight swung up to illuminate the metal ceiling that there was no dirt.

She looked behind her, but the tunnel was solid. She swiped one hand over her head, and it came back clean, and she knew she'd imagined the dirt splashing against her head like rain. It was a flashback.

"Sorry. It's nothing," she said, and he gave her one last perplexed glance before continuing.

The tunnel narrowed as it went, and there wasn't even enough room to put her hands on her hips without both elbows smashing the sides. Like the plastic tunnel in a hamster cage. They'd been walking for what felt like miles, although it was probably more like seventy-five feet. They had to be nearing the end.

She'd be aboveground again soon.

"We've got something up ahead," the ERT agent called.

"What is it?" Evelyn asked as she finally caught her breath and started moving.

"More blood."

Evelyn frowned, her hope dimming and the panic threatening again. "I was hoping you were going to say an exit."

"That, too," he said, and Evelyn moved faster, practically walking on his heels in her desperation to get out of the tunnel.

"Careful," he warned. "It's right up ahead. You have to watch where you step."

"Okay." She forced her feet to slow, and followed his careful instructions to walk around a puddle of blood. This one was much smaller than what they'd seen in the tunnel entrance, and there was a rag discarded next to it.

"Probably something that was used to wrap around the injury," the ERT agent suggested. "I bet it was re-wrapped here."

"So we're back to thinking Rolfe was injured," Evelyn said. "And not that someone was pulling a body through here."

"There's no evidence of anyone pulling a body through at all," he told her, his voice tight, maybe because he'd known Jen personally.

"And considering the space, it's unlikely she was carried out this way," Evelyn contributed.

"Yeah," he said shortly.

So they still didn't know what had happened to Jen. Evelyn frowned at the blood, remembering a different puddle inside the compound. A much bigger puddle in the hall that very first day. Jen's blood.

"They probably did remove her body right after Butler knocked me out," she said quietly, hoping they'd find her soon. Hoping they'd be able to give her family at least the closure of a body to bury.

"Probably," he agreed. "Careful. We're going up."

"Another stairwell?" she asked, unable to see around him in the tiny space.

"Nope. It just slants up until you're outside. But it's steep. Be careful."

She braced her hands on the ground, and angled her feet outward as she climbed up a steep slope, finally seeing light. The ERT agent in front of her offered a hugely gloved hand and pulled her up. In the fading light of dusk, she drew in deep lungfuls of freezing air. Around her were fir trees, much fuller than the spindly ones around the compound.

She turned back and glanced at the tunnel she'd just left, realizing that the first agent through had taken off a wooden covering to let them out. And that was hidden behind an evergreen bush, probably one Rolfe had planted to hide the exit. No one would've found this place without already knowing where it was.

Shading her eyes, she looked off into the distance at the compound. "How far are we? And *where* are we?"

"We're due west of the compound," one of the agents replied. "And this exit is approximately a hundred feet from where the protesters were gathered. Which makes it two hundred feet from the HRT perimeter and almost three hundred from the compound itself."

"That's quite a long tunnel to commission. And where it ends is far enough away that no one saw Rolfe exit," Evelyn muttered.

"Especially if he left in the middle of the night."

She looked around again and squinted. "Is that…?" She walked down the sloping ground, watching her step in snow that was half a foot lower here than it was by the compound, but still slippery. "Yep."

She pointed as the five ERT agents came up behind her. "A road. Not much of a road, but it's a way out."

The path was winding, hard-packed dirt. The snow was smashed down and there was a bare patch of land where a vehicle must have sat while most of the snow fell.

"Rolfe's getaway vehicle was parked here."

The ERT agent who'd led her through the tunnel sighed as he took out his cell phone. "I think you're right. But where the hell is he now?"

And what was he planning next?

"Mrs. Cartwright?" Evelyn held her credentials up to the door so the woman could see them. "I'm Special Agent Evelyn Baine, from the FBI."

She was late, and she was covered in dirt from

climbing out of the tunnel at the Butler Compound. But Lee Cartwright's mother had agreed to see her, and she didn't want to miss the chance to find out who Lee might have been passing information to inside the prison. Or if, by some chance, his nearly seventy-year-old mother was passing notes for him.

So she'd raced down the dangerous Montana roads into the tiny town—if you could call a place with a population of under two hundred an actual "town"—to meet Irene Cartwright. The woman lived in a one-story house behind a wall of pine trees in the middle of nowhere, and Evelyn had trekked up a rambling, un-plowed driveway rather than risk getting her car stuck.

"You're late," Irene croaked with the voice of a decades-long smoker, ignoring the credentials entirely. She looked older than seventy, with pure white hair that tumbled down her shoulders onto a thick knit sweater. Her face was a series of folds that drooped over light brown eyes, and creased around thin, papery lips. Something in her gaze reminded Evelyn of the barely contained fury she'd seen in Cartwright's eyes.

"I'm very sorry, ma'am. My investigation…"

"My time may not seem valuable, but I don't like to be kept waiting." Irene Cartwright scowled as she held open the door. "Come in. Take your boots off. I don't want snow everywhere."

As Evelyn stepped inside and peeled off her boots, grateful for the heat Irene was blasting on high, the woman headed into a living room off the entrance.

She called after her, "Don't dawdle. And don't touch anything. You're late, and my shows start soon. So hurry up and ask your questions."

Dropping her boots on a plastic tray in the entryway,

Evelyn hurried into the living room and sat on the chair across from Irene, who was studying her with obvious suspicion. Hoping to put her at ease, Evelyn said, "Thank you for seeing…"

"Let's just get down to it." Irene cut her off again. "Tell me what you want so we can get this over with. I don't want you FBI lackeys harassing me everywhere I go."

Evelyn tried to hide her surprise at the animosity in the woman's voice, but reminded herself that Lee Cartwright had gotten his hatred of the government from somewhere. Remembering his equal hatred of anyone who wasn't white, Evelyn tried not to show her discomfort.

"I just have a few questions about your visits to see your son," she began.

"Boy doesn't belong in jail," Irene said, folding her arms. "He's sorry for his mistakes."

His *mistakes*? He'd bombed three places of worship, killed two people, wounded dozens more.

Evelyn swallowed back her instant response. His mother's feelings had to be tied up with her memories of him as a baby, as a little boy she'd raised. Evelyn told herself that even someone like Lee Cartwright had people who loved him, and she chose her words carefully. "I spoke with him a week ago. He asked to speak with someone about a person who was copying his… mistakes."

Irene's eyes narrowed. "I'm visiting him this week. I'm going to tell him what you said. I don't think he asked to see anyone. Not *you*. You think you can trick an old woman?"

"No," Evelyn said, and as Irene's gnarled fingers

laced tightly together, she was suddenly reminded of her grandma. The woman who'd protect her from the whole world if she could.

"I'm not trying to trick you. You're right. He didn't ask for me. But he did ask for *someone* in law enforcement and I was available. He was trying to warn us. He didn't want anyone else to wind up in jail."

As she said the words, she straightened. That was it, she thought, recalling her visit with Lee Cartwright.

She'd assumed he didn't want a copycat to get credit, but what if he'd actually been making a plea for help? Her boss had sent her to interview Lee because she was exactly the kind of person he'd want to target. It would've been the perfect move if he wanted to brag about a copycat. But the wrong move if he wanted to *stop* a bombing.

She tried to conceal any hint of what she was thinking— or the fact that Irene might have given her a lead—as she leaned toward the woman. "Who was Lee trying to protect? Who was he trying to keep from ending up in jail, like him?"

Something flashed across Irene's face, and Evelyn knew she was right.

"No one," the woman said. "I—I thought you wanted to talk about Lee." She stood up, looking shakier than she had a few minutes earlier. "I'm not discussing anyone else. I want you to go."

"Mrs. Cartwright…"

"I want you to go," she screeched, jabbing a quivering hand toward the door.

"Who were you passing information to?" Evelyn asked. "Whoever it is, I can help. I can…"

"Get out! Get out, or I'm getting my shotgun! This is my land and…"

"Okay." Evelyn held up her hands and backed toward the door. She was armed, but there was no reason to get into a standoff with a seventy-year-old.

She didn't need to. If Irene was this upset, Evelyn knew she didn't have far to look.

Lee Cartwright had passed his bomb-making techniques to a family member.

15

"Other than his mother, Lee Cartwright doesn't have any family," Lucas told her.

"What?" Evelyn paused as she was shedding her heavy winter gear in Lucas's cubicle at the Salt Lake City office. "He must."

She sat in the middle of a pool of light, perched on an extra chair. The cubicle was lit up from Lucas's desk. The bullpen around her was dark, since everyone else had gone home for the night. She'd called Lucas back in, apparently just before he and his wife were about to climb into bed.

Lucas shrugged, rubbing his eyes so hard she cringed. "Maybe he was passing the information to a friend."

"No, I don't think so." Evelyn shook snow from her collar onto the floor of Lucas's cubicle. She had no idea how so much of it had managed to wedge itself under her winter gear, but it explained why she'd been freezing even with her many layers.

Lucas pulled his fists away from his face, leaving behind bloodshot eyes and reddened skin around them, then glanced at her. "Why not? Why does it have to be family?"

She thought about the way Irene Cartwright had shut down as soon as Evelyn had mentioned that Lee might be trying to protect someone. The woman had gone from spitting mad to nervous and panicked. She wanted to protect that person, too. "His mom wouldn't have been that worried about one of Lee's friends. It was someone who mattered to her, too. It was family. I'm sure of it."

Lucas sighed, and started typing again. "We could've waited to dig into this tomorrow. When you said 'family,' I expected it to be a quick hunt in the system. Then *boom*, we'd have a name we could hand off to the other teams. Hopefully a name that would match up with one of those pictures from the bombing."

Evelyn checked her watch, suddenly aware that it was now technically morning. Lucas had been working sixteen-hour days since she'd come out of the compound—and probably before that, too. When she'd called, his wife had muttered something about how he'd just gotten home before handing him the phone. She'd sounded exhausted—and so did Lucas. No wonder he looked like hell.

Evelyn figured she looked like hell, too. She certainly felt like it. She couldn't remember the last time she'd actually slept.

Last night, she'd returned to the hotel outside Salt Lake City that the FBI had booked for her, and someone had finally brought her overnight bag, along with her phone, credentials and weapon.

But even being armed, and having her own belongings back, she'd been restless and quick to lurch awake the previous night, as if she was still locked inside that compound. As if she was still at the mercy of a group of white supremacists and the unpredictable whims of their leader. As if at any moment someone might wake her up and then put a bullet in her, just for being an FBI agent.

Evelyn dropped her coat over the other chair in Lucas's cubicle and began unlacing her too-tight boots.

"Stop shaking snow everywhere," Lucas snapped, still typing away and looking more annoyed by the second. "I don't know what to tell you, Evelyn. But I think you're wrong. Because when I put in Cartwright, I come up with his father and mother, and that's it. No siblings for Lee, no siblings for either parent, no... Wait a second."

When he started typing faster, his head moving back and forth slightly as he searched, she finally demanded, "What? What did you find?"

"I can't believe this. You might be right." He shook his head. "What kind of mother passes bomb-making techniques from her incarcerated son to another family member? I've seen some stupid things in my years here, but that's crazy. It's like she wants them both locked up for the rest of their lives. But you have good instincts. I think he has a brother."

"You *think* he does?"

"A half brother," Lucas clarified. "Different last name, and they never lived together as far as I can tell, but... Yep." He stopped typing and looked up at her. "Same mother. She barely lived with the half brother, and never married his father. Apparently, the kid got shipped off to dad at an early age and never came back. Different last name."

"Nice find," Evelyn said.

"Yeah, I dug deeper into the mother, and the name popped up alongside hers a few times. I started pulling him up specifically, and found a funeral announcement for her father. Anyway, it listed this guy, the second son, and… What are you doing?"

While he'd been talking, Evelyn had plopped down in the chair, lacing her boots back up in a rush, trying to ignore the fact that her fingers still hadn't thawed from being outside half an hour ago. She'd gone from Cartwright's mother's house to a diner for some semblance of dinner, then made the long drive back to the Salt Lake City office. "What's his name? Where does he live?"

"Evelyn," Lucas said, leaning back in his chair as if he had no intention of going anywhere. "It's after midnight. You can't go visit this guy."

"Oh. Yeah." She dropped her laces without tying them off.

"Besides, if you're right, this guy isn't at home. He's driving around somewhere in a black truck. With a partner."

She leaned toward him. "We'd better pull up everything we can about him and get it out to the teams. Find him before he finds his next target."

Lucas nodded, sighing as he sat up again. "What we'd better do is make a pot of coffee."

"Okay," she said, even though she made no move to go and brew some. She wasn't even sure she knew how to make it, since she'd never been a coffee drinker. "What's this guy's name?"

"John Peters. That mean anything to you?"

"No." She rolled her shoulders, and got ready to work, to dig up everything she could about the guy. "But it will soon."

"Finally," Bobby sighed, lowering his window and practically sticking his head out to breathe in fresh, warm air.

John Peters glanced at him briefly, resisting the urge to roll his eyes at his young partner. The truth was, he felt it, too. Relief.

He knew Bobby was happy to leave the snow behind and get into warmer weather. The snow didn't bother John; it never had. He'd grown up in nothing but sunshine, with a father who couldn't stay out of trouble, who let everyone walk all over both of them, and he'd hated every minute of it. It wasn't until he'd gone back to see his mother, years and years later, in the frigid Montana mountains, that he'd felt a true sense of family. So, even if he'd never completely acclimated to it, the snow wasn't a problem for him.

But being cooped up in a truck for days on end was.

"We'll be there soon," John said, rolling up his sleeves and flipping the heat over to air-conditioning as the sun beat down on him. It might've felt like a sign if he believed in such things.

Bobby smiled, a huge grin that showed off teeth that were crooked but shiny and white. "They'll never expect it," he said, even sounding like a college kid.

He'd been so perfect for that first bomb. Too bad the security cameras had found him so quickly. But they'd recognized early on that was a possibility. John had a backup plan ready to go if it happened.

"They know what you look like now," John reminded him. "We need to be careful."

The footage had been released earlier in the week, grainy, still shots of Bobby placing the bomb, even an image of the two of them in the truck. He'd known that was a possibility, too, but hoped it wouldn't happen, especially not this fast. Of course, they'd tossed the decal from the truck in a garbage can as soon as they were out of the city, and he'd mucked up the license plate until he was positive no camera could read it. And luckily, his face had been too pixilated to be recognizable. Still, he'd felt a shock pass through him when he'd walked into an off-the-beaten-path gas station and seen himself on the news.

After that one surreal moment in the filthy gas station, staring slack-jawed at the image of himself on a tiny screen mounted on the ceiling, everything had become real. It had always been a given that he was never going home, but he hadn't let himself really think about it before then. Since he'd seen the news, though, he hadn't been able to think about much else.

He'd never see his mom again. Never see his half brother, his hero, the man who hadn't let "half" define their brotherly bond. They'd understand, though, even if he'd gotten too little time with his brother, not even knowing about his existence until he was an adult.

Still, he knew his mom and brother would both be proud of him, celebrate the way he was punishing the feds for everything they'd done to him and his family. For separating them after the three of them had finally bonded, by taking his brother away. But an ache had settled in his chest and refused to budge at the idea that he'd never see their faces again. At the idea that he'd never see their pride when they learned how he'd taken his own stand.

He'd either be in hiding for the rest of his life, or he'd be dead. He was just one small part of the whole story. But he was an essential part of the Freedom Uprising, and once it all came out, no one would ever forget his name.

"I'm still dropping off the present?" Bobby asked,

breaking into John's thoughts with his sarcastic term for their bombs.

John focused on the road, checked the speedometer. He didn't want to do something foolish, like get pulled over for speeding, or something careless, like not having a license plate. Too many great men had gone down that way, making small errors that ended up getting them caught. McVeigh, for one. He wasn't going to have his name added to that list. "No. I'm taking the bag in this time."

"But…"

"You're more likely to be recognized. You'll drive. I'll take point."

"I know they've got the pictures from the bombing everywhere on the news, but will the stupid pigs really expect us to be all the way across the country?" Bobby whined.

"We're not risking it. This has to go off without a hitch."

"But after the next one…"

"After that, it'll be someone else's turn to take up the cause." John left the freeway, avoiding the tolls as he continued heading southwest, slower now. He felt a smile stretch across his face as he imagined what was coming next.

It didn't even matter if he never got to see it, if by some cruel twist of fate he was arrested or killed along the way. He knew it could happen, and he'd resigned himself to it the best he could. It would be a small price to pay, if necessary. He was going to help change the course of history.

His anticipation must have been contagious, because

Bobby said, "They're never going to see it coming, are they?"

"Nope. We're going to make an impression." He grinned at the irony. "We have one final target, and we're going to hit it hard."

"No wonder this guy ended up falling for Butler's rhetoric," Evelyn said, speaking up a little to be heard over the sound of the Salt Lake City office morning buzz.

It had just hit 8:00 a.m. and agents were starting to swarm past them and into the bullpen. The office, which had been eerily silent for the past seven hours, was filling up with the low hum of agents chatting, the gurgling of coffee machines and the booting up of computers.

"What?" Lucas bolted upright, almost overturning his chair, and wiped a hand across his chin, as if he was afraid he'd been drooling in his sleep. He rubbed his eyes, then squinted at her, working his jaw. She could tell he was suppressing a yawn. "What time is it?"

She looked at the clock in the corner of the interagency coordination room where they'd moved a few hours earlier. "Eight. I've been digging up more on John Peters."

She should've been tired, too, but sometime during the night, researching the sad details of John Peters's life, she'd felt a rush she'd been missing lately. The rush of the chase. Of knowing she was onto something. An important piece of the puzzle. Maybe the final piece that would lead to an arrest.

Lucas stretched out in his chair, reaching for his coffee mug, then scowling at it, either because it was empty or because the coffee had cooled. "How long have I been out?"

Evelyn shrugged. "A couple of hours." It had actually been peaceful, the chance to work mostly alone in an FBI office. It had felt familiar to her. Before Cassie's case, she'd worked too much, because what else did she have back then besides her cases?

The thought made her frown. The truth was, she hadn't had a lot in her life. She'd worked hard since then to find some balance. But work had been her anchor for so long, her focus. Without the burning drive she'd once had for it, she'd begun to feel an emptiness inside her.

"What's wrong?" Lucas asked, sitting straighter and suddenly looking more awake, the investigator instinct stirring.

She tried to ignore the morose thoughts that had been plaguing her about her life. She needed to call her grandma. Nothing cheered her up like talking to her grandma, the one constant, stable force in her life since she was ten.

Between the nonstop investigation and Evelyn's calls taking place when her grandma was asleep, she hadn't spoken with Mabel in thirteen days, since the morning she'd left for Montana.

"Nothing's wrong." She handed him some notes and put her focus back where it belonged—on the case. "I think John Peters was the perfect patsy. When he was a few years old, his parents split—they'd never been married—and the dad took John. The dad was a loser any way you look at it. Dozens of arrests, usually for fights, and almost always on the losing side. Child Services investigated him a few times for neglect, but it never went anywhere. They came close to taking John away more than once—from what I could dig up, half the time the dad didn't even remember his own kid's name."

Lucas made a face, half disbelief, half disgust. "How could he not remember something like that?"

"He also had substance abuse problems," Evelyn said.

"Still, not remembering your son's name? Really?"

Evelyn shrugged. It was sad, but sadder was that she'd seen worse. She'd seen much worse. She'd even experienced worse, back when she'd lived with her alcoholic mom, before her grandparents had taken her in.

"All right," Lucas said, still looking uncomfortable, maybe because he had two sons of his own, which she'd recently learned. "Keep going. What else do we know about this guy?"

"Well, the dad was cut from the same cloth as Butler—survivalist, fringe militia. Only he wasn't accepted by them at all. So, John probably grew up surrounded by the propaganda, but with no stability, no real parent figure. When he got to Montana, Butler must've been exactly what he was looking for."

"But if he fell for Butler's supposed charms, why did he end up as part of Rolfe's master plan?" Lucas asked. She must have blanched, because he added, "Assuming you still think Rolfe's the one running things?"

"I do." The fact was, *she'd* fallen for Rolfe's charms, and she assumed John Peters had, too. Or at least Rolfe had fooled them both—as completely as he must have fooled the others.

She straightened her shoulders and pressed on, trying to ignore the doubt wriggling up. Was she still being fooled? Was there something going on here that she still wasn't seeing? What was Rolfe's endgame?

She pushed past the worry and put her focus back on John. First, find the bomber. Then worry about the mastermind. "Peters didn't come back to Montana until he was an adult. It looks like he met Lee shortly before his half brother went to prison. I think he suddenly found a connection he'd been desperately searching for all his life, and Butler—or Rolfe—tapped into that."

"So, what?" Lucas asked. "You think Lee introduced John and Butler? And then Rolfe recruited him out of the compound? Because I'm not sure the theory fits. If Lee and John were close, why didn't John ever visit him in jail?"

"My guess is that, at first, Lee didn't want a direct connection, since he was passing on his bomb-making skills. If John visited him, he'd be the obvious suspect as soon as a bomb went off with Lee's signature. But at the end, Lee was trying to protect him."

"How? He never even told you John's name."

"Yeah, well, that was our mistake. I think if Lee had gotten a local sheriff—a local white sheriff—he might have spilled. But he got me, because we thought he had an entirely different motivation for calling us."

Lucas frowned at her, looking unconvinced. "It seems to me that Lee Cartwright still believes in his 'cause.' Why would he dissuade his brother from joining it? For that matter, why would he try to stop him if he'd trained the guy?"

"I'm not saying he doesn't believe. But Lee Cartwright was a loner, Lucas. Jen told me that he fell out of favor with Butler a while back. It's possible he's not even the one who introduced his brother to Butler.

Maybe John followed in Lee's footsteps without Lee's help. Maybe Lee was flattered at first, then changed his mind."

Lucas shook his head, about to say something, but Evelyn continued quickly. "Lee bombed those churches and the mosque, got caught and now he's spending the rest of his life in jail. He may not be sorry, but I think he had a change of heart, at least as far as leading John down the same path. After Lee had been in prison for a few years, and it started to sink in that he really wasn't ever getting out. I think Lee actually did want to talk to someone to *prevent* this, to keep his half brother out of jail."

"Then why didn't he?" Lucas countered. "You were there. You talked to him. He shut you out, right?"

Evelyn nodded, regretting her dismissal of Lee's copycat claims once he refused to talk to her. "We made the wrong move. Lee Cartwright hates the federal government, and he hates anyone who isn't white. We thought he wanted to brag, and I would've looked like his preferred victim choice. If his intent really had been to brag about some copycat, that should've worked. But he didn't. He wanted help. He wanted to talk to a white, male, local sheriff. Not a biracial female FBI agent. He was never going to ask me for help. We misevaluated him. We made a mistake."

Lucas stared back at her, then shook his head again and said, "Well, we're paying for it now."

16

"We've got news," Fred Lanier announced over the speakerphone just as Evelyn walked into the Salt Lake City office interagency coordination room, where she and Lucas had taken to working lately.

"So do we," Lucas said. He looked refreshed after a few hours at home, presumably for another nap, a shower and a change of clothes. The lines on his prominent forehead had softened a little, the circles under his red-rimmed hazel eyes had diminished and the determination was back, showing in the tightness of his jaw, the alertness of his gaze.

She, on the other hand, felt as if she was walking underwater. She finally seemed to have kicked the cold she'd caught inside the Butler Compound, but lack of sleep was catching up with her. She should've gone to the hotel when Lucas had said he needed a break.

But the idea of returning to that sparse, tidy hotel, with its utilitarian furniture and so much stark whiteness— everything from the walls to the bedspread—made her feel penned in. Every time she lay down on that bed and closed her eyes, she had flashbacks of being in the compound, waiting to get shot like Jen.

Even after being at the hotel for four nights already, she couldn't seem to get used to that room. As they headed into the last week of November, she'd finally given in and purchased clothes and belongings to tide her over. She should have been acclimated by now. But she just felt restless.

Trying not to make any noise, she closed the office door behind her and took a seat.

"We put a rush on the DNA tests for the blood your ERT agents found inside that tunnel leading out of the Butler Compound." Fred's voice resounded in the large room.

"Did the DNA test get us a last name for this Rolfe guy?" Lucas asked hopefully, leaning toward the speakerphone.

"The blood didn't belong to him. It belonged to Special Agent Martinez." There was resignation and something else, something Evelyn couldn't quite identify, in Fred's tone.

"What?" Lucas gasped. "But the way those blood patterns looked in the pictures… I mean…"

"I agree." Fred spoke up before Lucas could say more as Evelyn gaped at the phone, wondering how Jen's blood had gotten in that tunnel.

Maybe it had been planted. But she couldn't think of a good reason for Butler or Rolfe to have done that.

"Considering the size of the tunnel, it would've been nearly impossible for someone to have carried Jen out of the compound that way, and there were no drag marks. The blood wasn't disturbed, so she wasn't dragged out," Fred continued.

"Then we think she could be alive?" Lucas asked, his eyes wide, his chest heaving, hands clutching the table.

"The blood pattern we saw suggests she traveled out of that tunnel under her own power," Fred said, his voice still solemn and tired. "I suspect she was badly injured, but walking."

Evelyn sank lower in her seat, shocked that Jen had survived the hit.

She flashed back to the instant Butler had pulled the trigger—the loud, overwhelming *boom* of the machine gun, the spray of red, the sound of Jen crashing to the floor. Evelyn could practically feel the stickiness of blood all over her as she'd slipped in it, the hard wood floor coming up to meet her as she'd slammed down, too. The crack as Butler's gun had smashed into her jaw. And then nothing at all. Nothing until she'd awakened in blood. So much blood.

How had Jen survived that?

"What does that mean?" Lucas pressed, anxiety creeping into his tone as his words came out faster and faster. "When do we think it happened? Was she inside that compound until the end or did they walk her out of there a week ago and kill her somewhere else? Do we have any leads?"

"We'll call you when we have more," Fred replied. "I know she was a colleague. I know this is hard for everyone at the Salt Lake City office, but we need to keep it under wraps for now. Okay?"

"Sure. Of course," Lucas said, dropping into his seat and staring blankly at the wall.

Evelyn studied him, wondering how well he'd known Jen. She wondered if Lucas was the one who'd been talking to Jen's family. If so, that meant he'd have to keep telling her husband—who called every day for updates—that they still didn't know any more, while sitting on this new development.

Lucas had told her that he and Jen hadn't been on the same squad. But that didn't mean they'd never worked together. Jen had been in the Bureau a long time, and by all accounts, she fit in well at the office. Back in Virginia, agents from BAU and HRT had a regular table at a nearby pub, and plenty of them were friends outside the office, too. Chances were, similar friendships had developed here. She had the sudden feeling that Lucas and Jen were closer than she'd thought.

As Lucas continued to frown and stare into the distance, Fred added, "Now we need to move on to the information you and the profiler dug up on this John Peters character."

Evelyn was about to speak up, to remind Fred that "the profiler's" name was Evelyn Baine, but he kept going.

"I need to know how actionable this new information is."

Lucas turned his attention back to the speakerphone on the table. "What do you mean? Peters is…"

"A possible match for the bomber or the driver," Fred interrupted. "Yes. I want your call on how solid you think this theory is. Don't get me wrong—you're doing good work over there. But this profiler we've brought in…"

Lucas cringed and glanced at her, and in that moment, Evelyn realized she hadn't spoken the whole time Fred had been on the call. He didn't know she was in the room.

Lucas appeared ready to say something, but Fred was already talking again. "She's got a lot of good theories. What bothers me most is that she can't commit.

Except for the initial bombing—which, let's be honest, could be a fluke. Butler might have talked about it because he was associated with someone or he heard rumblings in fringe militia circles and wanted to take credit. Now she's saying this Rolfe guy—who we still can't find—was really the leader. But is she one hundred percent sure? No."

"Sir…" Lucas started, avoiding her gaze.

Evelyn felt her face heat up, but it was more out of embarrassment than anger. She should've been furious that her professional assessment was being doubted, but she wasn't, because she doubted it herself.

"We finally got a clear image of the logo on the truck used in the bombing." Fred talked over Lucas. "And the logo's for a small plumbing company with some serious mob connections—a laundering operation. We can't connect that group to the two men in the images, but we're pursuing this angle a lot more strongly now. Obviously, it's still possible the logo was meant to throw us off, but to go with a real company? That would mean they'd need to know about the mob connections—which would also piss off the mob if it became public. It seems more likely that they just didn't expect the truck to be found on surveillance."

"Maybe, but…"

"So I'll put all the resources I can on John Peters, but I'm not there in Salt Lake. I need your honest assessment, Lucas. Is this profiler too traumatized by her experience inside the compound? Or is she truly onto something?"

Dark red splotched Lucas's cheeks as he closed his eyes, probably wondering how to respond diplomatically.

Evelyn saved him the trouble, trying to inject confidence into her voice. She couldn't guarantee anything she'd given them was one hundred percent accurate, but that was true of any lead. She *did* know she was onto something with Peters. "This is Evelyn Baine. Profiling isn't an exact science. But I was a special agent on a VCMO squad before I went to BAU, and from an investigative perspective, I can tell you Peters is a strong lead. We need to follow up on him."

There was a long pause, then some mumbling that sounded like creative swearing. Finally Fred said, "No offense meant, Evelyn. I think you're a valuable addition to the team. But there's been some concern expressed about your state of mind after your experience."

Evelyn glanced at Lucas and he put up his hands, shaking his head.

"It's understandable," Fred added, and Evelyn knew he was still talking about her mind-set after being a hostage.

"It's okay," she said before he could keep going. "You're right. I can't commit a hundred percent. That's how profiling works. It's never going to be a hundred percent. Just like an investigation doesn't have only one suspect. But we need to follow Peters."

"I agree," Lucas said. "We can't find the man, but we've found some of his history. He's never gone to see Lee in jail, but he's had some brief affiliations with fringe militia groups."

"Okay," Fred said, finality in his tone. "Then maybe you two need to visit Lee in jail again."

Evelyn looked at Lucas and nodded. It was time to go and see Cartwright a second time, and hope they could get more out of him. Hope that he'd help stop his half brother before John Peters found another target.

* * *

"Turn on the news," one of the agents working with Fred Lanier barked into the phone, then hung up without any more explanation.

Dread knotted Evelyn's stomach as Lucas glanced over at her from the driver's seat of his FBI-issued SUV. They'd been driving to the Montana State Prison to see Cartwright, a feat that had taken a day longer to arrange than expected. Lee hadn't wanted to see anyone. And the prison officials had been rule sticklers, wanting Lucas and Evelyn to wade through piles of paperwork before setting it up.

The only upside was she'd had a brief break to call Kyle, to actually talk to him. She'd spent most of the conversation assuring him that she was really okay, and then Lucas had come looking for her.

Now they were finally on their way to visit Cartwright again, but the roads were dangerous enough that Evelyn was beginning to wonder if they should turn back.

Lucas slowed the car on the icy roads winding through the remote Montana wilderness, then flicked on the radio. He didn't need to go to a news channel, because the song playing cut off mid-harmony and a news anchor jumped in. "A second bomb was detonated at an ATF office in San Francisco this afternoon."

"Shit!" Lucas smacked his big palm against the wheel and the horn blared.

The news anchor kept talking, but Lucas turned the volume down and picked up his phone instead, putting someone from the Salt Lake City office on speaker. "What do we know?"

"So far, not much," the frazzled voice of a woman

came back, chaos in the background. "But this time, someone noticed a suspicious person leaving a bag. Police were called. They arrived just when the bomb went off, which meant more casualties, but the man was spotted running from the scene, and we're supposed to be getting feeds from the area soon."

Evelyn nodded, even though no one could see her. Lucas had picked up his speed again, but instead of continuing toward the prison, he'd done a wild turnaround. The SUV slipped madly in the ice and snow before it gained traction, and he headed back.

"Shouldn't we keep going?" Evelyn asked, knowing that Cartwright had to have real information if he'd sought help before. The question was whether, this time, he'd actually hand it over. "Is there anything we can do from here?"

"I'm the head of the Salt Lake City's only terrorism squad," Lucas said. "I need to be back at the office *now*."

When the agent on the line stopped talking, Lucas shouted, "What else do we have?"

"Uh, well, I don't know if you've ever been to the ATF office in…"

"No." Lucas pushed down harder on the gas until Evelyn gripped the "oh, shit" bar above her head. "Give me numbers."

"We don't have numbers yet. We know the bomb went off about twenty minutes ago."

Evelyn stared at the dashboard clock, frowning. It was three in the afternoon, making it two in San Francisco. Not lunchtime. Not leaving time. Maybe the goal had been fewer casualties, but that seemed odd. They'd aimed to hit as many as possible in Chicago. Of course, this time, the police had been called. She wondered if the bombers had done it themselves, hoping to hit the responders.

It was a risk to the bomber, but somehow it fit. "They were going for the police," Evelyn suggested.

"We think so," the agent said. "Timing was right, and the San Francisco office has already learned that the 9-1-1 call came from a burn phone."

"Then why target an ATF building?" Lucas asked, taking his eyes off the road for a few seconds to look her way.

Evelyn shrugged. "Were there casualties inside the building, too?"

"Not that we've heard," the agent responded. "We have a few minor injuries inside. We also have some ATF agents who came outside when they heard the sirens approaching. We have at least a dozen injured between police, ATF and civilian—the building is in a commercial area—but we don't have any information on casualties yet."

"So is this a general sort of 'survivalists hate ATF' thing? Or does this Rolfe guy have a specific connection to Chicago and San Francisco?" Lucas asked.

"We don't know," the agent replied, her voice hesitant, as though she didn't understand why he was asking her.

"Talking to the profiler," Lucas said curtly.

Evelyn stared ahead, through the windshield, wipers furiously battling the snowflakes slapping onto the window, sounding more like ice than snow as they hit. Why ATF? And why those specific offices? The timing mattered, too, because they obviously wanted more than *just* ATF, if they were attacking areas where civilians and police would be among the casualties. Did they just not care who else was hurt, as long as it was on ATF's doorstep?

The thought lingered. It was as though they were saying it was ATF's fault. As though they wanted anyone caught in the crossfire—like the cops and the civilians—to hold a grudge against ATF, since the bomb had been "aimed" at them.

Evelyn told Lucas what she was thinking. "It's *possible* there were events involving ATF in Chicago and San Francisco. However, it's equally likely that there's just an ATF grudge."

Lucas scowled. "So it could be either option."

"Not exactly. I don't think it's general. I think it's a specific grudge. But specific to ATF. Not necessarily to Chicago and San Francisco."

"Okay," Lucas said, "then why?"

"The bombers—or rather, their leader—has something very specific he blames ATF for. My guess is that people died in the incident and he thinks ATF should've been blamed for *that*."

Lucas's hands tightened around the wheel, but he slowed down marginally to take a sharp curve. "Well, we can dig into any connections, but that doesn't really narrow it down a whole lot. Especially if this guy wasn't there, but just impacted in some way." He turned his attention back to the agent on the phone. "Any sign of the black truck?"

"What? Oh, not yet," the frazzled agent replied. "I'll let you know as soon as we get the footage. We do know that CNN is now reporting the first confirmed casualty. A police officer. Ah, jeez. He's twenty-two. He's brand-new on the force. Married a year ago, just had a baby girl. Damn it."

"Focus," Lucas snapped at her. "I want the bastards who did this to him. We say a prayer for him later. Right now, I want data. And I want it yesterday."

With every word, the SUV seemed to pick up more speed until Evelyn had to say, "Slow down." They weren't going to lock anyone away if they never made it back to the field office.

Lucas looked down at his speedometer and whatever it read made his lips tighten and his foot lift until Evelyn was no longer gripping the bar over her head so hard.

"Whoa," the agent on the phone said, then quickly, "We do have something, Evelyn."

Lucas frowned, probably wondering why his agent was talking to her.

The agent spoke up again before either of them could ask. "We got the footage." Her voice picked up, her tone higher-pitched. "It's that guy. The one you had us looking for."

Evelyn exchanged a glance with Lucas. "John Peters."

"Yes. He's running from the scene of the bomb. It's definitely him. He's the bomber."

"We've got something on Martinez," Fred Lanier said, and from the tone of his voice, Evelyn knew it wasn't good.

She looked across the long conference table in the San Francisco field office, where she and Lucas had flown late last night. This was the first time she'd been part of a task force of this magnitude, and the sheer amount of travel and work hours reminded her of cases she'd worked for BAU. It was the complete focus on one case that was different for her.

Typically, she'd be working from the BAU office in Aquia, usually on a dozen or so profiles at a time. Even if she flew somewhere for a specific case, she'd still have profiles pending. Often, she'd bring them with her and do them at the hotel after she finished working the current case. Usually she'd be in at least partial contact with Greg.

This time was different. This was a joint terrorism task force and she was working only this case. She was also the only profiler on the task force, and she wondered if Dan had allowed her to be assigned full-time simply because he didn't want her back in the office and on his nerves.

She was so busy hopping from one lead to the next, traveling from one city to the next, that she'd barely spoken to Greg in the past few days. She'd barely talked to Kyle or her grandma, either. She tried to tell herself it was because of the case, and not because she was avoiding any discussions about her career at the FBI.

Even though she was on the same JTTF she'd been on since she'd left the compound, it almost felt like a new case. The San Francisco office was packed with new members of the task force who'd assembled here and were coordinating with Fred in Chicago. They all looked up at his announcement about Jen, but most of them continued working. Most of them had worked with the San Francisco ATF office, and their fury that their colleagues and friends were being targeted fueled their work the way only a personal connection could.

She understood that all too well.

But as they continued working, she and Lucas went

completely still, waiting for the news from Lanier, whatever it was.

"Did you find Jen's body?" Lucas asked, and his voice cracked.

"Worse." Fred sighed.

Evelyn looked around at the other agents to see their reactions, wondering what could be worse than dead. A sick feeling welled up inside her at the idea that the cultists had left her alive long enough to walk her out of the compound, than done something horrible to her and killed her elsewhere. Evelyn's job had taught her the limitless possibilities of evil when it came to what one person was capable of doing to another. So she tried not to imagine at all, and just waited for Fred to tell them.

Lucas clenched his fists and leaned away from the phone as though he was warding off bad news.

"We don't have anything more on her whereabouts," Fred told them.

She saw her own relief reflected on Lucas's face. What Fred was saying probably meant they didn't have a final confirmation that she was dead. And if Jen had really managed to walk out of that compound after being hit with an AK-47, they had to work on the assumption she was still alive. And to do everything they could to keep her that way.

But if that wasn't it, what bad information could they have? The other agents in the room started setting down files, jabbing one another with elbows as they became aware something unusual was coming over the phone.

"We've found some…anomalies in Jen's personal life," Fred said slowly, as if he was choosing his words carefully.

Lucas's head popped up. "What does that mean?"

"She's got a bank account her husband knew nothing about that she opened within the past year. She opened it under a company she created that he also knew nothing about and, as far as we can tell, doesn't actually exist. She was definitely trying to hide it. And according to our white-collar team, in the past month, she started transferring money out of there in amounts that wouldn't raise any flags. She's been pulling that money into an account overseas. Another hidden account, under her maiden name."

When neither Evelyn nor Lucas replied, Fred added, "It's not good."

"What…" Evelyn cut herself off, trying to figure out what that meant, what question to ask. "What do you make of it?" She glanced over at Lucas, to see if he had an idea, but he just looked pale, his fingers tapping frantically against the table.

"Right now, we're trying not to jump to any conclusions," Fred told them.

"She was working with them," one of the San Francisco agents said, his cheeks mottled red, his fists clenched.

"No way," Lucas insisted loudly. "Jen hated that group. She *begged* us to investigate. She's the first one who warned us about the Butler Compound, and we didn't listen. There's no way she colluded with them."

The agent persisted. "Maybe they knew she was onto them and they offered her a choice. Keep coming after them and they'd come after her. Or take a payoff and help them. We've seen it before," he said.

"She'd never do that." Lucas leaned toward the agent, a hardness in his gaze that warned the man not to push it.

"We're looking at every angle," Fred said calmly.

"But we have to assume that Jen was involved in something she shouldn't have been. And that it might be connected to what's happening right now. So, we need to find out how she left that compound—and if she's still alive."

17

"This is bullshit," Lucas yelled. "Jen Martinez wasn't a traitor!"

"I'm not arguing with you," Evelyn said, holding out her hands.

But she wasn't sure what to believe. Her brief time with Jen hadn't set off any warning bells, no suggestion that she'd been in collusion with Butler. In fact, Evelyn had genuinely liked Jen, despite her rash actions at the compound.

Then again, Rolfe hadn't set off warning bells, either. She'd thought he was truly Butler's second-in-command, not a terrorist leader. She'd thought she could rely on him to keep her alive, to protect her from Butler.

Could she really trust her own judgment on this? Or was she too close to it all to be objective?

What if Jen *had* been working with them? Then Butler's shooting her didn't make much sense.

Unless Butler had been acting on his own when he shot her. It was certainly possible, considering how Rolfe had reacted. But Rolfe had seemed more concerned with keeping Evelyn from getting shot than with patching up Jen. On the other hand, given her condition, maybe it had been a surprise to them that Jen had lived through it. Maybe at that point, Rolfe figured Evelyn was his only remaining bargaining chip.

Could the shooting have been faked? Evelyn thought of the way Jen had gone down, of waking up in all that blood, and a shiver danced along her spine. The blood had sure felt real.

And she couldn't think of a good reason to fake Jen's death. So she could go underground for the group? But what purpose would she serve? And if she was really working for them, her bringing Evelyn there in the first place didn't make any sense. Not unless they'd wanted to guarantee an FBI presence at the compound. Maybe Rolfe had wanted to create an incident to distract everyone from his real plans—involving the bombs.

She frowned, sitting at the dingy table in the break room as she tried to work it out in her head.

"She tried to get us to investigate them." Lucas continued ranting, pacing back and forth in the break room. He'd pulled her out of the conference room after Fred's call, and hadn't stopped repeating the same arguments for the past fifteen minutes.

She'd spent most of that time battling shock. The money could be completely unrelated. Still, as Greg liked to say, coincidences happened but good investigators didn't lean on them. Because more often than not, if something looked suspicious, there was a reason.

The fact that Jen had apparently been able to walk out of that compound was strange. And Jen having a secret offshore account was suspicious. Despite the arguments Jen had made about investigating the compound, there was something here. And Lucas had to realize that, or he wouldn't be so shaken, regardless of what he was saying now.

"I know she was your friend," Evelyn said.

Lucas flushed. "I wouldn't say that exactly. But I'm the head of the counterterror squad and she brought me this group. More than once. I looked at it, didn't see anything and shut her down. She kept coming back, insisting I look again. No way would she do that if she was working for them!"

"What if she did it to divert suspicion, knowing you'd never believe her?"

"Come on," Lucas scoffed. "We brought BAU in on this last year. She was persistent as hell. Frankly, she was a pain in the ass about it. She tracked me down on my days off, at the gym, at the coffee shop. She wouldn't let it go until I heard her out."

"Really?" It shouldn't have surprised her, since Jen had tracked Evelyn down at the Montana State Prison to bring her to the compound. But somehow the idea of Jen chasing Lucas around town struck her as odd.

"Why do you think she came to get me at the prison? She took me straight to the compound." Lucas seemed ready to keep defending Jen's innocence, so Evelyn insisted, "Just hear me out. If it's not connected to Rolfe or Butler, why is she hiding money? Where did it come from? What's it for?"

"Fuck if I know." Lucas sighed, sinking down into the chair next to her, looking suddenly deflated. "Fred didn't say she *stole* the money. He said she was hiding it. Maybe she was siphoning money away from her family." He frowned after he said it, probably realizing how horrible that sounded, too.

"Maybe. But why?"

He shrugged, a brief lift of his shoulders, but there was something about the way his forehead lined with concentration.

"What aren't you telling me?" she pressed.

He got to his feet again, turning away from her as he poured himself a cup of coffee. "Nothing. But whatever's going on here, Jen isn't a traitor. She's not working with Butler." He swung back around, the cup hanging from his hand at an angle that made coffee slosh over the rim. "You saw her get shot! Why would they do that if she was working with them?"

"I don't know. I was wondering that myself. Do you think they faked it?"

Lucas shook his head, setting his coffee down without taking a sip. "That was real blood in the tunnel," he reminded her. "And it was Jen's blood. DNA confirmed it."

"Yeah, but why did she walk through that tunnel if she was a hostage?"

"That's what we'd all like to know," a new voice cut in.

Evelyn spun around and saw that one of the other JTTF agents had entered the room.

He picked up Lucas's newly poured coffee and started drinking it himself, calling over his shoulder as he headed out of the room again. "We'll have to worry about Jen later. You might want to get back into the conference room. We've got a lead on Peters."

"What do we have?" Lucas demanded as he opened the door to the interagency conference room and Evelyn rushed after him.

The agents inside glanced up as he came in, and then

someone pointed to the screen on the wall. The image on that screen had every agent in the room staring intently. Another surveillance image, this one from San Francisco. It had the same grainy texture as the images from Chicago, but captured Peters as he'd glanced across the street, directly at a brand-new security camera that had been installed a few days before. In his hand was another messenger bag, eerily similar to the one left in Chicago, down to the big, bold red sticker.

She couldn't read it from where she stood, but she knew exactly what it said. Freedom Uprising.

The image changed, zooming in on Peters's face. There was no question it was the same man Evelyn had seen when she and Lucas had pulled up pictures connected to people in Lee Cartwright's life. In Chicago, he'd had a reddish beard, but he'd shaved it off and looked more like the photographs she'd seen of him from when he'd first come to Montana. He actually looked a bit like Cartwright, except not as huge and not as angry. In the image on the screen, the expression on his face was one of pride.

Disgust threatened to choke her, and she shoved it back as she followed Lucas to the table. Anyone who'd take part in this kind of mission would believe in it. People like that would be proud of their actions, even now, with three confirmed dead from the new blast, and fifteen injuries, most of them serious.

Three police officers who'd never go home to their families. Two ATF agents whose careers were on hold for at least a year while they went through surgeries and rehabilitation. And ten civilians with injuries ranging from broken legs to possible brain damage.

And John Peters was proud.

She stared at the image, trying to imagine him the way he must have been when he'd arrived in Montana. A little lost. No real connections. Searching for purpose. The perfect recruit.

If she was right, Lee Cartwright, convicted bombmaker, racist thug, a man who'd attacked her while chained to the table, had tried to stop this.

She regretted that she'd been too caught up in his bad traits to see the good, but she couldn't focus on that. She couldn't go back and make a different choice in that jail and neither could Lee. He'd wanted to save his half brother from being locked up for the rest of his life like him. But it was way too late for that now.

"Did you get anything from the half brother?" one of the agents asked, and everyone turned toward Lucas.

Evelyn was about to tell them that she and Lucas had gotten the call about this latest bomb before they'd been able to see Cartwright again, but Lucas jumped in.

"I sent some agents to talk to him after we couldn't make it. He's being stubborn, giving us nothing. We're staying on him, though. If he genuinely wanted to help Peters before, maybe he'll help us find him now."

"He probably doesn't know where Peters is," an agent said.

Evelyn nodded. "He probably doesn't. But he might know what else they have planned. He might have an idea how we can bring Peters in peacefully."

"Cartwright is a long shot," Lucas said.

Although Evelyn didn't want to admit it, she had to agree. What could he do? It was too late to bring Peters in without landing him in jail. However, that was the least of Peters's worries, because life in jail was going to look like the sweeter deal when he was finally caught.

Chances were, Lee's next move would be to hope Peters *didn't* get caught, and to do anything he could to lead them in the wrong direction.

"We might not need Cartwright, anyway," the agent who'd come to get them in the break room announced, hitting a button and changing the image on the screen to show the black truck again.

This time, there was no logo, but otherwise the truck looked the same.

"We think the plumbing company logo was to throw us off track," the agent said. "It's a gutsy move, risking the wrath of the mob, but that seems to be what they did. Chicago's still investigating, just in case. They've got some guys from their organized-crime squads making arrests, trying to dig up any connections. So far, nothing. But we do have this." He changed the image once more, giving the room a close-up of the driver. In this shot, Peters was in the passenger seat and the bomber from Chicago was driving.

"Meet Bobby Durham," the agent said, pride in his voice as he pointed at the Chicago bomber. "We finally got a hit in the prison systems from that tattoo. This guy has done time on weapons charges. He's from Montana, too, and we can tie him back to the Butler Compound. Looks like he moved in there about a year ago. We presume these are the two men who left in the truck the night Evelyn and Jen arrived at the compound."

"What else do we have on Durham?" Lucas asked.

"We're running everything now. We're hoping to find some connection to San Francisco, maybe someplace nearby, where they'd lie low. What do you have on Jen?"

Lucas scowled. "The Chicago team is digging into

her finances. But I know Jen. I can give you my personal assurance. She had nothing to do with this. I promise you that."

Evelyn stared at him, trying not to gape. He'd told her that he and Jen weren't really friends, that she'd practically stalked him in her efforts to get him to look at the Butler Compound. She could tell he believed in her innocence. And that he felt guilty for not listening to her warnings before it was too late. But giving a room full of JTTF agents his personal guarantee could put a huge dent in his own career if he was wrong.

What did he know that he wasn't sharing?

Was Jen Martinez the key?

Evelyn sat on the bed in her tiny hotel room and studied the personnel file she'd finally convinced the FBI to email her. A squad of their best white-collar-fraud agents had spent a full day searching for more information on Jen's hidden money, and still no one had been able to make sense of it.

All they had were questions. Why would Jen alert the counterterror squad to the Butler Compound if she was connected? Why would she take Evelyn there if she was involved? And why would Butler—or Rolfe—let her go if she wasn't? Especially if she'd seen the driver, which made her a huge liability. Yet, the evidence said she'd walked out through that hidden tunnel under her own power. Had someone else walked beside her, forced her to do it?

The evidence also said she'd lost blood. Enough that the ERT agents at the scene had tagged her as "seriously injured." Butler could have been trying to kill her, but she'd lived; perhaps Rolfe was the one who'd brought her out. That was definitely plausible, particularly if Jen was working with Rolfe and not Butler. But that meant Butler had allowed her to live after he'd shot her, and she'd ended up in the tunnel underneath his room, which was strange.

Evelyn thought about the books they'd seen in Butler's room, the huge stack with the initials *RS* inside. It made her wonder if that had once been Rolfe's room, and Butler had swapped them while Rolfe was away from the compound, setting his plots in motion.

She pondered it, trying to remember the nuances of Butler and Rolfe's interactions. Although she'd never overheard Rolfe speaking angrily about a room, she wouldn't put it past Butler to flaunt his power.

So maybe it *had* been Rolfe's room, and that was why Jen had been led out through the tunnel. That still didn't explain why Butler would let it happen—unless Rolfe took her through after Butler was dead.

But if she hadn't left until the raid, she'd spent a week somewhere in that compound with a gunshot injury before walking out. And Evelyn hadn't seen or heard her at all, or heard anyone else mention her, except as already being dead. It was possible she'd been in Butler's room the whole time. But that meant she'd had no medical attention for a full week—and yet survived long enough to walk out.

If she'd gone through that tunnel immediately after being shot, that might explain how she'd lived. Once she was out, she might've been able to get medical attention, probably from someone willing to perform surgeries off-book and out-of-hospital. If that was the case, she might already be recuperating on some foreign beach near that offshore account. Although the money hadn't been touched, and as soon as the FBI started throwing the words *possible terrorism connection* around, the account had been frozen. But none of that answered *why*.

Another question—why would they keep her inside, bleeding to death, and then let her go? One possibility was that Rolfe had taken her far enough to get past the perimeter of FBI and police, and then killed her.

But if Jen was a simple hostage, nothing but insurance for Rolfe's escape, then the hidden money made no sense. Could it be a payoff? Perhaps to keep her mouth shut once Rolfe—or someone else—learned she'd found out about the compound's true purpose. Or she could've gotten the money because she'd been involved all along. Maybe the plan had always been to draw attention to the compound in order to distract from the bombers.

No matter how she looked at it, nothing added up.

Evelyn closed Jen's file, frustrated that it hadn't provided more answers. It told her Jen had joined the FBI young, that she'd been a strong agent with only one major flaw as far as the FBI was concerned—she had a tendency to go off-book.

That wasn't exactly something Evelyn could fault her for, since she had the same problem herself. It was partly why she was here in a crappy San Francisco hotel, instead of back at Aquia, settled in her cubicle at BAU, surrounded by new profile requests.

Evelyn stood and started to pace back and forth in the tiny room, five steps to one blank white wall and five steps to the other, thinking about Jen. She'd learned that the woman had always been a standout, which had probably made her an easy pick for the FBI Academy. From her years as a national champion swimmer who'd just missed being part of the Olympic team, to a summa cum laude student in law school who'd opted for the FBI instead of joining a high-profile law firm, she'd attracted plenty of interest. She'd met her husband in law school, and he was still practicing, although with less visibility than it seemed Jen would have had.

Their relationship looked solid, at least on paper. Evelyn had a call scheduled with him in a few minutes to see if that held up. Spouses were sometimes the last to know what was going on with their husband's or wife's work—but they were often the first to suspect when something wasn't right.

She picked up the phone and called him. Jen's husband answered on the first ring and she told him who she was, then apologized for not being able to meet him in person.

"That's okay. It's a long way from San Francisco," he said, exhaustion in his voice.

As a profiler, she rarely talked to the spouse of someone who was missing. Whenever she did, there was always a heavy mix of worry, hope and despair. But Jen's husband just sounded worn out, as if he didn't have the energy left for those emotions or any others.

She hesitated, curious about how he'd known she was in California, and he added, "I saw you on the news yesterday."

"Oh. Yes," she answered, still slow to recover as she wondered how he'd even known what she looked like. She'd gone to the site of the blast with some of the ERT agents, and there'd been a camera crew, so maybe they'd dug up her name somehow. Damn press. Her boss was going to love that.

Her phone buzzed, and she ignored the incoming text, trying to formulate the best way to start.

She let the silence stretch a little too long and he asked, "You wanted to know about Jen? Your voice mail said you had some questions."

"Yes. Sorry. I just wanted to find out if she seemed unusually distracted in the weeks leading up to the day she drove out to the Butler Compound. Or if she was talking about the group at all, if she ever mentioned the names Ward Butler or Rolfe."

"Rolfe who?"

"We don't have a last name."

"Is Rolfe part of the compound?"

"He could be connected," Evelyn hedged at his obvious interest, not wanting Jen's husband to go off on his own hunt.

"Nah, the name's not familiar," he said, the spark of interest she'd heard fading.

Evelyn frowned, not surprised that he hadn't heard the name. What did surprise her was that he seemed *less* interested now that she'd confirmed Rolfe might be part of the compound. What had he thought Rolfe was connected to?

She suddenly wished she was back in Montana, so she could see his face as she questioned him. Her phone buzzed with another new text, but she continued to ignore it. Because something here seemed off. "Is there anything else you're worried about with your wife?" Before he could answer, she hurried on, "Whatever it is, even if it seems minor, it could help us find her."

There was a pause, then he said, "No. We just want her home. No matter what."

No matter what? What the hell did that mean?

She remembered the way Lucas had acted when he'd suggested maybe Jen was simply siphoning money away from her own family, and not getting it as payoff from a terrorist. "Were the two of you arguing over finances at all?"

"Finances?" The surprise and confusion in his voice told her instantly that they hadn't been.

"No," he said slowly. "The FBI asked me about some account she supposedly had, but what does that have to do with her being missing? And what's being done to find her? First the news was reporting that she's dead." He choked on the word, then anger replaced the pain as his voice grew in volume. "And now the FBI is telling me she's *missing*. Does that actually mean dead and none of you have the balls to admit it to me?"

"Mr. Martinez, I promise you that we're telling you what we've learned." Evelyn raised her own voice as her phone kept buzzing at her. "She's missing. We can't account for her whereabouts, and yet at the same time, we have no evidence that she's dead." Nothing other than Evelyn seeing her shot with an AK-47. But considering the blood in that tunnel, there was a real chance she was still alive. Or at least *had been* alive.

"So you don't know," he summed up after a brief pause.

"We don't know," she confirmed softly. "I'm sorry. I wish we could give you a definite answer. Believe me, we have a lot of FBI resources on finding your wife. We can confirm that she was injured, which is why it's very important we find her as quickly as we can. That's also why it's important you be straight with me here. What aren't you telling me about your wife?"

The silence stretched on and on, finally broken by a buzzing on her phone again. Annoyed, Evelyn pulled the phone away from her ear and looked down at the screen. Three missed text messages from Lucas. Every single one was a simple statement.

Big break. Call NOW.

"Shit," she muttered.

"What?" Jen's husband asked.

Trying to hold back her impatience, she said, "Is there anything…?"

"No." He cut her off, and even though she *knew* he was lying, that there was definitely something he wasn't telling her, she couldn't press him on it now.

"I'm sorry," she told him. "I have to go."

She hung up and dialed Lucas, who answered with a furious, "Where have you been?" Not giving her a chance to reply, he said, "Pack up. Now. We think we found Peters and Durham. The FBI is sending your HRT buddies and we're going in to get the bastards!"

He hung up and she didn't have a chance to ask where they were, what their status was—armed, injured, barricaded?—or what the plan was to bring them in peacefully.

Knowing she wouldn't get any of that information until she was standing in front of the team, Evelyn grabbed the few belongings she'd taken out of her suitcase and stuffed them back in, then zipped it up and raced for the door without a backward glance. Chances were, she wouldn't be returning.

Maybe they'd get Peters and Durham in handcuffs, learn Rolfe's last name and location and track *him* down. And maybe they'd finally locate Jen.

Maybe this was finally the beginning of the end.

18

"Why aren't we waiting until they go into town for supplies?" Evelyn asked, wishing the question hadn't come out sounding quite so desperate. A room full of FBI agents and a handful of park rangers stared back at her.

She and Lucas had finally made it to the JTTF meeting at the edge of the King Range National Conservation Area on California's "Lost Coast." It had taken six hours by car, winding along steep, narrow roads. She'd feared an oncoming car would veer into Lucas's path at any second.

The closer they got, the more rain had come down in sheets. The talk radio station Lucas had put on kept breaking for weather advisories, warning people that "sneaker" waves were out in force, and telling everyone to stay away from the water's edge. It had all felt like a very, very bad omen.

Evelyn had tried not to focus on it, and instead spent most of the drive getting an update on what they knew while Lucas drove white-knuckled around sharp bends atop steep cliffs, avoiding the sudden deep puddles of water.

A pair of hikers had reported seeing Peters and Durham trekking inside the backcountry of the nationally protected forest, carrying big packs full of supplies. They'd recognized the men from the news, and once they had cell reception, they'd called it in to the FBI's hotline. By that time, no one knew where Peters or Durham might have gone, but a group of park rangers had set out, under strict orders to pull back as soon as they spotted the men. *If* they spotted the men, because eyewitness reports were notoriously unreliable.

Ten hours after that, the FBI had what they believed was a promising location for the suspects, and Lucas had gotten instructions to get up the coast, fast. HRT had received the call slightly later, but they'd arrived sooner, hitching a ride from the Air Force. Apparently, there were very few places to land a large plane around here, so they'd left a lot of gear behind. Instead, they'd come with the bare minimum—a small team of HRT agents and whatever they could carry into the forest on their backs.

Six of them were gathered at the other end of the tiny, dingy building that passed for a park ranger station. A pack of big men standing at rigid, almost military attention, with anticipation in their eyes. Evelyn had long ago learned that to be in HRT, you had to love the adrenaline rush of the most dangerous missions, and you had to be willing to run in when everyone else was running out.

From the middle of the group, wearing cargo pants and short sleeves despite the fifty-five-degree temperatures outside and the lack of heat inside, Kyle winked at her. She flushed, and averted her gaze from Kyle's too-blue eyes before anyone else noticed.

Still, she sensed Lucas's sideways glance as she said, "These men are from a compound where booby-trapping their own home with loaded guns and bear traps is normal. Is it really a good idea to go after them on their own turf?"

"This isn't their turf," a gruff park ranger, whose name Evelyn had never gotten, spoke up. "They shouldn't even be here. They obviously don't have passes."

Evelyn couldn't help herself. She glanced back at Kyle, knowing he'd find that funny, even in a situation like this. She could see a smile itching to break free at the thought of a pair of terrorists getting the approval to camp on BLM land.

She tried to scowl at him, but felt her own amusement bubble up.

"There's nothing funny about this," Fred Lanier, who'd flown in from Chicago with his core team, snapped.

Evelyn nodded, putting on her serious face as Fred continued. "We can't wait them out. These men are trained survivalists, and they're moving deep into inhospitable terrain. It's only going to get more inhospitable as we head into winter, and they're probably counting on that. They're wanted by the FBI. And their names and faces are plastered all over the news. They're not going into town, not for supplies or anything else, not unless—and until—they plan to set another bomb. They'll go even farther off grid. And they have the training to stay there for years. Right now, we know where they are. We're not sure how long we'll have that window, so we're acting on it before it's too late."

"But…"

Fred interrupted her. "We can't risk them getting away. We can't risk them setting off more bombs." The rest of the room stayed silent, and Evelyn could guess why. The HRT agents *wanted* to go in. The primary JTTF team was looking for a way to end this, and end it soon. Especially since many of them knew victims personally.

But Evelyn couldn't stop thinking of the bloodshed in that compound. Of all the men who'd died in there, a group that had very nearly included some HRT agents. A few of them had been seriously injured; there was a good chance they wouldn't be returning to HRT.

She imagined Kyle running back into battle with men trained by Rolfe and Butler, and she had to try again. "I'm just suggesting we wait until they come out of their camper or whatever..."

"They're not in a camper," the park ranger told her. "That would attract too much attention out here. We don't allow them."

"Okay, well, when they come out of their tents. We should consider waiting until they're on the move, not go in while they're hunkered at a specific spot that *they* chose. You don't have to be a profiler to know that as soon as they settle into one spot, they'll protect it. They'll have booby traps or safeguards or *something*. We need to catch them off guard."

Fred shook his head. "Normally, I'd agree with that," he said. "But they're our only connection to Rolfe, whoever he is, and our only possible link to Jen. Besides, you're the one who said we could be facing more bombs *and* more bombers. If you stand by that, there are other threats besides these two. And we can't sit on that. We need whatever information they have, and we need it immediately." He looked at her intently, as if daring her to back down now.

What argument could she make against that? She felt frustration build up, and a dread she couldn't explain at the idea of Kyle and his teammates going after Durham and Peters in their element.

This was going to end badly. She just knew it.

But all she could say was, "I guess we have no choice."

"We should've brought a park ranger with us," Gabe whispered as the team stopped yet again to check their compass.

They were in the middle of the King Range forest, and although the trek in had taken a few hours so far, they hadn't run into a single hiker. Probably a good thing, considering who they were chasing.

"We can handle it," Kyle said, keeping his own voice low. Besides, the park ranger they'd been coordinating with had seemed more concerned that Peters and Durham might violate Bureau of Land Management rules than the fact that they needed to be taken down.

As far as Kyle was concerned, Peters and Durham weren't leaving this forest except in handcuffs. Or, if it came to that, in body bags.

According to the coordinates the rangers had given them, they were getting close to where the bombers had to be hiding. HRT had a lot of training, and they'd been in forests and jungles in the US and overseas, but their targets weren't usually as well-trained as these particular paranoid survivalists.

They'd chosen their hiding spot well. The national forest got far fewer visitors this time of year, and there were parts of it that were accessible only to the very experienced camper. The chances of running into another human this deep in the park were slim. The chances of

Durham and Peters being prepared were high. HRT's experience at the Butler Compound told them that much. Any approach would have to be damn careful.

"This creek looks passable," someone said, and Kyle got his mind back in the present.

The sounds of birds chirping and water rushing echoed in his ears, and the scent of rain lodged in his nostrils. He felt as if he was in South America instead of northern California.

The creek ahead of them was fast-moving, but there was an old stone path constructed through it to the other side. Apparently, at one time this section of the forest had been part of a trail. But judging from the brushy overgrowth that hit Kyle mid-thigh, it had been years. And although the stones were flat, they were pretty close to the water, meaning they were going to be slippery.

"Are we sure this is the way?" Kyle asked. Peters and Durham were probably too smart to leave an obvious bushwhacking trail, but there were no signs at all anyone had been here in months.

"It's not the way they came, but it's the quickest way to get to them," their team leader replied. "At least, according to the park rangers." He gazed pensively at the creek a minute longer, then said, "We'll cross here. Hitch up."

The group, just a small, six-man team, hitched together their ropes and carabiners, connecting one man to the next, so anyone who fell in wouldn't instantly be swept away in the fast-moving water. Kyle was at the end of the group, all tethered together to cross the creek. He was about to step onto the path when he glanced to his right and up. And froze.

In front of him, Gabe kept walking. Kyle's combat

boots slipped on the slick rock and that almost sent both of them into the creek.

He threw his arms wide, hoping the quick movement wouldn't draw attention, and barely caught his balance. His heart thudded faster at the close call. "Psst. Look up."

As one, his teammates' heads turned and he could tell the second each of them had seen the pair of baby brown bears clinging to a tree trunk. One of the bears spotted them and climbed out over a branch, craning his head in curiosity.

"Cute," Gabe said, teeth clenched. "Anyone see mom?"

"Just keep going," Kyle muttered. If he had to shoot anything today, he'd prefer it be a terrorist rather than a mother bear determined to protect her cubs.

He picked up his pace a little, making it across the rocks and onto the relative safety of solid ground on the other side. But his gaze swiveled left and right, his hands lingering near his MP-5. Bears moved fast. And the high grasses and trees with vines and moss dangling from one to the next like a gigantic curtain obscured his view. Of bears or terrorists. Or whatever else might be out there.

He'd been warned to watch for rattlesnakes, too.

Suddenly, Gabe's fist went up in front of him and Kyle froze, wondering what his partner had seen.

He glanced around, without moving anything but his eyes. Animals—and people—responded to movement more than anything else. And HRT was dressed to blend in, wearing their regular flight suits with additional camouflage smeared over any exposed skin.

It took him longer than he'd like, but finally he saw

what Gabe had seen. Movement. About fifty feet away from them, and definitely not where the park rangers had marked on the map. There it was again. A glint of metal reflecting in the sunlight streaking down like little spotlights through the trees.

Peters and Durham? Or someone else?

"Slowly," their team leader instructed in a whisper over his bone mic. "We're going to get a closer look." Then he clicked off the mic; they wouldn't speak again unless absolutely necessary. Instead, they'd rely on their training and their methods. They didn't need to speak. They all knew their roles.

They lowered themselves, inch by painful inch, until they were lying flat on the ground, faces in the dirt. Kyle tried not to think about where that mother bear was, or the chance of shimmying face-first into a rattlesnake.

They were still tethered together, so the first thing he did once he was on the ground was to unhook the carabiner. He was careful to keep the metal underneath him so it wouldn't sparkle, sending off its own signal. As soon as he got it loose, he tucked it and the rope in one of his bags. Then he moved his weapon to a more comfortable position, ignoring the dampness creeping through his clothes, and started moving in a belly crawl toward the unknown targets ahead.

Normally, when he began a final approach like this, his mind cleared, and he got laser-focused on every tiny detail. But today, he pictured Evelyn, back in that park ranger station.

Dressed in her typical pantsuit, cut slightly too big to hide the gun at her hip, with her hair up in its usual too-tight bun. An expression of authority on her face, hiding something else underneath. Something that might've been nervousness. She'd looked so much the way she had the first day he'd met her, he'd been struck by the instant desire to walk over and tease her, ruffle some of that seriousness. Like he'd done a year and a half ago.

But things had changed dramatically since then. He'd hardly believed it when she'd agreed to his suggestion that the two of them go on vacation together, after she'd solved her friend's case. He *really* hadn't been able to believe it when she'd actually gone through with it.

She'd seemed happy. More carefree than he'd ever seen her. They'd had fun together. And although he'd already known that his feelings had become stronger than he wanted to admit, after that week on the beach, he'd been certain. He'd wanted to go straight to the Office of Professional Responsibility and announce that they were dating, put it out in the open. He'd brought it up, but as he'd expected, she hadn't agreed. So he'd settled for keeping things secret.

Now he wondered if he should've pushed the issue. Because after a few weeks back in her job at BAU, she hadn't slipped back into old routines as he'd feared. Instead, it was like she'd slipped into a whole new skin. Suddenly, she was missing all of her usual intense focus on her job, and her happiness seemed to have faded right along with it.

And he had no idea what to do about it. No idea how to help her find her passion for her job—for her life— again. Especially if he had to do it while pretending to the rest of the world that nothing had changed between them.

He scooted forward another slow inch, trying to get his head in the game as he spotted the tent up ahead. It was covered in leaves and moss from the forest. This wasn't a typical camper. This was someone who knew how to hide in plain sight. Someone with survivalist training.

His heart kicked up a notch and all worries about Evelyn were tucked away.

He paused, shifting his primary weapon so it would be easier to grab if he needed it. Then he slid forward again, until he was only a few feet from the tent's entrance. A few feet to the right of him was Gabe. A few feet to the left, another teammate.

They all stopped, listening. And then Kyle heard it. A whisper. He tried to make out the words, even as his instincts warned him something about that whisper was wrong.

He recognized the word in the same moment he realized why they felt wrong. Someone had said, "Now," but it hadn't come from inside the tent. They'd been flanked.

He didn't have time to warn his teammates, didn't have time to lift his weapon, before gunshots blasted through the air, coming from behind them.

"Shit!" Gabe rolled away from Kyle as bullets rained down between them, shooting dirt up into the air and filling Kyle's eyes.

He rolled left, feeling the sharp sting of a hit on his arm. His pulse jackknifed as he swung his weapon up and searched for a target.

He heard a teammate scream out a warning, felt blood rushing down his arm and wasted precious seconds glancing to make sure an artery hadn't been hit. Blood wasn't squirting, but his shirt was already soaked.

Nothing he could do about it now. He was on his back, facing the other direction, head up slightly with dirt clouding his vision as he searched desperately for a target. Finally, a flash as one of them took a shot, and another of his teammates screamed.

He lifted his gun and fired. From beside a huge red-wood, a figure dropped to the ground and didn't get up again.

His arm throbbed harder from the motion of pulling the trigger, which was more awkward than it should have been. Kyle ignored it and kept searching, knowing he was just as exposed as the man he'd shot.

Where was the second one?

His breath came faster as his eyes swept left and right, seeing nothing. He heard labored, heavy breathing from one side of him and a low moan from the other. If his teammates were making sounds like that, they were hurt. Worse than he was.

The gunshots had gone silent. Had someone hit the second man? He didn't think so, but then where the hell was the guy?

Vibrations suddenly rattled beneath him, the sound of something big thundering his way, and Kyle tipped his head back to find the bear he'd worried about earlier running straight at him.

He took his finger out from the trigger guard and rolled fast, praying the bear would race past him. He bumped Gabe, who was lying still—too still—on the ground, closer than he'd expected.

Then the bear veered toward him, and a gunshot rang out. He saw a flash of light from somewhere he knew none of his teammates had been positioned.

Kyle couldn't tell if the shot had been aimed at him or the bear, but it hit neither, and the bear veered again, this time away from him. It passed him so closely he felt the rush of air.

Then Kyle lifted his gun and fired, and the sound boomed even more loudly than he'd expected. It wasn't until new pain burst through him that he realized why. The rush of dampness in his arm got worse and he blinked as the world started to move. He thought he saw the second man drop as another gunshot rang out, although he couldn't be sure. He glanced over at his partner, but his vision wasn't right, and no matter how hard he stared, he couldn't tell if Gabe was moving.

He took a deep breath, and it felt as if the bear had sat down on his chest. He tried taking another, and then the world seemed to slip completely out from under him, and he couldn't feel anything, not even the burning pain in his arm.

19

"Any word from HRT?" Evelyn asked, trying to keep her knees from jiggling nervously under the desk.

She and Lucas were set up in a temporary space the park rangers had given them. The rest of the JTTF who'd flown in had gone back to the hotel, but she'd wanted to stick close. She couldn't really explain it, since news would probably come in by phone and not in person. But she'd asked to stay and Lucas had looked at her quizzically for a minute, then said he'd do the same.

Now he glanced at her from his own desk. "Have you seen me get a phone call?"

She frowned. "No, but…"

"It's the guy with the dimples, right?"

"Excuse me?" Heat rushed up Evelyn's neck. She knew he was talking about Kyle.

Lucas gave her a knowing grin. "The guy who was staring at you most of the meeting? You two have a thing?"

His grin widened, probably because she'd started fidgeting. Were they really that obvious?

"Never mind. I promise I'll tell you as soon as I hear something."

"Thanks."

"I don't have anything on the arrest, but I have something else. Check your email. We've had some news from the agents in Montana. Well, I guess it's mostly lack of news. They say they're pretty damn certain that none of those men inside the compound knew anything about the attacks. But we do have one interesting bit of information. Apparently, a week before Rolfe arrived, Butler was starting to get more and more verbose. Bragging about something big to come, about his growing power."

"He knew what was going to happen with the bombs," Evelyn said. "That's not news." Neither was the fact that the cultists had been in the dark, but she'd been hopeful they'd find someone—maybe a future recruit—who did. "So none of them suspected they were being groomed to be bombers?"

Lucas propped his elbows on his desk, rubbing red eyes and peering through the slats in the blinds at the slow drizzle outside. "I'm not sure they *were*. Being groomed, that is. I mean, I know that was the original plan, but listen to this. A few of them said something about Butler bragging about his *new room*."

Evelyn squinted at him. "So we're assuming the room with the tunnel *did* originally belong to Rolfe? And what does that have to do with the cultists being groomed as bombers?"

"I think Butler was having second thoughts about it all. I think he was getting high on his own power."

Evelyn nodded. Butler had grown more and more impressed with himself and his power during the siege. She'd seen it firsthand.

"I bet he started to wonder if he'd be better off forgetting Rolfe's plan and turning his compound into a genuine cult, with him as the leader."

"It fits," Evelyn admitted, remembering how Butler had threatened Rolfe, claiming that the cultists were loyal to *him*.

"So, the room," Lucas continued. "The few cultists who heard him talk about it didn't get why it was a big deal that he was taking this other guy's room. As far as they were concerned, it was Butler's place and Rolfe was just a guy with too many privileges. They'd never been in the part of the compound where Rolfe's and Butler's rooms were. They weren't allowed and it didn't seem to bother them. This was Butler's house. They were rent-free guests. Most of them thought he was an egomaniac, but he had the resources to provide all the security they needed for the coming...whatever."

"'Whatever' being?" Evelyn pressed. She hadn't gotten a clear sense of a united vision while she'd been there.

"Exactly what you said when we pulled you out of there," Lucas replied. "It's a mix. Some of them thought they were preparing for a Biblical Armageddon. Others expected a nuclear blast from some other country. A few thought it was going to be some kind of outbreak that would wipe out most of the country, and they'd need a place to hunker down and protect themselves and their supplies from the remaining, unprepared hordes. And yes, they actually said *hordes*. Anyway, they figured they'd be better off as a group, especially with Butler willing to foot the bills. Being a survivalist isn't cheap, at least not the way they were living. But for Butler, it didn't matter. He spent years building this place exactly how he wanted it, making sure it was far off the grid. He got his money legitimately, too. It doesn't look like he ever held down a job for long, but his parents invested well. They died a few years back and he inherited everything. He went from a survivalist and fringe militia member to a leader quickly after that. No clue what'll happen to it all now. Butler didn't believe in the legal system, so he didn't write up a will that we can find."

"Okay, so the room?" Evelyn asked. "Did he say *why* he was switching rooms?"

"No. They all seemed to think it had to do with this power he thought he was getting. A few of them said they'd gotten a little nervous about it. There were rumblings in the compound about people leaving, but no one did, not until Rolfe came, and then Peters and Durham left in that truck you saw the day you arrived."

Evelyn gritted her teeth. "The cultists finally admitted to knowing them?"

"Yeah. My agents tried a new tactic, which involved showing them pictures of the dead and injured from the blast sites, and suddenly the stonewalling stopped."

Evelyn slammed her fist into the desk, and pain shot up her arm. She glanced down at her hand, surprised. She hadn't intended to hit anything.

They should've used that tactic earlier. She should've *thought* of it earlier, and suggested the agents try it. As a profiler, that was her job. But it hadn't even occurred to her, and it should have. If the cultists really had nothing to do with the bombings, they would've been horrified. Survivalists who didn't know what they'd gotten into with Butler would protect their home against what they saw as an outside invasion, but they wouldn't go out and attack. They'd only defend what was theirs.

"It wouldn't have helped us a whole lot, anyway," Lucas said, although his voice lacked conviction. "The cultists knew the bombers only as John and Bobby. No last names. It was one of the compound rules, except when it came to Butler—probably part of his power trip."

"Or part of the plan to keep those who didn't pass muster in the dark about anyone who left the place."

"Maybe, at least originally. Anyway, even if we'd had descriptions, we wouldn't have had names. And considering how fast everything happened, I'm not sure descriptions would've gotten us far. But we did learn one interesting bit of information. Remember you said something about Jen—Martinez—saying the guy she'd recognized didn't fit? That he wasn't a survivalist?"

"Yeah." The memory rushed back, along with confusion. Obviously both Peters and Durham were survivalists. But she couldn't think of any reason for Jen to lie about that.

Why did nothing about Jen's situation hang together?

"The cultists agreed with her," Lucas interrupted her thoughts. "Not about Bobby. They said he was hardcore. But John? Every one of them made a comment about how he talked the talk, he had the shooting skills and knew how to live off the land, but they didn't think he was a true believer. They all seemed to think he was looking for friends more than he really had a prepper mind-set. That he liked the idea of survivalist skills for the wrong reasons, not as a way to keep himself safe, but as a way to hurt others."

Evelyn nodded slowly. "Okay. Well, that works. We know he was willing to bomb two buildings, so obviously he has no qualms about killing. If he was trying to join the group because he thought it was a way to win his brother's approval, then he wasn't in it because he wanted to be a survivalist. He was in it because he wanted his half brother's love."

"Yeah." Lucas rolled his shoulders. "Well, I don't know how much this helps us, but my agents said no one else had left the compound in almost a year, so that could be damn good news."

Evelyn nodded, surprised. "That *is* good news. But are they sure?"

"My agents don't think any of these guys are lying, not at this point. They aren't jumping up and down at the idea of helping federal agents obviously, but they know what kind of charges they're looking at after that firefight. None of them want to be implicated in the bombings. So, they're talking to us."

"Maybe the only one we need to worry about, besides Peters and Durham, is Rolfe," Evelyn concluded.

"I sure as hell hope so."

Something about her own conclusion felt wrong to her, but then again, she wasn't at her best and she knew it. There wasn't a single shred of evidence to suggest anyone else was involved. So maybe they'd gotten lucky, gotten involved just in time.

Or maybe that was why Jen had been part of it. Maybe Rolfe had *wanted* her there, wanted her to draw in the FBI. Rolfe had seen Butler's coming disobedience and decided to rid himself of the compound, and Butler, while providing a distraction from the bombings. Perhaps he'd planned to use the compound longer, but Butler's growing ego had prevented that.

She nodded to herself. The possibility of Jen being a traitor left a sour taste in her mouth. As much as she didn't like the idea, it did fit. They had to seriously consider it.

She told Lucas and he scowled at her.

"Hell, no! Besides, she started bitching about this group way before you're saying Butler developed his king mentality. And anyway, Jen would never…"

He cut himself off when his phone rang, and answered tersely, "Lucas here. What have you got?"

"Is it HRT?" Evelyn asked, leaning toward him across her desk. "Put them on speaker."

He scowled again, raising a hand to his other ear, but when she stood and started moving toward him, he put his phone on the desk and hit Speaker.

The instant high-pitched crackling almost made Evelyn cover her own ears. The reception was horrible, but she recognized the voice coming over the speaker. Kyle's team leader.

"We—ambush."

"What?" Lucas asked. "You're cutting out. We can't hear you."

"Extraction," the team leader said. "Medical. We have—dead. Need a helicopter." He listed some coordinates, but they came out too garbled.

Panic invaded Evelyn's chest. "Who?" she managed to choke out. "Who's dead?"

But the reception must have been bad on his end, because he continued. "And hurt—the helicopter…" Then he just repeated the coordinates until finally Lucas said, "I think I've got it," and ran out of the room to tell a park ranger.

"Who's dead?" Evelyn tried again. "Who is it?"

"Gabe," the HRT team leader said, "and Mac. And…"
Then the phone line went completely dead, too.

"Dead. Both dead."
The words rattled around in Kyle's brain as he tried to fight his way back to consciousness. His eyes didn't want to open, and the heavy weight on his chest made it hard to breathe.

"He's coming around," someone said, and Kyle felt a hand on his arm. "Take it easy. We're getting you out of here. Helicopter's on its way. We're moving you to a spot they can land."

If just breathing was this hard, he knew talking was going to be torture, but he had to find out. "Who's," he managed to rasp out, "dead?"

"None of ours," his teammate assured him, and Kyle realized he was being carried on some kind of make-shift backboard by two of his teammates.

But his partner wasn't one of them. "Gabe? Is he okay?"

A hand landed on his shoulder. "I'm fine," Gabe said, and Kyle turned his head, inch by painful inch.

Gabe was holding a compress against the back of his head, looking a little unsteady on his feet as he walked beside the backboard. He wasn't carrying any of his own gear, which meant he was hurt, too. But with only a six-man team, and two of them transporting him…

Kyle craned his head farther, trying to see who else was hurt, and spotted his team leader, with one arm looped around his partner's waist as he limped along.

He tried to figure out what else was wrong with this picture, and then he realized. "Peters and Durham?"

Every word made something damp and heavy rattle uncomfortably in his chest.

"Both dead," Gabe told him, his voice weak. "Neither of them's a threat anymore."

"What's wrong with…?"

"Save your voice," his team leader instructed, obviously anticipating his question. "Your partner rolled into a rock."

Kyle frowned, trying to make sense of that statement as he glanced down at his arm, hanging loosely off the board, blood soaked through the tourniquet someone had applied.

"When the gunshots started, I rolled away and hit my head," Gabe said ruefully. "Lost consciousness for a while, but it's probably not going to make anything worse. I already had a little brain damage," he joked, his grin looking way too forced.

If Kyle hadn't known Gabe was in bad shape, his expression would have cinched it. Instead of asking about his own condition—he knew his teammates would do everything they could to get him to a hospital alive—he tried to glance backward, wondering what had happened to the bear.

"The bear and her cubs took off," one of his teammates said. "They're fine."

"They're doing a lot better than Peters and Durham," Gabe added.

Kyle fought to pay attention, but moving his head had been a bad idea, and he could feel himself slipping back into darkness.

"They're not a threat anymore," Gabe continued as Kyle knew he was losing the battle.

"Yeah, but now we're out of leads for tracking down Rolfe," the team leader said.

The last thing Kyle heard before he lost consciousness again was his partner saying, "And for finding Jen."

20

"They want us back in Chicago," Lucas announced as he strode back into the hospital waiting room and sank onto the cracked plastic chair beside her. He'd left fifteen minutes earlier to take a call; the exhausted look on his face as soon as he'd seen the phone's readout had told her it was Fred Lanier calling.

Evelyn raised her head from between her hands and stared up at him incredulously. "I'm not leaving," she said, her words sounding throaty, as if she'd been crying.

She looked down at her lap again, even though she knew there was no reason to pretend. Lucas had followed her out of the park ranger station after that phone call. He'd seen her crying, thinking Kyle had died out in that damn forest.

It had been ninety long minutes before they'd gotten a follow-up, and she'd discovered it was the reception cutting out, that the HRT team leader had been telling her Gabe and Kyle were *injured*, that it was Peters and Durham who were dead.

It was a disaster for their case.

But all she could think of was Kyle, down the hall in

surgery. Still alive. So far. Gabe was having an MRI, to make sure everything was okay after he'd lost consciousness, and a third HRT agent Evelyn didn't know well was getting a broken leg casted.

But Kyle was in the worst shape. Gabe's explanation before they'd forced him to get in the MRI had been a jumbled mess of words involving a bear and an ambush. The doctors had been a little clearer. Kyle had been shot twice, once in the upper arm, and once in the space between his chest and shoulder. He'd lost a lot of blood, he had internal bleeding and they were going to "do everything they could."

It sounded ominous, and Evelyn wished she'd fought harder to keep HRT from going into that forest after Peters and Durham.

She leaned back against the painted concrete wall, her bun snagging on the uneven surface, and closed her eyes. An image of Kyle on the beach rose up in her mind. His blue eyes the color of the ocean. His feet bare in the sand, and his hand fitted to hers. His dimples showing as he grinned at her.

She knew the kinds of things he'd seen on the job, because she'd seen the same things. Some of them she still carried with her. He did, too. But somehow he managed to carry his load well. He'd made her laugh, even when she wasn't supposed to. He'd made her smile, even in the middle of a tough investigation. He'd made her think about a future that wasn't just about the job.

She'd spent the past month putting distance between them. Intentionally or not, she wasn't totally sure. But now she regretted every second she'd wasted.

Suddenly realizing that Lucas had been saying something, she opened her eyes. "What? Is there news?"

Lucas frowned at her. "No. I'm telling you that Fred is ordering us back to Chicago to rejoin the primary JTTF team. He wants us on a plane tonight."

"He thinks I'm just going to leave town when…"

"Does anyone know you're dating this guy?" Lucas interrupted. "Anyone besides me, that is?"

She shook her head silently.

"So, from their perspective, a fellow agent was hurt and you should want to go after who did it. There's nothing you can do here. They want you back on the case, working to catch whoever might be left in this plot."

"Going back to Chicago won't help me find Rolfe," Evelyn argued.

"Neither will sitting in a hospital waiting room. Trust me. I've been in your position—not knowing…" He trailed off, then finally said, "You'll feel better if you're out doing something on the case."

She opened her mouth to argue again, and shut it when her phone rang and the readout said, Dan Moore. Her boss at BAU was calling. She hadn't spoken to him since he'd cleared her to officially join the JTTF team.

She stared at it a minute, debated ignoring it, but she was already circling the drain as far as her boss was concerned. Holding in a curse, she pushed herself to her feet, strode out of the waiting room and answered.

"Evelyn, I heard about the mess in California," Dan said without preamble. "I'm sorry. I was told your friends were both injured."

"Uh, yes," Evelyn stuttered, surprised he'd even mentioned it. He wasn't ever intentionally cruel, but they'd never engaged in small talk, either. Besides, Kyle and Gabe had never been his favorite people, especially when they showed up at the BAU offices and distracted her and Greg.

Greg. Evelyn squeezed her eyes shut. She should've called him. He'd want to know about Gabe and Kyle—assuming Gabe hadn't asked one of his teammates to call his cousin. But knowing Gabe, he was probably waiting until he had the results of his MRI.

There was a pause, as though Dan was waiting for more details, but she was too busy wondering whether she should call Greg. And she couldn't bring herself to go into detail, anyway, not while they were still unsure as to whether Kyle was going to pull through.

"Anyway," Dan continued, "with the two suspects dead, it sounds like you've offered all the assistance you can to the task force."

Dan spoke again before she could disagree. "I just spoke to Fred Lanier. I know he wants you in Chicago, but unless you feel strongly that you can add something immediate to this investigation, we have other cases waiting. A lot of them. I want you back in Virginia. We need to talk about your job."

Evelyn stood shivering in her uncomfortable winter gear as snow fell all around her, obscuring her view and soaking her hair right through her hat. She'd come back to the compound as soon as her plane had landed in Montana, but as shades of pink and purple sank toward the skyline and the dark gray clouds dumped white on the world, she stood frozen. Both literally and figuratively.

She'd been back here since she'd been held hostage, but never by herself. Never with crime scene tape around the door, flapping in the wind, and no hint of

investigators or protesters. She'd never been afraid of
the dark, either, but as she stared at the massive, empty
building straight ahead, her boots seemed to get heavier,
stuck in the foot of snow.

As if Ward Butler was still inside, waiting for her.

She couldn't believe she'd convinced Dan to let her
return to Montana. Most of the JTTF team was in Chicago now, including Lucas. But apparently not all her
skills had deserted her, because she'd managed to make
a compelling enough case about her need to see Rolfe's
belongings. About her ability to do a different kind of
profiling—taking a known subject and predicting his
next move.

She supposed it helped that she'd accurately predicted the bombings from inside the compound. She
wished she felt as strongly as she'd argued that she
could track Rolfe down if she could just get a look at
the things he'd owned, the things he'd cared about and
kept close. Now that they knew Butler's room had originally been Rolfe's, that meant she was right about the
books marked *RS*. They *did* belong to Rolfe. She was
hoping they'd give her some insight, both into the man
himself and his long-term plans.

Not only had Dan gone for it, he'd agreed to break
the news to Fred Lanier. That was one pissing match
she was glad she didn't have to witness. Dan was her
ultimate boss, even when she was assigned elsewhere
for a case—and he was a damn good profiler himself.
Although she knew his decision would win out, Fred
Lanier wasn't exactly a lightweight.

Still, in some ways, she was only postponing the
inevitable by not returning home. Dan wanted to talk
about her position at BAU when she got back to Vir-

ginia, and she wasn't sure what she was going to say to him.

One problem at a time, Evelyn told herself, and started walking. The closer she got to the compound, the more she thought about the way she'd left it after being held hostage. She'd been in a daze, but with Kyle beside her, she'd felt safer than she had in more than a week.

He was going to be okay. She had to keep reminding herself of that, even after they'd finally let her go in and see him after his surgery. He'd been asleep then, and way too pale. Normally, whether he was joking around in her office, or getting ready to wade into a crowd of armed protesters, he looked strong and confident. Against the stark whiteness of that hospital bed, hooked up to various tubes and monitors, he'd seemed smaller, almost fragile.

The doctors had assured her—repeatedly—that he was going to live. She'd asked so many times that even Gabe had started looking at her sideways. And although she and Kyle had kept their relationship a secret from Gabe, she knew the two of them were close. She thought he'd suspected for some time. Now, he definitely knew something was going on.

He'd come into the hospital room a few minutes after her, telling her that his brain scan looked okay. That had saved her from having to make the decision about whether or not to call Greg for him. Which had also saved her from having to answer Greg's questions about how *she* was doing. She was grateful not to have to lie to him. Instead, she'd sat side by side with Gabe, mostly in silence, in Kyle's hospital room until morning. Until, finally, he'd opened his eyes, given her a tired smile and said, "Well, that didn't go as planned."

He'd been trying to make her laugh, to reassure her, but she'd still felt the residual worry. She'd carefully squeezed his hand while Gabe acted as if he hadn't noticed.

"I'm okay," Kyle had added. "Bears, bombers, bullets— they can only slow me down for so long."

She'd stared back at him quizzically, while Gabe gave her a brief rundown. Then Gabe had made some excuse about a phone call and left them alone.

Kyle had been fading from the medication again, but before he'd drifted back to sleep, she'd whispered, "Maybe we should just have stayed on that beach."

A few hours later, she'd forced herself to leave the hospital. She'd made the deal with Dan the night before, and she knew if she didn't fly to Montana soon, she'd be tempted not to leave at all.

Now, as she pushed open the compound door and it let out a high-pitched squeal, as though no one had touched it in years instead of less than a week, she wondered if she'd made the right choice. Rolfe had fooled her before. Would she be able to see through him now?

The only way to find out was to try.

She stepped inside, shivering. The place had been cold before, but now it was about the same temperature as outside. Without the big portable lights the FBI had brought in for ERT, the compound was dark and eerie, illuminated only by the thin beam from her flashlight.

It looked strange, empty, now. And not just because there were no people.

As she wandered through rooms that had once contained enough supplies to keep twenty people going through an entire winter, and enough weapons to arm them against any invading force, her footsteps echoed off the walls. It was all gone now, every bit of it cleared out and taken to an evidence warehouse where it could be cataloged and assessed.

The books weren't here anymore, either, but she'd be going to look at those later. First, she needed to look at the back bedroom with fresh eyes. Because the belongings weren't the only things that could give her clues. The room might, too.

As she walked through the main area and into the space where only Butler and Rolfe had been allowed, she couldn't help feeling tense. Even though the booby traps had all been cleared out, she glanced up at the place where a gun had once been rigged.

She could see the groove marks on the doorframe where the weapon had been wedged in, but the gun itself was gone. She kept going, forcing herself to move faster, ignoring the desire to turn around and run right back out the door. There was something ominous about this space, even with Butler gone and Rolfe in hiding. It was almost as though one of them was still in here, watching her.

"Ridiculous," she muttered, pushing open the door to Rolfe's bedroom first, the one where she'd been locked in the closet for days. True to their word, the ERT agents had torn up most of the floor, checking for a tunnel, but there wasn't one. The room was in the farthest corner, away from the doors. So was Butler's, on the opposite side. There was no obvious advantage to either location—without the tunnel.

Quickly crossing over to Butler's bedroom, she couldn't stop herself from staring at that tunnel. The board that had served as a door into the ground hung open, but in the darkness, it just looked like a big, yawning hole.

Could Jen have been down there the entire week?

The thought crept up on her. Evelyn hadn't seen Jen again after she'd been shot. Granted, her own ability to move around had been limited, but Jen definitely hadn't been in the main area. The other cultists believed her to be dead. And there'd been nowhere to hide. Especially not for someone with a serious gunshot wound.

Evelyn had also walked through the hallways in Butler and Rolfe's area, but the only place she'd never been until it was all over was Butler's room. So, if Jen hadn't left immediately after being shot, maybe she'd been here. Tied up in the main bedroom was possible, although that seemed unlikely, given Butler's antagonistic personality.

But if she'd been down in the tunnel, had it been as a hostage? Maybe she'd been tied up, so injured that she was unable to walk through the tunnel to the other side. Or maybe they'd dropped her down there, thinking she was going to bleed out, but instead she'd found her own way out. If she had, she'd never shown up at a hospital, a police station or an FBI office. Which meant, if she'd made it out without being under duress, she'd intentionally stayed away.

It was hard to imagine Jen as a traitor. But it was also hard to imagine a scenario in which she'd lived long enough to walk out of that tunnel and *not* been in cahoots with Butler or Rolfe.

Evelyn remembered the surprise on Jen's face when Butler had said her full name back on the day they'd shown up unannounced at the compound. Could Jen have been working just with Rolfe—and then he'd brought Butler in without her knowledge?

She sank to the ground in front of the tunnel leading out of the compound, shining her flashlight down into the claustrophobic space. Everything about Jen was confusing. She couldn't reconcile Butler shooting the agent, then keeping her alive in—or under—his room for a whole week. Unless maybe he'd thought she was his insurance, the way Rolfe seemed to think Evelyn was his?

Evelyn nodded to herself, standing. That felt right.

The problem was, Butler hadn't acted as if he needed *any* insurance against the FBI. So, maybe Butler was using Jen as insurance against *Rolfe*, the man whose room he'd stolen. But that only made sense if Jen had been working with Rolfe all along.

21

Evelyn sat cross-legged on the hard warehouse floor, surrounded by books. The FBI used this warehouse to store evidence, so another agent had already cataloged everything, and someone had looked through them once. They knew there was nothing obvious, no notes scribbled in margins about attack plans. But she was looking for something more subtle—the mental makeup of a terrorist.

If she had that—in theory—she wouldn't *need* plans of attack written on a napkin and hidden in a book. If she had that—in theory—she'd be able to *think* like Rolfe. She'd be able to figure out if there was going to be another attack, and if so, where it would happen.

JTTF was feeling pretty confident that they'd shut down the tactical side of the cell. The bombers were dead, the cultists said no one else had left the compound within the past few months—besides Rolfe, who came and went—so the prevailing theory was that the attacks were over. Yes, Rolfe was still a threat, but if he was recruiting bombers, would he actually become one himself? Or did he prefer to have others do the dirty work?

JTTF had asked her that question, and even without

developing a full profile on Rolfe, she'd known the answer immediately. He wasn't going to bomb anything himself. Not unless he truly felt he was at his endgame. And since they didn't even have his last name, she doubted he felt that cornered.

They'd released a sketch based on Evelyn's description. The hope was that either someone who knew him would recognize him, giving the task force a name, or someone would see the sketch and remember seeing him somewhere, giving them a location. They weren't going to quit until they found him, something they all knew could take a while. With his survivalist skills, there was a good chance he was doing exactly what Peters and Durham had done—hiding somewhere remote. But the level of tension had ratcheted down with Durham and Peters dead.

Evelyn wasn't so sure she agreed that the tactical element was really gone. The compound had been in place for several years. Her biggest worry was that Rolfe had recruited others even earlier than Peters and Durham, men who were waiting for their signal. The cultists who'd survived the raid had all been newer members, men who'd lived in the compound between three and nine months. Lucas had argued that more than nine months was a long time to wait, especially if Peters and Durham had immediately gone out and set bombs. He was right.

But Evelyn's profiler instincts were on alert. There were too many unanswered questions. Who was Rolfe? Where was Jen? Why had they targeted the ATF buildings? If Rolfe was out there somewhere, why hadn't he taken credit in some way, put out some kind of message about the attacks?

To her, it all screamed that there were more to come.

She looked around her at Rolfe's belongings and sighed. She was alone in the huge warehouse, but she hadn't wanted to lug all the books over to the Salt Lake City field office. She'd already gone through the entire stack from Butler's room once, searching for the initials *RS* in case anything in the stack had actually belonged to Butler. But the initials were inside every single book. Too bad Rolfe hadn't written his full name in there.

There were a lot of books, too. Four teetering piles, stacked around her in a circle so high she'd have to stand up to see over them.

Everything else that had been taken out of Butler's room had obviously belonged to Butler—the Bible she'd seen before, a huge case of weapons and extra supplies for one man to carry on his back in the Montana wilderness if he had to make a quick getaway.

Butler might have kept the books in his room because it was too much trouble to move them into the other bedroom. Or maybe as more of a power play, a way to show Rolfe that anything and everyone in the compound was under his control.

Rolfe hadn't tried to get them back. Which meant either he didn't care enough, or more likely he didn't plan to be there long enough for it to matter. Or maybe just because he *wanted* Butler high on his own power, hoping he'd incite something. Perhaps Rolfe had already decided that when the FBI came into the compound, as they inevitably would, he was going to get rid of Butler before he snuck out through the tunnel.

The thought shook her. She'd seen Butler yield to Rolfe's "suggestions," but she'd also seen him flaunt his power, his control of the men inside the compound. She was still convinced that Rolfe was the real puppet master. He'd known just how to play Butler, and he'd known just how to play her. A man like that wasn't going to give up because his two bombers were dead. A man like that was a long-term, strategic thinker.

Now, she needed to get inside his manipulative, evil mind and figure out what he'd planned next.

She glanced up and down the stacks of books, looking for one that seemed to be a favorite. Judging by the wrinkled, smudged and marked-up pages, a lot of the books were well-loved. It was time to find out why.

She reached for a psychology book first, a big, hardback textbook, something she'd read in her graduate studies in psychology. Not exactly pleasure reading, and not for the casual reader with no background in the subject.

But when she flipped it open, she discovered that not only had someone—presumably Rolfe—read it, he'd gone through and highlighted passages. Text on the theories behind thought control, and the mind-set of people who knowingly took on a mission deemed suicidal.

He'd been preparing to manipulate Butler's followers; that much was obvious. She'd known he was manipulative, and that he was relatively well-spoken and intelligent. But his reading material suggested either that he was *extremely* intelligent and self-motivated, or that he'd studied at a university at a high level. Or both.

It might be a way to track him.

She turned the book over, checking the back cover, hoping… Her breath caught as she spotted exactly what she wanted to find. A very worn sticker, showing where the book had been purchased.

She held the book up, squinting at it under the fluorescent lighting. The sticker had faded to almost nothing, but that was definitely the word *University*. She couldn't make out the rest of it, so she wasn't surprised it had been missed by whoever had logged the books.

Setting it down, she grabbed another book, this one on theoretical physics. The same sticker, and this one she could just make out.

She gaped at it, shocked. Rolfe—a presumed terrorist—had gone to one of the country's top universities. That meant he was even smarter than she'd realized, that he'd be damn hard to catch.

But she couldn't help smiling. Because it also meant she could track him. Rolfe wasn't a common name, and the university would have records.

She stood, careful not to tip any of the book piles, then raced out of the warehouse.

She was about to get a last name for Rolfe; she could feel it. This could change everything.

"Rolfe Shephard."

"What?" Lucas asked over some kind of commotion going on in the background.

"His name is Rolfe Shephard," Evelyn repeated.

"Seriously?" Lucas sounded impressed. "How the hell'd you get his last name? You've been back in Montana, what? A few hours? Jeez, we should've put you in charge of finding Jen."

"Jen?" Evelyn suddenly flashed back to her conversation with Jen's husband and his interest when she'd mentioned Rolfe's name—but his interest had fled once she'd said Rolfe had been at the compound. "You said she followed you around, outside the office, trying to convince you about this compound being dangerous, right?"

"Yeah, but what does that have to do with…?" He sighed. "Get back to Rolfe. How'd you find his name?"

"I tracked him down to his university, from the books we found in Butler's room. He finished graduate school—with a double major in psychology and mathematics—more than a decade ago. They threw privacy laws at me, but when I brought up the bombings, I got them to go through their records. He was the only *Rolfe* they'd had in the past twenty years. They faxed me a picture. It's definitely him."

"Okay," Lucas said slowly. "Psych and math? That's an interesting combination. On the math side, you think he could build bombs, too?"

"Probably. This guy was really, really intelligent. He graduated at the top of his class, but then never showed up for his graduation. I just got off the phone with the university, but I'm going to start looking into his background, see if it'll give me any idea where he might be now. Maybe I'll find a place where his path might have crossed Jen's," she added.

"You won't," Lucas said. "Don't waste time on that. How often do we have to debate this? She wouldn't beg us to investigate if she was involved."

"Not unless that was part of Rolfe's plan to get rid of Butler and create a press incident," Evelyn argued.

"Why is everyone so convinced she's a traitor?" Lucas snapped.

"Why are you so quick to defend her?" Evelyn asked quietly. As much as Evelyn hated to believe it herself— she'd liked Jen—it was the most logical explanation for how she'd gotten out of that compound alive. "I thought you said you weren't friends."

"We weren't. Not really. But that doesn't make her wrong."

"Is this guilt over ignoring her gut on this case or guilt over something else?" Evelyn asked, remembering Lucas's comment in the hospital waiting room that he knew what it was like to wonder if someone he cared about was going to make it. Could he have been talking about Jen? Could it have been more than just concern for a fellow agent?

"What exactly are you implying?" he demanded, his voice low and angry.

"Is it true, or did Jen's husband just suspect you were having an affair with her?" Evelyn asked as all the little things that had bothered her about her conversation with Jen's husband snapped into place. He'd lost interest in Rolfe when she said he was connected to the compound, because Jen's husband was looking for information about her affair. Maybe he'd even suspected she'd had more than one.

"How dare…?"

"He followed her," Evelyn said abruptly. It was logical—and it could even explain how he knew what she looked like, since the news channels *hadn't* gotten her name when she'd showed up in their shots at the bomb site in San Francisco. Fred Lanier had told her as much. Jen's husband had probably seen her meeting with Jen that day in the prison parking lot.

"I'm sure he followed his wife, who was—as you mentioned—following *you* all around town. He thought you two were having an affair." She tapped her fingers absently on the desk in the Salt Lake City field office's spare cubicle, wondering if the husband could've been involved with Jen's disappearance.

If Butler or Rolfe had shoved Jen down in that tunnel to get her out of the way, thinking she was going to bleed out, and she'd somehow managed to escape, get to her husband, maybe *he'd* made her disappear? She frowned. With the kind of injury Jen had, even if she'd taken the vehicle that had obviously been parked right outside the tunnel exit, that would've been a long way to drive.

Still… "Were you having an affair?" she asked Lucas again.

Lucas sighed. "It's irrelevant," he said softly, and she could tell by the sudden quiet that he'd left whatever conference room he'd been in.

"You've got to be kidding me! She's missing, and you're lying about a relationship with her?"

"Kind of throwing stones there, aren't you?" Lucas asked.

"Mac isn't missing," she replied, a lump in her throat every time she thought about Kyle. Even though he was okay, she kept remembering that moment when she'd believed he was gone.

She forced the memory aside and demanded, "So, Jen's offshore account. Did you know about it?"

"No! Not until it came out in the investigation. Why the hell would I have known about that? Are you accusing me of being a traitor now, too?"

Was she? "No. I'm asking why you lied to me."

"Oh, come on, Evelyn. It's none of your damn business."

"You told me she approached you about the compound, that she was so insistent she followed you around town, asking you to investigate."

"Yeah, so what? That's true."

"And then, what? It turned into a relationship?"

"It was an affair," he said angrily. "We're both married, in case you hadn't noticed. We both have kids. It was a mistake, and by the time all of this went down, it was over. It had *been* over, for months."

"Was it? Whose decision was it to end things?"

There was a brief pause, then Lucas said, "Mine."

"It wasn't mutual?"

"She didn't want to end it. She talked about leaving her husband, about me leaving my wife. That was…that was never going to happen. She got aggressive about it, started following me around again, this time about getting back together."

"Not about the compound?"

"No. But I'm not making that up. That's how it started. But after…she was still obsessed with the Butler Compound. Her boss had to keep warning her to stay away from the place. But she finally stopped coming to me about it."

"Did she threaten to go to your wife?"

"No. She wasn't like that."

Evelyn fell silent. Jen's affair with Lucas might explain her moving money. Maybe it wasn't a payoff, but an attempt to hide assets because she was planning to divorce her husband. And it sounded as if her husband had suspected.

If she'd made it down that tunnel, she probably couldn't have gotten all the way home without someone seeing her, or without losing so much blood that she'd be incapable of driving all that distance. But Lucas had only been up the hill, at TOC. It wasn't outside the realm of possibility that she could have run into *him* along the way.

It was possible, but she didn't think it was likely. There'd been a lot of FBI and police on the scene.

But what if she *had* run into him, as unlikely as it seemed? If he was trying to hide an affair gone sour, *he* had motive to make her disappear, too. And as an FBI agent, he had the know-how.

She honestly doubted he would ever have used it like that. But their affair definitely added a complication she hadn't expected.

It might mean nothing. Or it might explain the money, the disappearance or both.

"You need to inform the task force."

"Bullshit," Lucas said. "It's not relevant."

"Maybe it is," she argued. "It could be relevant in ways you never realized. What if Jen's offshore money had nothing to do with a payoff?"

"It didn't!" he exploded. Then he said, more quietly, "Shit."

"Just tell Fred, okay?"

"You know what this could do to my career? To my marriage? To *Jen's* marriage?"

"It might help us find her."

He let out a sigh that sounded like half frustration, half acceptance. "Fine. I'll tell him. Just let me handle it, okay? And give me anything else you've got on Rolfe."

"That's it so far."

"We'll get the name released to the public, along with the picture. Someone must've known him. You keep looking. We'll do the same. Call me if you find anything."

He hung up before she could press about Jen. She hoped he told Fred—so she wouldn't have to do it.

Greg was calling her.

Evelyn stared at the readout on her phone, unmoving. Greg wasn't involved with the JTTF. He hadn't been involved in the case since the standoff with Butler had ended. So he must be calling her about BAU. Maybe to do with her job, or her state of mind. Neither of which she was ready to talk about.

Still, it was Greg. Her closest friend in BAU. Her mentor. She couldn't ignore him.

She took a fortifying breath and picked up. "Greg, hi." She tried to sound upbeat but busy, rattling papers on her desk. It wasn't completely a lie; she *was* busy. The sooner they could track down Rolfe, the sooner this would all be over. "What's going on?"

"I heard from Gabe."

She dropped the papers, gripping the phone tighter. "What happened?" Before she'd left for her plane, she'd talked quietly with Gabe in the hallway of the hospital, asked him to call later and update her.

"Mac is fine, Evelyn. Gabe lost his phone, lost your number. He's actually on his way back here now, but he wanted me to let you know. Kyle's still in California. Sounds like he'll be good to fly in a few days."

"He's okay?" she asked, needing to hear it again.

"He's doing great, Gabe says. Anxious to get out of the hospital. They want to keep him a little longer for observation, but he's going to be fine. Off work for a while, but I'm sure he'll be back at Quantico the second he lands."

She'd been so busy worrying about whether or not

he'd be okay that it hadn't occurred to her what this could do to his job. An injury like that was going to put him out of HRT for months. And HRT was the most physically difficult unit in the entire Bureau. Would he even be able to go back once he'd healed? And if he was physically ready, would there still be a spot for him? Or would this case end his HRT career?

Here she'd been agonizing over whether or not she still wanted her job anymore, and Kyle might not have a choice. He loved HRT. It was part of who he was. He'd told her he planned to remain in the unit his entire FBI career, if he could. What would he do without it?

"You still there, Evelyn?" Greg asked.

"Yeah, yes," she stuttered.

"Good, because you need to call your grandma. She called the BAU office today, looking for you."

That was strange. Her grandma had never called BAU before. She had Evelyn's work number, of course, and so did the staff at the nursing home. But none of them had ever used it. They always called her cell phone.

"Did you talk to her?"

"Yeah, I picked up your line."

"Did she sound okay?"

"She sounded fine, Evelyn. Just worried about you. She said you haven't called her in weeks, and you usually *visit* a few times a week. She hadn't even known you were out of town."

Because when she'd left for Montana, she'd expected to be home the same day. Still, she'd tried to call her grandma and missed her every time. She should've tried again today. There was censure in Greg's voice, and she deserved it.

"I'll call her now."

"Good. Evelyn, is everything okay with you? I know…"

"I'm okay," she said. "Can we talk about it when I get home? I've actually got a big lead and I need to get back to it."

Greg knew when she was making excuses. She could hear it in his voice when he finally agreed. "Okay. But call your grandma first."

"I will," she promised. As soon as she hung up, that was what she did.

She tapped her fingers on the desk, faster and faster, as she waited for someone to pick up at the nurse's station. She could call her grandma directly, but she usually called them first, to find out how her grandma was doing that day. So she could prepare herself. Because, some days, Mabel Baine was sharp as ever. Other days, when the dementia had her in its grasp, she talked to Evelyn as though she was still twelve years old, and they were back in that big house in South Carolina where she'd grown up.

Today, the nurse at the front desk said, "Evelyn, your grandma's sleeping. But I'll tell her you called."

"Okay, thanks." Evelyn felt guilty that her timing was so bad, and even guiltier at how relieved she was not to have to talk to her grandma right now. Because her grandma would sense Evelyn was struggling. And she'd ask about it, meaning that Evelyn would have to give her some version of what had been going on.

She had to figure out what she wanted to do with her life, and she needed to stop feeling she was doing something wrong if the answer no longer included the FBI.

22

"Who are you, Rolfe Shephard?" Evelyn muttered as she sat in her borrowed cubicle in the Salt Lake City office.

It was the first step in answering an even more important question—*where* was Rolfe Shephard?

"Talking to yourself now?" a voice taunted from behind her.

Evelyn spun her chair around, recognizing that voice. "Lucas," she said, surprised. "What are you doing back here?"

"Oh, don't you know?" he asked, resentment in his tone. "I'm off the task force. I'm back here to work on *other* cases. Never mind that I head up the counter-terror squad, because there's a good chance I won't be doing that much longer, either. There's an OPR investigation pending."

"I'm sorry," Evelyn said. She *was* sorry he'd been kicked off the JTTF. He was a solid investigator, and she didn't want to put a dent in his career.

Still, she couldn't bring herself to regret asking him to report his affair with Jen. It could affect the investigation, and they both knew it. But she also recognized the irony. She was secretly dating another agent, too, and she hadn't reported it the way she should have.

"Yeah." Lucas raked a hand through his hair, suddenly looking more exhausted than annoyed. "Well, you may not believe this, but I knew nothing about the money. And the affair really has been over for a long time. Now, if I get suspended, my wife is sure as hell going to want to know why."

Evelyn stayed silent. What was there to say? That his wife deserved to know?

Lucas started to walk past, then he stopped and added, his voice strained, "Things may have ended between us, but I still care about her. I still want her to be found. I'm still praying that by some miracle she's alive. Just let me know if you find Jen, okay?"

She nodded. "Okay."

Lucas continued walking, head down, through the office. It was only 8:00 a.m., but she realized that the typical office noise had silenced at his arrival. Either news had gotten out about him and Jen, or everyone was wondering why he was back when the case clearly hadn't been closed.

There wasn't much she could do about it either way. She turned back to her laptop, and back to her search into Rolfe Shephard's life.

Three hours later, she leaned back in her chair, frustrated and confused. After Rolfe had graduated, he'd gone on to take prestigious positions at several top universities. But each job had lasted only a few years, and then eventually he'd dropped off the map entirely.

As far as she could tell, he'd had no questionable contacts during his time as a faculty member. No connections to any militia groups, fringe or otherwise. But the computer could only tell her so much. She picked up her phone and dialed a colleague of Rolfe's from his last faculty position.

That led her to the man who'd been the head of Rolfe's department more than a decade ago. After introducing herself and explaining the reason for her call, she asked hopefully, "Do you remember him?"

"Remember him?" Professor Lee snorted. "Hell, yes, I remember him. Probably one of the most brilliant mathematicians I ever met. Charming as hell, too, if he felt like it, which wasn't all that often—at least, not with other faculty. The story was different with his students. There were a lot of rumors about him and his female graduate students."

"Any complaints about him?" Evelyn asked when the professor paused.

"Sexual harassment type? Nah. Nothing like that. The women were attracted to his whole withdrawn-genius act. He'd give them that smile of his and they'd be all over him. At least, that's what the rumor mill said. But he was remote, removed, like he was above everyone around him. It drew people in initially, because of his intelligence, especially in an academic environment, and trust me, he knew how to manipulate. Eventually, though, the other faculty members started to resent him. Between his fake charm and his skills, there was jealousy, too. Still, we fought to keep him here—offered him tenure faster than anyone I've known, because there were so many universities that wanted to poach him. Then, one day, he just left. Boom. No notice or anything."

"Did you hear from him again? Do you have any idea where he went afterward?"

"Nope. Not a clue. We looked for him, both to try and get him back, and to give him his final paycheck if he refused. Never found him. Honestly, until you called today, I thought maybe something terrible had happened to him."

"Did the police look into it?"

"Oh, sure. We filed a report. But they said his place was cleared out, and apparently he'd given notice to his landlord, so that was the end of it. I protested a bit, asked them to keep digging, but they said it wasn't against the law to leave a job."

That was bizarre. He'd given notice to his landlord, but not his employer? "And as far as you knew, nothing had happened in his life to make him take off like that?"

"As far as I knew, everything was fine."

"Do you know if he had any sort of grudge against ATF?" The university was in California, so maybe he'd had a direct connection with that ATF office, after all. As soon as she'd uncovered Rolfe's full name, Fred had contacted the San Francisco ATF and asked them to run it, just in case. They hadn't gotten a hit, but that didn't mean he didn't hold a grudge.

"It wouldn't surprise me," the professor replied. "He always seemed pretty standard for what he was—you know, the stereotype of a genius professor. Remote, a little egotistical. But God forbid you get into a discussion about history with him. I made that mistake one day and discovered he *hated* the government. Don't ask me why, because I couldn't tell you. The first time he went on a rant about it, I vowed never to get into the topic with him again."

Evelyn digested that, turning to the main detail she

hadn't known but had started to suspect. "He was a genius?"

"To my mind, absolutely. His mom was MENSA, you know. And he must have been close himself."

"Really?" Evelyn sat up straighter, jotting notes as fast as she could. "Do you know her name? Or where I could find her?"

"I'm pretty sure she died quite a while ago."

Warning bells instantly went off in Evelyn's head. "What happened to her? When did she die?"

"No idea. I asked him about family, and Rolfe told me both his parents were dead. The only reason I know about his mom being MENSA is that he mentioned it in passing one day." The professor's tone was pensive. "Said it like it was a bad thing actually. I got the impression he and his mom didn't get along."

"Do you know why?"

"I wish I could tell you more, but like I said, he was a private guy. He could be charming if he wanted to, especially around women, but you never got any substantial details about him." He paused. "You're really telling me Rolfe's the person in that sketch the FBI released? That he's connected to those horrible bombings?"

"I am," Evelyn replied carefully. "Why? Does the sketch we released not resemble how you remember him? Or are you just surprised he's connected?"

"Well, no, he doesn't look the way I remember him," the professor said quickly. "Or obviously I would've called. Back then, he was heavier, and he didn't have all that curly hair, but almost a buzz cut. As for being surprised?" There was a heavy sigh. "Can't say I am. As much as we wanted him at this university for his academic potential, there was always something…off about him. You didn't really notice it at first. It kind of crept up on you slowly. A sense of menace underneath, I guess. Like he was a time bomb."

The professor drew in a sharp breath. "Sorry. Bad choice of words. But you know what I mean."

"I understand." She'd seen that menace up close and personal, and she'd seen the charm, too, something in the swagger that first time he'd appeared outside the compound that had made him seem more like a typical cult leader than Butler.

"I'm very sorry I can't help you locate him," the professor said. "But I'm happy to answer whatever I can. I just don't know much more."

"That's okay," Evelyn said, thanking him for his time. As she hung up, his words about Rolfe's parents rang in her mind. Both parents dead, and it sounded like he resented at least his mom. Could one or both of them have worked for the government? Could they be the source of his resentment? If so, could they lead her to Rolfe's next target—or his hideaway?

She dropped her notepad and started hunting for any reference to Rolfe's parents. Two hours later, just when she was rubbing weary eyes and thinking about trying a different route, Lucas came running across the office toward her.

He skidded to a stop next to her desk, and dropped a stack of photographs on her desk. They spilled in a messy pile, but Evelyn gaped at the top picture, then stared back at him.

It was a shot of her and Jen, taken in the Montana State Prison parking lot the day she'd arrived.

"What the hell is this?"

"Oh, it gets better," Lucas said, leaning over her and

lifting up the pictures, one by one. He held up the photo of her and Jen first. "Jen's husband hired a PI. He was following her."

"*That's* how he knew I was in San Francisco."

"Yeah," Lucas agreed.

Evelyn turned her chair to face him. "I thought you were off this case? Where did you get these?"

"Would you drop it if Kyle was missing?"

"I thought you and Jen were over?"

"Doesn't matter," he said. "I still want her found, and I refuse to sit by and do nothing while she's missing."

"So you went and talked to her *husband*? Do you really think that was a good idea?"

"He found *me*," Lucas said. "I went to lunch, my usual spot, and he approached me. Demanded to know... well, anyway, he admitted he'd hired a PI. Practically threw the photos at me. But you need to look at these." Lucas flipped to another image, one of him and Jen, and quickly moved past it.

Before he did, Evelyn caught a glimpse of the two of them at a gym. Lucas was in workout clothes, on the treadmill. Jen was in a suit, hands on hips. She seemed to be confronting Lucas.

The picture did suggest she was angry he'd ended things. But pictures could be deceiving. Were there other, more compromising images Lucas had pulled out of the stack?

Before she could ask, he continued to the next picture, another shot of him and Jen. In this one, they looked more friendly, holding take-out coffee cups and walking down the street together, deep in conversation. They could've been working, discussing a case. But that wasn't what captured Evelyn's attention.

She turned back to Lucas.

"Yep." He tapped the image triumphantly. "You're not seeing things. That's Rolfe Shephard in the background, and it's pretty damn clear that he's watching Jen."

"Tell me about this picture."

Evelyn stood in the office of Bruno Taglioni, private investigator, after she'd dropped a photograph of Jen and Lucas on his desk. It had taken her about five minutes to talk Jen's husband into giving her the name of his PI, and half an hour to drive to Bruno's office to confront him in person.

He glanced up at her, an expression of boredom on his heavily lined face. He couldn't have been more than fifty, but he looked a decade older, and the scabs on his knuckles suggested he'd lived hard, and still did.

"I'm with the FBI," she told him.

"I know," he said, going back to whatever he'd been typing when she walked into his office.

She reached over and pushed down the lid of his laptop so it almost smashed his fingers. "I'm not messing around here. I need answers."

He pulled his hands free and tipped his head back, looking undaunted. "This really how you want to get my cooperation, Ms. Baine?"

Her muscles tensed with frustration. If he knew her name, he probably knew what case she was investigating. "This really how you want to assist with a terrorism investigation?" she shot back.

"Fine, fine," he said. When he stood up, she realized that, although he was about double her width, he was only a few inches taller. "No need to get your panties in a twist."

She clamped her lips together, willing herself to keep quiet as he picked up the photo, then dropped it back on the table.

"I was hired by Mr. Martinez to follow his wife. He suspected an affair, possibly even more than one. I followed Mrs. Martinez around for a few weeks, took a bunch of pictures. Reported back to Mr. Martinez around mid-November. Right after I saw her meet up with you actually. Those were the final pictures I took."

"And what did you report?"

"My professional opinion is that she'd had an affair with this other agent, Lucas Halstrom, in the past. There was just a certain familiarity there." He shrugged. "But from everything I saw, there was nothing going on while I was following her. And I didn't see evidence of anyone else, but I think Mr. Martinez had gotten a little paranoid about it."

"Okay." That was good at least. Although she didn't really suspect Lucas of being involved in Jen's disappearance, at least this put to rest her lingering doubts that he'd been lying about the end of the affair.

She lifted up the picture again, pointing at the background, where people were walking by. Tapping Rolfe, who was partially hidden by a lamppost and held a camera in one hand, she asked, "Tell me about this guy."

Bruno took the picture, held it close to his face, then shook his head. "Don't know that guy."

"He doesn't look familiar? Maybe you saw him other times when you were surveilling Jen?"

"Nope."

Evelyn held in a sigh. "Do you have more pictures? Anything you didn't hand over to Mr. Martinez?"

"Oh, sure. A ton. I only gave him the highlights."

When he just stood there, she unclenched her teeth and asked, "Can I have them?"

He shrugged. "I guess so." He dug around in his desk drawer until he came up with a flash drive, which he put in her hand. "Good luck." Then he sat down, opened his laptop and went back to typing.

With a curt thank-you, Evelyn pushed the door open. Snowflakes flew into her face as she hurried to her car, head down. Once she was back in her rental, she flipped the heat on high, booted up her laptop and stuck in the flash drive.

She went through fifty or so pictures, beginning to wonder if it was a coincidence. If maybe Rolfe had passed through Salt Lake City on his way to the Butler Compound and happened to be in the same area as Jen.

She sure hadn't seemed to recognize him that day at the compound. If they'd been working together, it would be logical for her to fake it. But if he'd been following her for some reason, as a longtime veteran of the FBI she might have spotted him.

Then she went to a new picture, this one of Jen alone, going for a run through town, and there he was again, this time in a parked vehicle. A big black truck.

"Holy shit," Evelyn breathed. Rolfe Shephard had been trailing Jen before she'd ended up as a hostage at the compound. But why?

And did that make it more or less likely that Jen was involved in the terror plot? More or less likely that she was still alive? Or that she'd been dead since the day they were taken hostage?

* * *

"Why don't we have anything on this son of a bitch?" Fred demanded.

Evelyn held the phone away from her ear and cringed at his tone. "We do," she said calmly. "I told you about the professor…"

"Yeah, and that's all great, but I want something that'll tell us where he is, not what we already know—that he's an asshole."

It told them more than that, but Evelyn didn't get into it, because in the three days since she'd talked to the professor at the California university where Rolfe had last worked, she'd finally managed to get a lead on his mother. "We also learned his mom was MENSA, which is how I tracked her down," Evelyn told him.

"You did? Where is she?" Fred's anxiety seemed to vibrate from the phone.

"Well, she's been dead for a long time, but…"

"Did he kill her?"

"No. She died from congenital heart failure. But I figured out why we had so much trouble tracking down where he's lived. His dad was some kind of hard-core survivalist."

"What was his name?"

"I don't know yet," Evelyn said, frustrated by Fred's constant interruptions as much as by the fact that she didn't have an answer. "He lived completely off the grid, from what I can tell. Which is why I couldn't get a place of birth for Rolfe. It looks like he was born at home somewhere. He doesn't pop up in the system until he's about nine, just him and his mom."

"Where did they live? Anywhere he might go now?"

"Well, they lived in Chicago."

"Any connection to the ATF office there?"

"Not that I can find so far." Even though, as a profiler, running leads like this wasn't her typical role, she'd been assigned to figure out what made Rolfe tick. And that meant learning everything she could about him.

Meanwhile, in Chicago, Fred and his team were learning everything *they* could about Bobby Durham and John Peters, trying to connect them to any other possible bombers, or to Rolfe. They'd spoken with Lee Cartwright's mother repeatedly, until she'd hired a lawyer and started shouting harassment. Evelyn knew they'd also have to deal with the consequences of the shootout in California, and the two men's deaths.

The same antifederalist element who'd shown up to support Butler was crying foul over their deaths, claiming a cover-up. Luckily, unlike in Montana, there wasn't a whole lot of sympathy for the bombers, so it wasn't getting much momentum.

Still, Evelyn knew that all the men in HRT who'd been part of the takedown were under intense questioning, Kyle included. He'd flown back to Virginia yesterday, and she'd talked to him only briefly before he'd gotten on the plane. They'd barely had time to do more than ask if the other was okay. Both she and Kyle had said yes. And she was sure Kyle knew she was lying as much as she knew he was.

She held back a sigh. She missed him, missed the easy conversation, the comfortable chemistry they'd had on the beach. She wished she could rewind the past month and a half and return to that beach, before she'd gone back to work or come to Montana.

"Evelyn," Fred was saying.

"Sorry. What?"

"I said, what else do you have?"

"Right now, that's all. I'm…"

"Because there were six days between the Chicago bombing and the San Francisco attack."

"I know."

"And now we're about to hit eight days from San Francisco. I don't want to push my luck, but we're not seeing any signs that more are coming. We've had a whole team digging into anyone who was at the Butler Compound over the past year and left, and we've tracked down every single person whose name showed up on that list. From what we can tell, they're all clear. I don't think there are more bombers, Evelyn. I think we're just looking for Rolfe."

"It's possible…"

"And you pegged him as leadership, right? Not a bomber?"

"Yes, but that doesn't mean he won't stage an attack himself if he feels cornered."

"Does he? Feel cornered?" Fred asked. "Because I have to tell you, with his skills, this guy could disappear for years. We've got other threats. We've put Rolfe Shephard on the Most Wanted list, but if we're not looking at another imminent attack, I can't justify the sheer size of this task force for much longer. I've got other chatter I have to investigate."

"You have to be kidding me," Evelyn burst out.

"I'm not saying we're closing the case. There'll be a team on this for a long time to come. But there's a difference between a manhunt for potential bombers, and a manhunt for a wanted fugitive whose next move will be to hide in the woods for six years."

"I want to stay on Rolfe," Evelyn said.

"That's not really up to me."

It was up to Dan Moore. And Evelyn knew what the answer would be.

She'd be returning to Virginia.

23

Evelyn sat in her car, back in Virginia, in the BAU's silent parking lot, unmoving. The workday had started a few hours ago, but she hadn't gone in yet.

She was still on the case, but as Dan had said, "You don't need to be in Montana to dig into Rolfe Shephard's life. And we have other investigations waiting for profiles, too. We can't spare you full-time anymore."

Then he'd added, almost as an afterthought, "When you get back in, let's sit down and have a discussion about your role here at BAU."

He'd said it in an offhand way, as though they weren't talking about her entire future. She'd mumbled something affirmative, all the while having no idea how she was going to answer the questions that were coming.

A knock on her window made her jump, and when she glanced over, Greg's face was framed there, concern in his gaze. From his unbuttoned coat thrown over a coffee-stained suit, she guessed he'd already been working for a while, and had probably spotted her from the window and come outside to talk in private. Or to make sure she didn't start the car again and drive right out of here.

She turned off the engine and stepped outside, the forty-five-degree Virginia weather feeling ridiculously warm after Montana's below-freezing temperatures and nonstop snow. But she had a feeling her reception from Dan would be downright frigid.

Greg studied her a minute, and she knew exactly what he was doing.

She gave him a weary smile. "Stop profiling me."

"When did you get in?" Greg asked, reaching out and folding her in a hug.

She leaned into his arms, comfortable with him the way she might be with an older, overprotective brother. She'd gotten damn lucky when he'd been assigned as her training agent at BAU. "A few hours ago."

He pulled back, holding her at arm's length. "You look tired."

"Jet lag," she said, and it was partly true. She was working on almost no sleep, and had been for the past three weeks. "I stopped by to see my grandma after I landed, then I came straight here."

"Good," Greg said, and she knew he meant he was glad she'd finally spoken to her grandma.

She just nodded, busying herself grabbing her briefcase from the backseat so he wouldn't see her reaction. She'd needed to see her grandma. She'd hoped maybe talking things over with her would offer some clarity about what to do. But when she'd walked into her room, Mabel had peered up at her with a dazed look in her eyes, one Evelyn recognized too well. She'd forced a smile, and talked to her for an hour, as Mabel treated her like the twelve-year-old child her dementia had her believing Evelyn still was. Then Evelyn had kissed her on the cheek, promised to see her again soon and headed off to work.

Briefcase in hand, she pasted the best "everything's fine" expression she could manage on her face and slammed the car door, turning back around.

"You're in luck," Greg told her.

"Why's that?" She could use a little luck.

"Dan had a personal emergency. You're getting a reprieve."

Relief rushed through her so quickly she was embarrassed. "Is everything okay?"

"Yeah, he's not sick or anything like that. It's a family thing," Greg told her.

She stared at him quizzically. "What is it?"

"I can't get into details, Evelyn. I'm not even supposed to know."

She couldn't help being curious, but she let it go. "Okay. When's he supposed to be back?"

"A few days."

The relief grew stronger, and the painful grip she had on her briefcase handle began to relax. A few more days to figure out what she wanted to do about her role at BAU, and her place in the FBI in general. She'd hoped to avoid Dan as long as possible, but if he'd been in the office, that would've worked for no more than a few hours.

She increased her pace. "Let's go inside, then. I know Dan wants me back on other cases, too, but I'm close to getting somewhere with Rolfe. I can feel it."

"What I want to know," Greg said as he swiped his card on the BAU building's cipher lock and held the door open for her, "is why was Rolfe following Jen around?"

"I'd bet because he'd heard about her from Butler,

knew she kept coming out to the compound, nosing around, and he wanted to see what he was up against," Evelyn said. She'd told Greg about her discovery last night, before taking the red-eye home.

"Probably," Greg agreed. "But that puts a whole new perspective on their interaction, doesn't it? The fact that he already knew who she was and what she was doing when she drove into the Butler Compound?"

Evelyn stopped at the entrance into the bullpen, thinking back to that moment when Rolfe had rounded the corner of the compound. Jen hadn't seemed to know him. He hadn't acted as if he'd known her, either, but obviously he'd been faking.

"It also suggests that they genuinely weren't in cahoots, if Rolfe was following her because Butler said she'd been poking around the compound," Greg added.

"I know. And I'm glad." Very glad, in fact. Not just because she didn't want there to be a traitor in their ranks—especially a terrorist traitor—but because it meant her gut instinct on Jen hadn't been wrong. "But there's still something missing."

"Like what?"

Evelyn shrugged as the familiar sights and sounds of the BAU office filtered through. The smell of overcooked coffee and stale, dry air was pretty much the same as it was in the Salt Lake City office. And the Chicago office. And the San Francisco office. So was the drab gray carpeting, and the plain cubicles packed into the large bullpen. But the buzz of agents talking was different here, something to do with the solitary nature of profiling versus working on a squad, she supposed.

She focused on Greg again. "I don't know," she finally answered. "But why haven't we found a body? If they weren't in cahoots, he'd have no reason to keep her alive once he made it out of that compound."

"They're still searching the mountains," Greg reminded her. "But you know how big and remote that area is. Even the dogs haven't come up with anything. We might have to accept that we'll never find her body."

She turned to face him instead of entering the bullpen. "You think she's been dead the whole time?" Evelyn asked quietly.

Greg nodded. "I think they might have put her in that tunnel to keep her out of sight, expecting her not to survive, and she was stronger than they realized and got partway—or maybe even all the way—to the exit. If so, they probably caught her trying to escape and killed her. They know the mountains a hell of a lot better than she would. Otherwise, it's possible they held on to her until they left. Maybe Butler thought he was going with Rolfe until the last minute and that was his incentive not to finish her off. But once they made it out of that tunnel and past the HRT perimeter?" He shook his head. "At that point, she would've lost all value to them."

Evelyn couldn't contain her disappointment, although Greg was only saying what she'd already been thinking. But at least Jen had died a hero, trying to bring down a threat even when she'd been warned to stay away from it.

Anger at the FBI's refusal to put resources there before it was too late—including BAU, who'd profiled the Butler Compound as a low threat—rose up. Then, slowly, determination slid over the anger. She wasn't going to let Jen's death be in vain. She was going to find Rolfe, and she was going to bring him down.

"Hey, Evelyn," a voice said, and she raised her head, returning her attention to the room.

"Hi," she replied to the profiler who was walking away, engrossed in a file he was carrying.

She glanced over at Greg, who was giving her a knowing smile.

"I've missed that look," he said.

"What look?"

"Your 'I'm a hell of a profiler and nobody better stand in my way, because I'm on a mission' look."

She flushed, tried to make light of it. "I have a look that says all of that?"

"Yeah." He patted her on the arm and nodded toward the desk. "You had that drive from the moment you joined BAU, and I've been wondering where it went lately. Now, come on. Get back to work, and use it."

"I've got something," Evelyn announced, leaning back in her uncomfortable office chair, hearing the disbelief in her own voice.

Greg wheeled his chair around the wall that divided their cubicles. "I hope it's on that possible abduction case out of DC. That file's gotten passed around the office and none of us can get a good read on it. But I have a really bad feeling."

Evelyn spun to face him, blinking as she realized how strained her eyes had become after staring at her computer screen without a break all day. Her stomach grumbled and she checked the clock, discovering she'd long since missed lunch. In fact, the workday was almost gone, and she hadn't even noticed. Greg must have skipped lunch, too, maybe because Kyle and Gabe weren't here to insist he get out of the office.

She knew Gabe would be back at work within a few days, but Kyle was a different matter. He was home, but on leave while his injuries healed. After that, there was a big question mark in his future. But having seen him in between her investigation and his physical therapy appointments, she'd been shocked by how pale he still looked, how weak his arm still was. She couldn't believe he'd be able to return to HRT anytime soon—possibly not ever. Knowing how much he loved it, the thought physically hurt her.

"Evelyn?" Greg pressed.

"I haven't had a chance to look at that file yet."

She saw him glance at the stack of interoffice notes on her desk, which she hadn't gone through, either, then he squinted at the computer behind her. "Have you looked at any of the cases Dan left for you?"

"I'm following up on Rolfe. I…"

"You know you're going to have to put that case in rotation with the others, right? That you can't spend all day, every day, on it anymore? We've been *swamped* with profile requests, and between Vince retiring and you being gone for three weeks, everyone here is behind. Your caseload…"

"Greg," Evelyn interrupted when he showed no signs of slowing down. "I've got something big."

He frowned, and as he scooted his chair closer, she saw the darker-than-usual circles under his eyes. "What is it?"

"Rolfe's father. This guy has been off the grid most of his life, so it was really hard to track him." She pointed to the screen. "But here he is. Apparently, he was a seriously hard-core survivalist, which might be why we could never tie Rolfe to any survivalist or militia groups."

"Why?" Greg asked. "Because Rolfe didn't get along with his father?"

"Oh, no, I think he idolized his father. And I'm going to show you why. But I also think Rolfe was smart enough to hide his connections. He must've figured it would eventually become a way to track him, so he never joined."

When Greg seemed about to argue that point, she rushed on. "From what I can tell, his mom took him away from his father when he was about nine. That's when the two of them pop up on the grid. And *where* is the first place they pop up?"

Greg smiled at her, like a patient teacher who knew his student had the right answer. He'd given her that smile a lot back when he was training her.

"Where?"

"A Chicago hospital. She came in with two black eyes and a broken wrist. Rolfe seems to have been fine."

Greg's smile faded. "Rolfe's father beat his mother?"

"That's what it looks like."

"How did you even get this? Hospital records…"

"I didn't get it from hospital records," she interrupted. "It was part of a law enforcement report."

"The police got involved? Because of the domestic abuse?"

"Nope. I mean, yes, the police were the first on the scene, but it wasn't because of the abuse. It was because a man showed up at the hospital, and fired a rifle inside the building. No one was hurt, but he was threatening hospital staff, and he was looking for Rolfe and his mom."

"The father," Greg said.

"Yep. Apparently, she'd left him and taken the boy, but of course, he didn't believe in the federal government, or state government, either. He just wanted Rolfe back on his own terms. And guess who got involved next?"

Greg leaned forward, practically falling out of his chair as he stared at her computer. "ATF? The Chicago ATF that was bombed?"

"That's right. Because the gun he fired wasn't legally obtained. It was part of a big batch of weapons that had gone missing from a police bust. Anyway, there's a whole side story there, but it sent them after Rolfe's dad."

"I assume they arrested him?"

"Well, they tried. He went off the grid again. He didn't show up for years and years. In the meantime, Rolfe's mom tried to outrun him. She took Rolfe across the country, in fact. All the way to San Francisco."

"Seriously? And somehow Rolfe—or his dad—got on the ATF's radar again?"

"That's right. Once she got to San Francisco, I guess Rolfe's mom got a restraining order. So when she spotted her ex in town one day, she contacted the police. He still had an outstanding ATF warrant, so San Francisco ATF took the lead. They tried to make an arrest, and Rolfe's father opened fire. They shot back and killed him."

Greg nodded sadly. "And after all that, you think Rolfe idolized his father?"

"Yes. He followed his father's path, not his mother's. And the professor I talked to said he got the impression Rolfe didn't get along with his mom."

"Well, if he wanted to avenge his father, it explains the targets. I hope you're saying those are the only places Rolfe's dad had confrontations, though."

"According to all the evidence I've found, yes."

"That could be very good news. Hopefully that means we've seen the end of these bombings."

"Hopefully," Evelyn murmured, but she couldn't shake the feeling that it wasn't over.

She must have looked unconvinced, because Greg said, "At least you've got *one* piece of good news for sure."

"What's that?"

He smiled. "Dan's going to have to forgive you for not working on any of the other profiles today."

"This is great news, Evelyn," Fred Lanier said, his voice booming over her phone a few hours later.

The office had mostly cleared out by then. Even Greg had gone home, suggesting she take it easy and do the same on her first day back. But she'd been too engrossed in her search for more about Rolfe. Ultimately, she hadn't found anything else, so she'd called and told the head of the JTTF team about the connection between Rolfe's father and the two ATF offices that had been bombed. "Well, yes, but…"

"Two clear grudges, and unfortunately we were too late to prevent attacks there. But you're not seeing anything else? No other incidents with ATF or police and Rolfe's father?"

"No, but…"

"How deep into his background did you go?"

His constant habit of interrupting her was annoying, but even more annoying was his obvious desire to consider Rolfe a lower threat. He'd already been down-grading the threat level as the days went by with no more attacks. Now, eight days from the last bombing, with both bombers in custody and no indication that anything else was coming, Fred sounded calmer than she'd ever heard him.

She understood; they all wanted to put this threat behind them. And what she was handing over *did* suggest they could all relax a little bit.

Only she couldn't. Her profiler instinct, which felt as if it had gone dormant in the past month, was scream-ing right now.

"He and Butler built a whole compound for this."

"Did they?" Fred asked. "Hell, for all we know, But-ler created it, and Rolfe saw he could use it, and coerced Butler into turning the place into something different than he'd originally intended. After all, we know But-ler footed the bill."

"That's true," Evelyn said. "Either way is possible. Regardless, it became Rolfe's recruiting ground. I just don't think…"

"What? Two massive bombings isn't big enough for you, Baine?"

"That's not what I'm saying. But if he was going to find two men to bomb two locations, why bother with the recruiting site? Why not just go to some fringe mi-litia meetings, look for potential lone wolf terrorists and pull them out, offer them an opportunity?"

"I think we got lucky here, Baine. I'm sure Rolfe was planning to use that compound long-term, to keep taking recruits out of there for his missions. It's a damn good thing we shut that place down before he could get more recruits. My guess is that Rolfe's like a lot of

these guys. Once they get a taste of it, the original revenge targets aren't enough for them. They want more.
Isn't that how most of the people you go after operate?"

It was. Plenty of serial criminals started out thinking
they had one target they wanted to hit and then they'd
stop. Just one kill—someone they perceived as having
wronged them—and then the desire would go away.
The problem was, they liked it too much to stop. Once
they started, that desire only grew.

"Yes," Evelyn said, "but he didn't have to kill Butler. He'd been following Jen. He knew who she was. He
knew her suspicions about the place. He could've taken
her out before she ever arrived. He could've tried to save
the place. What makes you think that just because he
doesn't have a compound full of recruits anymore, the
need you talked about will go away?"

There was a pause, then he said, "I'm listening."

"Rolfe's still out there, Fred. Like you said, he's got
a taste for this now. He's not going to hide in the woods
for the rest of his life, content with what he's accom-
plished."

When she didn't continue, he said, "Okay. But going
by everything we got from the cultists, he's out of bombers. Did you find anyone who left the cult earlier than
Peters and Durham that you want us to look at?"

"No." And she'd tried. She had stacks of lists and
printed-out images all over her desk. Census information. Statements from local police. Photographs Jen had
taken of Butler and a few of his men coming into town
a year ago that had ended up in the original BAU file.

But it was too hard to tell. Not just to figure out
who'd left the compound, but accurately identifying
who'd lived there in the first place.

The census information had been a joke, it was so incomplete. The statements from police had included a lot of guesswork that was impossible to verify. And the men in Jen's picture had been too hard to identify—the only face she could put a name to was Butler. The men in his compound prided themselves on being off the grid, and she was discovering they'd been good at it.

"You said before that you saw Rolfe as a strategist. A leader, not a bomber. Do you think he'll actually take a bomb in somewhere himself?"

Evelyn considered it. He loved the power too much. He loved being in charge, the thrill of manipulation. He wanted someone else to do his dirty work. "Not unless he's desperate."

Fred was silent again. Finally he said, "I'm not sure what you're asking me to do here, Evelyn. We're not stopping our hunt for Rolfe. We've still got people digging into the cultists. But the more we find, the more it looks like we're no longer in a race against time, against another bomb. Now this is turning into a regular old fugitive manhunt."

When she didn't say anything, Fred added, "You've done a great job here. Thanks for all your help on this. But investigating Rolfe's background isn't your responsibility. We'll take over. Your boss called me yesterday before you got back, let me know how many other cases are on your plate. We'll be in touch if we need another profile."

Then he was gone, and Evelyn could just stare at the phone, wondering what she'd missed.

Because as much as she wished it was as straightforward as Fred believed, her instincts told her this wasn't the end. It was too big an operation to end with two bomb blasts that were simple revenge targets.

Rolfe might have gotten into this for his father, but she'd seen the gleam in his eyes inside that compound. He was in it for himself now, and judging by his exit from the Butler Compound while everyone around him was dying, he had something else planned.

There was going to be a grand finale.

24

"What are you after?" Evelyn muttered, talking to herself, or maybe to her computer screen. She had window after window open, all filled with information. She'd tried to research Rolfe and his father; there were a lot of dead ends.

But she *knew*—on some primitive level she couldn't really explain—that Rolfe wasn't finished. And she found herself taking up Jen's obsession, more with every day that passed.

She'd been at it for hours, casting furtive glances over her shoulder whenever she heard footsteps near her cubicle. In fact, she'd been at it for the past four days, against Fred's instructions, against her boss's orders.

Dan had returned to work today, looking tired and distracted. Rumor around the office was that he'd taken personal time because his wife was threatening divorce, but Evelyn wasn't sure how much stock she put in that. He'd said hello to her, promised to talk to her later, then disappeared into his office. She hadn't seen him since, and she'd been hoping she'd be able to continue avoiding him.

The rolling of wheels made Evelyn reach up and tap

her cursor, flipping her screen to another case she'd been assigned. That one would probably be coming home with her tonight, along with a stack of others she'd been neglecting because she couldn't get Rolfe Shephard out of her head.

Even at night, when she was trying to sleep, Rolfe's hazel eyes—so like her long-ago ex-boyfriend Marty Carlyle's—greeted her, taunted her. Disturbed her. She shook the image free and spun around in her chair.

Sure enough, there was Greg, who'd rolled his own chair over to her cubicle. He'd looked worn out since she'd come back from Montana, and she felt guilty since she knew it was partly because he'd taken on some of her caseload while she'd been assigned to the JTTF.

"Finish up whatever you're working on," Greg said. "We're going to lunch in half an hour."

Evelyn glanced at the clock and then back at Greg. "I'm still behind. I was going to eat at my desk."

"Not today, you're not. Mac's at Quantico this morning. Just to visit everyone—he's not back to work yet, which you probably know. But Gabe called earlier. We're taking him out to lunch like we used to."

It was an unspoken fact that he needed cheering up. It was also unspoken that she should already have known about Kyle's visit today.

She *had* known, or at least she'd known he was going to Quantico. She suspected lunch was Gabe's idea. Ever since he'd been injured, Kyle definitely hadn't been his usual carefree and charming self. He'd also been close-lipped about what was next for him.

It was uncharacteristic, and she wasn't sure if that was because things were strained between them or because he was afraid the answer wasn't going to include

HRT. Between her work and his therapy, she hadn't seen him in a few days.

She reached up and fussed nervously with her hair, and Greg gave her an encouraging smile. "It'll be fun. Like old times."

In "old times," Kyle would be teasing her, even mock-asking her out to see if he could make her blush or stammer. Now that they were *actually* dating, still in secret, and everything was so damn awkward, she doubted it would be anything like old times. But she smiled back, anyway, hoping.

Since the moment she'd thought Kyle had died in that forest, she'd known she wanted to make their relationship work. The distance she'd been putting between them lately had never been about Kyle, anyway. It had always been about her. About figuring out who she was and what she wanted.

Although, in the past few days, her desire to obsessively chase a profile had returned with a vengeance, her confidence hadn't. Was she still good enough? Or was Rolfe Shephard going to remain out of reach?

If she could find him, then maybe, just maybe, this was where she still belonged.

Apparently unable to read the thoughts running through her mind for once, Greg reminded her, "Thirty minutes," then wheeled back to his own cubicle.

She spun her chair around and stared at the new case on her screen. A possible abduction of a teenage girl. A case that legitimately needed a profile, and one so strange that it had puzzled most of the profilers in the office. Yes, Rolfe Shephard was out there, but so were other serial criminals. If she was going to remain in this job, those cases needed her attention, too.

Thirty more minutes, she vowed, checking her watch. She'd allow herself thirty more minutes to look into Rolfe's background, and then she'd take a break. She needed to see Kyle. And when she got back after lunch, she had to move on. She wasn't giving up on it, but she couldn't put off her other cases forever.

Because the second thing Dan Moore might want to talk to her about was whether she planned to stay at BAU—and panic erupted whenever she thought about having to answer that question. But the first thing he was going to ask was how her caseload was going. And if she said she hadn't started any of it since she'd returned, they might never get to the next question.

"Thirty minutes," she mumbled, and began searching again, this time looking into the fringe groups Rolfe's father had belonged to, on and off over the years. The groups had splintered so often it was difficult to track a specific person, and she was about to quit when she flipped past an offhand mention of a few members of one of those groups. They'd traveled hundreds of miles to take part in a protest.

Out of curiosity, she clicked on the image, and then stared in disbelief. It was Rolfe Shephard. The same curly blond hair, the same penetrating hazel eyes, the same lean build. Only it wasn't, because the grainy picture had been taken more than twenty years earlier.

Rolfe Shephard looked almost identical to the father who'd shaped his beliefs. Considering the way the professor had described Rolfe during his time in academia, Rolfe had changed his appearance after he'd left the university. Possibly to look more like his father. And apparently one of the last things Rolfe's father had done before his wife took his son and went into hiding was travel to Waco, Texas. Where he'd stood outside the Branch Davidian complex as it burned to the ground...

Her pulse picked up as she gazed at his face. The sheer fury there was unlike anything she'd ever seen. This was it. This was Rolfe's father's trigger.

This event was connected to why his wife had left. Maybe he'd been too obsessed with it? Maybe he'd told his son too much about it? Could it have become the reason for Rolfe's battle cry, too?

Words she'd heard Rolfe speak to Butler when she was locked in his closet came back to her, words about April 19. At the time, she hadn't thought much about it. Most antifederalists had strong feelings about April 19, because it was the date of the American Revolution's Battle of Lexington. A favorite event with anyone who didn't believe in the federal government.

But it was also the date of the Waco siege by the FBI, after ATF had failed to deliver a warrant on the people inside. And it was the date of the Oklahoma City bombing.

Evelyn grabbed her phone and dialed Fred without taking her eyes off the screen. "I think I know what Rolfe's going after next. And I think I know when it's going to happen."

"Ten minutes," Greg said, popping his head over their cubicle divider.

She turned, so he could see she had a phone pressed to her ear, and nodded at him. "I'll be ready," she mouthed.

Greg nodded and disappeared again, and she turned back to her call with Fred Lanier.

She'd just finished explaining to him what she'd

found on Rolfe's father, and about her suspicion that Rolfe was going to target the people involved in the standoff.

"My best guess is that he'll go after ATF in Texas on April 19, but I have to tell you, I'm worried I could be missing something here. It's a long time to wait between bombings, especially since the first two were close together. I'm going to dig a little more."

"All right," Fred told her. "Meanwhile, we're going to give the ATF branches a call, let them know to be on high alert starting now, just in case."

"Good," Evelyn said, although the relief she should have been feeling just wasn't there.

After hanging up with Fred, she stared at her computer, then glanced down at her watch. She had ten minutes and then she and Greg needed to leave.

"Shit," she heard Greg say with so much disappointment in his voice that she stood up and peered at him over the wall as he hung up the phone.

"What's wrong?"

He looked up at her and frowned. "I'm not sure I should be telling you this, but I just heard. Mac is out of HRT."

"What?"

"Gabe called me. Mac's rehab on his arm is going to take three months. And that's really, really optimistic. They're giving him a best-case scenario because he's in such good shape, and he's used to working so hard. But the team can't wait that long for an operator. You know how many critical missions they get. They need to be at full capacity."

She tried to fight back her dread. "That doesn't mean he can't go back once he's better."

"Maybe. He can try out again when he's up to speed. If a spot opens up. And you know that doesn't happen often—it's insanely competitive to get into HRT, and some of those guys stay there until they retire. I'm sure he'll try, if he can. But as of right now, his HRT career is finished."

"What's he going to do?" she asked in dismay.

"I don't know," Greg replied. "Gabe called to give me a heads-up. Mac *just* found out. He's going to need our support."

Evelyn nodded, and worry for Kyle warred with the persistent discomfort in her gut, telling her she was missing something crucial with Rolfe. Telling her that Rolfe wouldn't bomb two buildings in less than a week in November, and then go silent for four and a half months. It wasn't logical; it gave the FBI too much time to hunt him down. And in a way, it lessened the fear, lessened the impact, by giving the country time to recover between attacks.

"We've got ten minutes, right?" When he nodded, she said, "I'm going to make one more call and then we can go."

One last long-shot call to see if she could figure out what was bugging her. Grabbing her phone again, she dialed the professor she'd spoken to before.

"I wondered if you'd call again," he said when he answered.

"Do you have more you want to tell me?" she asked hopefully, even though she'd left him her direct number.

"Not anything specific, no, but I've been thinking about him since your…"

"I'm sorry," Evelyn said, cutting him off. "But can I just ask you a few questions? I'm in a bit of a time crunch." She glanced at her watch again, not wanting to be late. Not today.

"Okay," he replied, sounding a little miffed. "Go ahead, then."

She hunted for a question that might help her pinpoint what felt wrong to her. "You said you and Rolfe got into a discussion about history once, and you regretted it because he went on and on about hating the government. Can you tell me everything you recall about that incident?"

There was a pause that had Evelyn frowning at her watch, and got her foot tapping, no matter how much she tried to stop it. Finally, he spoke, slowly, as if he was trying to remember all the details.

"It started when I made a joke about the Boston Tea Party. And that just set him off. He went on this long rant about the American Revolution and the government and how their power was invalid. It was one of the craziest things I've ever heard in my life."

"Do you remember any specifics? Did he mention any dates?"

"Dates? I don't think so, no." Before Evelyn could move to the next question, he said, "Wait. It was close to Christmas. I think he *did* mention a date. Because right before this, we'd been talking about holiday plans. He said he hated this time of year, that it was his least favorite. I felt a little bad for him actually."

"Did he say why?" Evelyn asked, wondering if it mattered.

"Something about an anniversary."

"The anniversary of an event?" Evelyn's pulse began to race. Could there have been another run-in between Rolfe's father and ATF that she hadn't uncovered?

"I think it was his dad's death."

She frowned, trying to remember the time frame of the shootout with ATF. According to the report she'd read, he'd died during the event, but all she recalled was the year, which had been a few years after Rolfe and his mom had run away from him in Chicago. She propped the phone between her shoulder and her ear and opened up a search online. "What about ATF? Did he talk about them at all?"

"ATF? Hmm…no, I don't think so. He talked about some other agency, though. What was it? Hmm…"

Evelyn's foot-tapping grew faster, and as her internet search loaded, she checked the time again. Two minutes left.

"Gosh, I can't remember. It was some specialized unit I'd never heard of."

"Okay," Evelyn said as the search finally loaded and she scanned the article. Rolfe's father had engaged in that shootout with ATF fifteen years ago, in early December. The anniversary had just passed.

She let out a breath, relieved that she hadn't seen this a few days earlier. Because the day of his father's death would've been a likely date for a revenge bombing, a grand finale. She probably would've put everyone on high alert, and all for nothing, since the day had passed without incident.

Only… She leaned closer to the screen, noticing the word *later* in the sentence about his father dying of his wounds after the shootout. She clicked back, pulling up another article.

"I know!" the professor suddenly burst out, just as Evelyn's heart thumped hard, lodging somewhere near her throat.

Rolfe's father hadn't died in the shootout itself. He'd been rushed to the hospital, and he'd died a few days later. He'd died on today's date, exactly fifteen years ago.

"It was some specialized FBI unit! Whatever that group was that surrounded Waco."

The Hostage Rescue Team.

Evelyn hung up with a quick "Thank you," yelled at Greg to follow and ran for the door.

25

"It's going to be today," Evelyn panted into her phone as she pushed her foot down hard on the gas pedal, glad she had a siren to slap on her roof.

It lit up the road in front of her in swirls of blue and red, blaring its own kind of warning as she veered around vehicles at a dangerous speed. Lunchtime in the area around Quantico was a bad time to go anywhere fast. HRT was located on a Marine base, so getting in and out during rush hours was damn near impossible.

"What is?" Kyle asked, and she could hear the lingering disappointment in his voice about what he'd just learned. From the background noise, she could tell he was still at Quantico.

"Rolfe's final attack. It's going to be today," she said again. "And he's going after you guys. He's going after HRT."

"Why? I thought he was obsessed with ATF." Kyle sounded calmer than he should have, since she knew he was standing right inside the blast zone.

Beside her, Greg had one hand over his ear as he repeated the same information to someone else at Quantico on his own phone.

"No, not ATF," she blurted. "Not this time. It's about Waco, but Rolfe's father wasn't there for the ATF agents delivering warrants. He watched the place burn to the ground. He saw HRT. And his son's going after them—*you*—as revenge." Her words came out too fast, almost in a jumble, and she knew she sounded as panicked as she felt. How much time did they have? "You need to evacuate!"

"Evacuate an entire Marine base?" Kyle responded.

Evelyn swore. She was well aware of the size of the place, but she hadn't been thinking logistics. She'd been thinking of Kyle, and Gabe. And everyone else in HRT.

But Quantico wasn't just the home of the FBI's elite HRT unit. It was also where the FBI Academy for new agents in training was located. It was where a bunch of other specialty units worked—every part of the Critical Incident Response Group, *except* BAU, in fact.

And Quantico didn't just belong to the FBI, either. The DEA training facility was there, as well. And they were located on a big Marine base, complete with all the people you'd find on a Marine base. Like families.

It was fifty-five thousand acres of people, buildings and woods. Fifty-five thousand acres full of rich targets, if Rolfe Shephard could find a way inside. But knowing all the planning he'd put into this, the years of preparation, the lifetime of growing hatred, she was willing to bet he'd be able to find a way inside.

"Damn it, damn it, damn it." Evelyn slammed to a stop behind a big SUV, which itself was behind a huge line of nonmoving vehicles.

"Just stay calm," Greg said as he set his phone down, and somehow he sounded as though he was standing in the office going over a case file, not racing toward a site that was about to be bombed. "I just spoke to Gabe. Yankee's going to put a lockdown on over the public address system. Keep people in their houses."

"Greg, we need to get them out of there!"

"Evelyn, take a breath, okay? First of all, Quantico has security in place…"

"Which didn't stop the shootings a few years ago," she broke in.

"A bomb is a lot harder to get in here than a weapon already owned by a Marine who lived on the base to begin with," Greg reminded her, still sounding ridiculously calm. "And everyone at the gates has Rolfe's picture. They've had it since he went on the Most Wanted list. I don't think there's any way he could get in, but if he did, he's not going after Marines. He'll stick to his specific target, like he has in the past. We're better off keeping the families away from the FBI side of the base, rather than creating a mass panic."

Evelyn sucked in a deep breath, trying to calm her own raging nerves as she finally started moving again. "Okay. You're right." She spoke into the phone again, telling Kyle, too. "He'd target HRT specifically. We need to clear that whole area around HRT's buildings, evacuate everyone there. He *is* going after the people, so whatever he's planted is probably packed with projectiles, like the last bombs were. That's how Rolfe would have instructed everyone. It's probably why he wanted Peters in the first place, because of his connection to Cartwright."

"*If* he was able to get in here to plant something," Greg reminded her.

"We're heading over there now to check it out," Kyle told her. "But don't worry. Gabe already called and let them know to clear the place out. I don't believe we have any bomb techs on-site, but both Gabe and I have some training in disabling them from our time overseas."

Of course they did. Because it wasn't bad enough that Kyle and Gabe were at Quantico with the threat; they had to run *toward* the bomb instead of away from it.

Knowing Kyle was in danger was worse than being inside the Butler Compound, expecting a bullet to the head whenever Butler's patience ran out.

Evelyn slammed on the breaks again as traffic came to another standstill. The car in front of her did a three-point-turn into the grass and swung into the lane going the other way. Evelyn glanced over at the traffic leaving Quantico. Cars were moving at a regular rate, not streaming out as though they were fleeing from a bomb threat.

That meant Yankee had managed to keep the threat under wraps, and not create a panic. She told herself that was good news.

But up ahead, she finally saw the reason for the holdup. Yankee had obviously put measures in place to keep Rolfe out in case he hadn't arrived yet. Closing the entrance was the right move, but it wasn't helping her at the moment. Because no one was getting into Quantico.

"Damn it!" She whipped her wheel right and pulled her car as far off the road as she could, then put it in Park. Chances were, it wouldn't be here when she got back, but she ignored the blare of horns as she jumped out and ran toward the gate. Greg followed close behind.

She pulled her credentials out of her pocket and waved them at the guard, but he just nodded her through. "Evelyn, Greg, we've been expecting you." He pointed at a car idling next to the gate. "Get in and Special Agent Helen Doyle will take you where you need to be."

"Thanks." She pivoted, and Greg held the door open, letting her hop into the dark SUV.

As she scooted over to make room for him, she spoke into her phone. "Kyle? Where are you right now?"

There was no response.

Evelyn lowered her phone, glancing down to be sure the connection hadn't been lost, then tapped the back of her driver's seat. "Toward HRT."

The agent looked quickly back at her and nodded, then peeled away from the gate fast enough to slam Evelyn against her seat. In her ear, Kyle said, "Stay away from here, Evelyn!"

"I'm coming to help look…"

"Don't come anywhere near HRT's buildings! We found the bomb."

The car jolted to a stop, and since Evelyn hadn't bothered to buckle her seat belt, she flew forward, bumping her forehead on the back of the driver's seat. Beside her, Greg grabbed the handle on the door with one hand, and braced himself against the front seat with the other.

She'd barely managed to hang on to her phone, but the connection had gone dead. Because Kyle had hung up? Because something had happened?

"Why are we stopping? Go!" Evelyn demanded, and her voice came out screechy and desperate, not like a nearly eight-year veteran of the FBI. She couldn't even see the HRT buildings yet, positioned behind other buildings and trees.

Helen, who Evelyn vaguely remembered as one of the FBI Academy's best weapons instructors, replied, "I heard the person on the phone yelling at you to stay away from that spot."

"I don't care! We need to get over there. Hurry!"

The car didn't move and Greg turned to face Evelyn. "She's right. Do you know how to defuse a bomb?"

"No."

"Neither do I. If they've already located it, what are we going to do besides get in the way?"

Evelyn called Kyle back, but it went straight to voice mail. "We won't know what we can do until we get there."

"Or I can take you somewhere you can be useful," Helen suggested as Evelyn felt her heart racing out of control. "Where else can you help? The temporary command post? Back to the exit, in case this guy tries to leave? Where?"

Evelyn could hardly focus on her words. What had happened to Kyle? Were he and Gabe okay? She squinted out the front window, into the distance where she knew the HRT buildings were located. But she hadn't heard a *boom*, and the sky was clear and bright, a brilliant blue without a cloud. No black smoke, dust or debris crashing upward, like there would be at a blast site.

Could they have seen Rolfe? Identified him? Could he have snuck up on them, the way his bombers had done to the small HRT contingent in the forest?

She tapped the seat again, impatient to just get out and run. Except they weren't close enough. "Come on! We need to go."

"We need to go wherever Rolfe might be," Greg argued. "If they've found a bomb, he could be leaving that area now. We need to figure out his most likely route."

Evelyn turned to Greg to tell him she didn't know. And then, beyond the hood of the car, walking into the woods, she saw someone.

A man in dark pants and a sweatshirt, hands swinging as he glanced briefly back at the car over his shoulder. He seemed relaxed, out of place against Evelyn's own panic. And he looked familiar.

Why did he look so familiar?

Evelyn opened her car door and stepped out, never taking her eyes off the man as he started down a dirt trail into the woods. She'd been on that trail, a path that traveled a long way, a path Marines sometimes jogged on together in the mornings, a hidden path that led through the base.

She started to walk after him, vaguely registering that Greg had gotten out of the car behind her. Who was that man? Why did she recognize him? It wasn't Rolfe, so she shouldn't be worrying about him, but he set off all her warning bells.

There was something she recognized in the muscle-bound frame, the angular face with the pale blue eyes. And it wasn't just the strange menace in his gaze, a menace she'd encountered across too many interview tables. She'd seen him before. But where?

He wasn't FBI, of that she was certain. Did he live on the Marine base? Could she have recognized him just from being at Quantico from time to time, simply because he lived here? But if he did, why wasn't he back in his house, heeding the call that had come over the public address system, putting the whole base on lockdown?

He didn't belong here. That thought exploded in her

mind, like a bomb blast of its own. There was something in his too-casual stride that looked forced, as if he was trying to avoid notice. As if he was trying to blend in. As if he was somewhere he wasn't supposed to be. Or he'd just come from somewhere he wasn't supposed to be.

Evelyn was treading lightly, trying not to make any noise as she slipped the SIG Sauer out of her holster. She held it low, her finger resting beside the trigger guard the way she'd been trained.

Before she hurried into the woods along the trail, she glanced back at Greg. He walked in line directly behind her, minimizing the target he'd make, standard law enforcement practice. He had his own weapon out, his gaze steady, trusting her lead.

Evelyn nodded at him once, then tipped her head toward the trail. She held up one finger, then two and shrugged. She knew there was one man, but could he have a partner? Could Rolfe have been walking down that trail before she'd looked up and spotted his partner striding behind the cover of the trees?

She slunk forward, trying to move carefully, knowing that if this guy *did* work with Rolfe, he was a survivalist. He had more practice than she did at becoming invisible in the woods. And his weapons training was probably just as good as hers.

She clutched the SIG a little tighter as she moved behind a tree, peering onto the path where she'd seen him go.

The path was empty.

Her breath came faster as her eyes swept back and forth, searching for movement where it shouldn't be. She didn't see him. And that meant he'd definitely seen her. And he was definitely doing something wrong, or he wouldn't be hiding.

She suddenly wished she'd called it in before she got out of the car. But she didn't dare make noise now. She just pressed herself closer to the tree and kept searching.

Where the hell was he?

A twig snapped, and Evelyn registered it as coming from behind her and to her right. Greg was behind her to the left.

She ducked low as she scooted around the tree, trying to put it between her and the man, knowing she'd been flanked, knowing she'd become a target.

There was a loud blast and Evelyn panicked as she automatically spun in the direction of the HRT buildings, before she realized it had been a gunshot blast. A totally different sound, but she'd been so worried about Kyle and Gabe.

She swore, sliding in the old, dead leaves. On her knees, she scurried around the side of the tree, hoping it would provide cover, and wasted time glancing back at Greg, hoping he hadn't been hit.

Greg had taken cover behind a tree, too, but he nodded at her, then jutted his chin back toward the path.

Evelyn turned again. The man she'd been chasing had darted back onto the path after he'd taken that shot at her. He slid behind the cover of a tree on the other side of the path, and Evelyn knew Greg didn't have a shot.

She didn't, either, but no way was she letting that bastard get away. She pushed to her feet, and even though she knew she should wait him out, she also knew he was fast and he was better at using his surroundings to blend in than she was.

But with Kyle and Gabe having found a bomb set to

go off anytime, and with this guy—whoever he was—surely knowing how to disarm it, she couldn't wait.

She'd get one chance at this, and what she was about to do went against all her training, which said you didn't leave cover. You made the subject come to you. But she knew he'd try to escape if she waited. She hoped Greg would take her cue.

She slid out of her heels. Dampness instantly froze her bare feet, but she could run faster this way. Gripping her weapon in both hands, she jumped up, then raced left as fast as she could, angling her SIG toward the tree where she knew he was hiding.

She practically heard his surprise as he shifted behind that tree, moving backward to get out of her range, even as he lifted his own weapon and took aim.

There was no time to wait. Evelyn pulled the trigger, and then three loud blasts echoed through the trees, so close together she didn't know who had fired first.

Immediately after, a scream echoed down the secluded trail.

26

"The bomb has been defused."

Evelyn felt her shoulders slump in relief—without the tension that had been locked there from the second she'd raced out of the BAU office. Kyle and Gabe and anyone else who might still be close to that blast site were safe. "Are you sure?"

Kyle let out a short laugh that sounded anything but amused. "Yeah, I'm sure. Gabe and I disarmed it with about thirty seconds to spare."

Thirty seconds. Evelyn couldn't keep herself from glancing up, staring off into the distance where she could just see the HRT buildings. Everything seemed calm and peaceful, as it should.

She glanced down at the man lying in front of her, his skin way too pale, his eyes watering with pain. "I need an ambulance."

Worry instantly infused Kyle's voice. "Are you hurt?"

"No. But I caught the bomber." She was still trying to place him, but couldn't.

"You found Rolfe?" Kyle asked. "Where are you? We'll be right there."

"Not Rolfe," Evelyn said, looking around again, wondering if he was somewhere in the forest, watching and biding his time. Quantico had so many acres of woods, sometimes agents joked that there were more deer than federal agents. Rolfe would be right at home.

And the bombers he'd sent before had worked as a pair.

She stared down at the bomber, watching as Greg put pressure on his wound, even as he tried to fight it. After the gunshots had gone off, Evelyn had run over and kicked his primary weapon out of the way. She'd looked back to make sure Greg wasn't injured before checking the bomber for additional weapons.

Unsurprisingly, she'd found a second gun and a knife. Luckily, he'd been too injured to reach for either.

While Evelyn had put a tourniquet around his leg— where her bullet had hit—Greg had wrapped his suit jacket around the top of his chest—where Greg's bullet had struck. One of their bullets must have hit him first, throwing his own shot wide.

Evelyn had actually felt it whiz past her, close enough that it ripped through the sleeve of her suit, but somehow it hadn't touched the skin beneath. She hoped her luck wouldn't run out now.

"Where's Rolfe?" she demanded as the bomber's arms suddenly dropped, and he stopped fighting Greg.

He gave her a creepy, self-satisfied smile, blood on his teeth.

Evelyn frowned back at him. Why was there blood in his mouth? "He's hurt worse than he looks," she told Greg, who nodded somberly, as if he'd already known.

This guy wasn't going to make it long enough for the ambulance to get here. Then Evelyn realized Kyle was still on the line, still asking for her location. She gave it to him and hung up. She leaned close to the bomber as Greg pulled out his ID and called it in to someone.

"Where's Rolfe?" she demanded a second time, her face close to the bomber's. "This guy sent you to do his dirty work, and he's leaving you here to die! Are you going to let him get away with it?"

As he stared at her, his smile faded, but he didn't say a word; she suddenly realized why he'd looked so familiar. "You lived at the Butler Compound."

"Long…time…ago," he rasped out.

She'd seen him in a picture, not with Rolfe, but with Butler. It had been nearly a week ago, when she was going through the materials from BAU's files, which dated back from when they'd been asked to create the initial profile. Vince had provided it a year ago, but the picture had come from a good six months before that. It was something Jen had snapped of Butler and a small group of men on one of the rare times they'd come into town.

This man had been among them.

"Did you go to the compound for Rolfe or for Butler?" she asked, knowing she was losing him, and desperate for more information. "Who did you leave with? Where's your partner?"

He smiled again, and she resisted the urge to slap her hand down on the ground beside him. Instead, she gave him her own smile, trying to look serene, and she said, "Hear anything? Or rather, *don't* hear something?"

The cocky grin dropped away as he turned his head toward the direction of the HRT buildings.

"That's right. We defused it. And if you think your partner's getting away, think again."

His eyes drifted shut, then opened again slowly, as if

he was having trouble moving his eyelids. Evelyn heard the sound of an ambulance in the distance. Somehow she knew it wouldn't make it here in time.

"Never…find…Rolfe," he managed to whisper, then his eyes closed once more. They didn't open again.

Evelyn sat back on her heels and glanced at Greg, realizing suddenly that he'd stepped away and had been talking on the phone. And that Helen had come over, too.

"This guy was married to a Marine," Helen said. "I recognize him."

Greg held up the ID he'd taken off the would-be bomber and ended his call. "He's been here for a *year*. That's how long ago Rolfe put this plan in place."

"I think Rolfe's here today," Evelyn said, hearing the determination in her own voice. She wanted him behind bars, badly. "It makes sense. He wouldn't need two bombers. There's no need for a getaway vehicle, since this guy lived on base. Besides, there's less risk of error with only one, someone trusted, someone Rolfe picked out a long time ago, and trained. This was Rolfe's finale. He's here somewhere."

"No way he got inside Quantico," Helen insisted.

Standing up, Evelyn peered down the path, toward where Helen had left the car. She watched an ambulance race up, and skid to a stop, two paramedics leaping out. Behind it, she saw Kyle's familiar vehicle park only slightly more carefully.

"If he's not inside, he's nearby," she said. "He wouldn't miss this."

"By now, he knows it didn't go off," Greg reminded her.

As Helen walked over to talk to the paramedics, and Kyle and Gabe hurried toward her, Evelyn stared at the place that hadn't gone up in a huge blast. Where would Rolfe be? Unless he was actually inside the gates of Quantico, it would be difficult to see the HRT building. But he'd want to see the destruction.

"He's waiting to see the aftermath," she said as Kyle reached her side, looking her over as if he needed to make sure she was really okay.

"What?" Gabe asked. "What do you mean?"

"He'd be near the exit. Rolfe would be waiting for the panic. That's what he's looking for. He wants to create terror—he wants to watch the aftermath." Excitement charged through her as she spoke, suddenly certain she was right. "He's close. We can still catch him."

"He has to be here," Evelyn whispered from the back of a specialty, bulletproof van. She was sitting beside Greg, parked off the road a few hundred feet beyond the entrance, close to where her FBI vehicle still sat, abandoned. They were close to the woods, with a view of the entrance and its surroundings.

Cars drove past them, normal Quantico traffic they hadn't stemmed because they didn't want to spook Rolfe.

She glanced down at her watch. The bomb was supposed to have detonated over fifteen minutes ago. They'd been out here, beside the entrance, for five. Were they too late? Was she wrong? Was Rolfe somewhere else entirely?

"Don't worry," Greg said, taking her hand; as he did, Evelyn realized she'd been tapping it incessantly against the door. "The guys will find him."

"The guys" included Kyle and Gabe, and a small contingent of men from the other HRT team. They were currently wearing camo and skulking through the woods bordering the entrance on the other side of the street, searching.

Evelyn folded Greg's hand in hers, forcing herself not to squeeze as hard as she wanted to. HRT had gone after the men Rolfe had helped train, and it had ended Kyle's HRT career. It had very nearly ended his life. The incident had injured Gabe and another agent—and that agent probably wouldn't make it back to HRT, either. What would happen when they faced Rolfe himself?

"Mac shouldn't even be out there," Evelyn whispered. She hadn't dared speak the words when he'd insisted on joining the team. Hard as it had been, she'd kept her fear to herself, knowing he needed to go. Yankee had frowned at him, lips pursed, then finally gave one curt nod, approving it when they all knew it was against FBI policy.

She understood why he'd done it. Kyle had just helped disarm a bomb that could've taken out all of HRT. He'd been part of their team for years. She knew they were like family, and they couldn't deny him the chance to take down the man who'd done this to him. Not even when he was operating at half-capacity, with one arm in a sling.

In theory, with his training, Kyle was more deadly with the use of only one arm than most men who were armed with a crate of weapons. But Rolfe wasn't most men.

So, she understood Yankee's decision, but she didn't have to like it. She wanted Kyle beside her, safe, in the van. Ironically, it didn't stop her from wanting to be out in the woods herself, hunting down Rolfe, too.

"Kyle's not out there," Greg told her.

"What? But Yankee..."

"I know, but at the last minute, Gabe talked him out of it. He's in the other car."

Relieved, she glanced over at the base. Down the road a bit, she saw another vehicle just like this one. That vehicle held Yankee, who was giving instructions to HRT, and a few other agents, to keep an eye on the entrance from the other side.

Squinting down at the tiny radio clutched in her hand, she willed it to go on. Willed HRT to tell them they'd found Rolfe, that it was all over. When the radio stayed silent, she looked across the street, searching for any sign of movement. Any sign of HRT, or Rolfe. But she saw nothing. She knew she probably wouldn't, not until there were gunshots and someone walked out of the woods, victorious.

A sharp knock on the window behind her made her lurch in her seat, and she twisted around.

"Holy shit," Greg gasped as she gawked at the face in the window, half-hidden in the shade of the woods. "Is that...?"

"Jen," Evelyn said, her fingers gripping the handle of her SIG even as she dropped the radio in her pocket and reached out to open the door. Her mind worked overtime, trying to make sense of the ghost in front of her.

And Jen did look like a ghost. She was deathly pale, horribly thin—down at least fifteen pounds from when Evelyn had last seen her—and she had a patch of very short hair on one side of her head. Through it, Evelyn could see dark, jagged stitches. Someone had repaired a wound there, and it sure as hell hadn't been a medical professional. From the awkward way one arm was dangling at her side, the injury to her head wasn't the only one.

She saw Greg angle himself away from the open door, behind the protection of the vehicle wall, as Jen came into full view. His own gun was out of its holster and squared on Jen's chest.

"We thought you were dead," Evelyn burst out.

Jen's eyes, which looked dull and glassy, met hers. "I'm rigged," she said, then reached up and unbuttoned her coat, pulling it back to reveal a crude bomb strapped to her chest.

"Jen…"

"Step out of the car, Evelyn."

Jen's voice didn't sound right, and Evelyn studied her, not moving her hand from her weapon even though she knew that wouldn't help if the bomb went off. Jen was drugged, Evelyn realized—at the same moment she realized that Jen wasn't holding the bomb's trigger.

Evelyn focused hard, staring past Jen, into the dense woods. Rolfe was in there. Watching.

She'd been right about his endgame. She'd just been wrong about his final target.

Forcing herself not to glance backward, not to give away that HRT was across the street in case Rolfe didn't already know, Evelyn scooted toward the van door.

Greg grabbed her sleeve, but she shook him off and stepped outside with Jen. "Where's Rolfe?" she asked her as Greg stepped out, too.

She let her gun fall to her side, but didn't drop it. Beside her, Greg kept his weapon leveled on Jen.

"I'll show you," Jen said, then turned and walked slowly into the woods.

"What are we doing?" Greg muttered when she started to follow.

"Did you see that bomb?" Evelyn whispered back as

she slid her hand into her pocket and felt blindly for the button on her radio to transmit. "It doesn't matter if we follow or run away. If he detonates it, we're finished. And so is anyone driving past."

Greg's eyes lowered to her pocket and then rose again so quickly Evelyn almost missed it. He swore and followed her into the woods.

"Why are you doing this?" Evelyn called out to Jen, who was still walking with her slow, uneven gait.

"I'm sorry." She glanced back, tears in her eyes. "He threatened my kids, or I would've just let him blow me up before I walked over to that car and brought you into this. I'm so sorry."

Jen wasn't a traitor.

Evelyn nodded, telling Jen without words that she understood, just as Rolfe stepped out from behind a tree. He had a detonator in one hand, a pistol in the other and a smile on his face.

"I'd drop those guns," he advised, shaking the detonator back and forth.

"You press that button and you take yourself out, too," Greg reminded him, not letting go of his gun, but not aiming it at Rolfe, either.

Both she and Greg were good shots, but they weren't good enough to take him out without giving him time to press the button. Only HRT was that good.

Luckily, HRT was here. She and Greg just needed to distract Rolfe long enough for them to find a way to sneak up on him.

Rolfe shrugged at Greg. "But I'll get to take you with me," he snarled.

Evelyn wondered if it was really that easy for him. "You didn't accomplish what you set out to do here," she told him. "If you die today, you really think any-one else is going to carry on your mission? You really think anyone else cares about your father's obsessions?"

His gaze snapped to her, and Evelyn nodded. "Yeah, I know about Waco."

"Did you know she was there?" He jabbed the deto-nator toward Jen, who flinched.

Conversations from Evelyn's first meeting with Jen flashed through her mind, and she suddenly remem-bered the other agent talking about one of her very first assignments. She'd been at Waco—in her words, basi-cally getting coffee for the veterans. But she'd watched the place burn down; she'd even mentioned that a pro-tester had thrown something at her.

Could it have been Rolfe's father who'd done that, twenty-odd years ago?

"Is that why she's alive now?" Evelyn asked. Be-cause his grudge against Jen was so big that he wanted to make her suffer? So big that shooting her with an AK-47 and letting her bleed out wasn't enough? He wanted to blow her to pieces instead?

"Pure luck." Rolfe stepped closer, until she could see the gleam in his hazel eyes. "I was planning to take you, too—as insurance—but damn Butler grabbed you at the wrong time and dragged you out of my room. And after all the trouble I'd taken to keep you close, too. As luck would have it, this one was still alive down in that tunnel. I'd patched her up after he shot her, just in case, but I never thought she'd make it. Especially not when Ward tied her up and put her down there. But she's a fighter, this one."

He grinned at the agent, then back at Evelyn. "I was planning to kill her as soon as I saw the light at the end of that tunnel—" he couldn't seem to resist another grin "—but she ranted at me the whole way out. Compared me to the 'wackos at Waco.' I think those were her exact words. And then I knew I needed to keep her around for something special."

"So you brought her here. Why?" Evelyn asked, forcing herself to continue looking at Rolfe as a movement behind him caught her eyes. Please be HRT moving in, she prayed.

"I wanted her to watch," Rolfe said. "I wanted her to see what she hadn't stopped." He scowled, shook his head and pointed the gun at Evelyn. "You ruined that."

"Don't," Greg warned, aiming his own weapon at Rolfe.

Rolfe gave him a fleeting glance. "You move one more inch, and I press the detonator." He shifted his head back and forth, as if he was debating. "Or maybe I pull the trigger. Either way, you try to shoot that gun and someone's dead. Probably you."

Rolfe moved his gun over to point directly at Greg, and Greg slowly lowered his weapon. "You really want to take the chance?" Rolfe asked. "You try to save Evelyn here, and I kill you all. Your HRT friends included."

He gave them a huge smile, and Evelyn's gaze darted behind Rolfe and she realized HRT was close. But not so close they'd be able to take Rolfe out.

He was standing with his back directly against a huge tree, and she could see Gabe and two other agents fifty paces behind him, without an angle on him.

At his words, they all started to run, forgetting stealth, and going for pure speed. But she knew it wouldn't be enough.

Rolfe was pushing his finger down on the detonator.

Evelyn screamed at him to stop as she lifted her weapon, already knowing it was too late.

Then a blast came from somewhere behind her, and Rolfe dropped to the ground, dead.

Epilogue

Evelyn sat across from her grandma two days later, feeling a sense of peace she hadn't experienced in over a month. Not since she'd solved Cassie's case.

Mabel smiled back at her, a crooked smile because of the stroke she'd had when Evelyn was seventeen. It was a smile Evelyn loved, one she'd missed.

"You look different," Mabel told her as she rocked slowly back and forth in her favorite chair, one they'd shipped to the nursing home from South Carolina so many years ago.

"I *feel* different."

It was true. Something had changed in those final days as she'd hunted down Rolfe, as she'd felt the thrill of the chase come back. Her confidence had started to return with it, the knowledge that she *could* do this. And maybe most importantly, she felt a new sense of purpose.

She'd thought her obsession with catching Rolfe had been to avenge Jen's death. She was glad that wasn't the case, happy that the twist of fate that had kept her in Butler's Compound for the raid had also kept Jen alive.

But in the end, it wasn't important that her purpose

hadn't been accurate. Because it had reminded her that it wasn't all about Cassie. It had never been *completely* about Cassie.

The one driving force in her career had been her need to solve her friend's case. But there were a lot of people out there who had their own Cassies. People with someone dead or missing from their lives, people who needed closure. And Evelyn could give it to them.

"I'm staying at BAU," she told her grandma, and even though she'd never told Mabel she was thinking of leaving, her grandma nodded knowingly.

"Good. It's where you belong."

That was what she'd finally told Dan yesterday. When she'd come back into the office, they'd sat down for the discussion she'd been avoiding, and she'd let him know for sure. BAU was where she wanted to be.

Evelyn stood and gave her grandma a hug, then leaned back and told her, "There's someone I want you to meet."

Swallowing her nerves, she opened the door to her grandma's room and walked into the hallway, where Kyle was patiently waiting.

He still had a sling over one arm and he still looked exhausted from the shoot-out with Rolfe two days ago. She knew he was struggling with his own next career move, but she had faith that he'd figure it out, the way she had.

As she threaded her fingers through his, she remembered the instant Rolfe had fallen to the ground, a bullet high on his nose, in the one spot that would kill him instantly, no dying twitch. She'd spun around, wondering who'd taken the shot, and hadn't seen anyone.

Then Kyle's voice had come over her radio, asking

her to confirm that everyone was okay, and Gabe had rushed over and checked to be certain Rolfe was dead. Later, she'd learned that instead of going into the woods with his team the way he'd wanted, and instead of going into the second van as he'd originally planned, Kyle had gone back to Quantico. He'd gone looking for their new HRT sniper, because he'd "had a bad feeling about Rolfe's plan."

So when Rolfe had leaned against that tree, blocking him from the HRT operators, and pressed his finger to the detonator with such glee on his face, it hadn't mattered. Because perched underneath the car Evelyn had abandoned, an HRT sniper had eliminated the threat.

With Rolfe dead, the cell was finished. After they'd gotten the bomb off Jen, and brought her to a hospital to wean her off the cocktail of drugs Rolfe had forced into her to keep her compliant, Jen had confirmed it.

The agent had spent nineteen long days under Rolfe's control. During that time, Rolfe had told her a lot, including the fact that he'd been the one to kill Butler, as they'd suspected. He'd also confirmed that the compound had been his idea. Apparently, he'd talked Butler into putting in all the money, convincing him that his role would be monumental. Rolfe had thought it would be the perfect setup, that it would last for years, but then Butler had started getting greedy.

By then, Rolfe had already chosen Durham and Peters. He'd long ago selected his final bomber, who'd been interested in Butler's compound and Rolfe's ideology. Rolfe had groomed him for the position, had even personally done the research to find him a Quantico-based Marine to court and eventually marry—to provide them with access. So when Butler had begun getting high on his own power, Rolfe had begun to worry that he'd blow the whole thing.

He'd worried about Jen's interest from the first time he'd heard about it. Initially, he'd just been watching to be sure she wouldn't become a problem. When Butler had taken her and Evelyn hostage, Rolfe had seen his chance to get rid of Butler and distract the FBI all at once.

Jen said he'd actually thanked her for giving him an opening to dispose of Butler without compromising his bombers. As he'd stitched up her wounds, he'd threatened her family, bragged about his plans and then dosed her with enough drugs that she'd struggled to think coherently.

The doctors had needed to figure out what Rolfe had given Jen—he had a rudimentary knowledge of chemistry and had mixed his own drugs. But Jen was finally healing. She'd even be going home to her family soon. Her future with her husband was still in question; what wasn't in doubt was the whole family's happiness that she was alive.

Jen would undoubtedly be facing internal questioning before she was officially cleared to return to work, but Evelyn knew she'd be back in the field before long. After all, this was the agent who'd spotted a threat inside their borders that no one else had seen.

Lucas was going back to work soon, too. He wasn't heading up the counterterror squad anymore, and he had a letter of censure in his file, but he'd be moving on. He'd already gotten notice that he was transferring to a different field office. When he'd called to tell her, he'd said it was okay, that he was ready for a new start.

So was she. It was time for all of them to put this case behind them, Evelyn included.

She looked up at Kyle. "You ready to meet her?"

His smile wasn't quite the full-wattage grin from the beach, but there was honesty in his tone when he said, "I've been ready for this for a while."

"Good." She tugged on his hand, pulling him into the room. Looking back and forth between two of the most important people in her life, she told Mabel, "Grandma, this is Special Agent Kyle McKenzie."

She was moving forward, starting right now. She might've been lost for a while, wondering who she was without Cassie's case to solve, but she'd finally figured it out.

She was Evelyn Baine. Granddaughter of Mabel Baine, the woman who'd stand by her no matter what, who'd been doing it since Evelyn was ten years old. Girlfriend of Kyle McKenzie, a man who'd find a new path in the FBI, even if he wasn't sure of it himself.

Who was she? She was a hell of a profiler.

And she was ready for her next case.

* * * * *

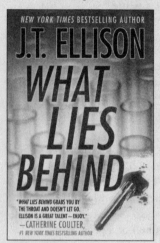

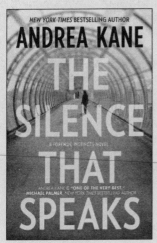

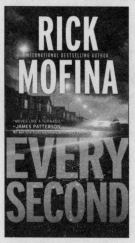

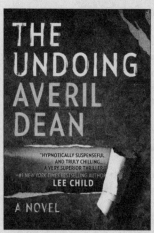

REQUEST YOUR FREE BOOKS!

2 FREE NOVELS
FROM THE SUSPENSE COLLECTION
PLUS 2 FREE GIFTS!

YES! Please send me 2 FREE novels from the Suspense Collection and my 2 FREE gifts (gifts are worth about $10). After receiving them, if I don't wish to receive any more books, I can return the shipping statement marked "cancel." If I don't cancel, I will receive 4 brand-new novels every month and be billed just $6.49 per book in the U.S. or $6.99 per book in Canada. That's a savings of at least 19% off the cover price. It's quite a bargain! Shipping and handling is just 50¢ per book in the U.S. and 75¢ per book in Canada.* I understand that accepting the 2 free books and gifts places me under no obligation to buy anything. I can always return a shipment and cancel at any time. Even if I never buy another book, the two free books and gifts are mine to keep forever.

191/391 MDN GH4Z

Name _____ (PLEASE PRINT) _____

Address _____ Apt. # _____

City _____ State/Prov. _____ Zip/Postal Code _____

Signature (if under 18, a parent or guardian must sign) _____

Mail to the **Reader Service:**
IN U.S.A.: P.O. Box 1867, Buffalo, NY 14240-1867
IN CANADA: P.O. Box 609, Fort Erie, Ontario L2A 5X3

Want to try two free books from another line?
Call 1-800-873-8635 or visit www.ReaderService.com.

* Terms and prices subject to change without notice. Prices do not include applicable taxes. Sales tax applicable in N.Y. Canadian residents will be charged applicable taxes. Offer not valid in Quebec. This offer is limited to one order per household. Not valid for current subscribers to the Suspense Collection or the Romance/Suspense Collection. All orders subject to credit approval. Credit or debit balances in a customer's account(s) may be offset by any other outstanding balance owed by or to the customer. Please allow 4 to 6 weeks for delivery. Offer available while quantities last.

Your Privacy—The Reader Service is committed to protecting your privacy. Our Privacy Policy is available online at www.ReaderService.com or upon request from the Reader Service.

We make a portion of our mailing list available to reputable third parties that offer products we believe may interest you. If you prefer that we not exchange your name with third parties, or if you wish to clarify or modify your communication preferences, please visit us at www.ReaderService.com/consumerschoice or write to us at Reader Service Preference Service, P.O. Box 9062, Buffalo, NY 14240-9062. Include your complete name and address.

SUS15